DEFENSELESS WOMAN

As Dane continued to advance, every muscle in Brittany's body tightened with fear. When she spoke her voice belied the brave front she presented. "What kind of man would force himself upon a defenseless woman?"

He cocked a brow skeptically. "Defenseless?" He jerked his head in the direction of the pitchfork she had thrown at him. "I hardly call that defenseless. And as for forcing myself on you . . . I hardly think that will be necessary."

Brittany's temper flared. "You conceited lout! Do you actually think I'd enjoy having you . . . touch me?"

His white teeth gleamed as he grinned. "We shall soon find out."

He shot out a hand, caught her roughly by the elbow, and yanked her forward into his steely embrace.

The feel of his hard, muscular body molded against hers sent a scorching heat throughout every inch of her. Brittany's head began to spin as her parted lips were crushed beneath his. . . .

DEFIANT SPITFIRE

KAY McMAHON

ZEBRA BOOKS

KENSINGTON PUBLISHING CORP.

ZEBRA BOOKS

are published by

Kensington Publishing Corp.
475 Park Avenue South
New York, NY 10016

First printing: April, 1988

Printed in the United States of America

Prologue

A gray, swirling fog clung heavily to the earth and encased everything within its reach. High overhead, rays of moonlight struggled to permeate the gloom and guide the passage of a coach-and-four along the deserted stretch of road. Up ahead, yellow shafts of light marked the traveler's destination through the dismal scenery. Quiet enshrouded their journey; the only sounds were the rattling of the carriage, the pounding of hooves against the hard-packed ground, and the drivers sharp command to the horses to quicken their pace. Time was of the utmost and secrecy a must, for danger lay at every turn. The completion of this meeting before identities were made was of extreme importance, lest the mission fail and all turn out to be for naught.

Inside the rented coach, a woman dressed in black, her face veiled in ebony lace, stared out from behind the leather shades at the dark countryside, her mouth set in a hard, hateful line. Five years had passed since the beginning of her plan, and before the summer waned, she hoped to see her revenge fulfilled. The bastard would pay for what he'd done! An evil smile parted her red lips as she thought about it. What made her scheme worth the wait was the beauty of it: he would never suspect what was happening until they slipped the hangman's noose around his neck, and only then would she tell him why. He would rue the day he'd walked into their lives. He'd turned from them when they'd needed him most.

The carriage lurched as the driver swung the team onto the road that led up the hillside to the mansion and the man who awaited her, and she dropped the leather flap back into place. Her only regret was that she saw no way to succeed with her plan without the help of this arrogant cretin. She needed his wealth and position. But what truly bothered her was that she no longer trusted anyone, and he was a stranger. Granted, he was being paid; but greed could turn any deal sour. She would have to watch him closely. At the first hint of betrayal, she would see him dead as well.

Chapter One

Boston, Massachusetts
Spring, 1767

Ebony darkness enshrouded the milling throng of protesters outside the courthouse. Their angry voices were raised against the injustices imposed by the Crown and they held their torches high to emphasize their disapproval. Red-coated British soldiers, muskets in hand, fought to disperse the crowd with warnings that they would find themselves imprisoned for their open defiance if their rebellious display did not come to end quickly. The threat only seemed to enrage them further.

The young woman fighting her way through the mass of people hurried her steps as she tugged on the hood of her cape, pulling it further down over her head to hide the bright, thick mane of golden hair. Brittany Lockwood had no intention of joining the rally. She was merely trying to reach the gaol, and the path took no other course but through this group of rebels.

Roan, her younger brother by five years, would have been standing in the middle of the throng had he not been accused of a crime and arrested. The message he had sent her had been simple, stating only that he needed her, and Brittany had left the tiny farmhouse she shared with him at the edge of town the moment the young messenger had told her where to find him. Theirs was a meager lot, it worsened since the death of their father a month ago, and she had had to travel the distance to the gaol on foot; the wagon they owned had a broken axle, yet even so, they had no horse to pull it.

Bitterness darkened the blue-gray of her eyes as she thought about their plight, and Brittany willed herself to concentrate on Roan and find a method to free him. They had no money nor anything worth selling except for the small plot of land their father had left them. As she neared the entrance to the stone building with its barred windows, she wondered what she could use to barter for his release . . . if indeed there was any hope of that. She doubted the Tories would sympathize with her need once she explained that only she and her brother lived on the farm and that she could not plant the spring crops alone. It was no secret that Roan Lockwood supported the rebel cause. Turning him loose to work the farm with his sister would not guarantee he'd stay out of trouble.

Mounting the wooden steps to the front door, Brittany steeled herself for what was inside. Although she had never had cause to visit the gaol before tonight, she had heard a good deal about it. The main floor was composed of three rooms. The largest was used by the gaolkeeper as his private quarters, while the two smaller ones segregated men from women. Handcuffs, leg irons, and chains were common-place, and no matter how cold the night, each prisoner had to bed down on the straw-covered stone floor with nothing more than a thin blanket. Yet that wasn't what brought the worried look to Brittany's lovely face; it was the knowledge that no matter what the crime, all prisoners—guilty or innocent, young or old, sick or healthy—were put into the same cell. Roan might have a strong will and a very stubborn nature, but spending any time in this place would surely have a permanent effect. Pausing with her hand on the doorknob, Brittany absently glanced back at the noisy crowd at the end of the street, thinking that this was perhaps what Roan needed. Maybe having a sampling of what he could expect as punishment for his open defiance of the law might curb his quick tongue. And then again, it might only sharpen it. Heaving an exasperated sigh, she twisted the knob and pushed the door open.

The stench of the place assailed Brittany's nostrils the moment she stepped inside, and she quickly raised a hand to cover her nose, praying she wouldn't retch. Directly in front of her at the end of a long, narrow corridor was a sealed metal door with a small barred window, and she assumed it opened to the place where the prisoners were housed. To her left at the end of a second passageway was another door, and she could barely make out the name Marlin Schmitt, no doubt the gaoler; this was where he resided. She decided to plead her case with him before seeking permission from the guard to see her brother.

Several moments passed before her summons was answered and the door opened to reveal a rather short, quite plump, balding man with wire-rimmed spectacles. He hadn't bothered to don his coat, and from the paper he held in his hand, Brittany concluded that her visit had come at the wrong time. The scowl on his face confirmed it.

"Please excuse the intrusion, sir," she began, and presented him with a polite curtsy. "But I've come about my brother."

"Have you now?" he sighed irritably. "And who might he be?"

"His name is Roan Lockwood, and he's only fifteen—"

"Lockwood, you say?" he interrupted, his thick brow wrinkling all the more as he tried to recall the young man and the charges brought against him. "Ah, yes. A dark haired youth with gray eyes?"

"Yes, sir," Brittany quickly nodded.

"His trial is set for the day after tomorrow." His manner

was cold and unfeeling as he started to push the door shut again.

"But, sir," Brittany replied before he had the chance. "I'm here about his release." This would be the hard part, and she knew it. What did she have to offer? She lowered her head and drew in a deep breath. Maybe—

"Release?" the gaolkeeper laughed. "There's never any release for a man accused of arson."

Brittany wasn't aware if Schmitt had said anything more before he closed the door on her or not. All she could hear was the hammering of her heart in her ears. Arson was a hanging offense! Dear God, if she couldn't prove his innocence, her brother was going to be hanged! It had to be a mistake. Roan would never do anything like that. Someone lied! Knotting her fist, she pressed it against the ache in her chest and turned around. She'd talk to Roan first and then decide what course of action to take. Maybe he knew who'd done this to him and she'd be able to find the evidence that would free him. Ignoring the sense of doom that seemed to close in around her, she raised her chin in the air and headed toward the locked metal door at the end of the other corridor.

"Is someone there?" she called out when no one responded to her determined pounding on the sealed portal. "Please, I must speak with my brother!" She gasped and staggered back a step when a face suddenly appeared between the bars, the man's identity lost in the shadows of the torch burning from behind him. "Are—are you the guard?"

"Yeah—what do you want?" came the gravelly reply before a meaty fist was raised to cover a yawn.

Brittany quickly realized that this man was under no obligation to do as she asked. She set her mind to finding a solution that would be swift and successful. "I'm here to see my brother," she said, her fingers crossed and hidden beneath the folds of her cape.

10

"At this hour?" he challenged. "Come back in the morning."

The dark shape disappeared and Brittany stretched up on tiptoe to peer inside. "I have Mr. Schmitt's consent," she called, wondering where the man had gone. All she could see of the interior in the small, vacant room were the stone floor and the blank wall on the other side. Several seconds ticked away, and she decided to add a little more to her lie. "I don't think he'd appreciate hearing that his guard sleeps on duty."

The face loomed before her again, and a moment later she heard the key rattle in the lock.

"Ain't much else to do," he grumbled, pulling the door open enough for her to step through. "Who is it ya wanna see?"

"Roan Lockwood," she answered before looking at him. And once she had, she was thankful that she'd left the hood of her cape pulled down close to her face, certain the poor deformed individual would see the shock registered in her eyes otherwise. His face was horribly pockmarked. One eyelid drooped, half-shut, and his left arm was smaller than his right, with only a stump where his hand should have been, except for what appeared to be his little finger. On this he had hooked the key ring. Yet none of this bothered Brittany as much as the way his lower lip sagged on one side and spittle ran down his chin. Repelled by the fact that he didn't try to wipe it off or worse yet, seem to care, she forced herself to study the floor. It was then she noticed that the sole of one shoe was twice as thick as the other, and her own problems suddenly seemed insignificant. "He's only fifteen," she went on to say as the guard selected another key and stuck it in the lock of a second door. "Perhaps because he's just a boy, Roan is being kept somewhere else?"

He shook his head dispassionately, swung the heavy door open, and reached for the torch hanging on the wall. "All criminals are kept in the same cell."

11

"But I heard there were rooms in the attic above Mr. Schmitt's quarters—"

"Just the real sick ones goes there," he answered flatly, leading the way into the long, narrow hallway on the other side of the door. He traveled only a yard or two, then paused and stuck the handle of the torch into a holder on the wall. "In there," he said, jutting a thumb over his shoulder toward the cell behind him.

Brittany started to thank him but he had already moved away and was heading back down the hall. She watched him until he had returned to the chair and sat down, propping it back against the wall behind him, his head lowered until his chin rested on his chest and his eyes closed. It was then that the odor of the place wafted up and gagged her a second time. Grabbing the edge of her cape, she pressed the cloth to her nose and turned her attention to finding Roan. The corridor in which she stood ran a length of fifty feet with a stone wall on one side and prison bars on the other. The light from the torch behind her cast indistinct shadows over the occupants of the cell, but she could see that most were lying on the floor, huddled beneath their blankets. A few were sitting up against the wall, the thin pieces of fabric tossed over their shoulders, their knees drawn to their chests with their arms folded over them and heads down. In this light it was hard for Brittany to tell if they were men or women until one of them moved, spotted her, and quickly came to his feet.

"Well, what have we here?" the tall figure bade in a deep rich voice as he came to stand near the bars and give her a long, leisurely once-over. "Old Schmitty hasn't softened in his old age, has he, and sent you to ease our discomfort in this foul place?"

The lewd suggestion sent a shiver down Brittany's spine and she stumbled back a step or two. "N-no," she managed to reply. "I-I'm here to see my brother."

"Oh?" he asked, moving into the light shining between the

bars. Although he was in need of a bath, a change of clothes, and a shave, there was a hint of good looks in his rugged features. "What's his name?"

"Roan . . . Roan Lockwood."

The man casually leaned a shoulder against the bars and slowly scanned the mass of sleeping prisoners until he seemed to recognize someone. Pushing himself up, he carefully picked a path through the snoring, unmoving bodies, then paused near the slight form of a young man who lay shivering in his blanket. Settling down on his haunches, he gave the boy a rough shake which brought the youth up on his knees in an instant.

"You Roan Lockwood?" the man asked and when the other nodded, he motioned toward Brittany. "Someone's here to see you."

"Brit?" the young man called. Shrugging out of the tattered cloth, he awkwardly came to his feet and hurried toward her. "Oh, Brit. I was so afraid you wouldn't get my message."

Their hands met between the bars and Brittany knew how frightened her brother was when he wouldn't let go of her hand.

"Mr. Schmitt said you've been accused of arson, Roan," she said, keeping her voice low. "How can that be? What happened?"

Neither noticed that the man who listened to their conversation had moved back to stand near the bars—far enough away not to draw their attention, but close enough to hear what was said.

"I don't know, Brit," he frowned. "I swear I had nothing to do with it. There was a rally protesting the Townshend Acts and I was standing there with them when two soldiers came up, grabbed my arm, and dragged me off to gaol. I had to ask the guard why I'd been arrested. I don't even know what building it was that I'm supposed to have burned." His grip on her hand tightened. "Brit," he whispered, tears glistening

13

in his gray eyes, "what am I going to do? If I'm found guilty, I'll be sentenced to hang."

"Hush," Brittany scowled. "Don't even think it. Your trial isn't for two days yet. It'll be enough time for me to figure something out."

"If you don't mind my sticking my nose in where it doesn't belong, miss," the stranger cut in, his back against the bars, "I'd say you haven't got enough time to turn around, let alone prove your brother's innocence." A devilish smile parted his lips and he cast the siblings a sidelong glance. "But I do have a suggestion that will solve the problem."

There was something about the man that made Brittany leery. Maybe it was his overeagerness to help someone he didn't even know. Or maybe it was simply the confident way he smiled. And if he had such a perfect suggestion to free Roan from prison, why didn't he use it to get himself out from behind bars? Softly arched brows came together in a suspicious frown as she stared silently back at him, inwardly deciding that she didn't want anything to do with him—and much less his suggestion.

"Thank you, but no," she replied, squeezing Roan's hand when he started to object. "We've been taking care of each other for some time now. We'll manage."

The stranger shrugged as if it didn't really matter to him. "Funny," he said, scratching his stubbled chin, "your brother acts as if this was his first time in jail."

"It is!" she exploded angrily. How dare he insinuate that this young boy was the sort who was always breaking the law!

The man turned to look her squarely in the eye, all sign of humor gone. "I don't mean to be rude, Miss Lockwood, but you haven't any idea of what kind of trouble your brother is in. England is fighting to retain its control of America, and they'll do whatever's necessary to ensure it. Your brother's life—whether he's guilty or innocent—is unimportant to them. They're not interested in him, except maybe to prove a point."

Brittany didn't like having to admit that the man made sense, but he did. "And what is that?"

"It's their way of telling the rebels that their defiance will not be tolerated—that *no one* is beyond their reach. They'll use his execution as an example, Miss Lockwood, and your cries of injustice will go unheard." He took a step closer, his dark brow furrowed. "You're not fighting the court here, miss. You're fighting England."

"Brit . . ." Roan whined, giving his sister's hand a shake.

"Hush, Roan," she said almost irritably and let go of him to wander aimlessly down the corridor. She needed time to think this through. Her father had been opposed to the revenues England was inforcing upon the colonies and talked at great length about it with her and Roan. What this stranger recited had been a close account of her father's feelings, and the eldest Lockwood had constantly warned his children to tread lightly where politics were concerned. Obviously his preaching had had little effect on Roan. And if what this man implied was true, then Roan's trial was merely a formality before he was hanged. Even the thought of it made her wince. She faced the stranger and asked, "What do you suggest?"

White teeth flashed with his smile. "Now you're thinking logically." He glanced over his shoulder at the sleeping prisoners, then motioned her near. "There's a midget who works the docks. His name is Aaron Dooley. Find him and tell him to take you to see Dane Remington." He paused a moment to rub one corner of his mouth as if he were attempting to hide his grin. "He and I have known each other for a long time. Tell him Brad sent you, and that you need his help."

"To do what?" Brittany frowned.

"Miss Lockwood," Brad warned, "I thought you'd figured it out by now. There's only one way to save your brother. Dane's going to have to break him out of prison."

Brittany's face paled. "What?" she breathed, straightening and taking a step backward. "He can't. That would be the same as admitting his guilt."

"It might look that way at first," Brad concurred. "But I can't see that you have any other choice. You need time to prove his innocence, and it's something you don't have. Hide him for a while until you've found the evidence you need, then take the information to the authorities."

Brittany had to admit there was no other way. If Roan was left in prison one more day, he'd be hanged the next. She looked at her brother. "All right. I'll do it. I'll do it for Roan. But I don't mind telling you," she added, glancing back at Brad, "that this whole plan makes me horribly uncomfortable."

"I can understand that, Miss Lockwood," he smiled softly, then let his eyes slowly travel the length of her. "You're not the type who breaks people out of prison. In fact, I doubt you've ever done anything that goes against the law."

His manner, the way he spoke so openly to her, bothered Brittany, and she decided it was time she left. Without thanking the man, she turned to her brother, squeezed his hand, and assured him that everything would be all right, that by tomorrow night they'd be together. What she didn't tell him was that nothing would ever be the same for them again.

Brittany hadn't been to the docks since she was a little girl, and only then because her father wouldn't leave her and Roan home alone while he visited one of the merchants to discuss the shipping of his goods to England. It hadn't changed much since then, except perhaps that it was more crowded and there was a great deal of tension in the air. Even though the hour was late and most everyone else was in bed for the night, the wharf was busy with activity. British soldiers seemed to outnumber the dockworkers loading and

16

unloading the huge ships anchored in the bay. There were small parties of protesters heckling the men in red uniforms. Tars fresh off the ships after weeks at sea were heading toward the pubs, where they could quench their thirst with a mug of ale and sate their desires with a woman to warm their bed. Brittany knew she didn't belong here, and if her need hadn't been so great, she would have turned around and raced for home. But she couldn't . . . she had to find the man called Dooley, then see about her brother's release.

Keeping the hood of her cape pulled down over her brow, she prayed no one would notice she walked the docks alone. She had no way to defend herself should she be mistaken for one of the back street trollops who frequented the area looking for a way to earn a little money. Brittany had never been intimate with a man, and the thought of allowing a perfect stranger—or even someone she knew, for that matter—to touch her, hold her, do things she couldn't even bring herself to imagine, chilled her to the bone. And then to ask for payment for having allowed it to happen—she shuddered, unable to understand how a woman—any woman—could do it.

With her head down and her thoughts elsewhere, Brittany didn't see the old man step in her way until it was too late and she had collided head-on with him, knocking the small crate he carried to the ground. The thin wood and fragile construction gave way under the abuse and spilled the contents on the cobblestones at her feet.

"Oh, I'm so sorry," she apologized, quickly stooping down to help gather his merchandise. "I hope nothing's ruined."

"I don't think so," he admitted, picking up the last small tin and shoving it back into the crate. Doubling his fist, he pounded the nails back into the holes where they had worked loose, turned the wooden box over just in case they didn't hold, and looked up at her. His gray brows came together instantly. "You shouldn't be here, miss—especially at this time of night."

17

"I know," Brittany agreed as she awkwardly tugged on her hood and hurriedly scanned the crowd of men moving around near them. "But I don't have a choice. I'm looking for someone and I was told I'd find him here at the docks. Maybe you know him. His name's Aaron Dooley."

"The midget," the old man replied, propping the crate on one hip so he could take her elbow and help her up again. This beautiful young woman had no business risking her safety—no matter how important she felt it was for her to walk the streets alone. "Everyone around here knows him."

"Have you seen him lately?"

"Yes. But are you sure that's who you want to talk to?"

Because of his size, Dooley couldn't get the kind of job most men had; therefore he had to resort to making a living any way he could. Most of the time he picked pockets or took payment for any information he had about someone. But he was best known for his association with the Remington brothers. He wasn't the sort a young lady with any sense deliberately went looking for.

All Brittany wanted to do was discuss business with this Remington character and then return home as quickly as possible, and as a result, she failed to hear the warning tone in the old man's voice. "Yes. He's the one. Would you tell me where to find him?"

His dark brown eyes discreetly took in the shape of the young lady standing beside him, and even though he didn't know who she was, he decided he wouldn't sleep well if he just sent her on her way to fend for herself. "I'll do more than that," he announced, hiking the box further up on his hip, "I'll take you to him."

Brittany was doubly thankful for the old man's help when their destination took them through an even rougher part of the docks. The buildings here were in need of repair, beggars slept in the street, rats chased in and out of discarded boxes and other debris, and the further they walked, the louder the voices from a nearby tavern became. No one had to tell

Brittany what would have happened to her had she come to this area alone. She cringed at the sound of a woman's shrill laughter.

"He is usually around here," the old man said as they paused near the opened door of a dilapidated warehouse and peeked inside at the darkness. "I think it's where he sleeps."

"Here?" Brittany questioned in surprise. Her family had never had much money, and there were a lot of things they'd had to do without, but her father always saw to it that his children were fed and kept warm on cold winter nights. Whatever did this poor soul do when the temperature dropped and the entire countryside was covered in a blanket of snow?

"Yes," the old man nodded. "Not much of a place to call home, is it?" He set down his crate and studied the street and the people milling about. "Last time I talked to him, he said he was coming here. But knowing him, he probably stopped off somewhere. No, wait—" He raised a hand and pointed at the tiny figure walking toward them from within the crowd moving down the street. "Here he comes."

Moonlight was all that graced this spot and at this distance Aaron Dooley looked like an eight-year-old child. But once Brittany could see his face in the ashen light, she knew otherwise. His dark brown hair was pulled back and tied with a ribbon at the nape of his neck. He wore a loose-fitting blue shirt and dark breeches, dark blue hose, and black shoes. In his hand, he carried his tricorn—something young boys didn't wear—and a leather pouch dangled from his waist. But it was the deep lines in his brow and around his mouth that gave away his age . . . that and the fact that he sported a pistol in his belt. The sight of it almost made her want to smile; she envisoned the clumsy way Aaron Dooley would have to hold it. Then she saw the hard look in his brown eyes and she decided that very few people laughed at this little man.

"Harris," he nodded, his voice surprisingly mellow rather

19

than high-pitched and nasal. "You waiting for me?"

"Yes," the old man replied, turning to Brittany. "I brought this young lady to see you."

A knot formed in Brittany's stomach when the little man's dark eyes fell upon her and she suddenly wondered if she had taken leave of her senses. She had let a man she'd never met before tonight talk her into asking for help from someone he claimed would be willing. Just because he'd convinced her of it, she had blindly walked right into the middle of God knows what. She drew in a deep breath and exhaled slowly before she turned to the old man and politely thanked him for his assistance. It wasn't until he'd left them that Brittany found the courage to face Aaron Dooley again.

"I was told you could take me to Dane Remington," she announced, deciding that there was no logic in avoiding the reason she'd come looking for him.

"Oh?" Dooley questioned, slowly walking past her toward an overturned barrel. After some difficulty, he pulled himself up on it and sat down to stare at her. He never liked craning his neck to look in someone's eyes, especially a woman's. But then, this wasn't just any woman. She had a beautiful face and he could see a bright yellow curl peeking out of the hood of her cape. "And who told you that?"

A chill slithered across her shoulders. Had that man back there in prison lied to her? She turned her head in the direction of the gaol as if half expecting to see it from this distance. Was this some sort of evil game he played? Why had he done it? And why had she fallen for it? Her throat constricted and she fought off the desire to cry and scream at the same time.

"I asked who told you that I could find Dane Remington."

His words broke her trance; but rather than being frightened, Brittany was angry. "Some buffoon who thought it would be fun to send me off chasing shadows." A breeze lifted one corner of her cape, drawing her eyes to it, and she irritably grabbed the cloth in one hand and yanked it around her, unaware that in doing so she'd given Dooley a clearer idea of the trim figure hidden beneath yards of fabric. "I hope he's in prison for the same reason as my brother. Because if he is, I'll stand in the front row and watch him hanged!"

"Who?" Dooley asked, his curiosity aroused.

"I don't know who he is," she stormed, heaving an exasperated sigh. "He simply told me to go to the docks, find a man named Aaron Dooley, and have him take me to Dane Remington." Her lip curled in an unflattering sneer. *Tell him Brad sent me,"* she mimicked derisively.

Dooley nearly fell off the barrel in his haste to get down. "Come with me," he ordered, grabbing a fistful of her cape.

"What? Why?" Her surprise turned to indignation. "Let go of me!" she snapped, slapping at his hand. "I'm through being played for a fool."

The little man's head came up and he glared back at her. "And that's just what you will be if you don't come with me right now!"

Brittany's anger lessened a mite as she cocked a questioning brow at him. "You mean he wasn't lying? You do know where to find Dane Remington?"

Dooley was growing impatient with her. Resting back on his heels, he jammed his tiny fists on his hips and said, "Of course I do. I always know where he is, but I'm not about to tell somebody I don't even know. Now are you coming with me of your own accord or do I have to use other methods?"

The idea that a man who hardly reached her waist could even suggest forcing her to do something against her will, let alone actually achieve it, made her laugh. "You?"

The midget seemed to grow two inches when he straightened his petite frame in a rage. With his chin lowered, his eyes blazing pure fire, his hand quickly moved to the butt of his pistol and before Brittany had even noticed, he had leveled the weapon on her and cocked the hammer.

"I might be little, but I should never be taken for granted."

He waved the muzzle toward the building on the opposite side of the street and Brittany quickly obeyed, too frightened to do anything else.

What have I gotten myself into? she silently moaned as she stumbled along, wondering if there was a single soul among the throng around them who would help her if she asked. *I've gone from a smooth talker to a maniac with a gun. What next? Roan, if your life didn't depend on this—* The thought was never finished, for once she looked up and saw what kind of establishment Dooley wanted her to enter, she realized her troubles had only just begun. She staggered to a stop and faced him.

"I—I can't go in there," she nervously told him, the smell of stale cigar smoke and ale floating out of the tavern to assail her.

"You can if you want to see Dane Remington," Dooley snarled, motioning toward the door. "And even if you've changed your mind, you're still going to talk to him."

Brittany's eyes lowered to the pistol he held pointed at her, certain he would use it if she argued. And if she were dead, Roan would have no one left to help him. Gritting her teeth, she gulped and turned around.

A gray haze encased the occupants of the tavern, and the pungent odor of unwashed bodies, beer, and tobacco smoke made Brittany's eyes burn. Yet what made her teeth suddenly chatter wasn't the rancid smell of the place, but the profligate goings-on of its patrons. There were several women in the crowded room, none of whom Brittany would call a lady. They all openly flirted, a couple of them exposed their bosoms to any man who wanted to see, and the rest drank ale like it was nothing more than goat's milk. It sickened her to see the way they behaved and almost made her ashamed of being a woman. The men weren't much better, for most of them were too drunk to stand up, some were engaged in seeing who could out-shout the other, and a fight had erupted in one corner. If for some reason she managed to live through this experience with nothing more than a crude education on how others chose to spend their time, she vowed she would get down on her knees every night and thank God for sparing her.

"Over there," Dooley ordered, giving her a shove in the direction of a group of men sitting around a table near the cold fireplace.

She staggered forward a step or two when suddenly someone latched onto the hood of her cape and yanked it off her head. Her bright golden curls tumbled free, and in the same instant, the earsplitting din hushed to a deafening quiet as all eyes centered on the beautiful blonde who had graced this lascivious den with her presence. Brittany was afraid to move, positive someone would make a grab for her and drag her upstairs, where she had seen one of the men take his female companion. Yet she also knew that the longer she stood there obviously unchaperoned, one, possibly even two, of these foul creatures would decide that she was theirs for the taking. Her assumption was correct, for the thought had barely crossed her mind when from out of nowhere a hand came up, tore the strings of her cape free from around her neck, and yanked the garment from her. Brittany made a desperate attempt to reclaim it but changed her mind once she saw the man who had taken possession. He appeared to have not had a bath in weeks. His thinning hair was matted to his head, his face was unshaven, and when he smiled suggestively at her, there was a dark, gaping hole where his teeth should have been. Brittany shrunk back; yet in doing so, she bumped into the trio of men behind her, all of whom were moving closer to make their claim on her. She screamed when one of them seized the neckline of her dress and started to pull her toward his smiling face, and the only thing that brought an abrupt end to his enjoyment was the explosion of gunfire and the lead ball that whizzed dangerously close to his head. He let go of Brittany in a flash, and before she could catch herself, she tumbled to the dirty floor.

"I didn't bring her in here for the likes of you," Dooley growled, a small puff of white smoke dissipating above his head as he jammed his pistol into his belt again and pulled a knife from in back of him. "And if you want to argue the point, I'll be more than happy to oblige." His brown eyes narrowed threateningly at the group who had been so bold, and without any hesitation they quickly stepped back. Aaron Dooley was ferocious with a blade.

Brittany would have liked to thank the midget for rescuing her, but she couldn't bring herself to say it. After all, *she* hadn't wanted to come inside in the first place. She knew what would happen, and she had tried to tell him so. But he had been too busy trying to prove that his stature didn't make any difference. Irritated with him and having failed to realize that the dangers which had threatened her only a moment ago were still very much alive, she pushed herself up, brushed off her hands, and regained ownership of her cape from the man who had stolen it. Giving him a damning scowl, she whirled the garment around her shoulders, tied it snugly at her neck, and nodded at Dooley to lead the way while she tucked the long strands of yellow hair back into the hood.

The inhabitants of the tavern resumed what they'd been doing before the little fracas, and the laughter, shouts, and noises from the crowd seemed even louder than before. The only exception was a group of five men sitting at the table where Dooley was headed. Every one of them concentrated his attention on the midget *and* the woman with him as the couple wedged their way through the mass of bodies blocking their path.

"Where did you find her, Dooley?" the one nearest him grinned once they had reached the table. "Or should I ask how much you had to pay her to be seen with you?" A chorus of laughter followed the comment, but Dooley didn't appear to be affected by it.

24

"She came looking for me, Drexler, if you must know," he sneered as he returned his knife to its scabbard. "When was the last time a woman came looking for you? In fact, I don't remember ever seeing you with a woman. What's the matter? Word get around that you like boys better?"

Brittany could feel a hot blush rise in her cheeks, and while everyone else guffawed over Dooley's remark, she pretended not to hear. Instead, she focused her attention on the little man as he crossed to a vacant chair, dragged it closer to the table, and climbed up on the seat. From there he proceeded to crawl over onto the table and sit down, where he crossed his short arms over his chest, silently daring his friend to say something else. When Drexler chose not to reply, but rather saluted the little man with his mug held high, Dooley twisted around and whispered to the man at the head of the table, one whose face was hidden from Brittany's view by a second man who had leaned in to listen. Whatever he told the pair must have been something they didn't want to hear, for the man who had eavesdropped quickly snapped his head around to stare at Brittany with a somewhat angry scowl on his face. But it was the other man, the one Dooley had turned to, that made her breath catch in her throat once his companion sat back and gave her an unrestricted view of him.

He sat with one arm draped over the back of the chair, his other arm on the table, his lean, brown fingers wrapped around the base of his mug. He wore a billowy ivory shirt that he hadn't bothered to tie at the throat, and it fell open to reveal a dark matting of hair on his muscular chest. His shoulders were wide and well defined under the gauzy material, something that made Brittany's heart beat a little faster. His thick, raven-black hair was pulled back off his face and tied at the nape of his neck with a ribbon, except for a defiant curl that fell against his dark brow. His jaw was square, his nose thin, his lips full and set in a hard line as he stared back at her. But it was the

25

emerald green of his eyes that caught and held Brittany's attention. Trimmed in sinfully thick, black lashes, his eyes seemed to pierce right through her, baring her soul and setting her nerves on edge. He was the most handsome man she had ever encountered, yet there was something about him—the dangerous look on his face, the way the muscle in his cheek flexed, and the flare of his nostrils, perhaps, that warned her to choose her words carefully. He didn't appear to be the sort who tolerated anything less than the truth from anyone. A shiver ran through her when he cocked his head to one side and looked her up and down as if he were appraising her worth. When he spoke, the deep, rich timbre of his voice sent a tingle across her shoulders and down her spine.

"Dooley tells me you were looking for Dane Remington."

Brittany gulped down the knot in her throat and forced herself to breathe. "Yes."

"Why?"

She nervously glanced about the group at the table staring at her, wondering what their reaction would be to her next comment. She wasn't about to tell anyone except Mr. Remington that she wanted him to get her brother out of gaol. If word got around, those at the prison would be waiting for them, and as a result, she very well might end up behind bars right alongside Roan. "That's between the two of us."

A hint of a smile touched one corner of the man's mouth and disappeared. Lifting his mug of ale, he took a drink, then studied the workmanship of the pewter cup he held for several moments before he set it down again. "He doesn't just talk to anyone without first knowing what it is they want." His green eyes found hers again.

Brittany could feel her body tremble, but she knew she had to stand fast to her decision. "Then he'll have to make an exception this time."

A flash of white teeth showed with his smile. "You've

26

never heard of Dane Remington before today, have you?" He waited for her to shake her head, then added, "Then perhaps you'll tell us how you knew to come here."

She couldn't explain why, but she sensed knowing the identity of the man in gaol with her brother was very important to these people. Even Dooley had wanted to know before he would take her to see Remington, and now as she thought about it, she couldn't remember if she had told him or not. Her confidence began to grow. She had something this man wanted, and she was going to use it to her advantage. "Someone gave me his name and told me where to look."

"Who?"

Brittany hoped the smile she felt tugging at the corners of her mouth didn't reflect itself in her eyes. "I'm to tell that to Mr. Remington and no one else."

His eyes held hers for a long while in a silent test of will, and in that moment the stranger seemed to recognize that he'd met a woman who wasn't afraid of him or of the situation in which she'd placed herself. In an unexpected show of temporary defeat, he pushed himself away from the table and stood up.

Brittany's heart raced wildly as she watched his long, lean frame grow to its full height. He was nearly a head taller than she. It suddenly occurred to her that if he wanted her to tell him everything she knew, he could simply encompass her slender throat with one huge hand and squeeze until she decided that her life was more important than her secrets. Her chin quivered as she watched him round the end of the table and walk toward her. Gripping the folds of her cape in an effort to stop her hands from shaking, she unconsciously lifted her eyes to look into his when he stood before her.

His slow, deliberate perusal of her from head to toe made Brittany's knees tremble. His nearness touched every inch of her. The heat of his body scorched hers. The manly scent of him muddled her courage, and she knew that if he raised a hand to her, every detail of the night's adventure would come spilling out in a rush of cowardice. Just when she thought she would have to decide, he surprised her by crossing his arms over his wide chest and saying, "And I don't suppose you'll tell us your name, either?"

Suddenly, Brittany knew she had the upper hand. He couldn't risk hurting her to get the information he wanted. "I think Mr. Remington should be the one to decide how important it is to know my name," she said, wondering if he sensed how frightened she was. "But I wasn't under the impression that it mattered one way or another. I was simply told he would help someone in trouble."

"And that's you?" he questioned with a vague smile.

In spite of her fear, Brittany laughed. "You don't give up, do you?"

He shrugged one broad shoulder. "It pays to be careful." Dropping his arms to his sides, he glanced back at the man he had left sitting next to Dooley. "See that we're not disturbed."

The other gave a nod of his head and grinned suggestively. "For as long as it takes," he replied.

A worried frown barely had time to knit Brittany's brow before the handsome stranger turned back to her, took her arm in a firm, yet unyielding grip, and shoved her toward the stairs at the back of the tavern. "Where are you taking me?" she demanded, her tone lacking the outrage she wanted.

"Someplace private," he answered dryly. They started up the steps.

"Look, whoever you are, I already told you that what I have to say will only be told to Mr. Remington. Threatening me isn't going to change that!"

He seemed not to hear, or at least not to be affected by her promise as he elbowed their way through the crowded hall at the top of the stairs. Reaching a door at the far end, he threw it open and pushed her through it. Brittany stumbled to a halt in the middle of the room, her eyes drawn to a huge bed that seemed to fill the entire space, and she started when she heard him close the door behind them. The pale light of the hurricane lamp on the nightstand cast an almost inviting glow across the bed's feathery softness, and she gulped down the fear that formed a knot in her throat and turned around.

The stranger stood with his back pressed against the door, his arms folded over his wide, muscular chest, his head cocked to one side as he stared back at her. The emerald color of his eyes had softened a bit, but Brittany could still see impatience gleaming in them. He wasn't in the mood for her stubbornness. She swallowed hard and backed away from him a step or two, wondering if perhaps she should tell him something other than the truth—anything that might appease him until she was given the opportunity to talk with Dane Remington.

"Suppose you start by telling me your name." Although the request was simply stated, it had a threatening edge to it.

"I-I already told you—"

"And I thought I made myself perfectly clear," he cut in. "*I'm* the one who decides how important your problem is."

If this man didn't trust Brittany, she certainly couldn't trust him. "All right," she conceded. "I'll tell you what it is I want Mr. Remington to do for me. But I'll tell only *him* my name." She forced herself not to look at him and went to stand at the window, where she gazed outside through the dirty panes at the street below, wondering if she'd break her neck or only sprain an ankle if she decided to throw herself from it. It had taken a lot of courage on her part to come this far, but she also knew it was beginning to run a little thin. If he suspected that her brave façade was simply that—a hoax, a deception, and nothing more, he very well could test it, and she'd be racing through the streets screaming like a madwoman. "There's a young boy being held in the gaol on false charges. I was told Mr. Remington would free him." She closed her eyes, praying her voice hadn't betrayed the nervousness she felt, and waited for his reply. When he didn't answer, she glanced at him.

He had left his vigil at the door to stand near the dresser, and she could see the thoughtful frown on his rugged brow. A long while passed before he looked at her again. "And this man who sent you to see me—where did you meet him?"

"In the gaol," she replied. "He was being held—" Suddenly Brittany realized what he had said. "Sent me to see you?" Her temper flared. "*You're* Dane Remington?"

Ignoring her question, he came to stand before her. "You mean you were inside the gaol?"

Brittany heatedly considered slapping his face for the trick he'd played. "Do you know how much time we wasted?" she hissed, her eyes flashing. "Why didn't you tell me who you were to begin with? My brother's trial is the day after tomorrow, and in all probability he'll be sentenced to hang! We only have twenty-four hours to do something."

Dane's dark brows gathered in a fierce frown. "And if you'd be still long enough to listen to what I have to say, we wouldn't be wasting any more of it."

He was silently daring her to say another word, and Brittany was sorely tempted. She wanted to tell him he was a cad, an insensitive degenerate who enjoyed playing games with someone who was at his mercy. But she didn't. Right now Roan's life depended on her being able to talk this man into doing what she wanted of him. She needed Dane Remington, but that didn't mean she had to like him. Straightening her spine, she brushed past him and went to stand on the other side of the room.

"All right," she answered stiffly as she toyed with the candle snuffer on top of the dresser, "what is it you wish to know?"

"What name did this man give you? The one who sent you here."

Brittany turned her head to look at him. "Why is that important?" The angry scowl she received silently told her that she was wasting time. "All he said was to tell you that

Brad sent me."

"What did he look like?"

His attitude irritated her. "Like he needed a bath and a shave. Mr. Remington, it was very dark in that gaol, and to tell you the truth, I doubt I'd recognize him again."

"How tall was he? You could tell that in the dark, couldn't you?"

Brittany's shoulders drooped. She couldn't understand why he was interested in knowing such a thing . . . it was her brother who needed help. "Not quite as tall as you." She faced him squarely and looked him up and down. "Nor as big." She waved a hand at him. "You know, as muscular or broad-shouldered. His hair was about the same shade as yours, though, but I couldn't tell what color his eyes were." Her own darkened. "Does that satisfy you?" she asked, not caring if there was an icy tone to her words. Maybe if he were made to realize how insignificant the information was, he'd stop asking such stupid questions. Her irritation with him grew when he turned his back on her and went to the window to stare outside, deep in thought. "Mr. Remington," she sighed when several minutes passed, "I fail to realize where any of this will lead us—"

"Describe the inside of the gaol to me," he interrupted, not bothering to turn around.

His rudeness provoked her and she decided to give it back to him. "What?" she sneered. "You mean you haven't been there yourself to know?" She smiled sarcastically when his head snapped around to glare at her.

"You want my help or not?"

The question stopped her cold. She lowered her gaze and said, "I wish I didn't, but I do."

"Then describe the inside of the building and we'll discuss how you're going to pay me later."

Brittany could feel the blood drain from her face. Pay him? She had no way of paying him. And he didn't look like the sort who would want to own farmland. Dear Lord, what was she going to do? Sickened by the thought, she staggered to the bed and sat down as she pushed the hood of her cape from her head and absently untied its strings. If only her father were alive . . . he'd know what to do. He'd have handled this whole affair without any trouble. She closed her eyes, willing the tears not to come. She was beginning to believe that her brother was right about their father's accident—that it was no accident at all—that it was merely a part in some heinous plot to get rid of the Lockwood family. And it all made sense. Her brother had been accused of a crime he hadn't committed and would probably be executed for it, and she had been tricked into coming here. This was no man who shared the room with her. He was Satan himself, and at any moment the entire place would burst into flames.

"So," his deep voice proclaimed as he came to stand next to her, "when it comes to the matter of money, your brother's life isn't so important anymore."

Brittany's eyes flew open. Sparks of pure rage glowed like burning coals in their gray depths. "How dare you!" she seethed, pushing the cape off her shoulders and coming to her feet. "Nothing in this world is more important to me than my brother, and if there were any *other* way for me to free him, I'd march right out of here."

His gaze took in everything: the thick golden strands of hair, the exquisite gray eyes, the pert little nose, the long, slender neck and heaving bosom, all the way down to the tattered hemline of her dress and up again. "Really?" he lazily challenged. "And what makes you so sure of that?"

"Because I don't have any money to buy the help I need." The muscles in her throat tightened and she quickly turned her eyes from his, thinking he might sense her frustration and mock her. "I obviously misunderstood your friend. I thought you'd help me—"

"For nothing?" he finished, masking the half-smile that touched his lips.

Brittany nodded but wouldn't look at him.

"Well, I think we might be able to work something out . . . provided, of course, you tell me everything I need to know."

A tear found its way to the corner of her eye, and when she blinked, it spilled over the rim of her dark lashes and fell to her chin. "Anything," she smiled hopefully. "I'll do anything you ask."

"Then start by telling me your name."

"Lockwood, Brittany Lockwood. My brother's name is Roan. He's only fifteen and he's accused of arson. But he didn't do it."

"And you decided to help him escape prison rather than prove his innocence."

"There isn't time," she moaned, following him across the room as he went back to stare out the window again. "You know how quick the courts are—especially with someone they think is fighting against the Crown. If we were rich, I could buy him the time we needed—or perhaps even buy his way out of trouble. But all we have is a small piece of farmland, one cow, a few chickens, and a lot of dreams."

"Are you telling me you and your brother are loyal to England?" he asked rather casually, his eyes a soft green.

"I'm loyal to my brother first," she firmly answered. "After that—" She shrugged. Her father had fought for America's freedom as best he could while he farmed his land and put food on the table. Roan wanted to follow in his footsteps. But as for her—she wasn't sure. She didn't like violence, and to have freedom, a person had to fight for it. "Does it make a difference?"

He smiled softly and Brittany thought how much more handsome he was when he did.

"Not really," he admitted. "I was just thinking how lucky the patriots would be to have you on their side. You have a very determined nature." He chuckled and stared outside again. "And a lot of courage. Now suppose you tell me what

33

I can expect to come up against once I'm inside the gaol."

"I'll do better than that," she said excitedly. "I'll draw you a map. Have you got some paper and a pen?"

Ten minutes later, Brittany had sketched a complete layout of the gaol and its grounds, all the way down to the place where the guard hung his keys while he napped. She also warned Dane that the gaol was located only a few hundred yards away from the courthouse and that there were always a dozen or so British soldiers stationed there. This information brought a deep frown to his brow and Brittany was quick with the suggestion that maybe his men could create a diversion that would keep the soldiers busy while he went inside. He seemed to like her idea although he didn't actually come out and say it, but she could tell by the way he nodded appreciatively that he intended to give it considerable thought.

"Is there something I can do to help?" she asked as she watched him fold the piece of parchment and tuck it inside his shirt. "Maybe I could be a part of the distraction. . . ." Her smooth brow wrinkled at his strange smile, and the flesh on her arms and across her shoulders tingled when his green eyes seemed to devour every inch of her.

"I'm afraid you'd distract the wrong men," he admitted, grinning. "Besides, if this doesn't work, you could wind up in gaol right alongside your brother."

Brittany was quick with her answer. "I'm not afraid, Mr. Remington."

His eyes raked over her a second time, clearly indicating his meaning. "You should be. British soldiers are no gentlemen when it comes to a woman with your kind of beauty."

His statement should have frightened her, but it didn't. He had paid her a very nice compliment, one she couldn't remember ever having gotten before, and it pleased her. She lowered her eyes, waiting until the warmth in her cheeks cooled. When she glanced up again, he was heading for the door.

"Wait," she called out to him. "We haven't discussed your fee."

A broad grin parted his lips as he stared back at her. "I'm no gentleman, either, Miss Lockwood," he said, opening the door and making a quiet exit.

The sound of the latch clicking shut behind him echoed all around Brittany as she stood mouth agape staring at the closed door.

Chapter Two

Fearful gray eyes watched the dying trails of sunset light fade beyond the single window in the gaol cell. The prisoner knew that when the pale light of morning spilled into this cold, dark room again, the guard would come to unlock the door. Time was running out for Roan Lockwood, and although he knew his sister loved him, he wondered if her absence meant she'd been unable to find Dane Remington and hadn't the courage to tell him. Huddled in the corner, his blanket tossed over his narrow shoulders, Roan crossed his arms over his drawn-up knees and rested his head against them, willing himself not to cry. Was this perhaps the way his father had felt just before he died? Had he known his executioners, the way Roan knew his? Heaving a trembling sigh, Roan lifted his head and laid it back against the wall behind him, his eyes closed. There had to have been more than one. Patrick Lockwood was not a little man; short, yes, but very stocky and as strong as the ox he used to plow the fields. One man could never get the better of him. And then there was the matter of the ax. If Patrick Lockwood had actually been crushed to death beneath the fallen tree, a tree he was supposed to have been cutting down, where was his ax? Granted, he had left the house that morning in the flatbed wagon intending to restock their supply of firewood, but never in his fifty-one years had he ever been careless when it came to felling trees. Roan had tried to tell his sister that, but her argument had always been the same—that that was why it was called an accident. It infuriated him to think that his sister could so easily dismiss their father's death, and it had been the reason why he'd spent a great deal of his time during the past month looking for clues that would prove otherwise.

"You scared, lad?"

Roan's eyes flew open when he realized the one who spoke was talking to him. "No," he snapped, squinting up at the man towering over him while he readjusted the thin piece of cloth covering his shoulders. "Just cold."

The dark figure stepped into the last light of day coming through the window and crouched down in front of him where Roan could see his face. "It's nothing to be ashamed of," Brad whispered as he pulled his own blanket off his back and tossed it over Roan's. Twisting around, he sat beside him. "I don't honestly know a single man who isn't afraid of being in prison or even a gaol like this one. It's just that most won't admit it."

"Are you afraid?" Roan asked, wondering why the man had suddenly decided to talk to him. Once Brittany had left the night before, he'd gone back to his place on the far side of the cell and pointedly ignored Roan. Today wasn't much different, except that several times Roan had caught the man looking at him. Roan couldn't say why, but he had the impression that this fellow inmate of his was watching out for him but didn't want Roan to know it.

"I was until last night," he confessed with a chuckle.

"Last night? What has last night got to do with it?"

Pulling up one knee, Brad laid his elbow across it and scratched his whiskered chin. "That's when your sister came."

"Brit? Why would her being here make a difference?"

A vague smile parted the other's lips. "Well, maybe if I

38

introduced myself, you'd understand. My name is Brad Remington."

"Remington?" Roan repeated in surprise as he sat up and looked his companion in the eye. "And Dane Remington is a relative of yours?"

Brad nodded. "My brother."

Roan continued to stare at the man for a moment before he fell back against the wall again, chuckling and shaking his head. "And you're not scared because you know he'll be coming for you."

"I do if your sister had the courage to look for him."

"Oh, I can guarantee you that," Roan assured him. "Brit wouldn't stop until she found him. What worries me is the possibility that she couldn't find him."

"Then stop worrying," Brad smiled. "I was to meet my brother at the docks five days ago, and if your sister did exactly as I told her, she would have talked to him within an hour after she left here."

They fell quiet for several moments, each envisioning Dane Remington's arrival and the method he'd use to free them. When Roan spoke again, his voice was low and childlike.

"I wish you'd said something sooner. I thought this would be my last day."

"I couldn't risk it," Brad whispered when one of the other inmates stood up to pace the floor and the path he chose brought him close enough to hear. "I didn't want anyone else to suspect what we're up to. Dane's success will depend on surprise, and if you had suddenly seemed very happy after your sister's visit, well. . . ."

Silence enshrouded the room again except for the occasional moans or fits of coughing by the others who shared the cell. They were a sorry lot, a group Roan didn't feel he deserved to be a part of, and for the first time since his arrival, he carefully studied each man, thinking perhaps he had been too quick to judge them. He was here because someone had mistaken him for someone else. He was innocent, and there was a strong possibility he wasn't the only one. A chill raced up his spine and he hugged the blankets tighter around him.

"Ever been in gaol before, Mr. Remington?"

His question brought a smile to his companion's lips. "Call me Brad," he instructed, "and the answer is yes . . . many times."

"What did you do to end up here?"

"I struck a British officer."

"You ain't serious?" Roan breathed in astonishment, pushing away from the wall. Twisting around, he crossed his legs in front of him, braced his elbows on his knees, and asked, "Why'd you do that?"

"I didn't like the way he was pushing an old man around. Of course, if I hadn't had too much to drink, I might not have done anything at all." He grinned over at the youth. "The price one pays for indulging in too much ale."

Brad's devil-may-care nature put Roan at ease. "Where you from?" he asked.

Brad shrugged. "Nowhere in particular. My brother has his own ship, and we sail around a great deal. Neither of us likes being in one place for very long."

"Have you ever been across the ocean?"

"Yeah. Several times. Have you?"

Roan heaved a disgusted sigh and settled back against the wall again. "Naw. Ain't never been anywhere. But I'd like to go sometime."

"Then why don't you?"

"'Cause I got my sister to take care of. Our papa died last month, and I'm the only one left to take care of her. She'd never last on her own. Course, if she got married. . . ." He let the sentence trail off as he imagined all kinds of exotic places he'd like to visit and missed the strange way Brad looked at him.

40

"You know, Roan," he said, "that might come true sooner than you think."

"Oh, yeah? Why do you say that?"

"Because once Dane gets us out of here, you won't be able to go back home. The authorities know where you live. You'll have to hide out until your sister can find the evidence you need to prove your innocence."

Obviously the youth hadn't considered that part of it, for his face suddenly paled and his brows gathered in a worried frown. "Yeah, I see what you mean."

Any further comment Brad might have wanted to make was interrupted by the sound of the metal door at the end of the corridor swinging open. Although the meals in gaol weren't even close to palatable, everyone agreed it was better than starving to death—barely—and at least it offered a break in the monotony. Both Brad and Roan stayed where they were, watching the turnkey carry in a torch which he jammed into the bracket on the wall, then turn and motion for a second man to follow. The smell of warm porridge preceded the other, and although it failed to completely mask the rank odor of the gaol, the inmates recognized that supper was about to be served and quickly left their places on the floor to stand by the bars, patiently awaiting their meager rations. Brad and Roan, however, decided to pass it up this time, thinking that before the night waned they would have the opportunity to eat something a lot more appetizing.

"Brad," Roan whispered as they watched the others gobble down their sparse sampling of stew, "do you have any idea what your brother has planned?"

Brad shook his head, a smile appearing from within the thick growth of beard. "But you can bet it will be dramatic. He enjoys showing up the Tories. Just be ready to move once it happens." One of the prisoners near them suddenly turned their way and vomited everything he had eaten, and Brad was quick to grab Roan's arm and pull him to another part of the cell. "God, this place is disgusting," he snarled as he pushed Roan back down on the floor and covered the boy's shoulders with both blankets. "You'd think men would have a little compassion for the sick. Even if they are criminals."

"Especially if there's a chance they aren't," Roan added.

Brad chuckled. "That applies only to you, son . . . not me." Settling down beside Roan, he laid his head back against the wall and closed his eyes, content to rest for a spell while he waited for his brother to make an appearance.

It was nearly midnight before everyone within the gaol had fallen into some kind of repose, whether it was deep sleep or fitful slumber. Even the guard had taken up his usual place in his chair, his chin resting on his chest, his bulgy eyes closed, content to spend the rest of the night right where he was. He had been asleep only a few minutes when an insistent rapping on the metal door startled him out of his dreams. Coming full awake, he could hear in the distance the angry shouts of a crowd on the street and wondered for a moment whether or not he had actually heard someone knocking.

His curiosity bade him to find out, and he awkwardly pushed himself up from the chair and went to the door. Standing on tiptoe, he squinted between the bars in the tiny window. There on the floor in the hallway sat a huge wicker basket, and from it came the warm, sweet smells of freshly baked breads and cinnamon rolls. During the five years he had been paid to stand guard over the gaol, no one had ever been kind enough to bring him something to eat in the middle of the night, and in all that time he had never been tempted to share the meal given its prisoners. This was rare indeed, and although he should have questioned who'd brought it and why, his desire to sample the food and find out if the donor had been thoughtful enough to include a bottle of wine turned him away from the door to get his keys. Rusty hinges squealed when he pushed the portal open all the way, and without the slightest delay he hurried to the basket, his thick-soled shoes clumping against the stone floor. A red-and-white checkered cloth covered the contents. He paused with outstretched hand, wondering why it had been necessary to use a basket large enough to accommodate enough rations for the entire group of prisoners, when suddenly the bright fabric jiggled and a pistol was thrust at his nose.

"Make one sound and I'll splatter your brains all over the wall," Dooley threatened in a harsh whisper as he climbed out from under the piles of bread and sweet rolls in the basket. "Anybody else here besides you?"

The turnkey's eyes nearly bugged out of his head as he stared at the black bore pointed at his face. "Just Mr. Schmitt, and he's in his quarters. D-don't shoot me, mister. I-I'll do whatever you want."

"Of course you will," Dooley sneered. "And you'll start by unlocking all the cell doors."

He jerked his head in that direction and waited until the gaoler had turned away from him before he glanced back over his shoulder and gave a short, soft whistle. Upon hearing the signal, Dane, Drexler, and three others stepped out from the second corridor where they had been waiting, pistols drawn. Motioning for Drexler to post guard should Schmitt decide to leave his quarters, Dane then led the rest of his group down the hall toward Dooley and his companion, and once the turnkey had unlocked the way, another member of the party clubbed the gaoler over the head. His pudgy frame crumpled to the floor in an unconscious heap.

"Grab the torch," Dane instructed and while Dooley climbed up on the chair to get it, he bent and retrieved the keys from the gaoler's limp fingers. "Dennis, you and Clay turn the women loose, but be sure and tell them to keep quiet."

"You got it, cap'n," the man assured him, following Dane into the corridor which led to the cells.

The bright light of the torch and the sounds of hurried

footsteps brought many of the prisoners out of their sleep and up on their feet, already sensing what was taking place. The first to reach the bars separating the rescue party from the inmates was Brad.

"I knew you'd come," he grinned at his brother.

Dane's glance quickly took in the other's appearance, and once he was satisfied that all Brad needed was some fresh air, he handed the keys to Clay and nodded at the lock before he answered. "Maybe you ought to tell me why you're in here first," he bade. "Then perhaps I'll change my mind about letting you out."

"I had a disagreement with a British officer," Brad replied with a smile. "And I'm sure you would have reacted the same way."

"You hit him."

Brad's smile widened, and he shrugged a shoulder. "He had it coming."

"I'm sure he did," Dane laughed.

The male prisoners, realizing this was their chance at freedom, quickly crowded the exit once Clay had unlocked the door and swung it wide. But before any were allowed to leave, Dane warned them that they must remain as quiet as possible. A group of nearly twenty soldiers were at the end of the block trying to break up a crowd of protesters, and if they wanted to sneak away unnoticed, they'd have to walk very casually. Everyone agreed, and as they started filing out, Dane grabbed his brother's arm through the bars when Brad took a step to follow.

"We'll be using a different way out," he whispered to him, watching Clay hand the keys to his partner as the pair moved down the corridor toward the women's cell.

It was Dane's plan to pay the warden a visit once the cells had been emptied out and from there leave the grounds through the back door of Schmitt's quarters. The other prisoners might have thought Dane was doing them a favor by turning them loose, but the truth of the matter was that he was simply using them as another decoy. Once their departure was noticed—and it surely would be because of the size of the crowd—the British soldiers would descend upon them with muskets cocked and ready. A large number of the group would make good their escape. Many of them would find themselves right back where they started. As for Brad Remington, he would be safely on his way to a place Dane had chosen to hide his brother for a few days until the authorities decided he wasn't worth looking for.

Roan was the last to leave the cell, and once he had reached the exit, he paused beside the man responsible for his release. "You must be Dane Remington," he said, shivering a little when the emerald eyes met his. He forced himself to smile. "My sister's the one who told you we were here." He nodded at Brad. "Me and your brother. I want to thank you for getting us out." A strange smile lifted one corner of the man's mouth, the purpose of which Roan couldn't understand. Figuring that he never would, he dismissed Dane Remington's odd reaction and started to turn away. A huge hand on his shoulder stopped him dead in his tracks.

"You're Roan Lockwood?"

"Y-yes, sir," he answered nervously, his worried gaze shifting from one brother to the other and back. The man's size was most intimidating to a young boy of fifteen, and although Roan couldn't say why, he had the feeling he might have done something wrong.

"Wait here," Dane instructed, giving him a gentle nudge toward Brad before he turned and glanced down the corridor for his men. Seeing that Clay and Dennis had already unlocked the door to the women's cell, he motioned for the pair to make a quick retreat, then nodded at Brad to bring Roan with them.

The group edged their way through the throng of people heading toward the front door. But once they'd reached the end of the passageway where Drexler and Dooley waited, they veered to the right and hurried toward the door at the end of the second hall. Pistols drawn, they crowded around Dane as he stood before the closed entryway, Clay and Dennis with their backs to them as they watched for unwanted company coming through the main entrance. Drexler and Dooley flanked both sides of Brad and Roan while Dane took the lead. Using the muzzle of his weapon, Dane rapped loudly on the sealed portal, the hammer cocked and a fist raised in anticipation. A moment later the door was swung open and Marlin Schmitt barely had time to see the hard knuckles thrown at his jaw before they connected and sent him reeling into a world of black unconsciousness.

"This ol' reprobate have a wife?" Dane asked as he guardedly pushed the door open all the way and surveyed the interior of the room, taking note of the huge desk and chair in one corner, the fireplace with its warm blaze against the opposite wall, and a door leading to an adjacent chamber.

Brad supplied the information. "Not that I've heard."

"Anybody else live here with him?"

The response was the same.

Stepping over the unmoving body on the floor, Dane motioned for Drexler and Clay to check the rest of the quarters. As they rushed off, he indicated to Dennis Holt that he and Brad should bind up the gaoler while Dane took the time to examine the papers lying on top of the desk. Within moments his orders had been carried through and the small party of men stood by silently awaiting further instructions. None of them seemed in much of a hurry to leave the building, and the longer Roan watched Dane Remington, the more he sensed there was another reason for breaking Brad out of gaol besides his being a Remington. Roan also suspected Dane and this odd assortment of renegades hadn't honestly cared whether he escaped or not and that the message his sister had taken to the man was merely a covert way of telling Dane that his brother was in trouble. Otherwise why would it matter to him what Marlin Schmitt had on his desk?

The gaoler's body was dragged to the middle of the room and the door to the hallway was shut and locked. Once Dane had satisfactorily gone over the documents on the desk, he picked up a candle and crossed to where the man lay. Coming down on one knee, he tilted the candle and allowed several drops of wax to fall on Schmitt's forehead. Roan watched the strange goings on without comment until he saw Dane withdraw a copper coin from his pocket and press it firmly into the wax.

"I'll be damned," he muttered with a smile. "You're—"

The emerald eyes shot up to silence Roan, and for a minute he thought that perhaps Dane Remington would kill him for what he had learned about him. The soft smile that parted his lips told Roan differently.

"Your payment for being freed from gaol is your pledge to keep my identity a secret, Roan," Dane advised as he came to his feet and returned the candle to its place. "Do I have it?"

Roan didn't hesitate in the least. "Yes, sir!" he exclaimed. "And I want you to know that if I can help—"

Dane shook his head. "You can help by staying out of trouble." The color of his eyes softened when he thought of who waited at home for the young man. "I think your sister needs you more than I do." The boy's disappointment shone clearly on his face, but Dane wasn't swayed by it. He knew he'd spend more time protecting the lad than helping the cause, and that was something he couldn't afford to do. He turned his attention on the dwarf. "Dooley, see that Mr. Lockwood makes it home all right."

"Aye, cap'n," the midget nodded, reaching up to grab Roan's elbow. "You heard the man, Roan. Time to go."

Stumbling toward the exit, Roan stopped once they neared it and turned back to look at Dane. "I just want you to know, sir, that if you ever change your mind—"

"I won't," Dane gently interrupted. "But thanks for the

47

offer." With a nod of his head toward the door, he motioned for the group to follow the pair and waited until everyone had gone before he gave the place a quick once-over and turned to make his own hasty exit.

The fire in the hearth had died to glowing embers, and the tiny, three-room house took on a chill. The woman who slept in a chair was stirred from her dreams. Brittany came awake with a start, her mind clouded with visions of her brother hanging from a tree, and she bolted to her feet before she realized it had only been a nightmare. Perspiration dotted her brow, and she raised a shaky hand to wipe it away. She hadn't meant to fall asleep, nor could she understand why she had. Roan hadn't come home yet, and it could mean only one thing: Dane Remington had changed his mind about helping them. Frustrated and a little angry, Brittany crossed to the fireplace and took the poker from its stand, irritated with herself for having allowed him to humiliate her as he had. Her only salvation had been in her handling of the affair once she'd followed him to the commons and confronted him at the table where his men sat by listening to every word she had to say. Although the others didn't seem to know what payment Dane Remington had requested in exchange for his help, Brittany told him she'd meet the price but only *after* Roan had been freed from gaol, and she'd gone on to liken her faith in him to her confidence that her brother would receive a fair trial. But since she had no one else to turn to, she would have to go against her better judgment in this case and take the chance that for once in his life he wasn't lying. With that she had turned on her heel and departed, failing to see the broad smile that flashed across his face.

Her journey home that night had been anything but pleasant. Several times along the way she'd been stopped by one man or another, some reeking of ale, some with money in their hands, asking for a tumble in bed with her if she didn't charge too much. She wasn't sure even now how she'd managed to get away from all of them, but those events weren't half as nerve-racking as her discovery that she was being followed.

The first time she noticed the man was when he accidentally bumped into someone trying to proposition her and knocked him out of the way. While he was busy apologizing for his carelessness—thus distracting the sot—Brittany hurried off without even bothering to look at him. About ten minutes later, she thought she saw him again when she stopped to fix her cloak. The breeze had caught the edge of her cape and whipped it off her shoulder. She had spun around trying to retrieve it before the garment fell and she spotted him standing just outside the circle of lamplight about fifty feet behind her. What drew her attention to him was that he'd stopped at precisely the same moment as she, something she found very curious. The entire evening had been one trial after another, and whether or not this incident was related didn't matter. She decided to find out for certain.

At the next corner—even though it took her in the opposite direction from her home—she changed course and hurried down the street past several darkened storefronts until she came to an alleyway. Checking first to make sure he hadn't rounded the last building at the crossroad and put himself in clear view of her, she dashed into the narrow passageway, raced to the first recessed doorway she saw, and ducked into its shadowed protection to wait. A moment later the same man rushed past the mouth of the alley as if he were in a hurry to catch up with someone, and it was then—when the light from a nearby streetlamp fell briefly on his face—that she remembered having seen him sitting at the table with Dane Remington.

At first it confused her. Why would he send someone after her? What had he hoped to gain? Was there a chance he hadn't believed her story and thought perhaps she'd been sent by one of his enemies to lure him away from his men?

The longer she thought about it, the angrier she became, and she unconsciously sucked in a deep breath with the intention of venting her wrath at the top of her lungs. What stopped her was the realization that in doing so she would reveal her hiding place, and the idea of outsmarting Dane Remington was far more appealing than satisfying the urge to scream. Shooting out of the blackened entryway, she'd raced off down the alley away from the spot where the man had been, and she hadn't stopped running until she was certain she'd lost him.

She'd spent a very restless night wondering if she'd done the right thing in escaping. When morning came and Roan hadn't returned home, she worried all the more. By suppertime she was nearly in tears, regretting her actions and certain Dane Remington had decided she couldn't be trusted. And now—

The tiny clock over the mantel struck one, jarring Brittany out of her thoughts. If her brother was to be spared, she'd have to be the one to do it, and she'd have to do it on her own. Tossing down the poker, she hurried to the cupboard where she'd hidden her father's pistol, thinking that if the gaoler had allowed her to visit Roan once before, he'd let her do it again. And after he unlocked the door, she'd level the gun on him. A confident smile parted her lips as she envisioned it, failing to recognize the danger she would face should she be confronted by two men; there wouldn't be enough time to reload the pistol.

Since her last trip through Boston had caused more problems than she cared to remember, Brittany decided it was time for a disguise. Roan and she were about the same size, and if she braided her hair and piled it high on top of her head underneath a hat—one with a floppy brim to help conceal her face—her trek to the gaol would probably be quite uneventful. No one would bother a young boy. Having made up her mind, she laid aside the pistol and started for Roan's bedroom and the place where he kept his clothes. But the distant thunder of horses' hooves stopped her midway across the room, and she froze, listening to the sound intensify as the visitors raced toward the house. Who could it possibly be at this hour? Absently she glanced at the clock as if the gesture would change night into day and render those descending upon the tiny building no threat but nothing more than weary travelers seeking directions to Boston. A tremor of fear shook her body and jolted her into action. Racing to the fireplace, she yanked the musket from the rack and went to the door. Swinging it wide, she stepped out into the moonlit night to face her guests, the musket aimed and her heart leaping to her throat once she saw the men dressed in the uniform of the British Army.

"Lower your weapon, Miss Lockwood," the tallest man instructed her. "We're not here to cause you harm . . . we're looking for your brother."

"Roan? But he's in gaol." The last was spoken hurriedly, for Brittany knew what it meant: Dane Remington had done as she'd asked, and her brother was free. If these soldiers thought she had anything to do with it, they'd arrest her on the spot. It was all she could do to keep from smiling and giving herself away. "I-I don't understand," she added, feigning confusion.

"We're not sure how it happened, Miss Lockwood," the soldier confessed, "but all the prisoners were released tonight, and we've been ordered to hunt them down." He dismounted and started toward her. "We'll have to search the grounds, Miss Lockwood. And I suggest you not interfere."

"He isn't here," she told him in all honesty, "but you're welcome to look. I have nothing to hide."

Glancing over his shoulder, he motioned for his men to check the barn and all other outbuildings while he went inside. As he walked past her into the house, Brittany lowered her eyes as though she respected his authority, while in truth she mocked it. Was this the feeling her father had

51

whenever he went against the Crown in defense of something he believed in? If so, it felt good. She remained perfectly still as she listened to the man walk through each room; she knew that he wouldn't find anything. Roan hadn't come home yet, and when he did, they'd decide where he could hide until she'd gathered the information she needed to prove his innocence. She wasn't going to simply stand back and let her brother hang for something he hadn't done. The sound of the soldier's footsteps coming toward her brought her out of her thoughts, and she quickly dismissed them to glance up at him, her lovely face twisted into a worried frown—one she truly didn't feel the need for.

"I don't think I have to remind you what will happen if we learn you're harboring a man charged with acts against the Crown, Miss Lockwood," he advised, looking down his nose at her. "It will be treated as an act of treason, and you'll be dealt with accordingly."

"Yes, sir," she whispered, dropping her gaze.

"Even though he's your brother, it will be your duty to inform us if he returns home or if you learn of his whereabouts."

And hell will freeze before I do, she thought defiantly.

"Do you understand?"

"Yes, sir," she replied.

Seeing that his men had returned from their assignment empty-handed, he nodded for them to mount their horses and brushed past her toward his own. Sitting rigid in the saddle, he cast her one last look and said simply, "Remember." Then, yanking back hard on the reins, he spun the animal around and kicked his heels in the horse's flanks, sending the group off in a rush.

The man's arrogance rankled, and she turned to watch his departure. Tempted to raise the musket and point it at his back as he rode away, she decided instead that perhaps it would be more fitting to put a bullet through one tip of his tricorn. Imagining his shock over her boldness, a smile broke the straight line of her mouth as she raised the weapon and took aim. Her finger moved to the trigger. Her thumb cocked the hammer. She squinted one eye, zeroed in on her target and fired. The click of metal against flint went unheard by the soldiers galloping down the lane, nor were they aware of the young woman who laughed at them. In her haste to protect herself against her unexpected company, Brittany had forgotten to load the musket.

"It's a shame you'll never know how close you came to having to explain how you got a hole in your hat," she sneered, lowering the gun and sighing heavily. "And how close I came to being thrown in gaol."

The cool night air encased her thinly clad frame and she shivered, reminded of the late hour and that she had no idea where Roan was. She went back in the house and closed the door. The fire in the hearth had all but gone out, and after she'd hung the musket where it belonged, she stooped before the glowing embers and added more logs until she had a roaring blaze. Roan wouldn't be spending the night, but at least before he left, her brother would have a warm meal in his belly.

The delicious aroma of stewed chicken bubbling in a thick broth and dotted with sourdough biscuits filled the tiny room a while later, and as it simmered in the pot, Brittany left the house long enough to go to the well for a pitcher of fresh, cool water. Her work had kept her too busy to think, but now as she raised the bucket and listened to the squeaking of the pulley, she was reminded of the hundreds of other times she had done it, and that from now on, she would be doing it solely for herself. Unshed tears burned the backs of her lids, and she angrily dared them to ruin her brave façade. Maybe it was hopeless to try to prove Roan's innocence when she was going up against the Crown, but, damn it, she had to try! She wouldn't—*couldn't*—just give up without a fight. And if worse came to worst, they would sell what little they had and find someplace else to live. She had heard that there was a lot of good farmland in Pennsylvania. And if that wasn't far enough away, they'd head south to Virginia. A soft smile replaced her need to cry when the name of Patrick Henry came to mind. He had the reputation of being the finest lawyer in all the colonies, and it was no secret that he openly opposed the British.

"By God, that's what we'll do," she announced aloud, as if her brother were standing beside her. If they couldn't find the evidence they needed to clear Roan's name, then they'd sell everything, go to Virginia, and hire Mr. Henry as their lawyer. From what she'd heard, he hadn't lost a case yet.

Excited with her decision, she hurriedly poured water into the pitcher and started back toward the house. Roan probably wouldn't like the idea of giving up their father's land, but once she explained its necessity, he'd understand; she was sure of it. Reaching out for the doorknob, she gave it a quick twist, pushed the portal open, and stepped inside without looking up, her mind filled with dreams of success. In the next instant, those dreams were shattered when a movement near the table in the middle of the room caught her eye, and for a brief second she feared the soldiers had returned to arrest her for what she was planning. Frightened nearly out of her wits before she recognized the young man sitting there helping himself to a meal, she let the water pitcher slip from her fingers and thud loudly against the floor.

"Roan!" she scolded through clenched teeth as she gave the door a hard shove. "What's the matter with you? I could have been carrying papa's gun instead of that pitcher and shot you right through the head."

"I'm sorry, Brit," he apologized sheepishly as he watched her pick up the pitcher and cross to the cupboard with it. "I didn't mean to scare you."

"How did you get in here?" she snapped, grabbing a towel to mop up the puddle of water.

He jerked his head toward the back room. "Through the

bedroom window."

"Well, you can't stay," she barked without looking at him. Falling to her knees, she angrily blotted up the water. "They're already looking for you. A band of British soldiers were here not more than an hour ago."

"I know," he whispered, fighting down the knot in his throat. Several moments passed while he watched her clean up the mess he had caused, and when she still continued to choose not to look at him, he drew up the courage to ask, "Brit, why are you angry with me?"

Her head came up instantly, and the pained look on his face tore at her heart. She wasn't angry with him; she was just angry. Her mood softened a little with the realization of how it must seem to him, and she rested back on her heels, smiling apologetically. "I'm not . . . I'm just scared," she confessed. "It was bad enough when Papa died so suddenly. But when I was told you'd been arrested for something that could get you hanged . . . well, I just realized how helpless we really are. We have no family, no friends—"

"But we do," Roan grinned. "We have Brad."

"Brad?"

"Brad Remington," Roan finished when he realized his sister had forgotten about the man she'd met in the gaol.

"You mean *Dane* Remington," she corrected, coming to her feet and crossing back to the cupboard. "And he's far from being our friend."

"No, Brit. I mean Brad Remington, Dane's brother. He's the one from gaol, the one who sent you to find the midget. Remember?" Brittany stood with her back to him, and Roan couldn't see the surprised look that came over her face or how quickly it turned to rage. Instead he mistook her silence to mean that he would have to explain further what went on inside the gaol after she'd left. He thought the entire episode amusing and he laughed as he picked up his fork and stabbed a piece of stewed chicken. "Brad said he didn't want to tell me that his brother was the one who was going to break us

55

out of gaol because he thought I might give it away." He popped a piece of meat in his mouth and added, "I probably would have, too. If I had known then what I know now. . . ." He chuckled and took another bite.

Brittany's hands shook as she squeezed the water from the towel into a bowl, wishing it were Dane Remington's neck she had in her hands. The moment she told him who it was who'd sent her, nothing else mattered. If she'd refused to agree to his conditions concerning payment, he'd have gone to the gaol anyway. He wasn't interested in *her* brother, but his own, the cad! He'd used her . . . they both had! Closing her eyes, she drew in a long, deep breath and let it out slowly, praying she could still the desire to take her father's musket from the rack, load it, and hunt the bastard down for the degrading trick he'd played.

"Brit? Are you all right?"

Roan's concern cooled her wrath a bit and she nodded. There was no need to tell him what had transpired between her and Dane Remington, but if the opportunity ever presented itself, she'd return the favor. The rogue would regret the day he'd tangled with her. "So," she began, turning around with a forced smile on her face, "tell me what happened. How did Brad's brother get the two of you out of gaol?" Coming to the table, she sat down in a chair opposite him.

"Well, I don't know exactly. I didn't have time to ask how they got the keys from the guard, but Mr. Remington told his men to turn everybody loose. I was going to follow them—"

"But he stopped you," Brittany cut in, thinking perhaps there was a decent bone in the scoundrel's body after all.

"Not really. I stopped to thank him for helping, and once he found out who I was, he told me to wait with Brad. We left through Schmitt's quarters while everyone else went out the front door."

Brittany's blue-gray eyes darkened, and rather than let

56

Roan notice her rage, she stood up and went to the fireplace. "So you're saying that he actually came to the gaol to free his brother, not you."

Roan couldn't see the importance of that particular distinction. "Well, yes. . . ." he admitted with a shrug. "But it doesn't really matter who he came for. He turned everybody loose."

"And sent them all marching out the front door while he and his brother and his men sneaked out the back." She whirled around and asked, "Now why do you suppose he did that?" She didn't give Roan time to answer. "I'll tell you why. Everyone else was a diversion. He sacrificed those people so his group could get away, and if you hadn't stopped to thank him, you'd have been one of those sacrifices. You could have wound up right back in gaol!"

Roan couldn't understand her anger. "I'm sorry, Brit, but I don't see it that way. I'm free, aren't I? Does it matter how?"

"Yes!" she shouted.

"Why?"

Brittany drew in a breath to explain that Dane Remington had agreed to help her only if she was willing to pay for it. But before she had voiced the statement, she realized Roan would ask what it was that they could possibly use as money when they didn't have any, and she quickly changed her mind about telling him. She didn't want her brother to know what the terms had been. Besides, as far as she was concerned, the man's actions had nullified the agreement. And there was the probability that she would never see him again, which would free her from any obligations she might have had.

Hoping to change the subject, she said, "We really don't have the time to discuss something we obviously disagree on, Roan. You've got to get out of here before the soldiers come back." She left her place by the hearth and went back to the cupboard. "I'll pack some food for you and give you papa's gun. Once you've found a place to hide out for a while, send word so I'll know where to find you once I've cleared your name."

"I think you should come with me, Brit," Roan replied, leaving the table to stand beside her. "It won't be safe for you here."

"I can't, Roan. If we both leave, who'll prove you had nothing to do with the burning of a building? I'll be all right."

"And what if you can't? What then?" he argued, touching her arm and drawing her eyes to his. "What if the person who set me up decides to use you next time?"

"I've already figured that out," she smiled encouragingly. "We'll hire Patrick Henry as our lawyer."

"Patrick—" Roan shook his head and went back to sit down. "And what are you going to use for money? He doesn't work for free, Brit. Besides, he lives in Williamsburg. It's a little too far to walk."

"I know," she agreed, setting aside the cloth bag she had started to fill with supplies. "We'll sell everything we have, then—"

"No!" Roan exploded, jumping to his feet. "You're not selling Papa's land because of me. I won't let you!" In a rage he rushed to the cupboard, yanked open the drawer, and retrieved his father's pistol. "I'd rather die first," he hissed, grabbing for the bag of food.

"Roan, wait!" Brittany pleaded when he ran for the front door and jerked it open. "Papa would understand. He'd do the same thing. Roan, please!"

But her brother would have no part of it. He had already dashed outside and was running toward the shelter of trees surrounding the small farmhouse. Brittany followed until she'd lost sight of him and realized the uselessness of trying. Roan had a stubborn streak that surpassed her own, and no amount of arguing would change his mind until he was ready to listen. She staggered to a halt and simply stood there staring into the darkness that had gobbled up her brother's thin, youthful shape, certain he would come home again once his temper cooled. Maybe, by then, she'd have good news.

Brittany rose early the next morning, fed the chickens, milked the cow, and stacked wood beside the hearth before she donned the best clothes she had and set out for town. Filled with hope and determination, she vowed not to return until she'd learned who'd accused her brother of arson, what building had been destroyed, and when the fire had occurred. From there she planned to build his alibi and draw a few conclusions as to why he'd been named in the crime.

But by the time the sun had painted a bright canvas of oranges and reds against the sky, Brittany was no further ahead than when she'd started. Depressed and exhausted, she'd headed home again, accepting a ride from a neighboring farmer in the back of his hay wagon. No one seemed to know anything, or at least they weren't willing to talk about it, and the whole situation, in her mind, hinted at something bigger than what appeared on the surface. Having expressed her thanks to the old man who'd made her journey a little less tiring, she waved goodbye to him as he started the wagon off down the road, leaving her to walk the last half-mile alone.

A chill was in the air by the time the house came into view, and Brittany was wishing she'd had the foresight to take along her cape. Hugging her arms to her, she ran the last hundred feet and hurried inside the house to start a fire. Twenty minutes later she sat before the hearth wrapped in a blanket and chewing on a crust of bread smeared with marmalade. The day hadn't been very productive, but she wasn't going to let it get her down. She'd try again tomorrow. Perhaps if she sat in on some of the trials at the courthouse, she might accidentally learn something that would be of use. It was worth a try.

Brittany had just about decided to retire for the night when she thought she heard a noise outside the window. Praying Roan, seeing the logic in her idea about hiring Mr. Henry, had come home to discuss it, she bolted to the window to peer outside. The sun had completely disappeared over the horizon, leaving behind only a hint of pale orange in the western sky and enough light to form eerie shadows among the trees. Brittany viewed the baroque scenery with some trepidation, wondering if there were truly something out there or if her mind had played tricks on her. Deciding it was the latter, since all she heard now was the rhythmic chirping of crickets and the occasional belch of a bullfrog, she started to turn away when she saw a dark figure move out from behind a tree and disappear through the open doorway in the barn. From this distance and because of the scarcity of light, she couldn't distinguish his size or even hope to recognize him, but she was reasonably certain it wasn't Roan. Whoever it was had obviously thought to make himself comfortable in her barn, for a moment later she saw the faint yellow light of the candle he had lit.

"Well, we'll just see about that," she fumed, rushing back to the fireplace and her father's musket. "You won't be as lucky as that arrogant soldier who was here. I'll make sure this damn thing's got a ball and powder in it this time."

Only a few minutes had elapsed before Brittany was on her way to the barn, the blanket draped over her shoulders and the leaded musket in her hands. It had been a long time since someone decided they could sleep in the Lockwood barn without permission, and Brittany's father had been the one to change the man's mind in much the same manner as Brittany planned to do. If whoever it was didn't have a good enough answer to suit her, she'd either send him on his way or shoot him if he argued. Yet, as she approached and could see the lantern with its flickering candlelight, some of her courage slipped and her steps faltered. It was almost as if the man were inviting her to walk right in—just as she'd planned to do. Changing her mind, Brittany decided it was probably wiser to circle around in back and come in through the other entrance, where she could catch him off guard.

To her dismay she found the back door closed, and she knew from past experience that the rusty hinges would squeal loudly once they were forced to move. Her only other choice was the door in the loft above her, but she quickly dismissed that idea; she didn't have the strength to pull herself up the rope and she'd have to leave the gun behind to do it. Torn by indecision, she simply stood there trying to figure out what to do when suddenly the problem was solved for her. The click of the latch sent her flying back around the corner of the barn and out of sight, and she held her breath while she listened to the door swing open on its squeaky hinges. Afraid to move and give herself away, she gingerly cocked the musket and waited for the man to appear, certain he'd had second thoughts about staying in the barn and at any moment would step out where she could see him. The silence grated on her nerves. The shadows remained unmoving, and Brittany suddenly realized that something was wrong—horribly wrong. If the intruder wanted to sleep in the barn, why would he open both doors and let in the chill night air? Was it possible he thought no one was home, had made plans to meet someone here, and was using this signal to them that it was safe to approach? She glanced back toward the house. Surely he would have smelled the fire from the hearth. Failing to trust her instinct to wait for a better opportunity to trap her unwelcomed guest, Brittany guardedly moved toward the back door to investigate.

The barn offered very few hiding places. On the whole it was one big open room with two stalls and a hay loft. From this angle Brittany couldn't see the man, but she also realized he couldn't see her. If she could get inside and spot him before he knew she was there, she'd have him at a disadvantage once she aimed her gun at him. Then she'd find out why he was here and order him off her property. Deciding that perhaps he had elected to stretch out in one of the stalls while he waited, she focused her attention in that direction and quietly stepped into the barn. But the moment

61

she'd cleared the doorway, a hand came around from in back of her and wrenched the musket from her fingers. She gasped as she spun around and staggered back several steps, certain the man intended to use the weapon on her and that her life was about to end.

"Good evening, Miss Lockwood," he greeted with a smile, and Brittany's fear turned to rage the instant she recognized him.

"You!" she choked out, her chest heaving and her tiny hands clenched into fists at her sides as she watched Dane Remington casually reach over and close the door. "You have a lot of nerve coming here. What do you want?"

He didn't answer but instead removed the piece of flint from the musket, thus rendering it useless, and leisurely strolled away from her.

"I asked what you're doing here," she demanded, shadowing his steps as he headed for the front of the barn and the opened doors. Upon reaching them, he pulled them shut, slid the bar in place, and turned around to toss the musket aside in a pile of hay before looking at her. The soft yellow light from the candle fell warmly on his handsome face, and even though she was furious with him, her heart pounded a little harder. She took a tentative step backward, willing herself to remain strong and firm where he was concerned. She mustn't let his masculinity intimidate her. "Well?"

"We have some unfinished business," he admitted, his eyes raking over her slender form draped in the blanket. "I've come to collect."

"Collect for what?" she hissed. "I don't owe you anything."

"Your brother's out of gaol, isn't he?" he challenged, his green eyes sparkling. "That was the deal, wasn't it?"

"As far as I'm concerned, Mr. Remington," she snapped, standing arms akimbo, "our deal is off. I know all about your brother being one of the prisoners, and even if I hadn't agreed to your slimy proposition, you'd have gone to the gaol anyway! If anything, you owe me. *I'm* the one who drew you a map, remember? I even suggested the diversion. Without my help, both our brothers would still be there."

He stared at her a moment, enjoying the sight of her beautiful blue-gray eyes, the delicate features of her nose and chin, the slight flush in her cheeks, the long, golden strands of hair falling about her face and shoulders, and the tenacious way she stood up to him. It had been a long while since he'd seen a woman so ravishing, and the thought of tossing her on her back brought a smile to his lips.

"That's true, Miss Lockwood," he lazily agreed. "But the truth of the matter is, I could have left him there."

Brittany saw the logic in what he said and had no answer in return; but she wasn't about to give up. "The way I see it, *Mr. Remington,*" she mocked, jerking the blanket off her shoulders and rolling it up in a ball, "is simply that you took advantage of the situation. If you'd been a gentleman, you'd have told me the truth as soon as you learned the name of the man who sent me. But you didn't. You pretended to be doing me a service for which you expected to be paid! Well, I shan't pay. And you, sir, are to leave my property this instant." An outstretched hand pointed the way.

Dane crossed his muscular arms over the wide expanse of his chest and grinned devilishly back at her. "And as I recall, I told you then that I was no gentleman."

Brittany could feel the argument leaning in his favor. She also realized he wasn't leaving until he had what he'd come for. She squared her shoulders and raised her chin determinedly . . . and most definitely not without a fight. "A bargain made in all honesty is one I would uphold. But ours was far from that and therefore cannot be considered binding. Or are you, sir, admitting you have no honor as well?" For a moment she thought she'd won when the smile disappeared from his lips. Then she noticed how his eyes gleamed.

"And were you so foolish to think you would find a man with honor—a gentleman besides—in a place where you found me?"

The flesh across the backs of her arms tingled and she worriedly hugged the blanket to her while covertly plotting her hasty retreat from the barn. "The place one chooses to inhabit does not necessarily indicate one's integrity."

"It does in this case," he replied, stepping in.

Brittany knew where she'd left the pitchfork and she didn't waste any time in retrieving it. Holding it in both hands, she raised the weapon in front of her and pointed it at Dane's chest. He, in turn, decided not to pursue her—for the moment, anyway.

"I think they imprisoned the wrong brother," she snapped, a false sense of victory giving her the courage to speak when her attacker quickly moved back a step to avoid the sharp tips she thrust at him. "And I suggest you vacate these premises before I decide to go to the authorities and inform them of the identity of the man responsible for turning the prisoners loose."

Dane shook his head as he unhurriedly slid his jacket off his shoulders. "That wouldn't be wise, Brittany," he sighed, tossing the coat over the top rail of the stall nearest him.

"I'm Miss Lockwood to you," she corrected icily. "And why not?"

He moved away from her as though he didn't have a worry in the world. "After tonight we'll know one another too well to call each other by our last names," he replied with a confident smile as he picked up the blanket she'd dropped, fanned it out over a soft bed of hay, and lay down on one hip. With his head propped up on his fist, he gave her a long, leisurely once-over and said, "And if you turn me in, I'll be forced to tell them who my accomplice was."

"You arrogant miscreant!" she stormed. "Do you mean to blackmail me?"

"No," he admitted. "Just to get what I have coming to

me." He raised a finger and motioned for her to join him on the blanket, but the strange smile that came over her lovely face told him that it wasn't going to be so easy.

"So you want what's coming to you?" she mocked, and Dane suddenly wished he'd chosen his words more carefully. "Well, you'll get no argument from me."

Before he could guess her intent, Brittany shifted the pitchfork to one hand, drew back, and sent it hurling toward him. Her accuracy surprised him, and he barely escaped injury as he jerked out of the way. His shirt sleeve wasn't so fortunate, and while he struggled to free the material from beneath the prong buried deeply in the dirt floor, she raced to pick up the musket and run to the closed front doors of the barn. There were more flints in the house, and she was determined to replace the one this rogue had thrown away, then finish the job she'd started. Maybe by killing him she'd have something to bargain with in exchange for Roan's freedom. However, it was a possibility she wasn't meant to explore. By the time she'd awkwardly slid the bar aside and was ready to shove the door open, Dane had given up trying to dislodge the pitchfork to gain his release, and instead simply yanked his arm free and sprang to his feet. He was on her in a flash, grabbing first the musket, then her wrist, spinning her back to the center of the room. Only then did Brittany realize the probability that she would not come out of this the winner, and she said the first thing that came to mind.

"I think I should warn you," she courageously declared as she backed away with each step he took, "Roan isn't the only brother I have. He doesn't live here anymore, but after I tell him what you tried to do to me, he'll hunt you down and kill you."

Dane smiled crookedly back at her; he didn't believe a word of it. "Not what I tried, Brittany. What I succeeded in doing." He threw the musket aside and continued to advance.

Every muscle in her body tightened with fear, and when she spoke her voice betrayed the brave front she wished to present him. "What kind of man would force himself upon a defenseless woman?"

He cocked a doubtful frown. "Defenseless?" He jerked his head in the direction of the pitchfork she'd thrown. "I hardly call that defenseless. And as for forcing myself on you . . ." He paused in his pursuit of her and shrugged a shoulder. "I don't think there'll be a struggle."

Brittany's temper flared. "You conceited lout! Do you actually think I'd enjoy having you . . . touch me?"

White teeth showed with his smile. "Shall we find out?"

Where once there had been hopelessness, Brittany now sensed victory. The man was deplorable, and if this were her only chance to experience passion, then she would leave this earth never having fully tasted of it, for she doubted his caress would do anything more than turn her blood to ice. "And what if I prove you wrong? What then? Say I allow you one kiss. Will you leave my property content in knowing you tried but failed?"

Dane thought about it for a moment while he studied the delicate line of her throat, her rounded bosom, and the sensuous curve of her waist and hip. "I doubt it will happen, but yes, I'll be content, *if* you prove me wrong."

Brittany braced herself for the most repugnant sensation she would ever have to endure, praying it would be over as quickly as possible. But a seed of worry took root in her brain as she watched his tall, muscular body move closer. It began to grow when the masculine scent of him assailed her nostrils. It blossomed into full, raging color once she felt the heat of his powerful frame before her, and Brittany suddenly realized how foolish she'd been. Certain he could read the apprehension in her eyes, she lowered her gaze, thinking that would be enough. It only made matters worse; for instead of distracting her thoughts about him, it merely intensified them. Her entire vision now consisted of the sinewy breadth

66

of a well-toned physique draped in a silky shirt. She blinked and dropped her gaze even lower, instantly regretting having done so when her eyes fell upon the tight-fitting breeches he wore and the bold evidence of his manliness. Her face flamed hotly, and she struggled to draw a breath and beg a moment to collect herself, knowing that if he touched her right now, she would pay dearly for thinking he would have no affect on her.

Dane had not missed the color that arose in her cheeks, nor had he failed to understand its cause. Though he'd found it difficult to believe, he sensed this beauty who stood trembling before him had somehow escaped the adventure of a young man's advances or even the pleasure of courtship. Had those very same been so blind to what she had to offer that they'd chosen not to woo her? The corner of his mouth twitched with a half smile. Or had she met their attempts with pitchfork in hand? That would indeed send any man running . . . but not him. And if he wanted to prove that, he'd better do it now while he had her at a disadvantage.

There had been only one other time in Brittany's life when she'd been alone with a man under the same circumstances. Except that he hadn't been a man but a thirteen-year-old boy and she a nervous, inexperienced twelve-year-old girl. They'd met in this very same barn with similar intentions—to share the excitement of a first kiss. It had been very pleasant, she recalled, until her father had accidentally walked in on them. He'd been more surprised than upset, and after he'd sent the young boy home, he'd tried to explain as best he could the dangers in doing what she'd done. She understood them perfectly—now. Realizing her mistake in giving Dane Remington the upper hand, positive he wouldn't stop with just a kiss, she started to take a step backward and insisted that he leave her farm immediately. But he had other ideas. As if he sensed what was on her mind, he shot out a hand, caught her roughly by the elbow, and yanked her forward into his steely embrace.

67

The shock of his forcefulness took her breath away, and Brittany opened her mouth to inhale. In that same moment, his hand came up from behind her and trapped the long strands of hair at the nape of her neck in his fingers while his other arm encircled her narrow waist and crushed her to him. The feel of his hard, muscular body against hers sent a scorching heat throughout every inch of her, and Brittany's head began to spin in anticipation of what he was about to do. In a daze, she watched his parted lips descend slowly upon hers. The instant they met, something inside her snapped and she came to life. Struggling with every ounce of strength she had, she frantically fought to break his hold on her, failing miserably; he was simply too powerful. Sliding her hands up between them, she pushed against his massive chest with all her might, merely succeeding in loosening the strings that laced the front of his shirt. When her fingertips met the iron flesh and crisp matting of hair beneath the silky fabric, a fire exploded within her, and she could feel herself weakening. Then his mouth twisted across hers, and Brittany's eyes flew open when his tongue traced the outline of her lips and then thrust inside. This wasn't how it was supposed to be! He wasn't playing fair. Finally in desperation she brought back her foot and kicked him squarely on the shin, instantly winning her freedom.

"You rogue!" she panted, stumbling back while Dane winced in pain. "You despicable, uneducated, lying barbarian! I want you off my property and I want you to leave right now. If you *ever* show up here again, I'll shoot you on sight! I have never in all my days met someone as detestable as you, and I pray to God I never will again." She raised a trembling hand and pointed at the exit. "Out!"

Dane had little doubt that she'd do as she promised should he be foolish enough to visit her again. But since he had no intention of seeing her after tonight, he would have to finish what he came for before he left. Without a word he started toward her, determined to take what he thought she owed him.

Brittany knew in that moment that her threats and insults hadn't touched him in the least. If anything they had spurred him on. "Don't come near me," she warned, stepping back while her mind hurriedly took inventory of the items in the barn. There had to be something she could use to change his mind and send him on his way. She continued to retreat until her shoulder struck an object hanging on the wall behind her. A quick glance revealed the thick leather ox harness and the vision of how Dane would look with it draped around his neck flashed to mind. Spinning, she yanked it from the hook and threw it at him, and while he clumsily tossed it aside, Brittany raced for the stall and the pitchfork she vowed would bring an end to Dane Remington's miserable life. But the tool remained firmly stuck in its place after several futile attempts to free it, and Brittany decided it was time to flee. If she could make it to the house, she could lock herself in. Surely Dane would lose interest after a while.

But her luck appeared to have come to an end when she turned to make good her intentions and found Dane blocking the narrow entryway to the stall. Rather than give way to tears and frantic pleading, Brittany straightened her slender frame and confronted him, her tiny fists resting on her hips.

"All right," she sighed, "I admit defeat. You're stronger, faster, and—God forgive me for saying this—smarter than I. However, I hate to think that all the talent between us should go to waste. You obviously want something I don't believe you deserve, and that puts us at a standstill. So why don't we take a moment to consider the alternatives?" A shiver ran through her when his eyes lowered to the buttons up the front of her dress and she could almost feel his fingers unfastening them. Hoping to distract him, she crossed her arms over her bosom. "Instead of working against each

69

other, why not work together? I was planning to go to the courthouse tomorrow and sit in on some of the trials. Perhaps I might learn something that would clear your brother. If I were able to do that, couldn't we then consider ourselves even?" She suspected he wasn't listening; his perusal of her lowered to her slim waist, her flat belly, and the yards of gathered cloth of her skirt. "Why was he arrested?" she asked, feeling the blush rise in her cheeks once his green eyes met hers again.

"For striking a British officer," he said lazily. "There were several witnesses and Brad doesn't deny it. He's guilty, Brittany; there's nothing to prove." He nodded toward the blanket on which she stood. "So why not have this over with, and then we can go our separate ways."

"Dear Lord in heaven," she moaned indignantly. "You make it sound like—like—"

"A business dealing," he finished. "It is. That's all it's ever been. That's all it ever will be." He smiled crookedly at her, one dark brow raised in question. "Surely you didn't think there was more to it than that?"

Although she would have preferred her first encounter with passion to have been coupled with love, she hardly expected the man with whom she shared it to be so indifferent about it. Her feelings were hurt, but more than that, she was insulted. "Of course not," she sneered. "How could I? Especially with you. In fact, I wouldn't even call this business. I'll think back on it as the one most sickening thing I ever had to do."

He smiled broadly at her declaration, then bowed as if surrendering to the truth. "Then why not get on with it?" he proposed.

"Because I don't want to!" she exploded, grasping the handle of the pitchfork. In a surprising show of strength, she yanked it loose. With it held in front of her, she charged him like a raging bull going in for the kill. Unfortunately, her matador deftly stepped out of the way as he reached out, secured the weapon in one hand and her arm in the other, and easily took the pitchfork away.

"Damn you!" she wailed, her tiny fists raining blows against his chest as he flung the pitchfork away, then clamped his arms around her and fell with her upon the blanket. "I hate you, Dane Remington," she cried. "Damn it, I hate you! *No-o-o!*" The last was wrenched from her in a scream of protest, for he had already worked her skirts up around her hips and his hand was bold upon her thigh. Pinned beneath him, she wiggled and squirmed to get loose. His breath was hot against her throat, and she squeezed her eyes shut to block out the sight of him while she strained to pull away. He seemed to have a hundred hands and thousands of fingers *all* quicker than her own as she fought to keep her clothing in place and her modesty intact.

"I'll see you hanged for this," she raged, shrieking when she felt the buttons pop loose on her dress and the lace strings on her camisole untwine. She screamed when his mouth, warm and moist, covered the peak of one naked breast while his hand worked the fastenings on his breeches free. Her entire body seemed aflame and though she fought every move he made, a strange stirring erupted in the pit of her belly and her shame mounted twofold. She mustn't find his advances exciting! She mustn't!

He rose above her for an instant, parting her thighs with his knee and pulling her undergarments out of the way with a quick swoop of one hand. Then he came to her, hot and hard, and Brittany gasped when he pressed the throbbing staff deep inside her. She lay paralyzed, enduring the first sharp piercing pain that made her wince before it ebbed into something almost pleasurable, and she vowed he would never know how fully, how sensuously he had touched her. He began to move, to caress her, to awaken in her the passion she had only dreamed about, and she bit her lip to stop the wanton desires that burned uncontrollably within her. But hard as she tried, she couldn't ignore the excitement

71

his touch aroused. The feel of his steely muscled frame pressed against her, the masculine scent of him, the burning kisses he trailed down her throat to her breast, then back to her lips—they all made passion build within her. His mouth moved hungrily against her while his broad frame moved ever quicker against her. The long, sleek thrust of his hips ignited a raging inferno within her and though she wished to deny it, he had awakened her womanly desires, and without realizing it she began to move beneath him. His heart thundered against her naked breasts, his breathing sounded in her ear, and just when she was beginning to wish it would go on forever, his long, muscular body shuddered in the glorious release of his ecstasy.

A tear found its way to the corner of her eye and moistened her tightly closed lashes when the thought that she had very nearly cried out her own pleasure in that moment of passion turned her heavenly bliss into shame. She lay frozen, willing herself not to move lest it already be too late for her to mask the traitorous yearnings of her young body, and waited for him to rise from her to secure his garments. But rather than have him recognize the humilia-tion which stained her cheeks scarlet, she readjusted her clothing, scrambled to her knees, and clutched the bodice of her dress to her bosom with trembling hands. Her gray eyes filled with unbridled rage pierced him.

"I'll see you rot in hell for this," she snarled, unaware of the fetching sight she presented. Golden locks of hair, sprinkled with pieces of straw, fell in wild disarray about her shoulders. Her cheeks were flushed, and her breasts threatened to spill from the fabric meant to hide them. "If it takes the rest of my life, I'll do it, I swear to God."

Tossing his jacket casually over one shoulder, Dane smiled back at her, oddly wishing this wouldn't be the last time their paths crossed. But he had other things on his mind, more important things than bedding a fiery wench such as this, and he had only come here to teach her a lesson.

His method, to her way of thinking, might have been extreme, but he wanted her to realize how foolish she'd been in making a deal with a stranger. "Good-bye, Brittany," he said. "And try to stay out of trouble. The next man you bargain with might not be so gentle."

Furious, Brittany sprang to her feet. He'd leave here with a knot on his head that wouldn't go away for days! She grabbed the first thing she could lay her hands on. Yet once she held the wooden mallet and had spun back to hurl it at him, Dane had already left the barn.

"Damn you!" she shouted into the darkness. "Damn you for what you've done!" Tears choked off any further exclamations, and caught unawares by the need to cry, Brittany slumped to her knees and gave way to her frustrations. It wasn't so much that he'd tricked her and forced payment from her that made her weep, nor was it even his cool indifference to her. It was the lingering warmth of his lips against her breast, the liquid fire she could still feel burning in her veins, and more than that the realization that he knew just how much his touch had affected her.

Chapter Three

Brittany had risen before the sun, done her chores, and promised herself that as soon as she returned home this afternoon she would cut firewood. More than a week had passed since Roan had left the house in a rage, and she'd spent every day at the courthouse in Boston rather than taking care of the farm. Not only was the supply of firewood running low, but the spring crops had yet to be planted. She realized that without the fall harvest, she wouldn't have enough money to survive the winter, but it was something that would just have to wait until she had Roan home with her again.

Once she had bathed, washed and dried her hair, and changed into a clean dress, she fixed herself a scant breakfast of hot cinnamon rolls and a glass of warm milk. Since she couldn't afford to buy something to eat in town, this would be the only meal she'd have until she'd returned home. Just the thought of going that long without food made her ravenous, and she attacked the meager sampling with zeal.

But while she ate, her thoughts began to wander, and just as they had for the past seven days, they came full circle and centered on the scoundrel who had plagued her every waking hour. Her desire to eat waned and the food upon her plate cooled, and in a rage she wadded up her napkin and threw it on the table. Bolting to her feet, she angrily began to clear away the dishes.

She had told herself over and over again to let the memories of what happened that night fade just as the warmth of his kiss had. She'd succeeded as long as the sun shone brightly overhead. Dusk was another matter entirely, for it had been then—when the lengthening shadows of evening masked his identity—that she'd been lured to the barn. Had she known who he was, it might have turned out differently. Suddenly, Brittany could almost see his handsome face and feel his strong arms wrapped around her, and a defiant, betraying smile touched her lips. Dane Remington was a rogue, a blackguard, a man who should be hanged for what he'd done to her. But the titillating excitement he'd stirred within her that night was something she would always remember, and she knew full well that had she known who'd awaited her, she'd have willingly gone to the barn anyway.

"You are such a fool, Brittany," she irritably told herself. "You're acting like it might have meant something to him." Without a care that she might break one of the dishes, she tossed them into the wash pan, went to the hearth for the kettle of hot water, and returned to the cupboard with it. "If it meant something to him," she admitted gruffly as she poured water into the pan, "he would have come back to see me before now. It was a matter of business, remember? He told you that—it was business then and it always would be." Yet she couldn't deny the glimmer of hope she felt. Maybe someday—just like Roan—he'd return.

Once Brittany had washed the dishes, dried them, and put them away, she set her mind on more important things as she grabbed her cape, whirled it over her shoulders, and tied the strings at her throat. Tomorrow was Sunday, which meant the courthouse would be closed. If she didn't uncover a useful bit of information today, she'd have to wait until Monday to try again. Each day that passed put more of a strain on her, and although she tried not to think about it, she was beginning to worry that something awful had happened to her brother and that it would be months before she learned of it. Yet even so, she wasn't going to give up her efforts to prove his innocence. She had, however, given up the idea of selling the farm and using the money to hire the Virginia lawyer.

The morning had started out bright and sunny. But as she left the house and started down the narrow lane to the main road into town, she noticed a gathering of gray clouds to the north. If she were lucky, the day would be nothing more than overcast and she'd have returned home before it rained. Better still, perhaps someone would offer her a ride.

Tension between the colonials and the soldiers sent to Boston from England had grown during the past seven days. Brittany had noticed the difference on her second visit into town. Now that a week had elapsed, it had become even more difficult to travel the streets without being pushed, shoved, and jostled about, even though she wanted no part of the constant demonstrations being held on nearly every street corner. What surprised her was that it wasn't just men voicing their dissatisfaction with the Crown and its rules, but women and children as well. Brittany could understand their disapproval—her father had talked often of it—but she felt it was something best left up to the men to handle. The women belonged at home with their children, where they'd be safe. She braced herself as she rounded the next corner. She had heard the angry voices of the crowd several minutes earlier and knew that today would be no different than yesterday. She'd have to fight her way through only to be confronted by one group after another until she reached the courthouse.

With her head down Brittany ignored most of the people milling about the street. If she appeared not to be a part of them, she might be able to avoid trouble. But she had no sooner decided on this strategy when someone within the group turned suddenly, bumped into her, and knocked her off the sidewalk and into the street. An excited shout from the driver of a passing rig and a quick hand upon the brake saved Brittany from certain harm; the alarm sent her scurrying out of the way before the team of dappled grays had trampled her. She turned to heatedly state her feelings to the one responsible. Her irritation only mounted when she discovered the person standing nearest her was a young lad of twelve or so with a very apologetic and frightened look upon his face. It was rather difficult to berate a child for doing something that had obviously been an accident. Yanking her cloak more tightly about her slender frame, she turned on her heel and stomped off without a word, edging her way back onto the sidewalk and moving at a quicker pace than before.

She had traveled only a short distance when she felt a hand grab her elbow and heard someone call her name. Surprised that she might actually know someone in this throng of protesters, she lifted startled eyes. It took her a moment to recognize the man, but once she had, she suddenly wished she'd stayed at home to cut firewood.

"Mister Ingram," she nodded, forcing herself to be polite. "I'm surprised to see you here."

Brittany had known Miles Ingram since she was a little girl. His father, Bartholomew, was a titled lord from London sent by the Crown years ago to keep order and to oversee the progress of their rebellious British colony, and both Miles and Bartholomew were known for their loyalty to England. To find Miles in the middle of a demonstration seemed quite unnatural. But then, Miles rarely did what was expected of him. The Ingrams were wealthy people and owned property adjacent to the Lockwood farm. They had been neighbors for many years, and although Brittany's father and the elder Ingram strongly disagreed on politics, they had still managed to be friends—not the type who visited each other regularly, but the kind who would never pass the other on the street without stopping to talk for a while or offer their help when the other needed it. As Brittany recalled, neither

her father nor Miles's had ever asked any assistance, and she assumed it was because both men were too proud to admit they needed it. As for Miles—well, Roan had told his sister years ago that he didn't like the man. He couldn't exactly say why, but as time passed, Roan grew to understand the lustful look in Miles's eyes whenever his gaze fell upon Brit. The two families might be from different classes, but Roan suspected that it didn't matter to Miles where Brit was concerned. He also guessed that marriage had never entered Miles's head, merely the hope that someday Brit would become his mistress. Thus Roan had repeatedly cautioned his sister to be careful if she ever found herself alone with Miles Ingram. She'd always taken her brother's warnings lightly, telling him that she doubted such a time would come. His words, however, stuck in her mind and now as she stood facing Miles, she wished the crowd at the corner was twice as big.

"It's quite by accident, I assure you," he smiled, the faint lines around his brown eyes deepening. "I was on my way to meet a business associate when a beautiful young woman stepped in front of my carriage." A bony hand rose to indicate the rig waiting at the curb, and Brittany suddenly realized he meant her.

"I apologize for that, Mr. Ingram. It was unintentional."

"Please call me Miles," he begged, clasping his wrist and letting his hands dangle in front of him. "We've known each other too long for formalities."

Brittany smiled uncomfortably as she covertly took in Miles's stately attire. He wasn't much taller than she, and his features were thin to a fault. His complexion was pale, his smile insincere, and his dark eyes lacked the genuine warmth in his words. His sandy blond hair showed only slightly at the temples beneath his white powdered periwig, and his narrow frame was clothed in dark brown breeches and coat, gold brocade waistcoat, beige ruffled shirt, and ivory hose. In his hand he held a three-cornered hat bedecked with a large white plume. He wasn't a very handsome man. He was plain—not striking in his appearance, but not unpleasant. He was nothing like Dane Rem— Brittany could feel the hot blush rise in her cheeks, and rather than have Miles notice, or worse, question the cause, she turned her face away from him, shielding her embarrassment with the hood of her cape.

"I'd like to express my sympathy over the loss of your father," he remarked, his thin face pinched into a frown. "It must be difficult for you without him, especially now that your brother isn't around to help with the farm."

Brittany couldn't be certain, but she thought she detected a hint of something akin to delight in Miles's statement. She cast him a sidelong glance.

"It's bloody awful what happened to him," Miles continued, failing to recognize her suspicious look. "Just bloody awful. If you ask me, I think he was set up."

"Do you?" Brittany asked, her tone icy. "And why is that?"

"Well," he went on, raising his pointed nose in the air as he sent a disapproving look to the riotous crowd behind them, "everyone knows these people will go to any lengths to have what they want." He turned a serious frown her way. "To the point of sacrificing one of their own."

Brittany didn't like having to admit it was possible, but what he said made sense, especially since she hadn't been able to find out any information to help clear her brother's name. Maybe Roan had been a sacrifice and she would spend the rest of her life trying to prove his innocence without succeeding. But suddenly, something else Miles said registered in her brain.

"You referred to Roan as 'one of their own.' What did you mean by that?" Her dislike of Miles Ingram intensified; no one attacked her family name and got away with it.

For a brief instant, Brittany could see an arrogant, almost hateful gleam in the man's eye before his face wrinkled in a somewhat atoning expression, as if what he'd said was to have been a secret. "I didn't mean to imply—well, I thought you knew—" He stopped, cleared his throat, then sighed heavily. "It's a well-known fact that Roan has been an active member of this group of rebels. He's been seen with them countless times—"

"Doing what?" she demanded. "Standing in a crowd? If that makes one guilty of treason, then you and I should be arrested, for that's exactly what we're doing." She jerked her head toward the mass of people who had drifted closer to them without Miles's knowledge.

Beads of perspiration dotted his upper lip despite the cool, crisp air, and he nervously blotted them away with a kerchief he pulled from his coat pocket. "Please don't misunderstand me. I wish to offer any help I can in clearing your brother. We're neighbors, Brittany. But more importantly, we're friends."

The bold use of her name when she hadn't given him permission upset her more than his sudden interest in Roan. Maybe her brother wasn't so far from the truth about Miles Ingram after all. Roan had never been one of Miles's friends in all the years they'd known each other. Why would he care about him now, unless there were some ulterior motive? The thought of it made her stomach churn. "Thank you for your generous offer, but there isn't much you can do," she replied, smiling sarcastically, though the gesture went unnoticed.

Miles's pale brown eyebrows lifted and fell with his surrender to the truth. "Perhaps not. But I can offer you the use of my carriage. The streets aren't safe these days for a woman such as yourself, especially unchaperoned . . . as you can well attest." He smiled pleasantly.

The thought of sitting alone with Miles inside the covered landau with no one to protect her was much more disagreeable than the idea of walking the rest of the way to the courthouse through the crowd. Noticing the milliner's shop over Miles's shoulder, she mocked, "You're too kind, sir. But I shan't need a ride, for I've come here to see about a new hat." At his puzzled look, she raised a finger and pointed past him. Without waiting for his comment, she quickly moved in the direction of the shop and called back as she left him, "Tell your father I asked about him."

She didn't stop until she'd opened the door to the tiny establishment, gone inside, and lost herself among the customers already there. From within their safety, she glanced back at the street through the front window and watched Miles until he had finally determined their visit was over and climbed back into the carriage. Maybe she was being unfair with him, since he had never truly made any advances toward her in all the years they'd known each other, but until Roan was living with her again, she knew she had to be careful. A woman alone was an open target to any man willing to take the chance, no matter how wealthy or poor he was. Dane Remington was a prime example of this. Brittany's shoulders sagged with the realization that the scoundrel had slipped into her thoughts again, and she quickly went to the door. There were more important things for her to do than feel sorry for herself.

As usual the courthouse steps were crowded with people who wanted to satisfy their curiosity, mock the judicial system, or simply be present when their friends or relatives were sentenced. Brittany had learned after the first day that if she was to be one of those allowed inside, she had to get there early. Because of her meeting with Miles, she was late. The doors were already open and a stream of observers was pouring in. Elbowing her way through the mass, she hurriedly and awkwardly climbed the steps and squeezed in through the doors just as they were being shoved closed again. Caught up in the flow, she was taken down the corridor and into the huge chamber where the general court was held. The seats were already filled and Brittany had to be content with standing at the back of the room and listening to most of what went on rather than seeing it, for even on tiptoe, it was impossible for her to see over the men crowded in front of her.

Sometime around noon court was recessed for an hour,

and while most of the observers left to get something to eat, Brittany chose to stay where she was. It had been difficult enough the first time to obtain a place in the courtroom. The afternoon crowd was always bigger and rougher, and since she'd planned to skip the noon meal anyway, there was no sense in leaving. Besides, if she were lucky, someone might vacate his seat and allow her the luxury of getting off her feet for the rest of the day. Edging her way through the men near her, she moved away from the wall and toward the cluster of benches, unaware of the brown eyes watching her. To her dismay no one would willingly give up his place to her, but even so, she decided that standing where she was now would at least give her an unrestricted view of the proceedings once court resumed.

Every muscle in her body ached and her stomach began telling her that it was time to eat. Ignoring both, she closed her eyes and tried to let her mind drift off to more pleasant things. It aggravated the situation when aromas of cold fried chicken and bread filled her nostrils. A groan tightened her throat once she saw that several of those who'd stayed behind had brought food with them and now sat contently filling their bellies. She realized it was all she could do to keep from reaching out and snatching a piece of what they ate when suddenly a bright red juicy apple was thrust in front of her.

"It isn't as filling," the deep voice beside her said, "but it will help."

Brittany didn't know whether to be embarrassed or grateful. She knew it was foolish to turn down the man's kindness for the sake of pride. "Thank you," she murmured, taking the apple and glancing at him from the corner of her eye. The half-smile on her lips disappeared. A tingling sensation raced across her shoulders and down her spine. He seemed oddly familiar, though she couldn't remember where she might have met him. Frowning, she considered his features for a moment, then asked, "Have we met before?"

83

His dark hair gleamed in the muted sunlight that shone through the windows as he turned his head to observe those standing nearest them. Convinced he and Brittany could talk without interruption or being overheard, he smiled warmly at her. "Once," he offered quietly. "About a week ago. I'm surprised you recognized me. I wasn't exactly dressed for company that day."

The sound of his deep, rich voice played upon the strings of her memory, faint and indistinct, but alarming. He was a very handsome man and well groomed, with the darkest brown eyes she had ever seen. How could she possibly forget meeting someone like him?

"I apologize, sir," she half whispered, dropping her gaze. "I can't seem to recall—"

"It's understandable, Miss Lockwood. I'm sure you've chosen not to remember having been there." He laughed softly. "I know I'm trying very hard." The man's attention was distracted for a moment when someone left his spot on the bench in front of them, and before anyone else could claim it, he blocked the way with his tall, muscular body and allowed Brittany to have it.

"Thank you," she smiled, sitting down. "And for the apple."

"You're doubly welcome," he replied with a polite dip of his head before moving to rest a hip on the railing directly behind her. Crossing his wrists and laying them on one thigh, he leaned slightly forward so that only she would hear what he had to say. "Did your brother make it home all right?"

His question didn't surprise her half as much as the discovery of who he was; for in that instant, the picture of Roan standing next to a bewhiskered man with whom he shared the cell exploded in her mind. Yet what bothered her more was the fact that this man's brother was Dane Remington. She gritted her teeth and willed herself not to jump to her feet, whirl around, and present him with a

84

stinging slap to the face.

"No thanks to you," she hissed, staring straight ahead.

Brad straightened in surprise. "I'm afraid I don't understand—"

"You and your brother would have left Roan there had he not stopped to thank you and remind you both that it should be the other way around." She studied the front of the courtroom again.

Brad mentally relived that night in gaol, trying to make some sense of what Miss Lockwood said. Failing that, he shrugged it off and elected to indulge himself for a moment and silently drink in her beauty while her eyes were turned away. The soft light of the cloudy day reflected itself in her long strands of golden hair and accentuated her finely boned profile. It had been dark the first time they met, but even so, Brad had gotten a glimpse of her loveliness in the torchlight and had decided then that she was the most breathtakingly exquisite woman he had ever seen. Looking at her now confirmed it. He smiled to himself as he thought of how many times a pretty face and womanly curves had gotten him into trouble. It was his weakness, Dane had told him, and Brad had to agree. While some men enjoyed inbibing a mug of ale or increasing their wealth, Brad always chose the company of women—married or single, rich or poor, didn't matter to him. He thrived on their demure manner, the musical tones of their voices, and their femininity, always looking to be of service to them in hopes of an intimate reward for his valor. It was what he had wanted from Brittany Lockwood, but her biting words just now raised considerable doubts about the possibility.

Lost in thought about the bliss he wished they could share, he failed to see a man who moved closer to him until a huge hand touched his shoulder and jolted him out of his reverie. He started to rise, ready to defend himself, thinking someone in the crowd had recognized him and sent a soldier to arrest him, but the firm grip on his shoulder held him down. He glanced up nervously in expectation of finding a gun pointed at him, and then let out a slow, thankful sigh as he saw Ernest Betts staring back at him.

The huge, brawny man was a member of Dane's crew, and the fact that he couldn't speak a word merely added to his menacing appearance. It had been his misfortune years before to be captured by pirates, and the evil captain had decided it would be interesting to see if Ernest Betts would bleed to death if someone cut out his tongue. It was an experience he would never forget, and because of it his temper always matched his fiery red hair. Brad saw impatience gleaming in the giant's brown eyes, but unable to figure out what he might have done, he shrugged and shook his head at Betts, who in turn nodded to someone on the opposite side of the room. There Brad saw Dane leaning back against the wall behind him, his arms crossed over his chest and a disapproving scowl on his face. Brad then knew exactly what he had done: he'd been told to stay away from the courthouse for his own safety. But having seen Miss Lockwood ascending the stairs, he'd lost all sense of caution and followed her, hoping for a moment when they could talk. His opportunity had come when he'd noticed the way she stared at those who ate, and as he passed by an old blind woman, he snatched the apple from her basket and approached Brittany. It had been foolish and he knew it. Smiling sheepishly at his brother, he lowered his gaze and rose to his feet. Brittany Lockwood would have to wait. Looking at her one last time, he turned and followed Betts out of the room.

Brittany wasn't aware of what went on behind her back, that a stranger had approached Brad Remington, that Dane had been standing not more than twenty feet away from her, or that all three men had left the building. She was too busy being angry. She had simply sat there trying to think of the most disparaging thing she could call Brad to his face. Striking him would draw too much attention, and she didn't want that. All she wanted really was to find Roan, her young, headstrong, rebellious brother. Suddenly, Brittany remembered that Roan had regarded Brad Remington as their friend. Was it possible Roan had gone looking for Brad, thinking that he might take him in? It would explain where Roan had disappeared to for the past week. Or maybe it took him that long to find Brad and once he had, Brad had sent him home again. Was that what Brad meant when he asked if Roan made it home all right? Filled with hope, she twisted on the bench to pose the question to him.

Her smooth brow furrowed instantly when she saw an old man standing where only a moment before Brad had been, and her irritation started anew. Brad had disappeared as noiselessly and stealthily as his brother had that night in the barn. Was it possible they were not truly men of flesh and blood, but demons come to plague her?

Her cheeks warmed instantly, for the memory of Dane renewed the feel of his rock-hard body pressed against her, the manly scent of him, and the heat of his lips kissing her. He was no illusion; he was a man, bold and challenging. Absently she raised the apple to her mouth and took a bite.

By late afternoon Brittany was no more the wiser to the charges brought against her brother. Neither Roan's name nor his case were even mentioned. It was as if he'd never existed and the incident hadn't happened. Miles Ingram's claim came to mind and she wondered if perhaps what he said was true—that Roan had been offered as a sacrifice for someone else's freedom. But who? And why? Was this other person so important to the rebels' cause that an innocent boy had to die?

While everyone else in the courtroom started filing out, Brittany remained where she was, trying to sort out the vague possibilities. Most of the trials had been over such minor things as how much a landowner had to pay to get back his runaway slave or whether or not a blacksmith was responsible for the broken wheel he had supposedly repaired only an hour earlier. However, the one trial that stuck in Brittany's mind had concerned an allegation charging a silversmith with treason for harboring a known criminal—a man who openly opposed the Crown. The arguments on the merchant's behalf had been to the effect that his visitor had yet to be charged with a crime and therefore couldn't be called a criminal. All of the evidence against him was hearsay. But the judge wasn't swayed and had sentenced the silversmith to be hanged at five o'clock this afternoon. It vividly reminded Brittany of what might have happened to Roan had he not escaped, and even though she didn't know the silversmith, the idea of a man hanging from a tree formed a knot in her stomach. She glanced up at the clock on the wall and took note of the time: the poor wretch had but a half-hour to live.

Executions in Boston were a public affair. The condemned man was driven to the hanging tree in a cart, his hands bound. The street was always crowded with onlookers. Some would mock him; others would throw rotten food at him. All in all, it was a deplorable sight, and one Brittany wished to avoid. Because of the late hour, it might already have begun, and that, coupled with her desire to be home before dark, made her rise and hurry to the door.

Her assumption was correct: the streets were already lined with people, and as she stood on the courthouse steps she could see the cart carrying the silversmith. It would be several minutes yet before he passed by, and Brittany quickly descended the stairs, thinking to push her way through the crowd and cross the street to the alley. From there she could head for home through the back streets and put a good distance between her and the gruesome ordeal before it was carried out. That was her plan. However, those standing in her path wouldn't oblige.

"Excuse me, please," she begged, fighting to wedge herself between two burly men. "Please allow me to pass. I must get through."

"We all wanna see, lady," one of the two snarled. "If ya wanted a better view, ya shoulda been here earlier. Be content where ya are."

"No, you don't understand," she argued, wincing when the mass of bodies pushed in from behind her, and someone stepped on her toe. "I don't want to see. I'm trying to get across the street."

"Can't get a better look from over there," the other mocked, slapping his companion playfully in the ribs. "For a shilling, I'll put ya on my shoulders."

The first man glanced back at her and grinned toothlessly when he saw the bright golden hair spilling out from the hood of her cape. "Hell, I'll do it for nothin'," he offered, starting to twist around toward her.

Brittany decided it was time she moved. Not caring how much it might hurt, she jabbed her elbow into the man's stomach, and when he fell back in obvious discomfort, she darted through the opening he'd made and lost herself among a group of women. Their attitude wasn't much better, and although she would have liked to have told them exactly what she thought of them, she elected to keep quiet and stand perfectly still. Once the cart rolled past where she stood and the throng of people moved to follow it, she could then be on her way home.

However, it didn't turn out as she'd planned. Instead of being left behind when the mob fell into step behind the cart, Brittany was swept along with them. And the harder she struggled to get free, the worse it became. It didn't take her long to realize that if she gave in to her predicament and allowed herself to be carried away with them, she'd endure fewer bruises and bumps. There was also the chance that once the mass of spectators gathered around the hanging tree, she then might be able to wriggle away and race for home. That too failed to materialize, for the throng continued to grow once they reached their destination and trapped her deeper within them. Admitting defeat, Brittany begrudgingly joined them in observation of the silversmith's execution.

She could hardly believe her eyes: a group of children scrambled up the tree where the condemned man was to be hanged, and now they fought and clawed each other for the best place to sit. The idea of watching a rope being placed around someone's neck and witnessing him jerk and twist once the cart was driven out from under him made her sick. Young children such as these should not be allowed to watch, let alone be so close . . . what was wrong with their mothers?

Brittany grimaced. They were probably the ones who wouldn't let her pass and complained because Brittany was standing in front of them. Had the entire town gone mad? Was *this* the only sort of entertainment they found fulfilling? Trying to center her attention on something else, she raised her chin and studied the overcast sky with its spattering of golds and reds where the setting sun fought to peek through. This only added to her frustrations: now it would be impossible for her to get home before dark, and from the looks of the swirling clouds overhead, there was a good chance she'd be soaked before she even left town.

The woman beside Brittany couldn't see well enough. Placing her hand on Brittany's shoulder, she leaned her weight on it and stretched up on tiptoe. Brittany's temper flared and she was just about ready to slap away the offending grip when her eyes caught sight of a group of men on horseback thundering down the cobblestone street toward the crowd. Their identities were hidden by the black, high-collared capes they wore and the dark tricorns pulled low over their foreheads, and while everyone around her scrambled out of the way, Brittany just stood there mesmerized.

The one who led the group had cast a spell over her unknowingly. Mounted on a coal-black stallion, the man had a tall, lean frame which flowed with the swift gait of the animal as if he were a part of it. His long, muscular legs hugged the steed as he leaned forward slightly in the saddle, one hand firmly gripping the reins, the other clutching a drawn pistol as he urged the beast onward. His shoulders were broad, his chest wide, his hips narrow, and the sight of his billowing cloak gave the illusion that he was a giant bird ready to swoop down and devour its prey. While he charged closer, narrowing the gap between them, something gnawed at Brittany's subconscious. An odd feeling stirred inside her and she lifted her eyes to look at his face. His attention was riveted on the small band of soldiers guarding the condemned man, and he allowed only a brief glimpse of his profile as he raced on by her. But even so, the black mask he wore disguised his features, and Brittany had to be content with her imaginings.

A round of shots were fired, scattering the crowd. Brittany just stood there watching, unable to comprehend what was going on. The soldiers who decided to stand their ground and fight back were shot; the rest were clubbed unconscious; it was all done in a matter of seconds. The noose had already been slipped around the silversmith's neck, though it hadn't been tightly secured, and with the explosion of gunfire, the jittery cart horse bolted, leaving the bound man to dangle from the rope. Brittany's eyes widened as she watched him twist and turn and struggle for his life, and in the next instant, the rider, the one who had caught her eye, spurred his steed. Grabbing the man around the waist, the stranger lifted him up enough to ease the tension on the rope while one of the children in the tree inched his way out along the branch. He produced a steel blade and its sharp edge quickly severed the thick hemp.

A second rider drew his horse in beside the first, pulled the silversmith down into the saddle in front of him, and rode off. His companion motioned to the boy in the tree. Brittany gasped as she watched the youngster jump into the outstretched arms.

Before the pair raced off in pursuit of their cohorts, the stranger edged his mount closer to the trunk of the tree. From where she stood, Brittany could tell only that he appeared to be nailing something on the rough bark with the butt of his pistol. A shout from one of his comrades warned him to hurry, and the stranger, with the young boy perched in front of him, spurred his stallion and sent him thundering off down the road.

Several minutes passed before a few of the men in the crowd approached the tree. Brittany followed as well, curious as to what the stranger had left behind.

"It's a coin!" one of them shouted while another worked the nail loose.

"What kind of coin?" someone else called out, and Brittany hurried to get closer before the inquisitive onlookers pushed ahead of her.

"Ain't the kind ya can use around here," the first answered once he had examined it. "It's made of copper."

"Copper?" a woman beside Brittany repeated.

"And I can tell you what's stamped on it," yet another voice replied. "I'll bet it reads 'Sons of Liberty.'"

The crowd around Brittany began to shove their way closer, all wanting to get a peak of it, and she decided she had had enough of being bumped and pawed and stepped on. Changing direction, she moved to the back of the group and out into the open.

"How'd you know that?" she heard someone ask.

"'Cause it ain't the first time he left it behind when he

92

wanted the Tories to know who was responsible."

"You sound as if you know him. What's his name?"

"Don't have any idea. But he's called the Dark Horseman."

Visions of the stranger cloaked in ebony and riding a black stallion lifted Brittany's eyes toward the road where he and his companions had gone. "The Dark Horseman," she whispered with a smile, feeling an excited tingle race through her. The Sons of Liberty were known for their secretiveness in dealing with oppressive British economic and political action. In order for the society to survive, its members never allowed anyone outside their organization to know their identity. No one here today knew the name of the Dark Horseman; Brittany didn't . . . and she doubted she'd ever see him again. Her smile deepened as she turned away from the crowd to go home. But she'd always remember the time she'd witnessed what he could do.

The threat of rain, with loud thunder and bright flashes of lightning, discouraged the protesters from continuing their demonstrations, and the streets of Boston emptied quickly. Only a few carriages dotted the streets Brittany had to travel, and although it made her journey a lot easier not to have to fight her way through a crowd, it also made her a bit nervous. It wasn't safe for a woman to walk alone, and now that practically everyone had gone inside, it was worse. If someone approached her, she'd have no one around to step in and help.

Her first thought about tomorrow, Sunday, had been that she'd have to wait a day before returning to the courthouse. Now she was glad of it; she needed the time to build up her courage again.

Word of what had happened was quickly reported to the governor of Boston, and before she'd reached the edge of town, patrols of British soldiers appeared at nearly every corner. Even though she hadn't actually taken part in the rescue of the silversmith, she was afraid the mere fact she was there would be enough reason for them to suspect her. Cold, alone, hungry, and frightened, Brittany pulled the hood of her cape down further over her forehead and quickened her pace. She'd be safe once she left town.

She'd traveled nearly an hour down the dark, deserted road before a light rain began to fall. Her thick woolen cloak kept her dry, but she knew that if she didn't hurry, it wouldn't be long before it started to soak through. It was another mile further to the Lockwood farm. The intense glare of lightning that lit up the entire sky seemed to transform the dark trees into devilish shapes ready to spring out at her. The crack of thunder overhead magnified her fears. Storms usually didn't bother Brittany, but she'd never before been caught outside in the middle of one. She hurried her steps, trying to ignore the pounding of her heart.

With her head down to shield her face from the cold rain, Brittany didn't see or hear the riders coming toward her until they were practically on top of her. Once she had, it was too late for her to find a place to hide and wait until they had passed on by. She also realized it would be impossible for her to disguise the fact that she was a woman alone. Praying that the need to find shelter from the impending downpour was more important to them than bothering with her, she gave their animals wide berth and stepped to the side of the road, her face averted and her gait hurried.

"You there," one of them called. "We'd like a word with you."

Brittany wanted to pretend she hadn't heard him, to keep on walking. She wished this was all a nightmare and that at any moment she'd wake up to find herself in bed. Reality, like a blinding glare of lightning, flashed before her when one of the men jerked his steed in front of her and blocked her path. Her worry increased when she raised her chin to see that they were British soldiers. Because of the trouble Roan was in, she assumed they would think she was a part of it and therefore have little mercy on her should her answers to their questions not be what they wanted to hear.

"State your name," the first demanded.

She swallowed and replied, "Lockwood, Brittany Lockwood."

"What are you doing here?"

"I'm on my way home, sir." She didn't like how the others had moved their horses in around her; the huge animals pinned her within the circle they had made.

"From where?"

"I was in Boston."

"Why?"

She knew she mustn't tell them the truth. "I went there to see about hiring someone to help me with the spring crops, sir."

The one who spoke glanced at the man nearest him and smiled. He hadn't believed her, and Brittany knew it. Just then, a clap of thunder exploded in the air and frightened the horses. For a moment she thought she could be crushed between the huge beasts as they jerked their heads and began sidestepping nervously. With outstretched hands she frantically pushed against the thigh of a stallion who'd come dangerously close while she looked for a way to escape.

"I think you should come with us, Miss Lockwood," the leader said as he nudged his horse in alongside her and prepared to help her up behind him.

"What for?" she demanded a little more sharply than she should have. "I haven't done anything." She twisted sideways out of his reach.

"Haven't you?" he challenged. "Your brother's wanted by the Crown—"

"He's innocent!" she exploded, yanking the hood of her cape out of another man's grasp.

"The governor suspects otherwise. And you've been seen

95

every day at the courthouse. Now a group of troublemakers has come along and freed a man sentenced to hang, and you were right in the middle of it. We think you know more than you let on, Miss Lockwood. So, why not make it easy on yourself—"

Brittany didn't wait around to hear the rest of what he had to say. With her opened palm she pulled back and slapped the arrogant bastard's horse across the nose, waited for him to rear his head, then darted out from within the circle of animals and raced off down the road. The men's excited shouts were barely audible over the rumble of thunder, but they were loud enough to let Brittany know that the men were coming after her, and she didn't waste effort looking back over her shoulder to confirm this. The trees on either side of the road seemed too sparse to do her any good; the soldiers could easily maneuver their horses out and around them, but at least it might slow them down a bit. Changing direction, she headed off into the woods.

She failed to recognize the difference between the sounds of gunfire and thunder. If she had, she might have stopped running to witness the approach of another man on horseback who galloped up behind the soldiers. With a pistol in each hand, he fired upon one and then another in the group, killing them both. The third was the recipient of the stranger's sword thrust between his ribs, while a fourth, the last in the group, decided to run for his life rather than tempt Fate.

Brittany's heart was pounding so loudly in her ears by now that she couldn't hear the racing sound of hoofbeats against the hard earth behind her. Her side ached and she was out of breath. The muscles in her legs were beginning to cramp, and the only thing that drove her on was the fact that no one had caught up to her yet. It was foolish to think she could outrun their horses, but that's exactly what she thought she'd done, and for the first time since she'd escaped them, she glanced back over her shoulder.

The shock of seeing the lone rider draped solely in black made her stumble, and she nearly fell. Lightning seared the ebony sky behind him, silhouetting the huge beast on which he rode and emphasizing the man's broad-shouldered frame and the cape flying out behind him. But the vision lasted only a split second, and before her eyes could adjust, Brittany wondered if she had imagined it. Lightning flashed again, and this time she knew he was real. But would he harm her? And where had the soldiers gone? Was this the one they called the Dark Horseman? Or was he something evil?

The events of the day had been exasperating; the soldiers' accusations and their attempts to arrest her had been more than she could tolerate. And whether this man intended to hurt her or not, Brittany decided she wasn't going to just stand there and let it happen. Spinning around, she raced off again, her skirts held high and her golden hair whipping out behind her. Within seconds the huge stallion overtook her, and she would have screamed when the strong, muscular arm came around her waist and yanked her off her feet had she not been too winded to vent her fear. Tears stung her eyes; panic tightened the muscles in her throat and chest. Lightning illuminated the sky and thunder roared overhead. And just when she thought he was about to kill her, the stranger slowed his beast, twisted her around in his powerful embrace, and gently deposited her on the animals broad back in front of him. In that moment, when he turned the steed back toward the road in the direction of home, Brittany realized this man had not planned to kill her, but to spare her from a terrible fate at the hands of the British soldiers.

"Who are you?" she asked in hardly more than a whisper. Her entire body tingled from the contact of his wide, sinewy chest and strong arms, which held her tight as he guided the stallion down the road. His deep, rumbling laughter reverberated in her ears, tickled each nerve, and spread a warmth throughout her despite the cold, stinging droplets of rain that seemed to be increasing in intensity. "Are you the one they call the Dark Horseman?" she pressed, twisting slightly to look back up at him.

The dark mask hid most of his face, but even in this dim light she could see the emerald shade of his eyes and recognize the smile glowing in them. Encouraged by his obvious good humor, she added, "Are you the one I saw rescue the silversmith from hanging?" She turned her head away and studied the road stretching out in front of them. "I must say, it was a rather foolhardy thing to do. It could have gone badly, and you and your men might have been captured. Then who would have come to your aid?" For some strange reason, she thought of Dane. "I know someone who would have helped if the price was high enough." She shrugged a delicate shoulder and shook her head. "Maybe not. His brother's life wouldn't have been at stake and that's all he really cares about."

Brittany missed the wide smile that came over his face, then disappeared.

She frowned suddenly. "What were you doing here?" she asked, turning her head toward him. "How is it you happened along when you did, and where are the rest of your men?"

But before there was time for him to answer, lightning flashed across the sky. It seemed to have severed the dark cloud hovering over them, splitting it in two and unleashing a turbulent downpour of fierce rain. Brittany squealed at the onslaught. The stranger grabbed the hood of her cape and tossed it back on her head, shielded her tiny body in the folds of his cloak, and spurred his animal into a gallop. They raced down the road as if the devil himself chased them, and the stranger didn't lessen their pace until the Lockwood farmhouse came into view. Reining in near the front door, he easily lifted Brittany from the saddle and set her on the ground.

Expecting him to dismount and follow her inside, she ran

for the door, opened it, and hurried in out of the rain. But when she turned back, she discovered much to her surprise and disappointment that he'd already spun the steed around and was galloping off. Within moments his tall dark shape disappeared into the blackness, where even the bright glaring flash of lightning overhead couldn't find him.

Chapter Four

Daylight waned into dusk. The golden orb of the sun dropped below the horizon and turned the bright warmth of the afternoon into the cool serenity of nighttime. Evening settled over the land and stretched its lengthening arms to encompass the countryside, and only the soft yellow light of a flickering candle permeated the darkness as Brittany left the barn and headed back toward the house. Unaware of what awaited her there, she turned the knob and pushed the door open wide, coming to an abrupt halt when she noticed the bright, cheery blaze burning in the hearth and the tall dark figure standing beside it. His black tricorn was pulled low over his brow, concealing his identity, but the dark cape he wore failed to hide his muscular build. Hypnotized by his presence, she stepped into the room, eager to have him hold her in his arms. It was what she wanted, but dared she hope for it? He turned then to face her, his emerald eyes sparkling through the narrow slits in the mask, and a smile curled the corners of his mouth when he saw her standing in the doorway.

"Why have you come?" she asked, her voice low and husky.

He moved toward her. "I've come for you," he whispered, shedding his cape and laying it aside. "I want you, Brittany. I have since the first time I saw you."

Her pulse quickened as she watched him take the tricorn from his head and toss it carelessly away. His raven-black hair glistened in the firelight and his thick-muscled thighs flexed with each step.

"Fate has brought us together, Brittany," he murmured, taking the lantern from her fingers, setting it aside and reaching past her to nudge the door quietly shut.

The same haunting question came to mind. "Who are you?" she asked, feeling the warmth of his nearness.

"I'm the vision in your dreams, your knight in shining armor, a gallant warrior sent to protect you, to love you. I have no name but these, and even they are of no importance. My only mission is to serve you, to see to your happiness. Allow me to do that for you, Brittany. Let me make love to you."

A tingling started in the pit of her stomach, and when she opened her mouth to speak, the words would not come. He stood much too close to her. Closing her eyes, she drew in a breath and moved away, puzzled by the revelation that she felt no shame, that what he asked of her was what she wanted, that if he pressed her, she would willingly give herself to him.

"It was meant to be," he said as if reading her thoughts. "You and I were destined to be together. Don't fight it, Brittany. Let me hold you, comfort you, love you."

His fingertips touched her arm and sent a branding heat throughout her body. Lifting her eyes to his, she saw the gentleness reflected in them and knew he spoke the truth. His arm slipped around her waist and pulled her close. He brushed her cheek with the back of his fingers, then curled them in the thick, golden locks of hair at the nape of her neck, drawing her face to his. His kiss was warm and tender, his embrace firm and strong, and Brittany's head began to spin. She had never imagined it could be like this. She slid her arms around him, feeling the strength in the hard muscles across his back and shoulders. She breathed in the masculine scent of him, reveled in the pleasure of his arms around her, and prayed this glorious rapture would never end.

His mouth slanted across hers and his tongue played upon her lips before pushing inside. Brittany found it both shocking and wildly exciting. Her pulse raced, her blood warmed, and when he bent to sweep her into his arms, she kicked off her shoes and clung so fiercely to him that she made him laugh as he carried her to the bedroom.

Moonlight trickled in and cast a silvery glow over the room, bathing the couple beside the bed in an ashen stream of light. Slipping his arm from under her knees, he slowly lowered her feet to the floor while he held her tightly against his broad chest. His opened mouth moved along the delicate curve of her throat while his fingers unfastened the buttons on her dress and slid it from her. His tongue dotted a molten path down her neck and across her shoulder and Brittany moaned in sheer ecstasy. His hands roamed freely over the firm mound of her breasts covered in lacy cloth, then down along her waist and hips, searing her flesh wherever he touched. His fingers untied the strings of her petticoats and let them fall, and when he dropped on one knee to pull off the frilly garters, then her hose, her breath caught in her throat. He trailed hot kisses up the length of her leg to her hip.

"I love you, Brittany," he murmured, rising before her. His wide hands delicately cupped her face and pulled her mouth to his, and Brittany's heart pounded frantically in her chest. "For all eternity," he vowed, kissing her chin, her cheek, the tip of her nose. "I am yours until the earth no longer exists—and beyond."

Warm hands found the lace strings of her camisole and worked them loose. The thin cloth was pushed aside, and his thumb played with a taut nipple while his mouth moved along her throat to the rapidly beating pulse at its base, then on to the silky flesh of her breast. Brittany, unaware of what

103

she was doing, entwined her fingers within the thick hair at the back of his head and pulled him closer, inviting him to taste the rose-hued peak. His tongue teased it, drew a moist circle around it, then withdrew when his mouth claimed it and sucked tenderly.

A fire exploded within her and raged uncontrollably. She moaned, then panted breathlessly as she felt him slip the camisole from her trembling body. He gently lowered her down upon the bed, and while he disrobed, Brittany watched him, unashamed and bold in her desire. Sinewy ripples across his arms and chest gleamed in the moonlight once he pulled the shirt off his shoulders and let it fall to the floor. A dark matting of hair followed the contour of his muscular build and narrowed to a thin line at his waist. She blinked when he kicked off his shoes, tugged at his hose, then slid the breeches from his lean hips. He was the most magnificent man she'd ever imagined, and he had vowed eternal love. Filled with happiness, she raised her arms to him and silently welcomed him into her embrace.

He parted her trembling thighs with his knee and braced the weight of his broad frame on his hands, placed on either side of her head. With slow deliberation he lowered his face to hers. Brittany wanted this moment to be the most special in her life, but her curiosity about his identity wouldn't allow her to ignore the mask he still wore. With his attention focused elsewhere, she slipped her arms around his neck, untied the knot in the black cloth, and pulled the silky fabric from his face. Brittany's blood turned to ice, her passion vanished, a scream lodged itself in her throat, and tears burned her eyes. It was Dane's face she saw! That wily scoundrel who had tricked her once before had somehow managed to fool her again. In a rage, she shoved him away and started to climb off the bed. But something had caught her ankle, pinning her down. Kicking wildly at it, she yanked herself free and tumbled painfully to the floor.

The impact of her tiny body connecting with the cold,

hard wooden planks jolted Brittany awake instantly. Her thin nightgown was drenched in perspiration. Her legs were entangled in the quilt she had dragged with her in her dreams, and her pillow lay in the corner of the room. It took her a full minute to realize where she was and that it had all been a nightmare, one she'd had repeatedly for the past two weeks.

"Will I ever be free of him?" she shouted, hurling the blanket away. Staggering to her feet, she grabbed her cotton robe from the chair and put it on as she hurriedly left her room. She'd make some tea; that always seemed to calm her. Maybe then she could go back to bed and get some rest. Her lip curled disgustedly as she poured water into the kettle, knowing that the only way she'd ever find peace was to learn Dane Remington had been murdered. And the way things were going, she was the most likely candidate to see it carried through.

Setting the pot on the floor next to the hearth, she irritably tossed a couple of logs onto the glowing embers in the fireplace, jabbed them with the poker two or three times until a bright blaze had erupted, then hung the kettle back on the hook. Settling back on the faded and tattered braid rug, she pulled her knees up to her chest and wrapped her arms around them. Resting her chin in the crevice they formed, she studied the flickering flames, unaware that early morning streaks of light were already staining the eastern sky. She was too busy trying to distract her thoughts from her waking dream. But as always, they drifted back to that night when the Dark Horseman had rescued her from the soldiers, and she remembered how he'd ridden off before she could properly thank him.

Visions of his magnificent form astride the black stallion brought a smile to her lips, and without realizing it she leaned on one hip and reached out for the coin lying on the end table near her. She had found it outside her door the next morning, near where he had reined in his horse, and she could only assume it had fallen out of his pocket. Holding it in the palm of her hand, she tilted it toward the firelight to study the raised figure of a horse and rider, his cape flowing out behind him, above which were inscribed the words, "Sons of Liberty." Theirs was a noble cause, though England looked upon them as mercenaries, troublemakers who would easily murder anyone who stood in their way.

She had seen what they could do that day on a street in Boston. They had shot and killed the British soldiers who were about to execute a man. Was it possible the silversmith was one of them? she wondered, her smooth brow wrinkling into a perplexed frown. Miles Ingram's words came to mind again and she held the coin at arm's length, suddenly discovering it had lost some of its fascination. Although her brother did not trust Miles Ingram, Brittany was never one to ignore anything someone said because of another's prejudice. Thus she always listened and then sorted out what she considered to be the truth. What Miles had told her two weeks ago might have been idle chatter, but now, as she reflected back upon his speculations, she began to wonder how far wrong he was. Could it be that these very same rebels had been the cause of Roan's problems? Miles had said he thought Roan had been set up to take the blame for someone else's crime, and that these people were known to make sacrifices. She laid the coin back on the corner of the table and stared at it. Was that the reason the Dark Horseman had come to her rescue—as a means of paying her back for what he had done to her brother? Brittany shook her head. That didn't make sense. If he was so callous as to frame Roan in the first place, he certainly wouldn't feel any guilt about it. She straightened suddenly when another thought struck her. How did the Dark Horseman know where she lived? She hadn't told him, and yet he had raced his stallion right to her doorstep. She thought for a minute: it was simple . . . he knew because Miles had been right about his suspicions!

"Damn!" she fumed. All this time she'd been looking in

106

the wrong direction. If she wanted to prove Roan's innocence, she'd have to start with the Sons of Liberty! But how? They were notorious for their secrecy!

"I'll talk to Miles," she announced, coming to her feet and heading back to her bedroom. After all, his father was being paid by the Crown to keep peace. If anyone knew the names of the rebels, Lord Ingram would. And Miles had a reputation for knowing everything that went on—political or private. A few minutes later she had changed out of her nightclothes and was coming back into the front room. With her head down as she concentrated on fastening the last two buttons on her dress, she failed to see the tall, slender figure standing near the hearth. He warmed his hands until he turned to look at her, and the movement of his dark cape caught her eye.

"Roan!" she gasped, a mixture of surprise and relief raising the pitch of her voice. "How—" Fearing for his safety, she raced across the room and peered out through the single window to make certain no one had followed him, then quickly closed the shutters and turned around. "Where have you been?"

His gray eyes warmed as he smiled back at her. "A lot of places."

Brittany wanted to be angry with him; she wanted to tell him in no uncertain terms how foolish he'd been in running away, and that during the three weeks he'd been gone, she'd done nothing but worry about him. But she couldn't; she was simply too happy to see him alive and safe. Without answering, she moved to him, put her arms around him, and tightly hugged him to her.

"I'm glad you're home," she whispered, tilting her head back to look into his eyes.

"I can't stay," he replied. "Not until this mess is cleared up, anyway. Besides," he added with a smile as he let go of her and went to the cupboard for a cup and a sprinkling of tea leaves, "I'm needed somewhere else." Returning to the hearth, he knelt and poured hot water into the cup.

"What could be more important than seeing that the crops are planted? I can't do it alone," she told him, watching him sit down on the narrow deacon's bench to sip his tea. "If there's no harvest next fall, we'll lose the farm. I thought my wanting to sell the place was what sent you running off to begin with. Now you act as if it doesn't matter."

"It matters," he disagreed. "It's just that—well, I can't do two things at one time, and right now it's too dangerous for me to stick around long enough to plant crops." He frowned and stared into his cup.

"Roan," she said, grabbing a chair and sitting down, "what's most important is proving you had nothing to do with the charges brought against you. And I think I've come up with a way to do it."

He looked up hopefully. "You have? How?"

Smiling, she reached over and patted his arm. "For the past couple of weeks, I've been going to the courthouse trying to learn what I could about your case. It's never been mentioned. What's more peculiar is that with one exception, not a single British officer has come looking for you."

"What are you saying?"

"I don't know exactly," she admitted. "But I'll tell you this: I think I've been looking in the wrong place. I don't think the Tories had anything to do with framing you."

"Then who did?"

Brittany shifted around more comfortably on the chair before she answered. "Something Miles Ingram said made me start to wonder—"

"Miles Ingram!" Roan exploded, roughly setting his teacup on the table and angrily rising to his feet. "When did you talk to that viper? I should have known he'd show up here as soon as he heard I was gone. I wish it wasn't a hanging offense . . . I'd kill the bastard."

"Roan, calm down," Brittany pleaded, tugging on her brother's hand and forcing him to sit back on the bench again. "He wasn't here. I ran into him in Boston a couple of weeks ago, and he offered to help us."

"Ha!" Roan mocked, collapsing against the back of the bench, his arms folded over his chest. "If he wants to help, you can bet there's something in it for him. He's never been known to do anything unless he gets paid first!"

"I know that," she agreed. "That's why I didn't suggest he could. But he said something that started me thinking."

"What?" Roan's anger was still quite evident.

"He agreed that you were set up. But he pointed out the strong possibility that it wasn't the Tories. He feels that the rebels had something to do with—"

"That's absurd!" he raged, jumping off the bench and going to the hearth, where he stared down at the crackling fire.

"Why? Because you believe in what they're doing and want to be a part of it?"

Roan spun around to glare at her, his young face looking much older than it had when he'd left the house so many weeks ago. "Not *want*, Brit. I *am* a part of what they're doing. I'm a messenger. I work for Paul Revere, and I run letters from here to New York and as far south as Philadelphia. And yes, I believe in what they're doing because it's right. Father believed in it, too, and if he were alive today he'd be proud of me!"

His tirade stung Brittany. She hadn't meant to imply that she thought her brother was foolish for fighting for what he believed. She'd simply wanted to point out there was a possibility he'd been used for the benefit of someone else. She loved her brother, and as far as she was concerned, no one—no matter what side of the issue they were on—would get away with trying to harm him. Swallowing the knot in her throat, she stood and looked him straight in the eye.

"I'm proud of you, too, Roan."

His rage vanished instantly. Stepping closer, he wrapped one arm around her shoulders and squeezed. "Thank you."

He hugged her again, then went back to the bench and sat down to finish his tea. But as he lifted the cup, he spotted the copper coin and picked it up to examine it. "Where'd you get this?" he asked, raising questioning eyes at her.

Brittany laughed. "You'd never believe it."

"Try me," he coaxed with a serious frown.

Deciding she would enjoy a cup of tea, Brittany had turned toward the hearth and therefore missed the concerned expression on his face. She sprinkled tea leaves in her cup and poured water into it, then returned to her chair.

Taking a sip of the hot brew, she began. "Because of our argument, I decided to spend as much time as I possibly could at the courthouse in Boston, figuring I might learn something that could help us. After court was adjourned one day, I went outside with the intention of going home. But instead, I was an unwilling witness to an execution."

"Whose?"

Brittany shook her head. "I don't remember his name, but he was a silversmith found guilty of harboring a criminal. Anyway, just as the hanging was about to be carried out, a group of men on horseback came riding in, cut him down, and rode off with him. But before their leader followed them, he nailed something to the tree. It turned out to be a coin just like that one."

"And you picked this one up from the ground?"

"No. . . ." She laughed at his befuddled look. "I found this one outside our door the next morning."

"What?" Roan gasped. "You mean he was here? Did you talk to him? Did he admit he was the Dark Horseman?"

"Yes, I talked to him. But he didn't say a word to me. You see, after they helped the silversmith escape, Governor Hutchinson ordered troops to hunt them down. It was my misfortune to meet up with a band of soldiers on my way home, and when they decided they wanted to take me back to Boston for questioning, I ran off. I can't honestly tell you what happened to the soldiers, but the next thing I knew, the

110

man on horseback swooped me up in his arms and brought me home. I kept asking him questions, but he wouldn't answer me, and once he set me on the ground, he spun his horse around and ran off. I didn't even thank him."

"Then he didn't give you this coin?" Roan asked, studying the words inscribed on it.

"No, I found it the next morning and assumed he dropped it."

"And he didn't tell you his name."

"No. As I said, he never spoke a word." Curious, Brittany sat forward in the chair. "Why do you ask?"

Roan shrugged, laid the coin back on the table, and hid a smile. "Oh, I was just wondering if he would admit who he was. I've met several people who are with the Sons of Liberty but I don't know their names—except for Mr. Revere."

"He's a silversmith too, isn't he?"

It suddenly dawned on Roan that he had done something he pledged not to do: reveal the identity of someone in the organization. His only solace was that he'd told the one person he could trust never to repeat it. He knew that, but he still had to be sure. "Brit, swear to me that you'll never tell anyone about Mr. Revere. It could mean his arrest, and I don't want his execution on my conscience."

Even before he spoke, Brittany knew what he was going to say; she'd read it in his eyes. "I'll never tell anyone, Roan. It might seem to you that I'm against this revolution, but I'm not. I understand what these men are trying to do. It's just that I wish there were a more peaceful way to achieve it." The vision of Patrick Lockwood flared up in her mind, and Brittany lowered her eyes. "I guess I'm just being selfish. With Papa gone, I want what's left of my family here at home with me. I'd like things back the way they were."

"They never can be again, Brit. You know that," Roan replied, reaching out for her hand. "Too much has changed for there to be any hope of it ever happening, and even if I'm

111

cleared of all charges, I wouldn't come home to stay. I'm a part of this now, and I won't stop until it's finished." He bent his head down, trying to look into his sister's face. "But I will promise you this: I'll find someone to help you take care of the farm. I wish I could do it myself, but you know it isn't safe for me here."

"Oh, Roan," she moaned irritably as she pushed his hand away and came to her feet. "I couldn't afford to pay for hired help and you know it. This farm has never earned enough to give us anything extra."

Roan had to agree, but the smile that sparkled in his eyes contradicted his sister's statement. "But you could afford to feed someone and give him a place to sleep in exchange for his help, couldn't you?"

She gave him a dubious look. "And what fool would do that?"

"Oh, there are more of them around than you think, Brit," he replied with an odd gleam in his eye. Rising, he picked up his teacup and returned it to the cupboard. "Besides, I'd sleep better knowing the farm and my big sister are being taken care of, since I won't be around to do it myself." He smiled warmly at her, then moved to the door. "I'll stop by and see you from time to time to make sure everything's all right. In the meanwhile, take care of yourself."

"Roan," she called, stopping him before he had stepped across the threshold, "I'll be perfectly safe. You're the one who must be careful. Promise me you won't do anything foolish."

"If you mean don't get myself killed, I promise. But being foolish comes naturally." He grinned devilishly at her, then disappeared into the early light of morning.

A lazy smile spread over Dane's face as he quietly sat by and watched his younger brother flirt with the harlot perched on his knee. Though many had told the brothers

112

how much alike they seemed, Dane knew otherwise: Brad had never had a serious moment in his life and always looked at each day as a new adventure, never worrying about tomorrow. There wasn't a woman in the world he wouldn't woo, and once he'd won her affection, he quickly and quietly made an exit. He wasn't the sort ever to settle down, though Dane didn't think of himself as the type who would, either. But Brad couldn't let a day pass without sharing the company of one woman or another, whether she was rich or poor, young or old, beautiful or homely. It didn't matter to him—only that she was willing. And those who showed no interest in him got special attention. They were a challenge, and Brad always enjoyed a good contest. Of all those Dane could remember, there wasn't a single woman who hadn't fallen victim to his brother's charm, and most of them had walked away with a broken heart. Dane had warned the scoundrel that someday he'd meet one who wouldn't play his games, and she was the one Brad had to be careful of. She would be the one to steal *his* heart, and Dane was hoping he'd be around to see it happen.

The laughter and loud voices in the pub drew Dane's attention away from his brother and the rest of his men, who sat leisurely around the table drinking ale; and for an instant the memory of another such time flashed to mind. Without realizing it, he glanced out at the crowd of merrymakers, half expecting to see Dooley walking toward him with a very shapely, very beautiful blonde following him. The surprise of such a thought made him blink, straighten in his chair, and frown. Memories of a woman had never haunted him before; why did they now? He looked over at Brad and the young redhead whose arms were wrapped around his neck. Maybe it was simply because he'd been thinking about all the women in his brother's life.

He raised his mug to his lips and took a swig, trying to shake off the strange feeling that tingled every nerve in his body. He couldn't afford the luxury of thinking about the

113

gentler sex, especially about Brittany Lockwood. She was trouble, though he couldn't say why, exactly. He'd realized it the first time he saw her. Maybe it was because he knew what Brad's reaction would be and he suspected Miss Lockwood would want nothing to do with his brother. He took another sip of ale and leaned back comfortably in his chair, his gaze absently sweeping the room until it settled in the direction of the front door.

Not only was Brittany Lockwood beautiful; she was very intelligent. She'd proven that when she spotted Drexler following her after she left the pub that day and then again when she managed to lose him. And she was very brave: she'd ignored the dangers she'd put herself in by coming to a place like the Bunch of Grapes. She'd taken the word of a stranger and gone looking for a man she'd never met—let alone trusted. She had to have been scared, but she didn't allow it to show. She'd stood her ground even when he'd threatened her. Her mistake had been in agreeing to his terms. A vague smile crossed his mouth as he thought about it. He hadn't honestly expected her to consent to such a proposition; he'd assumed it would send her flying. But it hadn't, and it was then that he appreciated her courage and recognized how desperate she was. She would do anything to save her brother.

Dane's eyes shifted to look at Brad. That was one thing they had in common. The difference was that Dane had ways of dealing with it that weren't so costly. Even though he didn't really know Brittany Lockwood, he sensed she wasn't the kind of woman who went around offering herself in exchange for a service, and he'd decided to teach her a lesson—a valuable lesson . . . and enjoy a blissful interlude in doing so. He knew of a lot of men who'd have agreed to help her, but her payment wouldn't have simply been a tumble in the hay. She would have suffered broken ribs and a bruised jaw, and possibly even paid for her recklessness with her life. He hoped what he'd done to her would convince her never to offer such payment again—no matter how just the cause.

Rowdy voices and a commotion interrupted his thoughts. A fight had broken out nearby, and rather than have one of the brawlers land in his lap, Dane quickly shifted in his chair, raised his foot, and planted the heel of his boot against the man's buttocks. Straightening his leg, he sent the poor fool flying back across the room and into the waiting arms of a friend before he lounged back in his chair to idly watch the two men continue their fight while he speculated on the winner. Before long his thoughts had drifted back to the sensuous young woman with the beautiful blond hair and determined nature.

A week had gone by after that sweet moment in the barn, and Dane had as usual forgotten about his own personal concerns since there were more pressing issues to consider. Rescuing John Jacobson was the single most important problem at hand. Dane had sent one of his men to the courthouse to confirm what he expected would be the silversmith's sentence, and from there they were to plot a way to see that it wasn't fulfilled. However, only a short time passed before the man returned to inform Dane that he'd seen Brad in town near the courthouse. Vowing he would beat some sense into his brother, Dane and Ernest Betts had gone after him. Everyone except Brad knew how dangerous it was for him to be anywhere someone might recognize him, and if Brad failed to understand that, Dane would see to it that Brad was taken to the ship and locked in his cabin for a time. It hadn't honestly surprised Dane to find his brother engaged in conversation with a lovely young woman, but the fact that she was Brittany Lockwood had. Seeing her again had renewed strange feelings, and for a moment he was tempted to join his brother. Chuckling, he raised his mug and took a drink, knowing that if he had, she probably would have created such a scene that both he and Brad would have wound up in gaol.

The next time he saw her had been an even bigger surprise. Once Jacobson's sentence had been announced and his execution set for five o'clock the same afternoon, Dane had gathered his men to discuss their plan. Dooley was to dress as a young boy, then mingle with the children who usually stood near the hanging tree. Once the cart carrying the condemned man rolled within view, Dooley was to climb up the huge oak and signal Dane. Surprise and confusion and the panic of the crowd would ensure that Dane and his men would reach Jacobson before the sentence was carried through.

What they hadn't counted on was the size of the crowd. Their travel was difficult; it took the mass of people longer to clear the way than Dane had originally thought, and if Dooley hadn't been sitting astraddle the tree branch, close enough to cut Jacobson down, their mission might have failed. Luckily, they arrived at the last possible moment to save the silversmith. While Brad and the others rode off with Jacobson, Dane lingered long enough to catch Dooley in his arms, then nail the coin to the tree trunk. But when he spun the horse around and prepared to chase after his cohorts, he caught sight of the lovely young woman standing alone in the middle of the street staring back at him. He couldn't imagine why Miss Lockwood was there. She had left him with the impression that she didn't approve of violence. Yet there she was, right in the middle of it.

Dane ordered another mug of ale from the barmaid and absently noticed that the fight had come to an end and that the two men were now laughing and playing a game of darts together. Brad and his harlot had disappeared, and Dane assumed they had gone upstairs. Clay Richardson and Rodney Drexler were deeply engaged in some sort of disagreement and Aaron Dooley was nowhere to be seen. Ernest Betts, as always, sat quietly in his chair, observing everything that went on inside the pub while he covertly watched for any signs of trouble. When this group wasn't enjoying their leisure time, they were risking their lives, but Dane always found his idle moments the least satisfying. Mildly irritated that he didn't have something to do, he slouched down in his chair, grabbed the full mug of ale, and reflected on the events of the evening he followed Brittany Lockwood home.

He'd had no intention of letting her know he was there. It was too much of a gamble for her to learn the identity of the Dark Horseman. She couldn't be trusted with such information, considering how she felt about him. But once he saw how the soldiers pushed their horses in around her, he knew he had to step in. It had been relatively easy for him to overpower the group since they hadn't seen him coming, and once the last of them raced off down the road, Dane spurred his stallion into the woods after Brittany. He'd wanted to tell her how foolish she'd been to walk home alone after dark, and that in doing so, she'd invited trouble. If he hadn't decided to follow her, she might have wound up in gaol—or flat on her back in the first barn the soldiers could find. He'd have liked telling her, but he couldn't. He was sure she'd recognize his voice.

What had surprised him was her remark about Dane Remington not helping someone unless his own brother's life was at stake, and he couldn't help but laugh at the irony of it. The sudden memory of her slender frame pressed against him as he guided the stallion down the road tingled the flesh across his chest and arms, and he sat up in an effort to still the sensation. There was something captivating about the blond-haired beauty that made the vision of her constantly intrude upon his thoughts. He mustn't let his infatuation cloud his mind; his mission in Boston was of the utmost importance and demanded his total concentration. Leaning forward on his elbows, he wrapped his hands around his mug and stared down at the amber brew. The vision of golden hair and gray-blue eyes flashed in his brain. Dane bolted from his chair to go to the hearth and focus his attention on the bright blaze burning there. A second later he was silently comparing the color of the flames to Brittany's silky locks when he suddenly wondered if she might not be a witch, one who had cast a spell on him.

"Cap'n Remington?" a soft voice beside him interrupted, and Dane quickly lifted his eyes, thankful for the distraction. He smiled warmly when he saw Cory Rison standing there. She was one woman on whom his brother had never successfully practiced his charms, and it was one of the reasons Dane respected her. She was no man's fool and had seen through Brad the first time he smiled seductively at her. She'd told him at the start that she was offering her help to the Remington brothers simply because their cousin Beau asked her to, and she said if Brad ever tried that foolishness on her again, she'd leave. Dane often wondered what changed Brad's mind—her threat, or the pistol she carried tucked in the belt of her breeches. To look at her, one would think she didn't find men attractive. She never wore a dress, silk hose, or frilly garters, but rather the attire of one of Dane's crew. Her dark brown hair was always in a braid that hung to her waist. Her expression was always serious, and her deep violet eyes would cut right through a man. Dane never worried about her taking care of herself. He had seen her defend herself with both sword and dagger, and she seldom came out of the fracas with anything more than a scratch. Her skill with the pistol was deadly. Of all those who stood beside him, Dane trusted Cory with his life and never doubted her faith in their cause.

"What is it, Cory?" he asked, noticing for the first time that despite her attire, she'd failed to disguise her womanly shape. The brown breeches she wore hugged her lanky thighs; the black, knee-high boots revealed the smooth curve of her calves; and the billowy white shirt fell in such a way over her bosom that a man would have to be blind not to realize she was a woman. Perhaps it was how she laid one hand on the butt of her pistol whenever she talked to someone that warned them to keep their distance.

"I just overheard a young boy asking if anyone had seen Dooley."

"Do you know who he is?"

Cory shook her head and glanced over at the entrance to the pub, unaware that Dane studied her profile. Though her features were thin, there was still a subtle beauty to them. "I figure he's somewhere around fourteen or fifteen, taller than me, with dark brown hair and really odd-colored eyes. He's across the street right now. Want me to bring him in?"

"Not right away," he replied, placing a hand on her shoulder and starting them both off toward the door. "I'll watch from here while you draw him into a conversation. If I recognize him, I'll signal to you. Then you can tell him you know where to find Dooley and bring him to see me. Understood?"

"Yes, sir," Cory nodded, hurrying off to do as bade.

Her tall, thin shape was lost for a time among the crowd milling about in front of the pub, before she reappeared on the other side of the street. Dane had to raise his chin in the air to see her, but the moment she approached a young lad who seemed eager to answer her questions, the face of Brittany Lockwood flared up again. Dane had seen Roan only one time, and then for only a few minutes, but he was sure the young man talking with Cory was Roan Lockwood. Curious as to why he needed to speak with Dooley, Dane waited for Cory to glance discreetly over at him. With a slight nod he gave his silent approval for Cory to escort the young man into the pub and stepped out of the doorway.

Roan had spent most of the morning searching the waterfront for the midget who could more than likely direct him to Dane Remington. At first he admitted it was possible no one knew a dwarf by the name of Aaron Dooley. The response to his question was always negative. After all, Boston was a large city. But when the hour approached noon and he was no closer to finding the man, Roan began to suspect that the people in this part of town were either protecting Dooley or simply didn't want to get involved. Then a rather pretty, queerly dressed young woman suddenly appeared, asking if he was the one looking for the midget. His first reaction was skeptical. Perhaps he should find out who this young woman was before he confessed to anything . . . especially since she didn't look like the type to do anyone any favors. But he had already wasted the morning searching for Dooley with little promise of his luck changing, and she was the only hope he had. Resting his hand on the butt of his hidden pistol, Roan nodded while staying alert for any sign of trouble.

An irritable frown creased his brow after she motioned for him to follow and stepped back into the street on her way to the pub on the other side. If Aaron Dooley was inside, it meant his suspicions were correct. No one other than this stranger was willing to tell him anything. Hesitant to place himself at a disadvantage by blindly doing as she instructed, he glanced up and down the steet before stepping off the curb. There was always the chance this strange creature worked for the British and he was about to walk right into a trap. Inhaling deeply, he let the air out in a rush and followed. He'd simply have to stay alert.

The young woman had disappeared into the crowded pub by the time Roan stepped through the door, and he could feel the perspiration pop out of every pore. Something was amiss; he could sense it. Deciding that perhaps it was wiser for him to seek out Mr. Revere's help than enter further, Roan turned on his heel, ready to vacate the pub, and came to an abrupt halt when he found the way blocked by the tallest, broadest, meanest looking man he had ever seen. Fear knotted his throat, and when he thought to sidestep the giant, he discovered that his feet seemed to be glued to the floor.

"A-allow me to pass, sir," he managed to say, but the imposing form only stood there staring back at him, his face void of expression. "D–did you hear me?" Roan gasped when a huge hand shot up and seized his arm, then twisted it behind his back while the man jerked Roan's pistol from his belt. His fear turned to rage. "Let go of me!" he demanded, struggling to wrench his arm free as the man shoved him backward through the crowd of onlookers who had quieted to watch. "You have no right—!" Suddenly he was thrown off balance, and before he could catch himself, he landed painfully on the floor. From this lowly perch he peered up at the group of men seated around him, his gray eyes searching for someone who might take pity on him. The girl dressed in breeches appeared before him again.

"Why are you looking for Dooley?" she asked, her violet eyes searing into him.

Roan began to tremble, but he fought hard not to show it. Dusting himself off, he came to his feet and faced her. "I was told he could take me to see Dane Remington." There was no sense in lying. And if he told them the truth, maybe they wouldn't kill him. His gaze shifted to the giant standing behind her.

"Dane Remington?" she repeated. "And why do you want to see him?"

Roan's courage began to grow. The girl obviously knew Mr. Remington or she wouldn't be looking at him so suspiciously. "I need to ask a favor of him."

The hard set of her mouth softened into a sarcastic smile. "And what makes you think he'd do it? Who are you, anyway?"

"Mr. Remington knows who I am, and that's all that matters. Besides," he sneered back at her, "he owes me."

"Oh, really?" she scoffed. "Well, I hate to be the one to tell you, but Mr. Remington doesn't owe anybody anything." Her cold gaze looked Roan up and down. "Especially a little boy like you."

Roan's chin came up and his gray eyes narrowed to fine slits. "Boy, is it? I'm more of a man than you can handle."

121

The group around them burst into laughter, and Cory's face flamed scarlet. No one in all her eighteen years had ever talked to her that way and lived to brag about it. Her hand moved to the butt of her pistol. "Well, suppose we just fix that," she threatened, pulling the weapon.

"Cory!" a deep voice from in back of Roan shouted. "Put that away."

Her eyes left Roan just long enough to look at the one who spoke, then settled dangerously on Roan again. Several moments passed while she apparently argued with herself over what her punishment would be if she didn't do as she'd been told. Finally, after what seemed an eternity to Roan, the young girl jammed the pistol back into her belt; but she wasn't through. "I think you just used up your favor, little boy," she hissed and started to move past him. But once she got close enough to Roan, she deliberately rammed her shoulder against his.

The contact spun him around. Enraged, he opened his mouth to hurl the first insult he could think of, spotted Dane standing near the hearth, and changed his mind. "She ought to be taught a lesson in manners," Roan barked with a jerk of his head toward Cory, who had elected to sit in a chair a few feet away from Dane.

"And who's gonna teach me?" she rallied. "You?"

Dane decided it was time he intervened before the real problems began. "That's enough," he warned quietly.

Roan wasn't paying any attention. "Yes, me. And I welcome the opportunity."

"Oh, do you?" she mocked, standing up again. "Then suppose we start right now. But I think I should warn you that *you'll* be the one learning a lesson."

Roan took a step forward. "All right. We'll start now. But get rid of your pistol first. Or need I worry that it's even loaded?" He answered his own question. "I doubt that it is. I imagine you carry it around just to make people think you're tough. Well, I'm not fooled by it."

"Of course you're not. You haven't the intelligence to recognize trouble even if it stares you in the face. Otherwise you wouldn't have come in here."

"Enough!" The command nearly rattled the roof, and the two who argued ceased their heated discussion in an instant, knowing the one who voiced his displeasure over their bickering would bring an end to their disagreement by a means neither of them would enjoy. Cory took her place in the chair again. Roan averted his gaze. Everyone else resumed what they had been doing before the pair had engaged in a verbal battle and Ernest Betts, Richardson, and Drexler moved in closer to hear what Dane had to say.

"Since you've gone to so much effort," he began, his green eyes darkening as he glared back at Roan, "I suggest you tell me what brought you here." He raised a hand and pointed at the chair near the end of the table.

"Yes, sir," Roan replied, sitting down.

"You can start by explaining why you think I owe you." It was quite possible Brittany had told her brother what had happened in the barn and Roan had come to collect whatever debt he felt Dane was obliged to pay. Leaning casually against the mantel, his shoulder pressed against its stone face and one foot resting on the slab, Dane crossed his arms over his chest and waited to hear what Roan had to say.

Roan was already regretting the way he'd approached the subject. He honestly didn't feel Dane Remington owed him anything. He took a deep breath and let it out slowly before he drew up the courage to look the man in the eye. "You don't really owe me, Mr. Remington. I said that only because I figured Dooley would take me to see you if he thought you did."

Dane's only response was a slight lift of one dark brow.

"I'm here to ask for help," he admitted, rubbing the back of his hand across his upper lip. "I thought perhaps you'd know someone who'd be able to help my sister plant crops and see to the care of our farm for a while." He lowered his gaze and nervously cleared his throat. "It isn't safe for me to be there now, and Brittany isn't capable of doing all the work by herself. We couldn't afford to give him anything more than three good meals a day and a warm place to sleep."

Dane's gaze shifted to Drexler, who smiled back. It was a well-known fact among the Sons of Liberty that its members helped each other out whenever they were in trouble, and Roan obviously knew it. Otherwise he wouldn't ask such a thing from a group of men who appeared to prefer a mug of ale to a hard day's work. The question was, how had he come by the knowledge? Roan had accidentally discovered the truth about Dane that night in the gaoler's office when Dane left his trademark behind, which meant he knew Dane was a member of the Sons of Liberty. But it wasn't enough. In order to know the activities of the society, one had to be a member.

"What have you been doing these past weeks?"

Roan knew the real reason Dane asked: he was testing him. And Roan's answer had to be exactly what Dane Remington wanted to hear or Roan would find himself back out on the street. "I've been doing a lot of traveling." The statement was vague enough to be of little interest to anyone eavesdropping. Its deeper meaning was clear to Dane.

"Anywhere in particular?"

"New York, mostly. Sometimes Philadelphia. I'm thinking about going as far south as Virginia sometime soon. It depends."

"On what?"

Roan had to hold back a smile. Dane Remington obviously understood. "The weather; I prefer traveling when the skies are stormy."

"You mean you enjoy . . . danger?"

Roan shrugged a shoulder. "It's a risk one has to take, traveling the way I do. Usually I outrun it, though."

Dane studied the boy for a moment, then left his place by the hearth and came to sit down on the edge of the table next

124

to him. "What do you suppose you'll do if you're ever caught in one?"

This time he did smile. "I don't plan on it ever happening. You see, there are plenty of places to hide."

Dane's green eyes softened as he stared at the young man. Roan Lockwood had a lot of courage, and he would be a welcome, needed addition to the cause. He also had the wit to pass messages covertly—as he'd done just now. His traveling meant he was a courier. The stormy skies indicated urgent news had to be delivered. Hiding from danger was his way of saying the British would never catch him.

"And how do you pay for a room along the way?"

"In silver," he quickly replied, and Dane instantly knew Roan Lockwood worked for Paul Revere, the silversmith.

"Well, Roan," he sighed, rising to return to the fireplace, where he leisurely stared down at the flames, "none of us are farmers, but I might know of someone hungry enough to work for a meal." He glanced back at the boy over his shoulder. "Does your sister know you've come here?"

"No, sir. I simply told her that I'd try to get her some help. I didn't say who or where I'd find it."

Dane was quiet for a moment. "Good," he finally replied. "And see that she never finds out. All right?"

"Yes, sir." Thinking the conversation had come to an end, Roan stood up. "Thank you, Mr. Remington. And if you ever need me for anything, I've got a friend who can always locate me."

Knowing Roan meant he should send word to someone in Paul Revere's shop, Dane smiled in return. "I'll keep it in mind," he said, watching Roan turn about as if to leave the inn. But when he started to pass by Ernest Betts, he paused and held out his hand, silently indicating he wanted the return of his pistol. The giant quickly obliged, and without a backward glance Roan pushed his way through the crowded room and disappeared out the front door.

"You've got a plan, don't you, cap'n?" Cory asked, leaving her chair to stand at Dane's side. The two of them stared after the young boy.

His smile broadened as he laid an arm across her delicate shoulders. "Have you ever milked a cow, Cory?"

The idea of giving up the adventurous life of a rebel didn't sit well with her, and she angrily shoved his arm away. "Yes, but I don't intend ever to do it again. If you're so determined to help that scalawag, then *you* go milk his sister's cow."

Dane's handsome features wrinkled into a playful, mocking pout. "But I don't know how."

Cory's eyes darkened with her rage. Whenever he did that to her, she knew she wasn't going to like what he had in mind.

Chapter Five

It was nearly noon before Brittany had managed to repair the broken harness strap. The hot May sun shone brightly overhead, and its warm rays beating down upon her shoulders and back as she worked outside near the barn convinced her that it was time for her to change into something a bit more comfortable than the long-sleeved woolen dress she wore. Laying aside her work, she straightened and shoved her tiny fists in the small of her back to ease the stiffness a mite, shivering when a trickle of perspiration ran down the valley between her breasts. Rubbing a knuckle over the spot, she shaded her eyes with her other hand and glanced up at the cloudless blue sky.

This had always been her favorite time of year, but this spring was different. Her father wasn't out in the fields; Roan wasn't cutting wood. And there was little hope she would ever be truly happy again. Her life had changed dramatically over the past two months, and what honestly frightened her was the chance that she might lose the farm on top of everything else. Because of the tax laws, everyone was suffering, no matter how large or small the farm. But Brittany wasn't one to give up without a fight, and now that she had fixed the harness, she would start plowing the fields this afternoon. The small apple orchard out back wouldn't bring in enough money to chase away the creditors or even appease them in the slightest. She needed the profits from her potato crop.

Part of Brittany's reason for working so hard was to get her mind off Roan. He wasn't any safer running messages for Mr. Revere than he'd be if he'd decided to come home. Either way, he was taking chances with the British. She could appreciate his need to join the cause; it was something he felt he had to do—just as she felt she had to continue her search for the evidence that would clear him. Sighing heavily, she dropped her arms to her sides and started toward the house. But she wouldn't be able to do that until after the potatoes were planted, the hole in the barn roof was mended, some wood was chopped, and she had replaced the old rope for a new one on the well.

Songbirds chirped merrily in the trees, and while Brittany walked toward the house, she lifted her eyes to look at them. Why couldn't her days be as uneventful as the sparrows? Why did everything have to be so complicated? Even her nights were haunted—plagued by the same dream she'd had since the first time she saw the Dark Horseman. They always ended in the same manner: she'd given herself to him and when the desire to know his identity got the better of her, she'd pull the mask from his face and see Dane Remington's emerald green eyes laughing back at her. She could explain why the thought of him being the Dark Horseman angered her, but she failed to comprehend the attraction she had for the other. He was a man, nothing more . . . like any other man she might happen to meet. Yet his mystery was what kindled sparks of curiosity in her. Or was it the strange yearnings she'd had lately to have a man hold her in his arms that constantly brought his image to mind? Shaking off the thought, she turned for the front door and had started to go inside when the rhythmical pounding of horse's hooves against the hard earth lifted her attention to the road.

A puzzled frown settled on her smooth brow and she

pursed her mouth disapprovingly. There astride a huge chestnut stallion—one who made the figure riding it appear more of a half-grown boy than a man in his late thirties—sat Miles Ingram. Brittany could not remember the last time he'd come to visit, if ever, and his sudden appearance made her wonder . . . and feel apprehensive. The dark cape he wore billowed behind him in the gentle breeze, and for a moment he was transformed into an evil vulture swooping down upon its prey, for indeed that was how he made her feel.

"Mr. Ingram," she nodded politely as he reined in his animal beside her, though being courteous was the least of her worries.

"Good afternoon, Brittany," he smiled, dismounting. Taking his tricorn from his head, he glanced up at the clear sky. "I believe it will be a beautiful day. Don't you agree?" His brown eyes raked over her, then settled on her face. "But it will pale in comparison to you."

Brittany forced herself to smile and thank him for the flattery, while in truth her stomach churned. Had it been anyone else, the words would have pleased her, since she was feeling anything but pretty lately. However, Miles Ingram wasn't known for being free with his compliments, and Brittany suspected he was merely trying to put her at ease before coming to the reason for his visit. She eyed him cautiously while he gave the house and yard a quick once-over.

"You seem to be faring well these days, now that you're forced to fend for yourself." He turned slightly and glanced back down the road he'd traveled. "Though I noticed on my way in that your fields are still unplowed."

"That won't be for very long," she answered simply.

"Oh?" He raised a fine eyebrow at her. "Do I take that to mean that Roan has come home?"

Brittany could almost hear the condescension in his voice. "It means the fields will be plowed and the crops planted."

"Then you've hired help?" The smile on his thin lips lacked the genuine interest he was trying to convey, and when he raised a hand to tug on his earlobe, the huge ruby ring he wore caught the sunlight and flashed in Brittany's eyes. "I can't honestly see how you can afford it. The amount of—"

"I'll manage, Mr. Ingram," she interrupted, fighting desperately to hold back what she really wanted to say. "Now, if you'll excuse me, I have more important things to do than stand around and gossip."

"Brittany, wait!" he pleaded, reaching out for her hand. He laughed uneasily when she pulled away from him and glared her disapproval. "I didn't mean to make you angry. And I haven't come here to gossip."

"Then why *are* you here, *Mr.* Ingram?" She stressed the title, hoping he would understand that their relationship didn't warrant the intimate use of her first name.

"I'm here because we're neighbors. And neighbors should help one another in their time of need."

A wisp of wind worked a single strand of blond hair loose from beneath his powdered wig and laid it across his pale forehead. It was the only time Brittany could recall that Miles Ingram wasn't absolutely perfect. The vision of him late at night after he had dressed for bed came to mind, and Brittany quickly turned her head, praying he wouldn't see the smile that lit up her face. He no doubt wore a white nightshirt that fell only to his ankles and left his bony feet sticking out. He probably didn't have a full head of hair and even so, what little he had more than likely stuck straight out in all directions. All in all, his appearance could be likened to that of a scarecrow with scrawny arms outstretched, sunken cheeks, and a blank expression on his face.

"Are you offering to help plow, Mr. Ingram?" she managed to ask, though she couldn't bring herself to look at him.

"What? I . . . ah . . . well. . . ." He stuttered and stammered a moment, readjusted the collar on his shirt, tugged

130

on the cuff of his jacket, then made a feeble attempt to trap the stray tendril under his wig again. "I . . . well, it's a novel idea and most noble, Brittany, but I think my solution is much better."

Interested, Brittany looked at him askance. "Really? And what might that be?"

The warm sunshine was beginning to make him perspire, and since Miles didn't like discussing business in such an informal way, he was bold to ask, "Might we talk about it inside? It's awfully hot—"

"But that wouldn't be proper, Mr. Ingram," Brittany replied, her eyes gleaming with devilish humor. Anything that made Miles uncomfortable pleased her.

His own brown orbs reflected his surprise. He had not meant to suggest he wished to place her in a compromising situation. He gulped nervously and extended a hand toward the huge oak in the middle of the yard. "Yes, of course. Then perhaps we could stand in the shade?"

Brittany would have liked to decline his invitation and send him on his way, but his statement had struck a curious vein, one she couldn't ignore. And there was always the chance it might be worth exploring. With a slight nod of her head, she moved toward the tree, Miles close on her heels.

"So, Mr. Ingram, suppose you tell me what it is you have in mind that will solve all my problems," she said, reaching up to pluck a leaf from a low-hanging branch.

Miles moved to stand near the trunk of the tree, fanning himself with his hat and wiping the beads of sweat from his brow. "I beg you listen to all I have to say before you judge. I have given this considerable thought, and once you've heard it all, I'm sure you'll agree." He peered over at her, awaiting her consent with a questioning look on his thin face, and smiled weakly once she had given it. "I realize you are accustomed to the hard labors of running a farm. You've lived here all your life. But you were never forced to do it alone until now. Your father and brother did the heavy work, while you did the lighter. Now you must do both. It will become too much for you, Brittany, and a lady such as yourself should not have to toil in the fields. You were meant for the finer things in life." A trickle of perspiration raced down his neck, and he irritably swiped it away with the back of his hand. "I'm sure you will admit—if only to yourself—that this farm is too small to offer much profit. Out of determination to prove you can, you will hold it together the first year. But after that it will become more difficult, and you will grow to despise the way it requires all your efforts. It will take its toll, Brittany. You'll be old before your time. You may even die alone."

Brittany's expression had remained stony throughout his entire narration while in her thoughts she'd had to begrudgingly agree with what he said. Yet there was no other choice as far as she could see. She dropped her gaze to the delicate leaf she twirled in her fingers. "And what is your proposal?" she asked quietly, sensing she wouldn't like what she heard.

"Before I answer, allow me to explain a little further," he urged. "You and I both know that a great deal of your eastern property along the coast is marshy and therefore unusable. What little is left, you farm. What I propose is that you sell the few acres you have and move into Boston, where a lady—"

"Sell it?" she cut in, her temper rising. "And to whom do you suggest I sell it?" She threw the leaf away. "You, perhaps? Well, let me tell you something, Mr. Ingram. This worthless property belonged to my father . . . it was his dream. As a child back in London he pledged to someday own land in the colonies and raise his family here. That's what he did, and the only way I'd even consider selling it would be if my brother's life depended on it. But I will never sell it just to live in grand style in a house somewhere in Boston!" Whirling away from him, she started toward the front door. "Good day, Mr. Ingram," she threw back over

132

her shoulder without breaking stride.

"Brittany, please!" he called, chasing after her. "You've misunderstood my intent. I'm not offering because I expect to gain anything. I simply wanted to help you."

"I don't need your help. I've already come up with an idea that far outdoes yours." She paused at the threshold and glared back at him, a silent challenge darkening the gray-blue depths of her eyes. "And I won't have to sell my father's farm to do it."

Miles stopped short and glanced about the place as if expecting the answer to present itself. "How?" he demanded in a sudden change of mood. He didn't like having to play the milksop . . . not for Brittany or anyone else.

Brittany's temper cooled a bit once she realized he'd asked a question she couldn't answer. She had no plan, no way to save the farm. Without help she would be forced to sell it sooner or later. But Miles Ingram would never know . . . not until the last. And she certainly wouldn't sell it to him. Lifting her chin in the air, she looked down her nose at him and opened her mouth to request that he leave her property immediately. He didn't deserve an explanation. But before she'd drawn a breath to bid him farewell, the noisy rattling of a horse and cart coming down the road diverted her attention from the matter at hand.

"Good God!" Miles exclaimed. "Who are they?"

Brittany wondered much the same thing, but she wasn't about to let him know it, and rather than say anything that might give away her thoughts, she just stood there, watching. The two-wheeled cart was loaded down with various household items that hinted its owners moved around a great deal. Iron pots, hung by rope and draped over the side, clanked loudly against the wooden planks of the small wagon each time a wheel hit a rut. Wicker baskets filled the inside, a chair tied across them. Cloth bundles filled the rest of the cart, but none of this was of as much interest to Brittany as the man who drove the cart. He sat hunched over on the seat, his head lowered. Yet even so, Brittany could see the black eye patch. His face was covered with a dark growth of thick beard, his black eyebrows were bushy, and there was an ugly wart on his nose. The hands which held the reins were dirty, his clothes soiled and torn, and the faded brown cape draped over his shoulders lay uneven. Brittany had to force herself to pull her eyes away from the disfiguring hump in the middle of his back. The hat he wore looked as if it had never been removed from dirt-caked hair, and Brittany suddenly found herself wondering if he ever bathed.

"You, there!" she heard Miles shout. "Turn that thing around and find some other road to travel."

A single dark green eye glanced up at the one who spoke, but no words passed the stranger's lips. With a grunt, he pulled back on the reins and brought the horse and cart to a halt. It was then that Brittany noticed the steed, and she frowned. A thread-bare blanket was tossed over his back and the stranger had plopped a straw hat on the animal's head. He needed to be curried and his long legs, mane, and tail washed clean of the dried mud, but underneath it all, Brittany could see the makings of a fine stallion. Was this beggar blind as well that he would treat such a horse with so little regard? What she wouldn't give to own an animal like this one.

"Are you deaf, man?" Miles spoke again. "I ordered you to leave."

Just then a head popped up from between the wicker baskets in the cart. A young face was turned their way and a second later a tall, lanky figure jumped to the ground.

"'Ello, gov'na," the young boy sang as he approached Miles. "Me and me friend 'ere 'ave come about the job. Would ye be the one I speak to?"

Miles's milk-white complexion paled all the more as he turned to confront Brittany. "Surely, you don't—you wouldn't consider—oh, Brittany, you mustn't—"

Miles was right. She shouldn't, wouldn't, and mustn't

consider hiring these poor wretches for fear they would steal everything they could lay their hands on, but Miles would never know it . . . let him think what he liked. As soon as he'd gone, she'd advise the pair that they'd come to the wrong place. Until then— She smiled crookedly and shrugged a shoulder at Miles Ingram, falsely indicating that his assumption was correct.

"But look at them!" he snorted indignantly. "Brittany, you must give my offer a great deal of thought. Your father would understand—and even approve—of selling this land rather than—"

"I'm sorry, Mr. Ingram," she calmly cut in, "but I've made up my mind. However, *if* I decide otherwise, you'll be the first to know." She smiled dearly at him. "Good day, Mr. Ingram."

Miles sputtered and fumed for a moment, and then, realizing their conversation had reached its limit, shoved his hat back on his head, grabbed the reins of his horse, and pulled himself up in the saddle. He gave the filthy cretins one last disapproving look and spun his animal around.

"I don't think he likes us too much," the youngster observed as he watched Miles race off down the road, his coattails flying behind him. "Is he a friend of yers?"

Brittany took the opportunity to study the youth while his back was turned and couldn't shake off a peculiar feeling she had about him. He wasn't much taller than she and quite underdeveloped for a boy she guessed was near her own age. He had yet to experience the nuisance of shaving, for his jaw was smooth and clean. His voice was high-pitched, his features thin, and his hands free of any telltale signs of hard labor. He was a puzzling sort. But then, so was his companion. Unwittingly her gaze drifted to that one, and a chill slithered up her spine when she found his gaze already upon her. She swallowed the lump in her throat and looked back at the boy.

"I hope you haven't traveled too far," she began, frowning

when he glanced over at her. His deep violet eyes held little humor and seemed as if they should belong to a man twice his age, one who had seen many things and experienced even more. They were hardly the eyes of a child. She cleared her throat and began again. "What I mean is that I hope you haven't come here under false pretenses. I did not post notice of work to be done. In fact—"

"Ye can't pay for it," he finished, his gaze traveling the length of her as though they'd just met again after an absence of years and he wished to see if she'd changed. "We were told that, and that ye'd be willin' to pay with warm meals and shelter over our 'eads."

Brittany started to object, since she honestly preferred doing the work on her own to having this seedy pair living underfoot. But before she'd opened her mouth, the youth moved away from her and stared off in the direction of the barn.

"Zachary and me will sleep in there. We'll eat at dawn, noon, and after sundown." He faced her again. "We won't bother ye, and ye won't bother us." He turned as if dismissing her and waved at his companion to pull the cart around, indicating the place where they would be staying.

"Wait just a minute, young man." Brittany's fear of them turned to anger. "Has it occurred to you that maybe I don't want your help?"

He wore a tricorn pushed back on his head, and the feather in it fluttered abruptly when he jerked back to look at her. He sucked in a sharp breath to say something, changed his mind, and snapped his mouth shut again. When the cart rolled near enough, he grabbed the side of it and swung himself up in back, there to sit with his legs dangling over the end, his hands gripping the wooden planking and a dark scowl twisting his face as he stared back at her. Obviously, they weren't taking no for an answer. Dumbfounded, Brittany stood by quietly watching them as Zachary guided the horse and its cart to the side of the barn. From there they began to unload their belongings and carry them inside. They were staying whether she liked it or not.

Brittany had never had to deal with the likes of these two strangers before. They made her nervous and she would have liked ushering them off the place at gunpoint. But by late afternoon they had fixed the hole in the barn roof, replaced the rope in the well, and gone off to the fields to plow as much of the earth as they could before dark. Neither of them spoke a word to her again, yet without asking they seemed to know what needed to be done and which task was most important. She hated admitting she needed them and even more that she appreciated their help, and it wasn't until early in the evening, after she had fixed a tray of food for them and had started toward the barn with it, that she figured out why they had been so insistent on working for her.

"Roan sent you, didn't he?" she asked once Zachary had taken his plate and retreated to a dark corner to eat alone.

The boy poured himself a cup of tea, picked up his food, and settled himself on an overturned bucket, the plate balanced on his knees. "Don't know no Roan, lovey," he replied and popped a piece of meat into his mouth.

"Roan Lockwood . . . he's my brother. He told me he knew of someone who would work here for meals and a bed."

The dark violet eyes glanced up at her. "Sorry . . . ain't never 'eard of 'im." He busied himself with eating again and completely ignored her.

Realizing he no longer wanted to talk, Brittany backed toward the doors, her gaze shifting from the youth to the hunchback and finally the floor. Once she reached the exit, she paused to ask, "Might I know your name, since it appears you'll be living here for a while?"

Without looking up, the boy muttered, "Cory."

"Cory," Brittany repeated. "And do you have a last name?"

He stuffed a biscuit in his mouth, chomped on it for a moment, then looked at her. "Like I said 'fore. We don't bother ye and—"

"And I don't bother you," she finished with a sarcastic smile. "I remember."

"See that ye do," came the caustic reply.

Brittany's spine stiffened. If he were only a few inches shorter and a pound or two lighter, she'd be tempted to teach him some manners. After all, it was her food he was eating and her barn where he intended to sleep. Maybe he'd worked for the privilege, but it gave him no right to be rude.

"Well, then. Since we're setting down ground rules, here are a few of my own. If you don't like them, you're free to go." She waited until Cory frowned up at her. "Good. I see I have your attention. You're to stay away from the house. If I see that you're not working up to capacity, I won't feed you. Each morning after the crops are planted, I'll give you a list of jobs to do. If they aren't done, you don't eat. You'll do your own laundry." Her gaze slowly and deliberately took in his dirty attire. "That is, of course, if you ever wash those rags you wear."

Deep laughter from the corner of the barn instantly drew her eyes to the hunchback and she could see his huge frame shake with mirth.

"And that goes for your friend." She glared at Cory again. "We shall not speak to one another except when there's a need, and only then at mealtimes. Do I make myself clear?"

Cory's face was by now bright red. In a rage he jumped to his feet, accidentally spilling his plate on the straw-covered floor and knocking over his cup of tea. His fists were clenched at his sides and in all appearances seemed ready to do battle—whether physical or verbal, Brittany wasn't sure. But she wasn't about to back down, either.

"Do I take this to mean you disagree?" She held out a hand toward the exit. "If so, there's the door."

"I'll tell you what it means," he began, cut short by the

138

hunchback's loud clearing of his throat. Dark, blazing eyes sought out his companion in the shadows, his argument on the tip of his tongue. But Zachary wanted no part of it and concentrated on his meal again. Taking it as a silent warning to hold his words, Cory suddenly elected to go for a walk. Brushing past Brittany, the youth disappeared into the darkness outside the barn.

Nearly a week passed and in all that time, Brittany and the young boy said hardly two words to one another. Every morning after breakfast, she would watch the pair from her window as they took the ox and headed for the fields. At noon sometimes, they'd already be waiting in the barn for their meal, then eat it in a rush and hurry back to work. Sunset brought them back exhausted and oftentimes lacking the energy to lift their forks. She admired their stamina and wondered at the true source which drove them. They didn't owe her anything, yet they worked as if the farm belonged to them and it would be their loss if the creditors came to collect.

By the beginning of the second week the fields were ready for planting, and it was Brittany's turn to help. Donning a large, wide-brimmed bonnet to protect her face and neck from the hot rays of the sun, she appeared in the barn one morning ready to do her share.

"Ye goin' somewhere?" Cory asked as he took his plate from the tray. Zachary, as always, had found his spot in the corner and ate quietly, though his gaze never left the beautiful blonde standing near the doorway.

"I guess you could say that," she smiled, enthusiastic that at last she would be able to do something other than the cooking, laundry, or chopping wood. "I'm going to help with the planting."

"Like 'ell!" Cory exploded. "Ain't no place for a woman and we don't want ye there."

Brittany wasn't giving in. "Three pair of hands will get it done that much quicker," she calmly argued. "And the sooner it's planted, the better."

"And 'oo will be fixin' our meals if ye are out in the fields?"

"I will," she guaranteed him. "I'll work a few hours in the morning and again in the afternoon. You'll be fed, if that's what you're worried about."

Cory's angry glance told Brittany that he didn't approve, and when he glanced over at Zachary and the hunchback nodded in return, the boy's irritation only deepened. "Be sure ye stay out of me way," he grumbled, sitting down with his food.

That evening after everyone had eaten and Brittany had washed, dried, and put away the dishes, she decided to go for a stroll in the cool night air. The day had been very productive for the group. They had planted nearly two acres of potatoes and by the end of the week they could start with the wheat. By then the first harvest of hay would be ready and the prospects of a favorable yield this summer looked good. Brittany knew she had Cory and Zachary to thank for it, and maybe they didn't want to hear it, but she decided to tell them anyway. Changing direction, she headed for the barn.

The pair was odd. During the time they'd lived and worked on the farm, they'd never been willing to talk about anything besides business. She still didn't know their last names, where they came from, or what they planned to do once they decided to leave. And not once had she heard Zachary mutter a word. But stranger than that was the observation Brittany made about their attire. Cory never went without his hat, and Zachary always wore his coat. She assumed the latter was self-conscious about his deformity, but she also figured comfort would overrule his pride in the hot noonday sun. It never did. As for Cory, the boy's ill temper had eased a little toward her, and Brittany hoped it was because she had proven to the boy that she was willing to work just as hard and as long as he. It might have been the reason, but it wasn't enough to convince him that Brittany wasn't his enemy. He was nicer to her, but he still wouldn't talk freely.

She could hear the young boy's voice speaking to the hunchback as she neared the half-opened front doors of the barn. She hadn't planned to eavesdrop, but something he said piqued her interest, and she paused a moment to listen.

"So, what does Hancock think about it?"

Hancock? Brittany wondered. Her father often talked of John Hancock. Might Cory be referring to the same man? She took a step closer, wanting to hear more and suddenly realized that the boy had asked Zachary a question, one he couldn't answer with a nod of his head. She had assumed the hunchback *couldn't* speak. Now, she knew differently.

"And what about Dr. Warren?"

Brittany straightened. They *had* to be talking about John Hancock! Dr. Warren, Joseph Warren, was suspected of being a member of the Sons of Liberty! Who were these people? she silently demanded, stepping up to the door and peeking inside. The young boy was standing in the middle of the room with his back to Brittany. Zachary was lying in one of the stalls and from this angle all she could see of him were his feet and legs. If he answered Cory, Brittany wasn't aware of it, for her attention was riveted on the young, lanky shape shimmying out of his dirty jacket. The coat took flight as Cory tossed it aside, then reached up for his hat. Pulling it from his head, he proceeded to shake out the waist-length braid he'd stuffed beneath the tattered tricorn, and Brittany's mouth fell open. Cory turned to plop the headgear on a nearby nail and unwittingly gave Brittany a clear view of his profile. He was no boy! Cory was a woman! Unable to fathom why she chose to keep it a secret, Brittany started to grasp the edge of the door and swing it open. There was a lot to be explained, and they would have it out right now! But Cory's next question stopped her cold.

"And what about Miss Lockwood? How long do you think we can go on fooling her? You're the one who said you weren't sure if she could be trusted, and I have to admit she doesn't strike me as stupid."

Brittany strained to hear Zachary's reply, but she was too far away from him to make any sense of what he said. Stepping back from the doorway lest Cory turn and discover her there, Brittany contemplated her alternatives. Storming into the place and demanding the truth from the pair would only stir up resentment for her eavesdropping and draw them into the silence of before. Nay . . . she would have to find other means of learning their identity, and even more so, their purpose in coming to her farm. They had admitted Roan hadn't sent them. In fact, they didn't know him.

Then who were these two? The lantern was extinguished, plummeting the interior of the barn into darkness and startling Brittany into awareness. She mustn't let them know she was here, that she'd heard what Cory said, and that she was onto their little game. She had to have time to figure out why they'd chosen her farm as cover. Glancing back at the house, she decided it would have to wait until morning, since there wasn't much she could do about it now. She'd get a good night's rest, fix them breakfast, don her only decent dress and go to Boston. She'd ask around until she found someone who knew of a girl named Cory and her hunchbacked friend.

Bright streams of moonlight trickled in through Brittany's window and hit her full in the face as she lay awake in bed. She hadn't been able to fall asleep as she'd planned, and when the mattress seemed to develop lumps in it, she tossed off the covers and went to look outside. The moon was high overhead and she guessed the hour was somewhere near midnight. Thinking a cup of hot tea might relax her, she picked up her cotton robe from the chair, hurriedly donned it, and went into the other room. She'd just gotten the kindling in the fireplace to glow when she thought she heard a horse whinny on the road out front. Crossing to the window, she espied—much to her surprise and pleasure—the figure of a man on horseback, his wide shoulders draped in a flowing black cape. He moved with grace as he spurred the stallion and sent the steed racing off down the road.

"The Dark Horseman," Brittany breathed, watching until his tall, muscular shape vanished into the darkness. What was he doing here? She shifted her attention to the barn. Was it possible Cory and the hunchback were friends of his? A new thought struck her . . . were they perhaps spies for the British, and had he learned of their whereabouts? But if that were true, surely he would have taken them with him. Or maybe he'd simply brought a swift and quiet end to their lives. The idea of finding two dead bodies in her barn turned Brittany's stomach . . . but leaving them there wouldn't make them disappear. Tightening the sash around her waist, she moved toward the door, silently praying she was wrong.

The earth was cool beneath her bare feet as she crossed the front yard and moved toward the ominous dark shape silhouetted in the moonlight. It seemed to take on a strange, almost eerie form and hardly resembled the place where she'd spent many hours as a child laughing and playing with her younger brother. From there she'd observed her father hard at work, and there she'd taken refuge when she had gone there to cry the day her mother died. For a brief instant she remembered the last time she'd been drawn to the barn in the middle of the night and her steps faltered: Dane Remington had been waiting there for her. Every inch of her flesh tingled with the memory of his touch, the feel of his rock-hard muscles beneath her fingertips, and the branding fire of his kisses. She hadn't been able to put that experience from her thoughts, though her strenuous work of late had dulled it to some degree. Yet every now and then that rapturous moment flared up to confuse her. She would subconsciously allow herself to daydream about it, conjure up images of the day he would suddenly appear on her doorstep with open arms and a pledge of eternal love upon his lips, then have it all shatter into the stark fragments of reality. He would never come back to her! She had been simply one brief encounter among what she was sure had been many!

"Damn him," she muttered, changing course and heading toward the side of the barn and the broken board where she could peek inside without being seen. If he ever did come back—under whatever circumstances—she would be the one to shun him!

The interior of the barn was lost in shadow for the most part, but moonlight shining in through the opened loft door fell across the stall where Zachary usually slept. It was empty. Shifting, she strained to see the spot where Cory bedded down and discovered it, too, was vacant. Puzzled, she decided to get a closer look and circled around to the back door. Finding it ajar, she entered as quietly as possible.

"This is very peculiar," she murmured with a frown as she stood in the middle of the room and stared down at the blankets, wicker baskets, and the rest of their belongings. "Surely they wouldn't leave all this behind." She glanced up at the front doors. Or perhaps they'd heard the Dark Horseman's approach and ran away before he'd found them. Hurrying outside, she rounded the barn to the corral where Zachary had kept his horse only to find it empty as well. Yet to one side stood their cart.

She shook her head and turned back toward the house. Cory and Zachary disappearing without taking their things with them. The young man she thought was a boy turning out to be a woman. The mute actually speaking. The last person she expected to find outside her door was the Dark Horseman. There had to be some connection; she just didn't know what it was. Maybe Roan could figure it out, she mused as she crossed the yard and went back into the house. After all, he was working with the Sons of Liberty, which meant there was always the chance he might know their activities and who was involved in them. Dropping her robe on the chair, she crawled into bed and pulled the covers up under her chin. She'd still go to Boston tomorrow, but instead of looking for someone who knew Cory, she'd find her brother. She'd unravel this mystery if it took the rest of the summer to do it!

It seemed as though she'd slept only a few minutes when the thunderous pounding on the front door of her house made her bolt upright in bed. Bright morning sunlight poured into the room; it was very clear that she'd overslept, and she scrambled off the mattress to don her robe. The insistent knocking sounded again.

"Just a minute!" she shouted as she yanked the sash around her waist and tied it in a knot. Whoever it was had a lot of nerve paying her a visit at this ungodly hour, and she wouldn't hesitate to tell them so. Darting through the front room, she seized the knob and swung the door wide open. The reprimand she'd hastily rehearsed in her head vanished the instant she saw Cory standing at the threshold glaring back at her.

"Me and Zachary want our breakfast," the boy hissed, looking Brittany up and down. "Or are ye sick?"

Brittany was sure her face must be the color of her white cotton robe, and it took her a second to collect her wits. Unconsciously glancing back toward her bedroom, she wondered if she hadn't dreamed the entire episode of the night before. Her dream about the Dark Horseman being Dane Remington had always been real enough. "No, I'm fine," she mumbled.

"Then if it ain't too much trouble, could ye be fixin' us somethin' before we starve to death?"

Maybe the part about seeing the mysterious night rider near the house and then her trip to the barn to find Cory and Zachary gone had been a dream. She was sure she'd seen the boy take off his hat and let the long braid fall free. It couldn't all have been her imagination! With a curious frown on her lovely face, she turned her attention on the one who stood waiting for an answer.

"Do you ever take off that hat, Cory?" she asked before she realized it.

His violet eyes glanced up at the pointed brim shading his brow. "Never," came the curt reply. "And what's that got to do with eatin'?"

"You mean you sleep in it?" she ventured further.

Cory's thin face wrinkled with a sneer. "I do everything with it on. Even take a bath. Now, are ye gonna fix us breakfast or not?"

Although Cory's words were tipped with his usual sarcasm, Brittany noticed an uneasiness in his manner, as if he were anxious to leave and have their conversation come to an end. "I'll bring something for you in a few minutes," she told him, certain now that everything about last night had really happened.

Rather than close the door on Cory, she watched until the trickster moved away and started back toward the barn. Stepping out of the doorway and bending slightly, Brittany tried to peek beneath the edge of Corys hat and see her hair at the nape of her neck as she walked away. But the collar on the young woman's coat covered enough of it to make it impossible for Brittany to be absolutely certain. Shrugging it off since she figured she'd find out some other way, Brittany went back inside to change her clothes and fix breakfast. Now she was more determined than ever to find Roan.

"I won't be helping in the fields today," she announced to the pair a short while later as they took their usual places to eat.

"Good," Cory muttered into her cup of tea.

"I'll be going to Boston to visit with a friend of mine," she continued, her gaze focused on the young woman garbed in boy's clothing. "I have some information I think he will find helpful."

If her statement bothered Cory, she didn't show it. "Like what, lovey? 'Ow to make a nuisance of yerself?" She glanced over at Zachary and laughed at her own insulting humor. The hunchback nodded, smiled, then concentranted on his food.

"No," Brittany admitted. "But it will make a few people very uncomfortable once it's learned." She grinned sardonically. "In fact, I imagine it will cause quite an uproar. But I'm sure you're not interested." Mild disappointment showed briefly on her face when Cory simply continued to eat rather than comment. She decided to try something else and set her gaze on the hunchback. "Zachary. What would you like to have for dinner tonight?"

A dark green eye looked up at her, and Brittany was sure she'd tricked him into saying something when he opened his mouth and drew a breath. But instead of answering, he merely shook his head and bent over his plate again. These two were very good at their deception, and it would take a lot more than casual conversation to trip them up. But then that would make it too easy, and Brittany didn't expect that. She had given this situation a great deal of thought while she prepared breakfast and had decided that her second guess about the pair was correct, that they were British spies and the Dark Horseman had learned of their hiding place. She didn't appreciate the fact that Cory and her friend had put Brittany in the middle of something she'd prefer not being in and figured the only way to solve the problem was to get rid of them.

Thus her plan. She'd given the pair just the vaguest hints that she had some vital information that would cause a lot of problems for someone. Since this pair hadn't or couldn't confide in her, she assumed it was because they thought she was on the opposing side. Therefore it would be essential for them to follow her to her friend's house, eavesdrop on what was said, and then report back to their leader. Of course,

147

Brittany had no such information, but Cory wouldn't know that. And once she'd followed Brittany into the crowded streets of Boston, Brittany would turn the trick around and follow Cory after Cory thought Brittany had gotten away from her. Then, after Brittany discovered who was giving Cory orders, Brittany would go to the one man she felt she could trust: Paul Revere.

"I packed a lunch for the two of you and when I'm ready to leave, I'll bring it here to the barn." She cast each one a final glance, saw that they both seemed more interested in what they ate than anything she had to say, and turned around to leave. Was it possible she was wrong about the whole thing? Knowing she couldn't just ask them, she walked outside and headed back to the house.

"Well, even if I am, I still need to speak to Mr. Revere," she told herself as she wrapped last night's leftover fried chicken in a napkin and put it in the basket next to the biscuits and jar of apple jelly. Ten minutes later she had donned her bonnet, draped a shawl over her shoulders, and stepped back out into the bright sunshine once more, the basket hooked on one arm. But when she lifted her gaze in the direction of the barn, she staggered to a stop, unable to believe her eyes, for there, only a few short yards further on, sat Zachary in the cart, the reins in his hands, and Cory standing alongside the horse, stroking its velvety nose.

"Too far to walk," Cory explained without looking at Brittany. "'Sides, Zachary and me need supplies."

Brittany doubted that but didn't say anything. It was merely an excuse, one that would allow Zachary to stay with her as long as possible . . . or at least until she advised him of where she was going. It was much easier giving her a ride than trying to follow her through the woods. What surprised her was that Cory had elected to stay behind. A finely arched brow rose with Brittany's suspicion that perhaps Cory had other plans, such as meeting someone later. This way she wouldn't have to cover up her disappearance. Suddenly,

Brittany was torn between going to Boston and staying at home to catch Cory in the act. But to do the latter would only raise questions from Cory that Brittany couldn't answer. Grabbing for her shawl when the wind threatened to pull it from her shoulders, she decided to go through with her original plan. She was sure there would be other times when she could trap the young woman. Without comment she handed the basket to Cory and climbed up on the seat beside Zachary.

About twenty minutes later and a mile or so down the road, Brittany was wishing she'd declined the offer of a ride. Sitting so close to Zachary made her nervous, and his continued silence didn't help ease things. During his stay on the farm, Brittany hadn't spent much time with him, since he always seemed to want to keep his distance. Because of it, she had learned nothing about him and noticed even less. Now as they sat shoulder to shoulder and came into contact whenever a wheel bounced over a rut in the road, she began to discover curious things about him. There was a strength in his well-muscled arm that she wouldn't have guessed possible from his movements. He handled the horse with authority and ease, and without making a sound. His hands weren't gnarled or wrinkled as she'd expected them to be, but rather appeared to be the hands of a healthy, young man in his thirties. His dark beard wasn't quite the same color as his hair, and as she peered covertly over at him from behind her hat brim, she could have sworn that the eye patch had been on his other eye the first time they met. She already knew he could talk; what she couldn't understand was the need for hiding his and Cory's identities. She was no threat to them . . . or was she? Frowning, she concentrated on the road stretching out before them.

By the time they reached the outskirts of the city, Brittany had worked herself into such a frenzy that she was contemplating jumping from the cart and running away as fast as she could. The only reason she didn't was that she realized it wouldn't do any good. If Cory and the hunchback were part of a bigger gang, it wouldn't take much for one of them to find her. Paul Revere didn't owe her anything, so she doubted he would offer refuge, and she had no idea where to find Roan. Yet more than that, she knew she mustn't turn her back on whatever it was they were doing. Her father would have been ashamed of her cowardice.

For you, Papa, she silently pledged as Zachary guided their cart along the cobblestone street leading past Long Wharf and into the less respectable part of Boston and the place where all her troubles had begun. There had been countless times over the past few weeks that Brittany had cursed her decision to go to Dane Remington for help. It seemed that after that, things had only gotten worse for her. But there really hadn't been much of a choice: she could have either accepted his help or let Roan hang for something he hadn't done.

Suddenly a shot rent the air and jolted Brittany out of her musings. Terrified that she and Zachary had unwillingly ridden into the middle of trouble, she grabbed his coat sleeve and hung on while she quickly and fearfully looked all around them for a clue to the assailant's whereabouts. Another shot was fired and this time Brittany screamed.

"Zachary, get us out of here!"

The hunchback apparently agreed with her. Before she could ask again, he slapped the reins across the stallion's rump and sent the cumbersome rig rattling off down the cobblestones. However, his choice of direction wasn't what Brittany expected—or wanted.

"Where are you going?" she shrieked when he urged the horse to take them toward the crowd of people at the end of the street. "Zachary! Turn this cart around—!" Anything else she wished to add came out in a horrified screech and she decided to hang onto the wooden seat rather than get hurled to the ground. Zachary wasn't stopping for anyone; she didn't even hear his angry command at the steed to hurry. All that caught and held her attention was the small party of soldiers in the midst of the crowd up ahead, their weapons lowered on the mass of people and raucous shouts to disband trailing from their lips. Brittany couldn't understand why Zachary wanted to be in the center of the riot until their noisy approach urgently warned those blocking their path to move and the way opened up to reveal an injured man lying in the street.

Sensing the new arrival had come to help, the throng of people quickly and strategically pushed in around the soldiers, separating them from the fallen man, and once the cart clamored to a halt, three within the group lifted the other and placed him in the rig behind Brittany. His coat was saturated with blood, but his wound didn't interest her as much as who he was. Did Zachary know Brad Remington so well that he would risk his own life as well as hers to save him? She was about to voice the question when the hunchback violently snapped the reins and set the rig and its occupants racing down the street at breakneck speed.

They rounded the first corner they came to, flew down the avenue, turned a second time, traveled two more blocks, and went into an alley. The narrow corridor was vacant and just when Brittany thought they would change direction again, Zachary hauled back on the reins and brought the cart to an awkward, sliding halt in front of a sealed doorway at the end of the alley. Without glancing her way or back at his passenger, the hunchback agilely jumped to the ground and descended upon the entrance, loudly banging his fist against the wooden planks until the latch clicked and the door was swung open. Brittany couldn't hear if Zachary said anything to the man who answered the excited summons, but both quickly came to the back of the cart and hastily lifted Brad in their arms. Brittany sat by breathlessly as she watched the pair carry the unconscious man inside, wondering if she was supposed to follow them or wait in the cart for Zachary. Her answer came a moment later when the hunchback reap-

151

peared in the doorway and motioned her to come with him. Hesitant at first, she just sat there staring back at him. She didn't want to be a part of this; her trip to Boston had been innocent, and now because of Zachary, the authorities would be looking for her as well as for Brad Remington. She straightened her spine and said, "I think it's best you took me home."

Zachary's bushy eyebrows lowered in a fierce frown and his green eye darkened with displeasure over her decree. He jerked his head toward the door again.

"I think not. I have no reason to hide. What you did had nothing to do with me, and if the soldiers come to arrest me, I'll tell them so." She raised her pert little nose in the air and silently waited for him to do as he was told. But instead of climbing into the cart beside her, Zachary rounded the back of it and came to stand next to her.

"Get out of the rig, Miss Lockwood, before I drag you from it," he warned in a deep, rich voice that belied his grubby appearance. Yet the threat of his statement wasn't what made Brittany's head spin or sent her pulse racing.

"You lying, deceitful cur!" she raged, jerking clear of Dane when he reached out to grab her wrist. Sliding across the seat, she jumped to the ground on the other side of the cart. He quickly followed and was on her in a flash. "You lay a hand on me, Dane Remington, and I'll scream so loud the entire garrison of British soldiers will be down on you before you have time to turn around," she spat, pulling away from him. The wall behind her prevented her from going any further.

"Then I suggest you listen, because you're in this up to your pretty little neck whether you want it that way or not. *If* we're lucky, those soldiers back there didn't have the chance to recognize you before we rode off. We won't know that for a while, but if that's the case, then you may return home . . . later, after we're sure. Until then it's safer for you to stay here." He cocked a brow at her accusingly. "Unless, of course, you know something I don't."

Confused by his statement, she frowned. "Such as?"

If he intended to answer, the angry shouts of men somewhere close by cut him short. Obviously fearing they would soon be discovered, he roughly took Brittany's elbow and shoved her toward the doorway. Caught off balance, she stumbled inside when he pushed her through the opening and spun back around in time to see him close the door between them. A second later she heard his sharp command and the rattling of the cart as he sped away.

a friend, or a foe. Then when Dane left the room
that she needed a place to hide for a while, no matter

Chapter Six

Bernard Patterson was a cobbler by trade and had lived and worked in Boston for nearly his entire life. He never married and enjoyed the solitude of being alone. It had always been relatively peaceful in his neighborhood, and he had shared a friendship with practically everyone who owned property around him. He had been happy until King George III decided to tighten his hold on the American colonies. Boston received most of the attention and before long the colonials retaliated. Everyone's business suffered, including Bernard Patterson's. Because of it, he was only too eager to help fight against the injustice. His health had prevented him from physically joining the activities of the Sons of Liberty, but it didn't stop him from opening his home to a member in trouble. It was why Dane Remington brought his wounded brother here and why Bernard hadn't hesitated in the least to cloister Brad away in the attic, where he'd be safe until he'd healed from his injury.

What surprised him had been the beautiful young woman Dane had brought along. Bernard had never met Brittany Lockwood before today. He didn't know if she was aware of Bernard's involvement in the organization, if she was a member, a friend, or a foe. Thus when Dane left, explaining only that she needed a place to hide for a while, Bernard decided not to reveal his secret. He would wait until Dane returned as he'd said he would.

Brittany had remained near the back door of the cobbler's shop long after that scoundrel Dane Remington had left her there, arguing with herself whether or not she should make a hasty exit before the owner returned from wherever he'd gone. She wanted to quietly disappear just to spite the blackguard who'd brought her here. On the other hand, she knew the kind of trouble she'd be in if she did and then have the misfortune to meet up with the soldiers who were looking for Brad. If she'd been recognized, they more than likely wouldn't believe her story and would probably throw her in gaol. After all hadn't her brother been charged with arson? To their way of thinking, criminal acts run in a family. Completely frustrated and feeling helpless, Brittany untied the strings on her bonnet and pulled it from her head as she turned around to study the interior of the place.

The room, though small, had a cozy atmosphere. Next to the fireplace were a rocking chair and footstool, and beside them was a table draped in lacy white cloth. On top was a brass candle holder, a white taper, a pair of spectacles, an ashtray with a smoldering pipe, and an opened book with a tobacco pouch marking the page. A light blue braided rug covered the floor. A settee and coffee table sat opposite the rocker. A huge cupboard bedecked with blue willowware china filled one wall, across from which a staircase led to the second story. Near the door, beside Brittany, were a dropleaf table and two chairs. No windows graced the room and the only light came from the doorway opposite her. A thin curtain covered the entryway, but through it she could see the adjacent room and recognized the tools of a cobbler. Was the man who lived and worked here related to the Remington brothers? she wondered, her gaze drifting to the stairs.

Suddenly she remembered how badly Brad had been wounded. Had it been Dane up there bleeding to death, she would have set aside her bonnet and settled herself comfortably in a chair to wait. She moved toward the steps, excusing her desire to help Brad simply because he had never tricked her the way his brother had. In fact, if it hadn't been for Brad, Roan might be dead at this very moment.

"Sir?" she called up to the old man who answered the door. "May I be of some help?"

Several moments of silence followed before his short, pudgy figure appeared at the top of the stairs. "Yes," he replied. "Make sure the key is turned in the lock and start a fire. We'll be needing some hot water." He cocked his gray head to one side. "Unless you know more about doctoring than me. I've never removed a bullet before."

Brittany hadn't either. But whenever there had been an accident on the farm and her father or Roan had needed tending to, it had been her responsibility. "The closest I've ever come was setting a broken arm."

"That's more than I've ever done," he admitted. "And my eyesight ain't what it should be."

"Why not send for a doctor?"

Wiping his hands on a towel, the old man glanced off toward his right as if looking at his patient. "Can't. It's too dangerous."

Brittany surmised it had something to do with why Brad was in the crowd on the street in the first place, but she wasn't going to ask. "Then I guess it's up to you and me," she told him, starting up the steps. "What little help we can offer him is better than none at all, I suppose." She stopped on the last tread and introduced herself. "I'm Brittany Lockwood."

"Bernard Patterson," he smiled in return, then held out a hand toward the ladder propped against the wall. "I've hidden him in the attic," he explained. "And I suppose you should stay there with him until Dane says it's safe to come out."

The mention of his name made her lip curl into a sneer, and rather than explain her reaction, she quickly mounted the final step and walked toward the ladder before Bernard noticed. There was a trap door in the ceiling, one that would be fairly unnoticeable once it was lowered into place, and she had to agree that if someone wanted to get lost for a time, this was the ideal place to do it.

"Well," she said, resting a hand on one of the rungs, "I guess we'd better get started."

"Will you be able to get up there by yourself?" Bernard questioned. "With all your skirts in the way?"

Brittany smiled encouragingly. "I live on a farm, Mr. Patterson. I can't even begin to guess how many times I've climbed a ladder—just like this one—to get into the the barn loft. I'll manage. Now why don't you see about the hot water, some bandages, and something very sharp and pointed I can use to probe for the bullet. Oh, and bring a bottle of whiskey, if you have some. If we're lucky, maybe he'll drink enough to pass out."

Bernard's pale green eyes brightened in obvious relief that someone else would be taking over the task of seeing to Brad's wound. Without another word he hurried down the stairs after the supplies.

The flame from a single candle flickered in the attic and cast a faint yellow glow about the walls and ceiling. Brittany had pulled herself up the ladder and stood staring over at the cot where the sleeping man lay. There was no other furniture except the straight-backed chair beside the bed, and Brittany decided to ask Mr. Patterson if he had a small table she could use. If Brad was to recover, she would have to have everything within reach. Even so she wasn't too sure it would be enough. It was dry and dusty smelling here . . . not the kind of place where a sick person could get well again. He'd need bright, warm sunshine and a breath of fresh air. Once she had approached the bed, she absently hooked her bonnet on the finial of the chair and sat down to make her examination and determine the seriousness of his injury.

Mr. Patterson had already removed Brad's coat and

unbuttoned his shirt front, and Brittany could see the very ugly, deep hole in Brad's shoulder just below the collarbone. Assuming the bullet hadn't passed all the way through, she realized how difficult and painful it would be for Brad as well as herself. With only an old man to hold him down, Brad would have to be tied to the bed and possibly even gagged to keep him from screaming and being overheard by the wrong person.

Whether he sensed someone was sitting next to him or not, Brad stirred, then opened his pain-filled brown eyes. Seeing Brittany there confused him, and he blinked several times to make sure he was truly awake and not dreaming. The pain in his shoulder convinced him that he wasn't imagining the beautiful blonde staring down at him and although it took a great deal of effort, he smiled back at her.

"It appears you've gotten yourself into trouble again, Mr. Remington," Brittany grinned. "A bit more serious this time, however." Bending, she picked up his jacket to see if there was a hole in its back as well, indicating that there would be no need to get him drunk. A frown darkened her eyes. "I'm afraid you're in for a rough go of it. I'm going to have to get the bullet out."

Brad closed his eyes and nodded.

"I sent Mr. Patterson after some whiskey and I want you to drink as much of it as you can. Will you do that for me?"

He nodded again.

"After you've rested, maybe you'll tell me how you managed to get yourself in such a predicament," she continued. "I would have thought spending a few nights in gaol would have cured you. Apparently it didn't."

He smiled over at her and opened his eyes again. "Dane?" he managed to ask.

"He'll be here later," she told him, certain that he would, and stood to unfold the blanket that was draped over the back of her chair. Fanning it out, she let it fall over Brad's legs and stomach, deciding one wouldn't do; she'd have to ask Mr. Patterson for all he could spare. Sliding the chair closer, she sat down again to study his wound.

"What—are you—doing here?" Brad whispered, his eyes warming at the sight of her. She was without question the most beautiful woman he'd ever seen.

Brad recalled how angry he'd gotten when Dane announced that Cory and he would be going to the Lockwood farm for a while, and that Brad was to stay away. He couldn't understand what difference it made who went, since Dane planned to disguise himself anyway. The look his older brother gave him told Brad more than if Dane had actually tried to explain, and Brad reluctantly had to agree. His infatuation with Brittany Lockwood would have given away his identity.

"It's a long story," she said, lifting the hem of her skirt to tear off a strip of her petticoat. She pressed it against the wound in an effort to slow the bleeding. "But I'm sure you know most of it. *Zachary* and I,"—she stressed the name Dane had used with obvious indignation—"were on our way into town when we heard gunshots. The next thing I knew, some men were tossing you in the back of our cart and we were racing through the streets as if every building was on fire and we stood in its path. He brought you here and told me to stay with you."

"Told?" Brad frowned. Part of the disguise was that Dane couldn't utter a sound, and it was the main reason Brad hadn't been allowed to go. It had always been very difficult for him to keep his mouth shut for very long.

Unaware of how a simple touch would affect the young man, Brittany laid her hand on his brow. "You're warm," she observed, then glanced back in the direction of the ladder. "I wish Mr. Patterson would hurry."

Not as warm as I could be if I didn't have this damn bullet in me, he mused with a vague smile. Maybe his brother didn't trust Brittany, but Brad didn't care. As soon as he was well. . . . Besides, what better way to find out what's going

160

on inside a woman's head than to ask her in the heat of passion? Love is blind, so they say, and if given the chance, Brittany would tell Brad everything he wanted to know for the sake of love. He had done it before, countless times, and Brittany would be no exception.

Feeling weak and a little dizzy, Brad closed his eyes when Brittany left his side to take the things Bernard Patterson carried up the ladder. In the darkness of his half-conscious state, he listened to the two of them move about the room preparing for the surgery they were about to perform. Vaguely he heard Brittany instruct her companion to heat the blade of a large knife in the coals—no doubt to cauterize the hole in his flesh once the bullet had been removed. The tinkling of glass made him open his eyes again, and he smiled appreciatively when he saw Brittany hold out a glass of whiskey to him. Helping him to sit up a little, she held the back of his head in one hand and lifted the dark liquid to his lips.

"Drink it all," she ordered softly. "You're going to need it."

Brad eagerly obliged her. The pain in his shoulder was excruciating and the burning warmth of the whiskey helped take his mind off it. Once he had drained his glass, she refilled it and urged him to drink more. After a short time, Brad's vision blurred. He wasn't sure if it was the whiskey he drank or the pain which shot through his chest that made him teeter on the brink of unconsciousness. He downed another glass at Brittany's insistence and before his head hit the pillow again, he had tumbled into dark oblivion.

"We'd better hurry," she said, glancing up at Bernard, who'd stood beside her all the while, ready to do whatever she might ask. "Do you think you can hold him down? Or should we bind him?"

"Let's try it without," Bernard replied, frowning. "The lad's uncomfortable enough as it is."

"All right," Brittany consented, picking up the narrow,

long-bladed knife Bernard had supplied for her. Gulping down the wave of nausea that had suddenly overcome her, she took a deep breath to calm her nerves and leaned over the unmoving body, ready to begin.

The entire procedure took only fifteen minutes, but to Brittany it seemed like forever. Luckily for her and Brad, the bullet hadn't penetrated as deeply as she'd first thought. He stirred and mumbled incoherently when she first inserted the tip of the blade and all Bernard had to do was hold Brad's arms when he tried to push Brittany away. He moaned in pain when she dug deeper, and Bernard had to practically sit on the patient when Brad fought to sit up. The whole affair turned her stomach, and before she touched the red-hot blade to his wound to cauterize it, she paused long enough to catch her breath. The stench of burning flesh gagged everyone. But the moment Brittany had finished with Brad, he fell into a deep sleep, content with having her wash away the blood with a warm, damp cloth, bandage the shoulder, and cover him with another blanket so he could rest.

"You sure you've never done that before?" Bernard asked while Brittany washed her hands in the bowl.

"Never," she sighed, smiling. "And I pray I never will again."

"Well, you did a good job. I doubt Doc Warren could have done better." He handed her a towel and asked, "May I fix you some tea and something to eat?"

"I'd love a cup of tea, but I think I'd better wait to eat until my stomach settles down."

"Then a cup of tea it is," he smiled knowingly. "If you'd like, you may come downstairs while I heat up the water. But I must ask that if someone knocks on the door, you'll wait up here until I tell you it's safe. All right?"

Brittany would have preferred going home, but there were several reasons why she decided against it for the moment. First of all, it was very possible that she'd been recognized by the soldiers and that they were at this minute looking for her.

If that were true, she'd be safer traveling the road home in the dark. Second, she wanted to make certain Brad would be all right. But more than anything, she wanted to have it out with his brother, and she was reasonably sure Dane would return to Mr. Patterson's before very long.

"Agreed," she nodded, then led the way when Bernard held out a hand toward the ladder.

A short time later the two of them were sitting before the fire sharing a cup of tea and a quiet moment together. There were a lot of things Brittany wanted to ask Mr. Patterson, but she doubted he would answer them. He had no reason to trust her, even though she'd shown up at his door with Brad and Dane Remington; obviously it must seem to him that she was a friend of theirs. Perhaps after he talked with Dane he would be more willing to confide in her. Settling herself in the rocker, cup in hand, she stared over at the bright flames.

"Do you live near Boston, Miss Lockwood?"

Brittany nodded and set aside her teacup. "Along the coast, north of the city. Our property runs adjacent to the Ingram estate. You've heard of Bartholomew and Miles Ingram, haven't you?"

Bernard quickly raised his cup to his mouth and took a drink. "Yes," he admitted after a moment. "Are they friends of yours as well as neighbors?"

Brittany thought that was a rather odd question. Couldn't he tell just by looking at her that she didn't have the wealth it would take to be friends with the Ingrams? "Papa and Mr. Ingram were—after a fashion. They talked whenever they ran into each other in town. But we never dined with them, if that's what you mean. Why do you ask?"

Bernard shrugged and started to answer, but the soft rapping on the back door brought him to his feet in a hurry. He was about to wave her toward the staircase when the knocking sounded again . . . this time in a set pattern, one Bernard recognized as a signal. "It's Dane Remington," he whispered, motioning for her to stay put before he crossed to the door and unlocked it. Opening it a crack, he peeked outside to make certain, then moved aside and opened it all the way.

Brittany's heart pounded in her chest the instant she saw his tall, dark figure fill the doorway, then step across the threshold and into the room. He was dressed in dark blue, and when he took the tricorn from his head, his raven-black hair caught the firelight and shimmered. He had discarded the clothes of the hunchback, the beard, and the eye patch, and for a moment she wondered how she could have been so easily fooled. The vision of him had burned itself into her memory, and she would have sworn she'd have recognized him the instant she saw him again. She hadn't, though; his disguise had been complete. What upset her more than being duped was his need for it in the first place.

"How's Brad?" he asked Bernard with only a brief glance her way.

"He's resting quietly," he said, closing the door again and turning the key in the lock. "And you can thank Miss Lockwood for that. She's the one who fixed him up."

Dane's green eyes found her, and even though he didn't say it, Brittany could see by the way he looked at her that he was indeed grateful. "He has a lot to thank me for," she told Bernard, though her gaze never left Dane. "If I hadn't wanted to go to Boston this morning, his brother might have bled to death right there in the street. But I suppose he blames me for that. You see, I'm the one who told him his brother was being held in gaol. If I hadn't, he wouldn't have gotten Brad out, and Brad wouldn't have gotten shot. Isn't that the way you see it, Mr. Remington?"

Bernard hadn't missed the innuendo in Brittany's statement, but he couldn't understand it, either. Dane obviously did. With a half-smile he turned toward the stairs and mounted them silently. He returned a few minutes later, talked quietly with the shoemaker, then headed for the door on his way out again. Brittany immediately came to her feet.

164

"We need to talk, Mr. Remington," she called, stopping him before his hand touched the key in the lock. "Because of you, there's a good chance I'm in as much trouble as your brother."

Sensing that what she had to say didn't concern him, Bernard excused himself and hurried into the other room.

"And perhaps you're better off not knowing anything more than you already do," Dane pointed out with a sideways glance over his shoulder at her.

"Which is absolutely nothing." Her chin came up and she took a step toward him. "Whatever possessed you to come to the farm? Did Roan send you? And why the disguises? To fool me? Well, you didn't, not for long. Who is Cory really? Your woman?"

With each added question Dane's eyes darkened. Brittany deserved some sort of explanation, but her arrogance grated on his nerves. Glancing toward the curtained entryway to make sure Bernard hadn't overheard her, Dane turned, reached for Brittany's arm, and roughly shoved her toward the stairs. Just because her brother was fighting for the cause didn't mean Brittany could be trusted. He had seen how Miles Ingram wished to protect her from the two strangers who rode onto her farm that day; there was more to it than just being neighborly. He also knew Miles had to have an accomplice, and right now all the evidence pointed to her.

"Let go of me!" Brittany demanded when he bruised the tender flesh around her wrist. "I'm quite capable of walking on my own."

"And taking care of yourself?" he rallied hotly once they had reached the top of the stairs. He gave her a shove toward the middle of the room. "Your brother didn't think so, or he wouldn't have come to me asking for help."

Brittany didn't like being pushed around, especially by this rogue. "I would have managed . . . somehow. And even if I hadn't been able to hold onto the farm, Miles would have given me a fair price for it." She didn't believe that; she'd just said the first thing that had come to mind.

The faded blue cotton dress she wore was reflected in her pale blue-gray eyes and contrasted with the rosy blush in her cheeks. It was easy to see what attracted Brad. If he weren't so involved in other things just now, he'd be tempted to give Brad *and* Miles Ingram a little competition.

Dane's frown deepened. What was he saying? He didn't have the time nor the inclination to play games . . . especially with Brittany Lockwood. Granted, she was very beautiful, and he would probably enjoy tossing her on her back again in a more pleasurable spot than a mound of hay, but as he looked at her, he doubted it would end there. He was already allowing thoughts of her to distract him, and with the kind of work he had to do, his mind had to be clear, not clouded with insignificant musings about a woman.

That was probably the reason his brother was lying upstairs in bed suffering from a gunshot wound. It wouldn't surprise him to learn that Brad had been following a pretty, shapely young woman when he wandered unknowingly into the middle of a dangerous situation, one that resulted in his having to be hidden away somewhere until the authorities lost interest in finding him. Sometimes taking care of his brother was like having a five-year-old boy around.

Now things were even more complicated. He had Brittany to watch out for as well. And what made it even more difficult for him was that he couldn't trust her to tell her the truth about what he was doing and why.

"I apologize for bringing you into this," he said, "but it couldn't be helped. I saw Brad go down and knew no one there would help him. I'm sure you'd have done the same thing if he'd been your brother."

Brittany had expected him to tell her it was none of her business, not apologize to her. Taken aback by his unexpected behavior, she simply stood there staring at him, mouth agape, unable to reply.

"As for the disguises," he continued, crossing to the tiny

166

window in Bernard's bedroom and looking out at the street below, "I know you wouldn't accept our help if you knew who we were. As for Cory being my woman. . . ." He smiled at the thought of how angry Cory would be to hear her name linked in innuendo with his or that of any man, and he turned back to look at Brittany. "Cory belongs to no one. She likes it that way." He raised a dark brow at her. "You'd do well to learn from her."

Brittany wasn't sure, but she thought he had insulted her. "What is that supposed to mean?"

"Simply that you should be careful who you choose as friends."

"Oh, I am," she retorted acidly. "I don't count you among them."

The vaguest of smiles touched his mouth and disappeared. "Maybe you should. I don't want anything from you."

"Really?" she mocked. "Then why did you and Cory come to the farm? You must have wanted something out of it or you wouldn't have wasted your time."

Crossing his arms over his wide chest, Dane leaned a shoulder against the window frame and casually looked outside again. "I did it because your brother asked for help. I felt I owed him."

"For what?"

"For letting me know that Brad was in gaol."

Brittany's cheeks flamed with her rage. "How soon you forget," she spat. "*I* was the one who paid for that bit of knowledge."

"No," he corrected as he studied something of interest outside the window. "You paid for his release." He shifted his attention to her lovely face. "And your stupidity."

The deep, piercing greenness of his eyes seemed to touch her very soul, and Brittany shivered in spite of herself. It had been nearly a month since their tryst in the barn, but she could remember every second of it as if it had been only yesterday. She could feel the warmth of his touch, the

167

branding fire of his kiss, the rock-hard muscles of his arms and shoulders as she fought to push him from her. Worst of all, she could remember the passion he had stirred in her, and she'd been unable, after all this time, to forget it. She didn't like being in the same room with him. Nor did she like being called stupid.

"If what I did for my brother was stupid, then what you did for Brad could be deemed the same, wouldn't you agree?" She cocked a brow at him and waited. When he didn't answer, she admitted, "The only thing stupid about what I did was to go to you for help. I should have found someone else, a man with morals, one who wouldn't take advantage of a situation."

"Like Miles Ingram?" he asked.

There was no way of knowing for certain, but Brittany sensed he didn't approve of Miles Ingram. Bernard Patterson had behaved much the same way when she'd mentioned Miles's name. It had bothered her that he seemed interested in whether or not her family and his were friends. It bothered her even more now that Dane implied it as well.

"Mr. Ingram is a gentleman, sir," she replied. "And a gentleman wouldn't suggest the sort of payment you required."

The corner of Dane's mouth lifted. "And would a gentleman like Miles Ingram have the nerve to break your brother out of gaol? I imagine that's the reason you didn't go to him first. I doubt he would do anything more strenuous than opening a box of snuff or selecting what color hose he should wear, not risk his life helping your brother."

Brittany didn't know why, but she felt she should defend Miles. "Of course, he wouldn't do it himself. He'd hire someone who would."

"And what do you suppose would be the fee for doing something like that?" His eyes freely roamed the length of her from head to toe and back again. "And how would you have paid? The cost wouldn't have been cheap."

"As well I can attest," she barked. "However, I'm certain Miles wouldn't have asked what you thought it worth."

Dane's green eyes lowered to her heaving bosom. "Oh? Then I would say the man's a fool."

"And you, sir, are an unprincipled cad."

A flash of white teeth showed with his smile. "I've been called worse," he confessed, lifting his gaze to her face again. Suddenly, a movement from outside the window in the street below caught Dane's eye. A group of British soldiers were making a door-to-door search, and they were about to knock on the back door of the cobbler's shop. Without bothering to tell her what he saw, Dane hurriedly closed the distance between them and grabbed her elbow.

"What—?" Her angry demand to know his intent was cut short when he quickly covered her mouth with his hand.

"Soldiers," he whispered in her ear.

The loud pounding on the door below them confirmed his declaration, and Brittany instantly recognized the danger she was in. Twisting free of him, she hurried to the ladder and climbed up the rungs ahead of Dane. Together they pulled the ladder up after them and sealed the trap door just as Bernard answered the summons. All they could hear were the muffled, demanding voices of his visitors, followed by the sounds of footsteps on the stairs and in the bedroom below them. Brittany pressed the back of her hand to her mouth, closed her eyes, and sank to the floor. She had never been so frightened in all her life. Several minutes passed while they waited and listened, and after what seemed an eternity, the back door slammed shut behind the soldiers, marking their departure and an end to their need to hide.

"I've got to go home," she whispered as Dane quietly crossed the room toward his brother's cot. "If I was recognized, they'll be sending someone to the farm to confirm it. If I'm already there, they'd have no way of proving I ever left." She rose to her feet and hurried after him when he ignored what she'd said. "Did you hear me? I must go home."

He studied his brother's sleeping face a moment longer, then turned to her. "It's too late for that now, I'm afraid. You'll have to stay here for a few days."

"But if I do, I'll never be able to go home again. My disappearance will only strengthen their suspicions. Don't you see that?"

Oddly enough, Dane found himself fighting off the urge to kiss her. Her anger and frustration had heightened the color in her cheeks, made her eyes sparkle, and added a healthy glow to her skin. The long, slim column of her neck looked inviting, and he wished he could press his lips against the velvety flesh of her throat and entwine his fingers through the thick locks of her golden hair. But he couldn't, and he knew it. She'd never allow him the luxury. "Not if we get you an alibi."

The smooth arch of her brows crimped into a frown. "What kind of alibi? Visiting relatives or a sick friend? I have neither, Mr. Remington."

"I'll think of something," he said and walked past her toward the trap door, where he knelt down to lift off the cover.

"And while you are thinking, what happens to my farm? The chores won't wait. There are chickens to be fed, a cow to milk—"

"Cory will see to it."

"Cory," she spat in disgust as she watched him move the ladder and slide it into place. "I'd prefer Cory and her hunchbacked friend find work elsewhere. As a matter of fact, Mr. Remington," she hurriedly went on when Dane twisted around and put a foot on the first rung of the ladder, "I insist upon it. Both you and Cory were well paid for the work you'd done, and if you think otherwise, then consider what I did for Brad as making us even. Agreed?"

Dane paused a moment to look at her. "Stay here until I come back for you. We'll discuss whether or not Cory and I should find other work then."

Brittany's stubborn streak surfaced. "Nothing you can say will change my mind. I want you and Cory off my farm."

"Even if it means the crops will rot in the fields?"

"It's a chance I'm willing to take just to be rid of you." Her gray-blue eyes flashed as she glared back at him, and when his darkened a bit, some of her defiance slipped a little.

"Stay put," was all he said before he descended the ladder and disappeared from sight.

Brittany stood staring at the aperture through which Dane had left for a long while afterward. She wondered at the feelings which stirred inside her. She was proud of the way she'd stood up to him, even though it appeared he hadn't been affected by it. She was glad he'd decided to leave when he had.

Yet, she felt a strange emptiness now. She truly wanted him and his friend to leave the farm, but she honestly didn't look forward to it. Dane had an unexplainable magnetism about him that made it impossible for her to get him off her mind—even when they hadn't been together for more than a short while. Sinking to her knees, she sat on one hip and stared at the square shaft of light coming up from the room below, oddly wishing Dane had more he wanted to say and would appear on the ladder again at any moment. The clicking of the latch at the back door to Bernard Patterson's shop told her he didn't, and Brittany marveled over how disappointed she was.

Miles Ingram never liked being out after dark; too many things could happen. His horse could stumble and toss him; he could lose his way wandering about in the shadows and have to spend the night outside, damp and uncomfortable, rather than tucked away on silk sheets and a soft mound of feathers. And there were always snakes slithering about the woods. One of the nasty little vipers could bite him, and he'd be dead before anybody missed him. Yet the note his trusted butler had given him said it was urgent and that he should go to the edge of the marsh as soon as possible. He was to come alone and on foot, since a man could travel more quietly and more deftly through the trees than a horse and rider. The secrecy of their rendezvous was of more importance than Miles's well-being.

The distance from the mansion to the meeting place was more than a mile. By the time he moved out of view of the huge manor and entered the cover of trees leading to the swamp, he was wishing he had ridden his horse at least this far. He had fallen down twice already. He had heard something moving about in the tall grasses, and a pebble had somehow wedged itself inside his shoe. The night air was hot and humid, and he was perspiring so badly that he felt as if he had taken his bath with his clothes on. All in all, he was extremely miserable.

"This had better be worth it," he fumed when he snagged his hose on a prickly bush. Cursing under his breath, he hopped to a fallen tree trunk and sat down to pull out the thorn embedded in his flesh, vowing that *he* would be the one to choose the spot of their next meeting. Swatting at a mosquito, he wondered if all this would ever pay off. He had heard many promises, but they had delivered very little, and the only reason he didn't tell his cohort to go back to wherever she'd come from was simply that he was greedy at heart—and something of a gambler. If there was even a slight chance of making money out of all this *and* the possibility of having Brittany Lockwood at his mercy, then he'd go along—for a while, anyway. But something had better happen fairly soon or he'd turn his partner over to his father and deny everything. After all, he hadn't really done anything yet, and he could always claim he'd agreed to the proposal out of loyalty to the Crown and as a means of entrapping a spy.

An owl hooted from somewhere in the branches high

overhead and Miles nearly fell off the tree trunk. They were such eerie creatures. It seemed to him that their sole reason for being on this earth was to frighten people who were stupid enough to go wandering about in the dark. One never heard them sing; they didn't eat seeds or worms like most birds, but preyed on small rodents. They were flesh eaters, and Miles always worried that it would be his misfortune to be around when the pickings were slim and they chose to attack a victim of much larger scale—like himself. Shaking the tiny stone from his shoe, he clumsily jammed his foot back inside and stood up. Well, not tonight, he silently vowed as he started off toward his destination again.

Until this moment, when he paused at the edge of the marshland on the Lockwood property, he hadn't given much thought to the possibility that the note he'd received could have been part of a trap. He cursed his foolishness in not having at least armed himself with some kind of weapon or instructed Charles, his butler, to come along. The man could have hidden somewhere close by should Miles have needed his help. But it was too late to change the odds in his favor, and he didn't relish the thought of trekking all the way back home for a pistol. When he finally walked through the front door of the manor again, he had no intention of leaving until daylight guaranteed his safety.

The snapping of a twig spun Miles around, his eyes wide, his heart pounding in his chest. He didn't know if he should stand his ground or flee. Should he come face-to-face with a large, vicious animal—whether of the two- or four-legged kind—he didn't want to give up without a fight; but he didn't want to appear the fool if the intruder was only Millicent Ashburn. He sensed she already thought of him that way, and he certainly didn't want to do anything that would confirm such notions. Taking a deep breath, he gritted his teeth, focused his attention on the sound, and braced himself for whatever was about to unfold.

"Really, Miles," came a soft-pitched voice from the

shadows, "you look as if you're standing in court awaiting sentence. Relax . . . it's only me."

Her announcement didn't lessen the pain in his chest; nor did it strike a humorous vein . . . Miles Ingram didn't have a single one. "Miss Ashburn. The least you could have done was call out, rather than sneak up on me like that. A man could die of apoplexy." He staggered to a huge rock and sat down. "And next time I suggest we meet somewhere a little more . . . appropriate, shall we say?" He could hear her moving about, but she elected to stay far enough away from him that he couldn't get a very good view of her.

"And where would that be? Your parlor, perhaps? Or how about the courthouse in Boston? Why don't we just tell the whole world what we're doing?" Her tone was hard and cold.

"I didn't mean a place like that," he sneered. "Just somewhere comfortable. An out-of-the-way little inn where no one would recognize us."

"And how far would we have to travel to be assured of that? Maine?"

The rustling of leaves beneath her feet as she moved to stand behind him tempted Miles to turn around. In all their meetings, he had never been allowed to see her face. It was a part of their deal, she'd told him. She didn't trust him any more than he trusted her, and it was her only insurance of walking away from their bargain should something go wrong. He didn't appreciate her having such an advantage, but there was little he could do about it right now. What she didn't know was that he planned to change that part of it as soon as possible. Somehow he'd trick her. He just hadn't determined the method yet.

"All right, suppose you tell me why you felt the need for us to meet at this ungodly hour." He slapped the back of his neck, killing the mosquito before it drew any more blood. "And in such a deplorable place."

Her smile went unseen. Little did Miles know how much

Millicent enjoyed watching him suffer. It was the main reason she'd sent word for him to meet her here. Folding her arms, she leaned comfortably against the trunk of an oak. "When was the last time you visited Miss Lockwood?"

Miles shrugged. "I don't know . . . two or three weeks ago."

"Are you aware that she has help planting her crops?"

Miles straightened and turned sideways on the rock, carefully avoiding looking at her. He didn't know whether she had a pistol with her or not—or if she'd use it should he turn all the way around. "You mean those two beggars? Did she actually hire them?"

"Yes, damn you!" she exploded. "And you should have known that! It's your part of the bargain to take care of her! Must I do everything?"

Her tirade angered him. "If you think you can, go right ahead. It wouldn't bother me in the least, since all I've gotten from you so far is a lot of empty promises. Where's all the money I'm suppose to be 'raking in'? You told me months ago that you had a way of smuggling goods into the colonies so that neither the British nor the rebels would know of it."

"I also told you that we had to get rid of Miss Lockwood and her brother before we could," she rallied.

"Well, Roan is gone," he countered.

"Through pure luck and nothing else! Have you any idea how close his sister came to finding out the truth about the charges brought against him? It wouldn't have taken her very long to figure out you were behind it. Then where would we have been?"

"No further than we are now!" he raged, jumping to his feet and taking a few steps away from her. Turning back to the shadowed figure watching him, he snarled, "I think we'd better just forget about this entire arrangement."

Millicent wanted to agree, to tell the bloody milksop to go to hell with all the rest of his kind. But she couldn't. Everything was beginning to fall into place, even though

Miles couldn't see it. It had taken her some time to win the trust of the others involved in her scheme, to acquire their confidence enough to be told all she needed to make the whole thing work. She had done that. It was the reason she'd sent for Miles. And if the success of her plan didn't depend largely on his help, she'd pull the pistol she'd brought with her and blow his head off. But the desire to see the greater goal achieved stilled her want to kill him—for the moment, anyway. Gritting her teeth, she gulped down her pride and said, "I apologize for losing my temper, Mr. Ingram. I've been under a strain, and I let it get to me. If you'll be kind enough to listen for a moment longer, I'll explain the real reason I asked you to meet with me."

Miles couldn't name it, but something about this woman—her temper, her need for secrecy, perhaps—frightened him. To hear her apologize took him aback completely. Befuddled, he merely stood staring at her slender shape veiled in the darkness of night without uttering a word.

Millicent took his silence to mean consent. What surprised her was that he didn't have some derisive comment to make. He was lucky he didn't show his arrogance and smile at her. A flash of white teeth would have been all it took for her to change her mind. Uneasy with the way he stared at her, she moved behind the tree out of sight as she said, "A ship carrying English goods will be anchoring offshore on the other side of the marsh within a few hours. I hope you're ready for them. Otherwise they'll take the merchandise elsewhere and I'll be forced to find another partner."

"My God," Miles moaned. "I should have been told earlier!"

"There was no way. I didn't find out myself until a little while ago, and this was the first chance I had to get away. Can you take the goods or not?"

Miles wasn't sure exactly how he would manage it on such

176

short notice, but this was too good an opportunity to let pass by. Besides, his father had decided to spend the night in Boston. If he worked until sunup, he just might be able to handle it. But he'd have to hurry. "Yes. Yes, I'll take them. Do they know where to go?"

"They've been given their instructions."

"Then I must return home immediately. There's a lot to do."

"Mr. Ingram," she called, stopping him when he turned to depart, "I don't think I have to tell you how risky this will be. If you owned the Lockwood farm, it would be no trouble at all. I suggest you pay Miss Lockwood another visit."

Miles's shoulders dropped. "I already told you she won't sell."

"Then think of something else. Kill her if you have to, but get her off that farm!"

Miles's milk-white complexion paled even more. The last thing he would ever do to Brittany was kill her! He wanted her—whether as a wife or mistress didn't matter. But he would never see her dead because of his lust for money. "I'll take care of it," he half-whispered.

"See that you do. Otherwise . . ."

Her words trailed off, but Miles knew what she implied. Brittany's life was unimportant to Millicent Ashburn; it meant everything to him. He'd pay Brittany a visit as soon as possible. Staggering back, he turned and hurried off toward home, cursing the day he let this little bitch into his life.

The soldiers never came again, and it should have soothed Brittany's nerves; it didn't. In fact, it only made the waiting that much more intolerable. By late evening, the tiny attic room had turned from a safe haven into a prison, and only because she'd finally gotten Bernard to admit that the soldiers who had searched the place earlier were only looking for a wounded man—a man whose identity they didn't know—not a hunchback and blond-haired woman who helped in his escape. Apparently the crowd that had pushed in around the soldiers when Dane moved the cart next to his brother had been enough to restrict their view of the rescuers. That meant it was safe for Brittany to go home. Bernard, however, didn't agree and pleaded with her to wait for Dane's approval, vowing he would return to the cobbler's home before nightfall. But like the soldiers, Dane didn't show up again.

Brittany had managed to take her mind off her impatience when Brad awoke sometime around sunset asking for a glass of water. It took nearly all his energy just to ask, and once she'd fulfilled his request, he tumbled off to sleep again. His brow was fevered and she'd spent the next hour wiping his face and neck with a cool, wet cloth. She ate the sparse meal Bernard had graciously offered, then told him it was better for her to stay close to Brad should he awake and want something rather than sit by the fire in Bernard's parlor as he'd invited her to do. She'd doubted Brad would stir again before morning, but she'd said it in hopes that Bernard would retire early and before Dane came to call. While the old man slept, she planned to leave his hospitality and go home—with or without Dane's permission.

She had no way of knowing, but she guessed it was around ten o'clock when Bernard stuck his head through the opening in the attic floor to ask if she'd like to lie down for a while; he'd awaken her later and they'd take turns sitting up with Brad. She declined, telling him she wasn't really tired but that he should nap first if he wanted. Admitting that the day had been exhausting, he bade her good night for a spell and climbed back down the ladder. Twenty minutes later Brittany was lying on her stomach, peeking down through the trap door at him. Still fully clothed, he had stretched out on his bed with a blanket drawn up over him. His eyes were closed and he was snoring, an indication that if she planned to leave, she'd better hurry and do so quietly.

The streets of Boston were relatively empty when Brittany left Bernard's place, heading away from the docks at a brisk pace. On this route it would take longer for her to get home, but she knew traveling through the residential part of town would be safer than on the avenue leading past the pubs and inns frequented by sailors and dock workers. Luckily the night was warm and clear, and she didn't need the shawl she'd apparently left behind in the cart. The full moon lit the way down the darker streets and within a half-hour she had left Boston and was on the road home.

The trip was long enough to give her plenty of time to think. As always, Dane Remington came to mind, and she silently went over their earlier conversation. His excuse for showing up on her farm was that he felt he owed Roan. Brittany found that unlikely. A man who had the nerve to require a woman's virtue as payment for his help couldn't possibly have a conscience and therefore feel any need to meet his obligations. He was right when he said he needed a disguise. She would have ordered him off her property if she'd known who he was. But why had Cory dressed as a boy? She didn't know the woman. She never would have expected to see someone like Cory with Dane Remington, and that puzzled her.

Spotting a stick lying by the side of the road, she bent and picked it up to use as a walking cane. Absently watching the tip of it stab the soft soil each time she took a step, she was curious about why Dane and Cory had really come to her farm. If she sent them away, she'd never learn the real reason. Perhaps she should let them continue to work for her. Not only would she have a harvest in the fall which would stall off the creditors a while longer, but she just might stumble across something they said or did that would give her a clue. She didn't know why, but she sensed Dane Remington and his group of misfits were mixed up in something that had to be kept secret. Her eyes narrowed and she jabbed the stick a little harder against the ground. It was no doubt something evil, she mused with a snide grin. And what better way to get even with him than by finding out what it was and turning him over to whoever was interested?

Brittany laughed devilishly at the idea, then suddenly remembered seeing the Dark Horseman on the road in front of her house and mused how she'd thought then that Zachary and Cory were the ones he was after. She'd already decided they were spies for the British and were using her place to hide out for a while. She was rather convinced of it when she went to the barn and found it empty. Yet now that she knew who Zachary really was, it didn't quite fit. If Dane worked for the British, why had it been necessary for him to break his brother out of gaol? Couldn't he have just told someone, and have Brad released?

A chilling thought suddenly struck her, and Brittany stopped in the middle of the road to look back over her shoulder: maybe Brad had been put in the gaol with the rest of the rebels—like her brother—to learn whatever he could about the revolt. Dear God, the whole affair could have been planned. It was a good way for the Remingtons to win the confidence of people like Roan and Paul Revere and to trick them into thinking they were on their side! It had fooled Roan.

"That can't be," she said aloud and started down the road again. "Why would they shoot one of their own?" Tossing the stick away, she thought, *But then, how could they have known he was one of them when he was standing in the middle of a riotous crowd? It could have been a mistake.*

The pounding hooves behind her spun Brittany around. When she saw the horse and rider bearing down on her, she didn't know whether to scream, turn and run, or hide in the trees at the side of the road. The stallion raced from shadow into moonlight, and the moment the platinum light hit the man's handsome face, Brittany's fear deepened. She could almost see the rage glowing in Dane's green eyes before he caught up to her, and with all the thoughts that had been going through her head about his being a spy, she half-expected him to pull out his pistol and shoot her where she stood. But he didn't. Instead, he yanked back hard on the reins and brought his steed to a halt beside her.

"I gave you more credit than this, Brittany Lockwood," he growled, one hand resting on the pommel of his saddle, the other midway down his thigh as he leaned forward to glare into her frightened eyes. "I thought you'd have realized by now how dangerous it is for a beautiful young woman to be out alone after dark. Or even in broad daylight, for that matter."

Brittany didn't like the tone of his voice. He sounded as if he were talking to a child who had run away from home. "Until a second ago, I was perfectly safe. Now I'm not so sure."

Dane wouldn't dignify her comment with a reply. Sliding back off the saddle and onto the horse's rump, he held out a hand to her. "Come on. I'm taking you home."

"Thank you, no," she replied, lifting her chin. "I prefer to walk." Giving him a mocking smile, she turned and started down the road again.

Dane watched her until she'd walked on ahead a hundred feet or so, thinking that she was the most stubborn woman he'd ever met, and one who wasn't intimidated by him. His first reaction was irritation: it annoyed him when someone blatantly ignored his orders. It usually meant wasting time having to convince them that their health was in jeopardy if they disobeyed for very long. And time was something he didn't have.

But the longer he thought about it, the more he could see the humorous side of it. A lazy smile parted his lips as he studied the gentle sway of her rounded hips. Moonlight bathed her slender form in an ashen glow as if daring him to touch the sensuous curves hidden beneath the cotton dress, and Dane suddenly decided to test her tenacity. Sliding back into the saddle, he nudged his horse and slowly followed

Brittany down the road ribboned in black and silver. If she wanted to walk, he'd let her.

Brittany hadn't realized how exhausting her day had been until she glanced over her shoulder at Dane with the intention of snubbing him and saw how relaxed and comfortable he was astride his stallion. The smirk on his handsome face and the slight nod he gave infuriated her, and she jerked back around to concentrate on the path she took. Every muscle in her body ached, and she longed to be home again, where she could kick off her shoes and lie down on the soft feather mattress in her bedroom. But she wasn't going to let him know. Squaring her shoulders, she raised her chin and hurried her pace.

About a half-hour later she neared the fork in the road. The lane to the right led home, the one to the left toward the Ingram estate. Brittany had just about had enough of Dane Remington and his subtle way of proving a point. He had not only kept his mount within five feet of her the entire trip, but once he had leisurely swung a leg over the horse's neck and proceeded to light up a cheroot. To all appearances he seemed bored and quite unaware of how tiring the journey had been for her. She also realized that part of his game was to provoke her. Looking at the thick stand of trees dividing her from the yard outside her home and realizing his horse was too large to follow her through them, Brittany set her steps in that direction without so much as a backward glance.

"I hope there aren't any snakes in there," he called after her, amused by her ploy to be rid of him.

"There aren't," she returned confidently. "The only viper out at this time of night is riding a horse."

Dane chuckled openly at her insult. Her quick wit was unusual for a woman—at least the kind of woman he was used to—and he found it refreshing. With a click of his tongue and a nudge of his heels, he cantered off down the road toward the farm.

Brittany watched him go and smiled at her cunning. If she had known it would work so easily, she'd have moved into the cover of dense oak much sooner and rid herself of his presence from the start. Stepping back out onto the lane where the way was less restrictive, she relaxed and set her pace at a comfortable rate.

A short time later the house came into view and Brittany smiled when she saw it, relieved to be home again. It felt as if she'd been away for a month. Crossing the front yard, she glanced over at the barn and saw the faint light coming from inside. Apparently Dane had decided to retire rather than wait for her to return, and she was glad. She wasn't in the mood to talk to him right now. All she wanted was to go to bed. She'd figure out what to do about her unwelcome company in the morning. Seizing the doorknob, she freed the latch and stepped inside.

The room was lost in darkness except for the small amount of light coming in through the window. Brittany gingerly felt her way around the furniture toward her bedroom door. Moonlight trickled in through the window and fell invitingly on the bed. Not bothering with her clothes, she stepped out of her shoes, crossed to the fourposter, and tumbled upon the feathery mattress. In a matter of moments she had fallen asleep.

A warm night breeze tickled her face and played with the tendril of hair lying across her nose. She stirred, stretched languidly, and rolled onto her stomach. A sweet smile graced her lips and she murmured in her half-conscious state. Airy dreams filled her head. The world outside her room didn't exist. The troubles of her day were gone. In their place was the vision of a man, a tall, muscular, handsome man with broad shoulders, dark hair, and a gleaming white smile. He stood in the doorway of her bedroom watching her, his sleek, sinewy body bathed in the platinum streams of light, his face hidden in the shadows. She knew why he had come. He wanted her as he always had and her heart beat a little faster

183

at the thought. Sitting up, she watched him cross the threshold, round the end of the bed, and come to stand next to her, his wide-shouldered frame casting a shadow across her and making it impossible for her to see his face, the smile on his lips, and the look of sensuous yearning in his eyes. He held a hand out to her and she quickly took it, allowing him to draw her off the bed and into his arms.

Their parted lips met urgently, as if their time together was short and they might never have this chance again. Long, lean fingers entrapped the golden strands of hair at the nape of her neck and his other hand pressed against the small of her back to pull her close. She entwined her arms around him and reveled in the strength of the muscles across his back. The manly scent of him filled her nostrils, drugged her mind, and set her blood on fire. Their tongues touched and their kiss became fevered and passionate. Each experienced a rapturous joy of which neither could get enough. His nimble fingers worked the buttons on her dress free and slid both dress and lacy white petticoats down her slender hips and willowy legs to the floor. She unfastened his shirt front and glided the garment off his shoulders. His lips trailed a moist path down her chin and neck, across her shoulder, and up her throat to the lobe of one ear while he whispered sweet words of love against the velvety smoothness of her skin.

Her world careened dizzily when he stripped away her camisole, then shed the rest of his own attire and swept her up in his arms. She was hot and cold, excited and frightened, willing and timid all at the same time. And when his lips found hers again and he gently lay with her upon the cushion of down, his naked flesh touching the full length of hers, she wondered if this was a dream at all, or the wild yearnings of her heart come true.

Suddenly, she feared that the man who held her, caressed her, and kissed her while his thumb teased the peak of one breast would vanish as stealthily as an early morning mist when sunlight warmed the earth. Or worse, she feared she would see his face and know he was the scoundrel who plagued her very soul of late rather than the mysterious rider cloaked in black. Afraid the truth would not be what she wanted and wishing to delay knowing it for certain, she wrapped her arms around him and pulled him down, meeting his lips with hers in an ardent embrace. The feeling of his nakedness against her trembling body sent her pulse and mind soaring. She moaned in ecstasy when his opened mouth found her breast and his hand the smooth contour of her hip and thigh. Anxious to blend their souls as one, she moved beneath him and welcomed the manly boldness of him deep within her. She gasped in the sheer pleasure of it when he pressed the fullness of his manhood long and hard against the arching of her hips. At first he seemed to tease her, play with her, drink in the knowledge of her willingness when he would not move. Thinking it to mean he wasn't sure, she locked her fingers in his dark hair and pulled his mouth to hers, their tongues clashing, their hearts beating wildly, their passion exploding in a raging fire of desire.

His breathing quickened, as did hers. He thrust his throbbing staff deeper and with long, sleek penetration lifted her beyond the heights of her imaginings to a world she little knew existed and never wanted to leave. Her womanly instincts took over and she moved against him as she felt the thunderous pounding of his heart against her naked breast and heard his ragged breathing in her ear. She could taste him, feel him, touch him, smell the masculine scent of him, and as their passion exploded into rapturous glory, she knew it was real, that she truly held him in her arms, possessed him, and had made love to him.

All too soon it ended. They lay breathless and panting in each other's embrace. Snuggling close within the circle of his arm, she closed her eyes and blissfully drifted off to sleep.

Chapter Seven

The morning sunlight that fell in through the window lay heavily against Brittany's eyelids, penetrating her dreams and bringing her to a slow, pleasant wakefulness. A smile curled her lips as she happily recalled the sweet moments of the evening past, the feel of him, his gentleness, his boldness, the courage it had taken for him to come to her. Suddenly her eyes flew open and she bolted upright in bed. With the coverlet clutched tightly against her, she hurriedly scanned the room, frowning once she found that both it and her bed were empty. It had to have been a dream, but it seemed so real that she wasn't sure what had happened.

Her fantasy had always started out the way it had last night, but she always woke before it had gone too far. He had always worn a black mask. She had always taken it from him. And he had always been Dane Remington and not the Dark Horseman! Huddled up against the headboard, she closed her eyes and tried to recall everything that transpired from the minute she crossed the yard and came into the house. The room had been dark, so she had had to feel her way to her bedroom. She had seen the moonlight falling on her bed and remembered crossing to it and collapsing on the mattress fully clothed except for her shoes. She opened her eyes and looked down at the floor, relieved to see the shoes lying there. At least that much of it had been true. But what about her clothes? She couldn't remember shedding them herself, only that he had done it for her. Brittany chewed nervously on her lower lip. If it wasn't a dream—and it appeared it wasn't—who was the man who came to her room in the middle of the night? Brittany's head jerked toward the door. Dear God, it couldn't have been Dane! She would have known! She would have stopped him!

And what if it was? she wondered, tears springing to her eyes. What would he think of her? Worse than that, what would he expect from her now that she had seemed willing to lie with him? Pulling her knees up to her chest, she wrapped one arm around them and nibbled on her thumbnail as she stared at the vacant doorway. Would he come to her room every night thinking he had the right? She could hear a rooster crowing in the yard and realized that Dane was more than likely up and dressed by now, probably on his way to the house. Flipping off the covers, she scrambled from the bed and hurriedly pulled on her chemise, silently vowing that he would not find her in a state of undress as though she were waiting for him. She would appear as if nothing out of the ordinary had happened. After all, she wasn't really certain it had.

It took her longer than usual to fix breakfast. Her hands shook so badly that she kept dropping things and had to stop to clean up the mess. It was going to be difficult for her to pretend, but until she knew for certain, it was all she could do. She would have liked staying away from him, but if the vision she had last night had been nothing more than a dream, he would find her behavior strange and question it. Yet if it wasn't and they truly had made love, her aloofness would be one way of telling him that she didn't want it to happen again. Having filled two plates with portions of scrambled eggs and pancakes, she leaned heavily against the table and closed her eyes. It was all so confusing. She was almost positive that she had spent the night in someone's arms, but she couldn't understand how she could have been so casual about it at the time. She wasn't accustomed to letting men into her bed. With a throaty growl she lifted the tray and turned for the door.

Dane had been awake now for over an hour. He'd washed and shaved, had changed into the clean clothes he'd brought with him the day he arrived on the farm as Zachary, and was lying on a bed of straw staring up at the rafters in the barn. A smile touched his lips as he thought about what had happened last night and how surprised he'd been when Brittany didn't scream the second she saw him standing in the doorway of her bedroom. He had gone to the house to discuss his plans for his brother after he'd taken Cory back to Boston. He knew Brittany would be asleep, and he intended only to wake her and ask that they talk in the parlor. But once he saw her lying on the bed, her golden hair fanned out across the pillow, the moonlight trailing in through the window caressing her pale skin, he forgot why he had come. Thinking about the image even now made his blood warm. Crossing his wrists behind his head, he closed his eyes and sucked in a deep, long breath as if to recall the soft fragrance of her silky mane and the sweet scent of her flesh. He couldn't imagine what had possessed him to go to her once she'd opened her eyes and sat up, but he had. And when he held out a hand to her, she took it, eagerly drawing herself up into his arms. He ran his tongue over his lips, reliving the titillating sensation he had felt then when she kissed him. She had ignited a fire in him that he couldn't control . . . and didn't want to. Brittany wasn't the first woman he had been with, but he had to admit she was the only one he would find difficult to forget.

Opening his eyes, he sat up and leaned back against the

wall, one knee bent, his arm draped over it. Thinking about what they had done caused him great discomfort, and he decided he should concentrate on something else. But he couldn't. He was simply too captivated by her beauty and apparent willingness to let him make love to her to consider anything else. He had wanted to ask her what had changed her mind about him. He had been reasonably certain she hated even having to look at him, and all of a sudden she was kissing him, caressing him, responding to his advances. And once their passion had faded, she had curled up against him and fallen asleep as though it were something she did every night. He had enjoyed the feel of her supple curves against him and liked the idea of waking up next to her in the morning. But his confusion over why she had allowed him in her bed in the first place chased him away before dawn.

"Women," he muttered to himself. "They're fickle."

A shadow crossed the stream of sunlight coming into the barn through the front doors, and Dane hurriedly rose to his feet. He'd let her be the one to explain. In fact, if she chose not even to mention last night, then neither would he. It would soon become a faint memory where he was concerned. Yet once she had stepped into view and he saw the radiant glow of her flushed cheeks, her thick golden hair, the sensuous curves draped in pink cotton, and her exquisite blue-gray eyes looking shyly back at him, he wondered if he'd ever be able to forget Brittany Lockwood.

Her heart started pounding the instant she saw him standing there. He looked even more handsome than he had the last time. And seeing him here in the barn without the eye patch, beard, and hump reminded her of the night he had lured her here for the payment he thought he deserved. Feeling a blush rise in her cheeks, she quickly looked away. "Where's Cory?" she asked with a frown once she realized they were alone.

It wasn't exactly what he expected her to say, but he hadn't

190

thought she would just come right out and talk about last night, either. Obviously she needed a moment or two to work up her courage. "I took her back to Boston last night to stay with Brad."

Unable to meet his eyes, Brittany stepped further into the wide room and set the tray down on the grain barrel. "Does this mean she won't be coming back?" She and Cory might have had their differences, but at least with her around, Brittany figured perhaps Dane would be reluctant to try something.

The look of near-panic in her eyes when she glanced his way almost made him smile. Apparently what had happened between them was too embarrassing for her to talk about. Crossing to the tray and his plate of food, he picked it up and returned to his place on the straw-covered floor. "Not for a while, anyway. At least not until Brad's able to travel."

A frown wrinkled her brow, and for a moment she forgot about them being the only two in the barn. "You make it sound like Cory will be bringing your brother here."

Chewing on a mouthful of pancake, he smiled lopsidedly. "That's right," he admitted and dropped his gaze to his plate of food again.

"Oh, no, it isn't," she rallied, crossing the short distance it took to stand before him, her tiny fists on each hip. "And you have a lot of nerve making decisions that concern me without even bothering to ask. I don't know what kind of trouble he's in, but I want no part of it. It was bad enough getting me involved the way you did, and now you're telling me that it was just the beginning. Well, I've got news for you, Dane Remington. I won't do it!" Her temper flared when he continued to eat as if he hadn't heard a word. "Are you listening to me?"

Sparking green eyes glanced up at her. "I heard, but I'm not listening." He took another bite of his breakfast.

Brittany's spine stiffened. "Am I to take that to mean you

don't care what I say? That you're going to bring your brother here without my permission?"

"Something like that," he replied without looking at her.

"Well, we'll just see about that," she retorted, turning around and heading toward the doors.

"Brittany," he called before she had traveled two steps. "I think you'd better hear me out before you do something you'll later regret."

She didn't like the tone of his voice nor the threat of his words. She paused and glanced back over her shoulder at him. He lounged comfortably on his bed of straw, his ankles crossed, his upper torso propped on an elbow as he lay on one hip and casually ate off his plate. His dark hair gleamed in the morning light and his rugged features took on a healthy glow. The muscles across his shoulders strained the seams of his white shirt and where he had neglected to fasten the top three buttons she could see the dark matting of hair on his chest. The sight of him made her pulse quicken, and Brittany wondered—providing the man last night had been Dane and if it truly happened—how she could not have possibly known the instant she saw him standing in the doorway. He wasn't the sort a woman could easily forget. Her mouth crimped into a sneer. That was, of course, if he wasn't wearing a disguise. She forced herself to concentrate on what he had said and asked, "And what might that be?"

Swallowing the last bite of food, he shoved away the plate and looked up. "I need a place that's safe where my brother can rest and get better, a place away from Boston where the authorities won't think to look."

"So you've decided to bring him here . . . to my farm . . . to the home of a young woman whose brother is accused of arson and is wanted by the Crown. That isn't a wise choice, Mr. Remington. Surely you can see that."

"When was the last time anyone came here looking for Roan?"

192

Brittany shrugged a shoulder. "I don't know. Two or three weeks ago . . . why?"

"Your brother is one among many the British have to contend with. If they didn't find him within the first week, they'd have given up by now. They won't be coming back."

She raised her nose in the air and looked smugly back at him. "Not unless someone told them there was a criminal hiding out on my farm." She expected to see his eyes darken in rage. She wanted him to plead with her. *She* wanted to be the one to make all the decisions. But rather than jumping to his feet and hurling angry words at her, Dane simply lay there smiling back at her. A long moment passed before he pushed himself up, grabbed the plate off the floor, and returned it to the tray.

"When Roan came to see you that day, did he tell you how to contact him?" he asked, folding his arms over his wide chest. He smiled when she refused to answer. "I'm reasonably sure he did. You're his sister, and he can trust you. He knew you'd never do anything to jeopardize his freedom. Even if you disagree with what he's doing."

The shock of his statement sent a hundred thoughts racing through her head. He was implying that she didn't approve of Roan working with the Sons of Liberty and that she supported the British rule. He also made it sound as though he favored England's control over the colonies. Yet if he did, why was Brad shot by British soldiers, why did Dane need a safe place to hide him, and why had he helped Roan if he disagreed with the revolt? One minute it appeared he was on England's side and the next he hinted at working with the patriots. He couldn't do both . . . or could he? The confused frown faded from her smooth brow. Yes . . . he could. He could be doing both—and be paid for it. The bastard was a double spy! A slow rage erupted deep inside her, but somehow Brittany managed to control it. And he thought she was too stupid to figure it out!

193

"Why do you ask?" she questioned acidly. "Did you think I'd tell you?"

Dane had noticed the mixture of emotions she felt reflect themselves in her beautiful gray-blue eyes, and he wondered what had brought them on. Was she possibly torn between her loyalty to Roan and to the Crown? Didn't she know how to handle it? This kind of traitor was the most dangerous . . . one could and usually would change direction without warning and at a most crucial time. He'd have to be very careful. "I wasn't asking really . . . merely warning. Your brother came to me asking for help and in doing so revealed why he needed it—that he had duties elsewhere and could not see to those at home. I agreed because I felt I owed him that much, and I will continue simply because I gave my word. However, the debt does not equal the work I've done, and therefore I wish to even the score: safe lodgings for Brad until he is well."

"And if I say you nay," she countered hotly, "then you will tell those who are interested in learning where they can find him. That, sir, is blackmail."

Dane shrugged a wide shoulder. "Perhaps. But I see it as a trade: my brother's freedom for Roan's." He truly had no intention of turning her brother over to the authorities. Roan was too valuable to the cause. He merely wanted to ensure Brittany's silence about Brad, and threatening her brother was the only way of doing it. She obviously cared more about Roan than anything else in her life.

"You are the lowest of vermin, Dane Remington," she spat, glancing toward the wall and the spade used to shovel manure. Rushing to it, she jerked it from its nail, seized it in both hands, and spun around, ready to attack. "I'm willing to make a trade. Your life for Roan's freedom."

Dane had expected to make her angry. He hadn't thought she'd try to kill him. Tensing his muscles, he turned slightly to one side and prepared to make a grab for her weapon the moment she swung it at him. The first assault came dangerously close to his head, but Dane merely leaned back out of the way and watched it whiz on by. The second launch came close on the heels of the first when Brittany, realizing she had missed, brought the shovel around with a backward swoop. It too missed the target, but that didn't stop her from trying a third time. Thinking to trick him, she chose a different spot and lowered her weapon, planning to strike him on the knee. If she connected, he'd more than likely lose his balance, and while he tumbled to the floor, she'd move in for the kill.

Dane's first reaction to this blonde vamp's plan to murder him had been one of surprise. It quickly changed to one of survival when she took the first swing. But with each added blow, the situation in which he found himself became rather amusing. Her blue-gray eyes had turned the color of dark, flinty steel. Her lovely mouth was pressed in a hard line. Her cheeks glowed with her rage, and her chest heaved with each angry breath she took. She was the most ravishing beauty he had ever seen, but her desire to bring about his end by splitting his skull open with the blade of a shovel made him smile. He had faced many men with more threatening weapons, and the worst they had done was blacken his eye or bruise his ribs. Unlike Brad, Dane had managed to evade the bullets fired at him as well as the men who wished to arrest him. His skill and quickness had kept him out of trouble, and Brittany Lockwood, though she didn't know it, had very little hope of succeeding where others had failed. Concentrating on her eyes, he knew before she took another swing just where she intended to land the blow when she looked down at his knees. Once he disarmed her, he'd have to tell her what she had done wrong. Right now, however, he had to plan his strategy. Watching her twist around and take aim, he braced himself for the attack, ready to jump the handle and blade once she hurled it at him.

Certain the battle was about to come to an end, Brittany swung her weapon as hard as she could at her victim, thinking the blow would knock him off his feet. Much to her surprise and chagrin, however, Dane agilely bounded over the metal end of the shovel and escaped without harm. Brittany wasn't so lucky. The force behind her assault spun her around until her back was to him and Dane seized the opportunity to become the aggressor. Springing forward, he caught her around the waist and tumbled with her onto a pile of straw. Brittany had managed to hang onto the spade, but not for long. Before she had struggled to sit up, Dane had wrenched the shovel from her hands and tossed it out of reach on the other side of the room.

"Damn you," she shrieked, jabbing her elbow in his side when his grip around her middle tightened. "Let go of me!"

"And have you find another weapon to finish the job?" he bantered, enjoying the soft curves he held within the circle of his arm.

"If not now, then later," she promised, still struggling to free herself. She gasped when she suddenly found herself trapped beneath him, the bed of straw cushioning her slender frame, her hands pinned on either side of her head, his lean, muscular body pressing close above her. The devilish humor she saw sparkling in his green eyes made her shiver and clearly marked her foolishness in thinking she could win against this rogue. "You're a cad, Dane Remington—a vile, unprincipled cur. A true gentleman would not treat a lady in such a manner." She thought to play upon his honor, if he did indeed have any.

"And a lady would not have tried to bash in my head with a shovel," he corrected lightly, tightening his hold around her wrists when she wriggled to break free of him.

"Had she not been threatened with blackmail, she would have had no want to see you dead." She relaxed a moment to regain her strength and let her meaning sink in.

196

"Had this lady been of kind heart, she would have willingly agreed to house a wounded man, not summon the authorities." He cocked a brow at her, challenging her to deny it.

"And had she been asked, rather than told, she might have found it in her heart to open her door to him." She squirmed, trying to push him from her. "To *him,*" she rallied. "But not his brother and all he chose to bring along."

The fragrance of her hair and the sweet smell of hay attacked Dane's senses and stirred his blood. She was a fiery vixen with a quick wit and tongue to match, and he suddenly found himself wondering how her father had dealt with her moods. A wicked grin parted his lips as he began to lower his head. Never in the fashion he had in mind, he concluded.

Brittany stiffened the instant she realized that Dane was about to kiss her and that it probably wouldn't stop there. She had to change his mind, set his thoughts on other things, trick him into turning her loose. Swallowing the knot of worry that had formed in her throat, she drew in a breath and said, "And a true gentleman wouldn't force himself on a lady." The warmth of his breath touched her cheek when he laughed.

"Most assuredly," he agreed, resting on his elbows with his lips only an inch away from hers. "On that we concur. The problem is, however, whether or not I can be counted as one." He smiled crookedly. "What do you say?"

Brittany failed to see the trap he had set. "I think not," she snapped. "You are a scoundrel, a cowardly beggar who takes pleasure in tormenting women. How many before me have found themselves yielding to you in much the same manner, Dane Remington?"

"Yielding, you say?"

The whiteness of his smile made her tremble. It also sparked her rage anew. "Only because there is no other way to be free of you. How is it possible for you to sleep

197

peacefully at night knowing what you've done? I would think the guilt would haunt your dreams. Or will you admit you have no conscience?"

Dane shifted onto one hip but still held her trapped beneath a long, lean leg. He pulled one of her arms under him so she could not strike him or wiggle loose, while the other he clutched tightly in one hand. His green eyes raked over her, touching her, devouring the soft curves and feasting on the silken flesh of her long, slender neck and the valley between her breasts where the cotton dress lay open. After a long while he lifted his eyes to meet hers. "Aye. I have a conscience, Brittany. The vision of the night we spent here often comes to mind. But guilt is never a part of it. We struck a bargain, and the price was met. 'Twas nothing more."

"And what excuse can you give for today? You just admitted the price was met, so why do you force yourself upon me now? I don't owe you anything. I never did!"

Her abrupt change in mood from the evening past confused Dane. She had been so willing then and now she wanted nothing to do with him. If given the chance, she'd kill him. Was it a game she played? He studied the beautiful face glaring back at him and fought the urge to kiss away her anger. She spoke of guilt . . . was it possible she meant her own? Had he caught her in a weak moment? Did she now wish to lay the blame on him while denying that the passion she experienced had been real? This lovely creature imprisoned in his arms was many-faceted and stirred a strange desire deep within him to unravel the mystery which enshrouded her. He failed to understand how her loyalties could be divided between the beliefs of her father and brother and that of the Crown. She struggled to hang onto the farm but wanted to turn away the help that would ensure against her losing it. She met his passion openly and freely, and yet within the short span of time from night to dawn, she put it from her mind as though it never happened. He could see the naked desire in her eyes while with her lips she cursed him. Was she a witch? Had she bewitched him? Was he playing with the kind of fire that would not only burn his fingers but scorch his soul as well? It was in moments like these that Dane wished he had his brother's devil-may-care attitude toward women—and life, for that matter. If he did, he'd ignore the subtle warning that stabbed at his subconscious and turn the heat of wrath, which glowed hotly in her eyes, to that of unbridled desire, then bask in the warm embers of their passion once it had waned. A lazy smile parted his lips. And why not? What could it hurt this one time?

"I have no excuse, Brittany Lockwood," he murmured, leaning down. "Nor do you."

A scream lodged in her throat when Dane's opened mouth covered hers. The branding heat of his kiss seared her and set her aflame. The feel of his body clouded her mind, crushed her will to be free of him, set wild imaginings coursing through her. As his lips moved hungrily over hers, Brittany relived the sensation from another time. But the memory wasn't vague as though it happened long ago; it seemed closer, almost as if— Brittany's eyes flew open. The man who had shared her bed last night was kissing her right now! A throaty growl erupted, and with surprising strength she tore free of his hold and raked her nails over his suntanned cheek.

"You—you despicable guttersnipe!" she howled when Dane jerked up on his knees and gingerly ran his fingertips over the bloody furrows. "It was you!" In a rage she shoved him from her and scrambled to her feet. She made a most fetching sight, with long strands of golden hair falling about her shoulders in loose array, sprinkled with bits of straw. Her chest heaved with her indignation and her gray-blue eyes flashed sparks of hatred. "How dare you pretend to be someone else and slither your way into my bed? Did you think I'd never figure it out? Did you think I'd be fooled the first time you kissed me?"

From his lowly place on the floor, Dane sat quietly staring back at her, wondering at her tirade and curious as to whom she meant she had expected to find at her bedroom door. One dark brow rose disapprovingly. Surely, she hadn't planned to meet—no, not him—God, how could any woman find Miles Ingram attractive enough to do anything more with him than discuss the weather?

"Answer me, damn you! What did you hope to prove?"

Brushing the straw from his clothing, he slowly came to his feet. Touching his cheek once more, he looked at the blood on his fingertips, then settled his attention on her. He didn't feel she deserved an explanation, but it was probably the only way he'd get her to voice the identity of the man she had waited for. "I wasn't trying to prove anything, Miss Lockwood," he replied, dusting off the sleeve of his shirt. "After I returned from taking Cory to Boston, I decided we should talk things over."

"Ha!" she cut in. "You certainly have a strange way of talking!"

Dane didn't like the undertone of her words, and he gritted his teeth to keep his anger in check. "Had I known," he went on, his voice low and dangerous, "that you were expecting company, I would have waited until this morning. Maybe next time you'll post a sign." He lowered his chin and frowned angrily. "You might even consider locking the door!"

"And you might have the decency to knock the next time before you come barging in!" she rallied.

"There won't be a next time," he bellowed.

Brittany honestly couldn't explain why, but she felt insulted. Stiffening, she decided he wouldn't have the last word. "Good!" she shouted with an arrogant toss of her silky mane that sent the long, golden tresses bouncing over her shoulders. "See that there isn't." Thinking their discussion had come to an end, she started past him and gasped when he shot out a huge hand and caught her arm.

"Who were you expecting to come to your room last night, Brittany?"

His question shocked her. It sounded almost as if he was jealous, and Brittany simply stood there staring back at the emerald greenness of his eyes as he glared at her. Yet what caused her inability to answer wasn't his bold inquiry but rather the surprise that he thought she had actually been waiting for someone—that what had happened between them was planned for someone else. In her mind she hurriedly went back over the words she had said, trying to sort out his reason for asking. Failing that, she felt her temper flare again and she yanked away from him.

"And what makes you think I was waiting for anyone?" she demanded.

The muscle in his cheek flexed as he held his anger at bay. "You asked why I pretended to be someone else. Whether you admit it or not, you implied you were expecting company. I want to know who."

Brittany understood now. What she had meant was that in her dreams the Dark Horseman always came to her room. She had thought she was dreaming when Dane appeared, that Dane was the Dark Horseman. She hadn't been waiting for anyone. Her rage had been because she felt she'd been tricked, even used by this man who now had the audacity to demand an explanation. A mocking half-smile wrinkled one corner of her mouth as she stared at him. She knew that nothing she said would convince him of her innocence, and since he seemed to take offense to his failure to be the one she wanted, she decided to let him go on thinking whatever he liked.

"And by what right do you ask?" Her tone was cool . . . her words were icy. "What makes you think I'd be willing to tell you anything? Who are you to me that you feel

201

you deserve to know anything about my private life?"

Dane's eyes seemed to darken even more. "Who, Brittany?" he repeated. "Who were you expecting in your bed last night?"

She cocked her head and laughed. "That's something you'll never know," she whispered, delighting in the anger she saw tighten the muscles across his chest and arms, in the way the vein in his neck popped out, in the way he gnashed his teeth as he glared at her.

Dane stood mute for several seconds, failing to understand why the knowledge of her lover's name was so important to him. He had his suspicion and it wouldn't be difficult to prove. Yet he wanted to hear it from her own lips. His gaze lowered to her tiny mouth, and he suddenly wanted to feel her lying beneath him again, struggling and hurling vile names at him. This too confused him. She was like a poison in his system, one he knew he should rid himself of, but at the same time he wanted more. If he had any sense at all, he'd get on his horse and ride away before it was too late. Too late for what? he mused, drinking in the vision of her where sunlight sparkled in her golden hair, added a deep blue radiance to her beautiful eyes, and lightly kissed the fairness of her smooth skin. His anger faded and in its place his passion stirred.

"I think I already know," he murmured, stepping in. "Maybe not *who* you were expecting, but who you *wanted* there."

Brittany moved back quickly. Her heart thumped loudly in her chest and her flesh tingled. She glanced past him toward the door and knew she couldn't reach it before he was on her. And even if she succeeded, she doubted he would let her go. He'd probably follow her right into the house.

"Tell me I'm wrong when I say you were expecting a *real* man to take you in his arms and not some milksop with fancy clothes and proper manners. Tell me you don't prefer to be

202

taken rather than wooed into bed, Brittany." He kept moving until he had her backed up against the wall with no place to run. "Tell me your heart isn't pounding wildly at this moment and that you'd rather I stepped aside and let you pass. Try to convince me that it isn't passion I see glowing in your eyes."

Brittany tried to speak but the words wouldn't come. Everything he said was true, yet she didn't feel them about him. How could she? He wasn't what a woman should look for in a man. He had no integrity, no manners, little regard for authority and even less for the wishes of a woman. He was proving that now. Afraid to move in one direction or the other lest he think she wanted him to stop her, Brittany gulped down her fear and drew in a breath.

"If I tell you all these things, will you allow me to pass?" Her voice lacked the strength and conviction her words meant to imply.

Dane's eyes lowered to her trembling mouth, down her creamy-white throat, and onto the rounded bosom straining against the bodice of her dress. A bright yellow curl lay invitingly upon the firm mound covered in cotton, and Dane slowly reached up to entwine its silken strands around his finger. "Maybe," he replied. "But it would depend on whether or not I believe you."

Her brow furrowed irritably. "Then I stand little chance," she snapped. "'Tis obvious what you have in mind."

He lifted his eyes to look at her. "And what is that?"

Her own eyes widened at his boldness in asking her to state his intentions as if they were discussing something as unimportant as what she should prepare for supper.

Dane chuckled at the outrage he saw burning in her eyes. He raised a hand and leaned it against the wall near her head while he leisurely studied the delicate structure of her face, then settled on her lips. "So tell me, Brittany. Say you aren't longing to have me take you in my arms and lie with you

203

upon this humble bed of straw." He nodded over his shoulder at the mound of hay behind them.

"If you must know, *Mr. Remington,* I would prefer to be wooed the way any lady would. To lie upon a bed of straw would liken ours to the basic desires of sheep." Her anger deepened when he threw back his head and laughed loudly at her comparison. "A *gentleman* wouldn't even consider it."

Rubbing his thumb against the corner of his mouth in an effort to mask his humor, he forced down a smile and replied, "And we always come back to the question of whether or not I'm a gentleman. Or should I say it's what you keep asking. As I recall, that day you came to see me at the pub and we discussed the terms of my agreeing to get your brother out of gaol, I told you then that I was no gentleman. A few minutes ago you agreed. So why do you constantly bring it up? Are you hoping to strike a vein of guilt? To save you the effort, I'll admit there isn't one. I can't remember feeling guilty about anything I've done." He leaned a little closer and lifted a stray tendril of hair off her brow. "And why should I feel guilty about doing something you obviously want me to do?"

He was standing much too close. The heat of his body penetrated the thin cotton dress she wore as if she stood naked before him. Her knees went suddenly weak and her heart hammered in her ears. She didn't know why—it was against her strict upbringing, and the desire for revenge for how he'd tricked her—but she did want him to kiss her, hold her, make love to her. She steeled herself against the desire, blinked, then said in hardly more than a whisper, "On that much we agree. You are no gentleman." She clamped her teeth together to stop the quivering of her chin. "But hear this," she managed to continue. "Even if you rode to my door in an elegant carriage, dressed in the finest cloth with the manners of a titled lord, I would still turn you away. You are a rogue, and I would do better to spend my days alone than

204

yield to your ways."

A taunting grin parted his lips. "Knowing what you do about the pleasures to be had held in a man's arms? I think not, Brittany." The warmth of his breath fell upon her ear when he leaned in to nibble on her lobe.

"I will forget," she vowed, closing her eyes when a shiver raced down her spine.

"If you live five score and ten, it might fade," he murmured, his lips moving along the fragile line of her jaw. "But you will never forget."

His opened mouth captured hers when she made to deny the possibility and her world reeled. Her want to break the trance and the embrace vanished when his arm slipped around her waist and brought her full against his hardened frame. The heat of the iron thews beneath his shirt scorched her and sent a raging fire coursing through every inch of her. He pulled her away from the wall and with his free hand leisurely roamed the slender length of her back to her buttocks, drawing her hips against his. The evidence of his desire was hot and hard against her thigh, and the feel of it was like a blast of cold winter wind. She twisted free of his branding kiss.

"Dane . . . don't," she pleaded, gasping for breath. "Please. You mustn't." She tried to push away from him, but his grip tightened and in the next instant, before she could object, he turned with her and lowered her back upon the pile of hay. His lips were pressed against hers again, bruising, demanding, fervent in his desire to spark her passion while his fingers unfastened the buttons up the front of her dress. A gentle morning breeze caressed her skin but failed to cool her fevered flesh where his lips traced a hot path of kisses down her throat. His other hand was on her thigh, pulling up the hem of her skirts, and Brittany quickly grabbed his wrist, praying she could stop him. His strength far surpassed her own and within seconds the branding heat of his long, lean

205

fingers touched her naked flesh, starting at her knee and working upward on the inside of her thigh.

"Dane!" she shrieked, using both hands to push his away. He kept coming.

Tears flooded her eyes. Panic singed every nerve. He meant to have her and there was nothing she could do to stop him. The strings on her camisole fell loose, and Brittany changed objectives. Seizing the lacy cloth in both hands, she yanked the material back to hide her gleaming breasts from his kisses. Dane was not discouraged in the least. Grabbing her wrists, he tore her fingers from their hold on the thin fabric, shifted his weight, and placed his knees between her thighs and lowered his head. A fire exploded from somewhere deep inside her when his opened mouth, warm and moist, captured the taut peak of one breast, and even though her mind called out for him to bring an end to this blissful torture, her body betrayed her. She was fighting an inner battle, one her heart was winning.

This means nothing to him, she inwardly cried. *He'll laugh about it later. He'll mock you. He'll taunt your willingness if you give in. Make him stop before it's too late . . . before he's won your passion and your dreams.*

Suddenly an idea came to mind, and while she strained against the hand working to pull her clothes from her, she gasped for air and proclaimed tearfully, "You'll pay for this, Dane Remington! If you don't stop right now, I'll send word to the Dark Horseman."

His head came up immediately, and Brittany thrived on her victory.

"In fact, *I'll* be the one to tell him where to find you!"

He had an odd look about him, one Brittany couldn't quite comprehend. But it didn't matter. She had found his weakness, his fear. She could see it in his eyes. Pushing him from her, she clasped the front of her dress together and awkwardly sat up. Tucking her legs beneath her, she

206

readjusted the hem of her skirts and bravely glared back at him.

"I'm not a simple-minded milkmaid. I know he's looking for you. What other reason would bring him here in the middle of the night?" She struggled with the strings on her camisole and while she hooked the buttons on her dress, she added, "I saw him, so don't deny it. And don't tell me he wasn't looking for you and Cory. The two of you were gone when I came to the barn. I don't know how but someone must have warned you that he was on his way, and you two ran off like the cowards you are." Feeling much safer now that she had the obvious advantage, she clumsily stood up and shook the straw from her skirts. "In fact, I think it's best if you leave my farm, Mr. Remington. I don't like being caught in the middle of something I don't even understand, let alone, agree with." She threw him a challenging look for the first time since her tirade began, expecting to see at least a speck of worry in his dark green eyes, but instead found him smiling back at her.

He sat quite at ease on one hip, a knee drawn up and his wrist dangling over it. His head was cocked to one side. His raven-black hair was ruffled and sprinkled with bits of straw. His white shirt lay open to the breastbone and exposed not only the dark matting of curls but the sinewy strength of his broad chest. And he seemed anything but worried. In truth, at that moment she thought he looked very much like a swarthy pirate and only lacked a gold earring in one lobe to complete his attire. His manners surely attested to the possibility.

"What else has your snooping afforded you?" he asked lazily.

"Snoop—snooping!" she exploded. "This is *my* house, *my* property. I can do whatever I wish around here!" The rosy flush in her cheeks darkened. "And right now I wish you'd take your belongings and leave!"

Dane slowly shook his head and pushed himself up. "My apologies, Miss Lockwood," he mocked, "but I won't be able to oblige you. I gave Roan my word that I'd stay until I wasn't needed anymore. You wouldn't want me to go back on my word, would you?" He smiled rakishly.

"Your word," she spat indignantly. "Your word means as much to me as this damnable revolution. It's already taken my father *and* my brother, and now, because of it, I'm forced to put up with you!"

Dane's humor disappeared with her mention of Patrick Lockwood. As far as he knew the eldest Lockwood had never joined the rebels working against the Crown. What had she meant about the revolt taking her father? Dusting off his clothes and combing his fingers through his dark hair, he started toward her. "I'll make you a deal, Brittany," he said, chuckling at the way she quickly backed away from him. "If you promise not to snoop anymore, I'll leave you alone. I'll be the perfect gentleman so that you may go about forgetting the kind of pleasures that could have been yours . . . if you're able. In return, you'll have a harvest this fall, I'll have kept my word, and we'll both be happy."

Brittany liked his proposal but at the same time doubted he'd live up to it. Her conscience warned her to tell him no, but she knew she wouldn't be able to handle the harvest all by herself.

"What about your brother and Cory?"

Dane had only offered a deal as a way to make peace with her. If she set her mind on having him leave the farm, it would only cause trouble for him, since he'd be staying no matter what she said. Her question told him he had won.

"You could use the extra help, and Brad needs a place to rest up for a while."

"A place to hide is more like it," she rallied, irritably

208

plucking bits of straw from her long hair.

Dane nodded. "But no one will think to look for him here. You weren't recognized."

Angry gray eyes glared over at him. "And what about Zachary? His shape was much more recognizable than that of a young woman wearing a bonnet."

"Zachary doesn't exist. You and I know that. The authorities can go on looking for him for eternity and never find him. Only you and Cory knew about him." His confident smile was short-lived when Brittany cocked a brow at him.

"And Miles Ingram."

Until now, Dane had forgotten about Miles having been at the farm the day he and Cory arrived. Granted, Ingram might be able to connect Brittany with the hunchback in the cart who rescued Brad, but he didn't honestly see it as a threat. The only people who witnessed the affair were protesters. They wouldn't turn over one of their own. Yet on the other hand, if a group of British soldiers suddenly appeared at Brittany's doorstep, Dane's suspicions about Miles Ingram would only increase. But rather than let Brittany in on his thoughts, he shrugged a wide shoulder and said, "I was under the impression Mr. Ingram liked you." His green eyes sparkled mischievously. "A lot. I don't think he'd put you in any danger."

Brittany wasn't sure if she could agree with that. She hadn't been very sociable where Miles Ingram was concerned. "Perhaps," she frowned, thinking she'd much prefer trying to make it on her own rather than allow this knave to continue living here. And consenting to Brad's joining them would only deepen the evidence against her should Miles Ingram take offense to her treatment of him and send soldiers to search her farm. However, she mused hopefully, there was always the possibility she could uncover the real reason Dane wanted to stay. If what she suspected about him was true, she'd clear her name and possibly Roan's by presenting the facts about Dane and his cohorts to whoever was interested. Feeling a little better about her decision, she glanced up at Dane and smiled sarcastically.

"All right, *Mr.* Remington, we have a deal. But only until after the harvest is in. Then I expect you to leave. Agreed?"

Brittany's trim figure and golden hair were silhouetted in the bright sunlight shining through the open barn doors behind her, and Dane wondered if he'd be able to stick to their bargain. She was the most alluring woman he had ever seen. It would be much easier for him to forget about her if he left, but he couldn't. He was here for a reason and it had nothing to do with harvesting crops. A vague smile crossed his lips. There were other harvests he'd rather reap. But Brittany made it quite clear she wanted nothing to do with him. It's what she said. He knew otherwise.

"Agreed," he finally answered.

Brittany gave a mental sigh of relief. If he hadn't consented to her conditions, she would have been forced to take other measures. What worried her was that she didn't know what they were. Now, however, she had him right where she wanted him, and he was too ignorant to realize it. She'd enjoy watching him play right into her hands.

"Then I suggest you get to work. There's still several more acres to be planted."

"Yes, madam," he grinned, his green eyes casually traveling down the length of her slender shape. He wished he'd finished what he started, then discussed their differences. Well, there was always tomorrow. Or the next day. Sooner or later she'd give in to her desires. Turning away from her, Dane unfastened the front of his shirt and pulled it off his shoulders. Right now he'd change into something more suitable for working in the fields.

Brittany's heart skipped a beat the moment the white linen cloth slid down his wide, muscular back and the bright streams of sunshine caressed his bronze, well-built, half-naked physique. Finding it difficult to draw a breath, she staggered back toward the doors and her escape. Upon reaching them she turned and raced from the barn toward the house, cursing her decision to let him stay with each hurried step she took.

Chapter Eight

Brittany tried avoiding Dane the rest of the day. She fixed him a cold lunch of potato salad, rolls and jelly, a slice of ham, and a cherry tart for dessert, put it in a covered basket, and set it in the barn before he returned from the fields at noon so that she wouldn't have to talk to him, much less look at him. But around the time he was expected to come strolling down the lane toward the barn, she was standing near the window in the parlor peeking out from behind a half-closed shutter, waiting for him to make an appearance. Worry knit her brow after a while when it was well past noon and he had yet to show himself. *Maybe he's changed his mind and decided to go on back to Boston,* she mused, somewhat disappointed.

"Good," she proclaimed aloud, turning back to her chores.

A moment later she was at the window again.

Another twenty minutes passed, during which Brittany paced the floor, several times going to the door ready to swing it open and check the barn. She'd never get anything done if she didn't satisfy her curiosity. Afraid he'd walk in while she was there, Brittany had let go of the doorknob each time she had touched it. Simply on the chance he was just working late, she couldn't risk his discovering that she cared one way or another if he stayed or left the farm. Finally, after what seemed an eternity, the deafening silence that had hammered in her ears for the past hour was broken by the sound of someone whistling a bright, airy tune outside on the lane, and she flew to the window to see who it was, unaware of the pleased smile which spread across her face once she recognized Dane's tall, lanky frame. Her glee was only momentary, however, once she realized how happy it made her to learn she had been wrong about him. What difference did it make to her whether or not he stayed? He was a rogue and a liar. His brother and their friends were mixed up in the revolt in some way and just having Dane here on the farm would make it appear that she too was involved. The whole situation was crazy, and if she hadn't already made up her mind to find out exactly what he was up to, she'd tell him to pack up his things and find someone else to torment. From now on she'd ignore him.

It was nearly dusk by the time she saw him casually walking across the front yard on his way to the barn again. Brittany had wisely elected not to light a candle until after he had returned so that she could watch for him by the window without being seen. She had left his supper in the basket again and didn't plan to go back after the dirty dishes until morning—after he had left for the fields. He had to prove he could keep his word before she'd put herself in that predicament again. Crossing to the cupboard, she picked up her plate of food and a fork and returned to her vigil by the window, her attention focused on the pale light coming from the barn. She didn't have to be sitting in the same room with him to see what he was doing. More than likely he had spread out in one of the stalls to eat his supper, his legs stretched out in front of him, his upper torso propped up on one elbow, his emerald eyes concentrating on what he ate, and his coal-black hair glistening in the candlelight. She might not like Dane Remington, but she had to admit she thought he was the most handsome man she had ever seen . . . well, almost. The Dark Horseman could easily be ranked higher.

The candle was suddenly extinguished and Brittany jumped as if she thought he knew what was going on in her head right then and didn't want her watching him. Laughing at the absurdity of the idea, she absently set aside her untouched plate of food, leaned a temple against the window frame, and stared out at the dark barn.

I wonder if he sleeps without a shirt, she mused with a vague smile, vividly recalling the last vision she had of him there in the barn. It was certainly possible. He wasn't modest, and the nights had become increasingly warmer since the first day of June. In fact, now that she thought about it, both the days and nights were warmer than usual, and that always seemed to mean a hot summer was sure to follow. The distant hooting of an owl interrupted her train of thought and Brittany decided it was time she went to bed, too. Forgetting about the supper she hadn't eaten, she turned to the door, made sure it was locked, and headed toward her bedroom. A few minutes later, she was lying wide awake in bed, staring up at the ceiling.

Dane always loved the smell of hay. It was one of the things he remembered most clearly about his cousin Beau's plantation in Virginia; that and the peacefulness of it. But Dane had never enjoyed staying in one place for very long and it had been part of the reason he had purchased a frigate with his share of the inheritance from his father's estate. He liked the colonies but he could never accept the idea of leaving his English homeland for good. This way he could do both. Brad had gone along simply because he wasn't ready to settle down either, and America offered a whole new scope of possibilities—not to mention women. As Dane lay there on the hay, his wrists crossed behind his head, his eyes staring up at the odd shapes the moonlight created in the

215

rafters, he realized that the time he had already spent here on the Lockwood farm was the longest he had ever spent anywhere—with the exception of his childhood. What puzzled him about it was that he wasn't in any particular hurry to leave; he couldn't honestly explain why. He didn't really like farming; he preferred the open seas or the rolling hills of a great estate—much like the one where he and Brad grew up. He liked his freedom and his solitude. A smile kinked his mouth. He also loved a good fight. Or maybe fighting for something in which he believed—like the rebellion. It truly wasn't his battle to fight. His roots were really with England. But he disagreed with their policies and the way they went about enforcing them. Their taxes hurt the little people, like Brittany's father and Bernard Patterson.

Thinking of Brittany again, he vented a long sigh and closed his eyes. He doubted he'd ever smell the sweet aroma of hay again and not think of the moments the two of them had shared here in the barn. And more than anything, he prayed she wasn't mixed up with the spying that was going on in this part of Boston.

Perspiration dampened Brittany's face and neck and prevented her from sleeping peacefully. Flipping off the thin sheet, she swung her feet to the floor and stood up. A soft breeze lifted the hem of the curtains on her bedroom window but failed to mitigate the stifling heat. Thirsty, she headed into the front room for the bucket of water, her gossamer nightgown clinging to her back and breasts. Her shoulders drooped in disgust when she found the pail empty. It meant she'd have to go to the well if she wanted to quench her thirst. Grabbing its rope handle, she headed toward the door. Maybe the short walk in the night air would cool her off enough that she'd be able to go back to sleep.

The damp grass beneath her feet felt good as she walked toward the well. Moonlight lit the way and a chorus of chirping crickets soothed her irritation and unwittingly brought back fond memories. There were many warm nights when the young family living in the tiny farmhouse had sought comfort out-of-doors, and those times were some of the best she could recall. Her father would drag the rocker from the parlor and set it outside near the front door while Brittany and Roan spread out a blanket in the grass close by. All three would study the bright, twinkling stars overhead and wonder if a pair of them might be the eyes of God watching over them. It never took very long for the little girl and her younger brother to fall asleep, and Patrick Lockwood would carry them back to their beds.

Now that Brittany was a grown woman, she understood why her father sat outside in the rocker all alone. It had nothing to do with the warm nights and his inability to sleep; he was simply missing his wife, and staring up at the heavens gave him comfort. It was his way of being with her. Brittany hadn't really gotten to know her mother. She'd died of a fever when Brittany was only seven years old. But she missed her just the same. She missed her even more now that she was full grown. There were so many confusing thoughts going through her head of late that she longed to have someone to talk to. Roan wouldn't be any help; he was a man. It was Brittany's feelings as a woman that puzzled her, and Roan would have no way of understanding them, much less explaining them to her. And Roan was busy with other things, more important things than the emotions of his older sister.

She listened to the pulley squeal as she lowered the bucket into the well and her gaze drifted across the yard to the barn, silhouetted in the ashen streams of midnight. Until Dane Remington entered her life, she hadn't given much thought to men and romance. She had been content with the way things were. She had already made up her mind to live out her days on her father's farm, to see it prosper the way he always dreamed it would. It was obvious to her that Roan had chosen a different endeavor and would probably never be satisfied with living on a farm. The responsibility had fallen on her shoulders.

A sadness darkened the gray of her eyes as she thought about the magnitude of it all. The taxes the Crown imposed on the import and export of goods left little profit; without it, it became increasingly more difficult for her to buy the supplies she needed to keep the farm running smoothly. If Dane and Cory hadn't offered their help in exchange for meals and a bed, the crops still wouldn't be planted and she'd already be facing the possibility of losing the farm this fall.

And what about next year? she sighed thoughtfully. Who would help her then? Dane didn't strike her as the type to stick around, nor did she want him to. He was a threat to her sanity. Her determination to succeed on her own returned, and she absently straightened her slender frame. Yet deep inside her she experienced a strange twinge of emptiness. Forcing herself to forget about it, she turned back to the well, preparing to raise the bucket, when out of the corner of her eye she spotted a movement among the trees. She couldn't distinguish what it was—man or beast—but an inner sense warned her of danger. Ducking down behind the stone well to conceal the gleaming whiteness of her nightgown, she peered over the edge to watch and listen and suddenly cursed the loudness of the crickets and the tree frog who seemed oblivious to the intrusion. The rustling of dried leaves upon the ground drew her attention to one particular spot, but she still couldn't see anything. Then—for just the briefest of moments—she espied a dark shape—too small to be a man, but certainly not that of an animal, for it walked on two legs. A child? Brittany's eyes widened at the discovery. What in all of God's creation would a child be doing out at this time of night, sneaking around in the woods alone? The street urchins of Boston never ventured this far from town. Could he—or she—be lost? Looking for food? A place to spend the night? Or something to steal?

There's not much worth stealing around here, she thought, disgruntled.

The figure disappeared among the shadows for a moment, then reappeared about ten feet further on, and Brittany speculated from the direction in which the child went that he was leaving the farm. Deciding that it didn't matter why the youngster had chosen her place to visit, she stood up and called to him. Her father had taught her and Roan to be hospitable, and besides, it wasn't safe for a young child to be roaming about after dark. But the child apparently didn't agree. The instant he heard her summons, he bolted and ran deeper into the trees.

"Wait!" she shouted, rounding the well to chase after him, "I'm not going to hurt you. I wanted to offer you food and shelter for the night."

The youth wanted nothing to do with her and within seconds had vanished into the woods. Brittany, forgetting that she hadn't any shoes on, raced after him. It took most of her energy to dart in and out of the low-hanging branches and gingerly pick a path for her bare feet while trying to catch sight of the youngster again. She followed for nearly fifteen minutes before she stubbed her toe on a rock and tumbled to the leafy ground. Tears burned her eyes, but she stubbornly refused to cry. She did, however, vow to wring the urchin's scrawny neck if she ever got her hands on him. Pulling herself up on a decayed log, she clasped her foot and rubbed the injured extremity while she glanced about the wooded area ribboned in ebony and platinum.

"I hope you go hungry the rest of the night," she muttered when she failed to see him anywhere. "Or better still, I hope a bear eats you for breakfast."

Her anger and pain in her toe both lessened after a while, and as she sat there on the log looking up through tree branches at the starlit night, she found the whole situation rather amusing. If she had had any sense about her, she would have returned to the house for her robe and slippers and a lantern to light the way. She certainly wouldn't have gone off chasing after a half-visible little ragamuffin who didn't want her help. But she had, and now she'd have to stumble her way back home. Wincing as she stood up and put weight on her foot, she silently cursed her stupidity and hobbled off in the direction of home—or so she thought. About twenty minutes later she paused to lean against a huge oak and settle on some sort of plan. She didn't know how it could have happened, but she was lost. She had played in these woods as a child hundreds of times and had never managed to get herself so turned around as she had now.

"Well, Brit," she scolded, looking up through the trees, "let's see if you can get a bearing on where you are and which direction you should take."

Her father had often told her that if she ever got lost she should look for the North Star and then decide which way was home. Of course, he hadn't explained how she should do it when there were so many branches and leaves in the way. But then he never expected her to be this foolish, either. Studying the few stars she could see, she half-heartedly listened to the night sounds while she calculated her position and which path she should take. Several minutes passed, during which time she became more confused than ever. But what brought the frown to her lovely brow wasn't the delay in going home, but rather the sudden silence that seemed to close in on her.

Instinctively, she crouched down beside the tall oak and hurriedly surveyed her surroundings. The crickets no longer sang, the tree frogs had ceased their methodical croaking, and even the gentle breeze had seemed to stop. The hair on the back of her neck tingled and her heart pounded so loudly in her ears she doubted she'd hear cannon fire if it exploded right next to her. Then, in the shadowy darkness some ten yards to her left, she spotted the figure of a man moving parallel with where she hid. Seconds later she heard the muffled clip-clop of horse's hooves and the squeaky wheels of a cart before the pair appeared in the muted streams of moonlight about fifty feet behind the man.

It wasn't uncommon for men to travel at night. What made this group different was the fact that the animal's hooves were bound in heavy cloth to cut down on the noise and the wheels on the cart had burlap wrapped around the rims. They were traveling at night because they didn't want anyone to see them—or hear them. Who were they? And what were they doing on her property? Moving around to the back of the tree, she slowly came to her feet and peeked out from behind it, hoping to get a clear view of the man's face. Distance, darkness, and the way he kept his head down made it impossible. Thinking she'd have better luck seeing the driver of the cart if she moved a little closer, she lifted the hem of her gown and started to move out. Before she had taken two steps, a huge hand came up from in back of her and firmly covered her mouth while a strong, muscular arm encircled her waist and lifted her from her feet. The contact of her tiny body with the rock-hard muscles of the man's chest, who held her imprisoned against him, took her breath away. The sound of his deep, rich voice in her ear nearly caused her to faint.

"Be quiet, Brittany," Dane whispered, "or we'll both wind up dead."

She wasn't sure if she should be grateful it was Dane who held her or not. But he didn't have to explain why it was important for them to keep their presence a secret from these men. She had already guessed they were up to no good. Nodding her consent, she expected him to let go of her. He didn't, and Brittany started to squirm.

"Hold still," he warned through gritted teeth, his eyes trained on the men moving away from them.

"Then let go of me!" she demanded, though the words came out in a muffled cry.

During her attempts to free herself, Dane's arm tightened around her middle and pressed up against her bosom. She didn't have to look to know what the result was. She could feel the neckline of her nightgown slipping downward and the warm breeze that touched her near-naked breasts. If Dane noticed, she doubted he would care who watched and would probably take her right there under the stars with dried leaves as their bed. She stopped fighting him instantly, praying the intruders would leave before it was too late.

Dane hadn't realized he was holding his breath until the men and their cart finally disappeared into the shadows and the squeaking of wheels faded into the distance. He hadn't come to the woods with the intention of finding strangers . . . he had come looking for Brittany. He had heard her call out to someone and could only assume she had seen Dooley heading away from the barn. He wasn't worried about her ever catching up to the little man. Dooley was too quick and deft for that. What Dane didn't want her to do was recognize him. She'd demand to know why he was there, and Dane would have to lie. All she really knew about Aaron Dooley was that he had known where to find the man Brad had sent her after. Dane doubted she had made the connection beyond that, but if she got close enough to Dooley to realize that she wasn't chasing a young boy but a dwarf, it wouldn't take her a second to figure out who he was. And that meant trouble.

He had finally gotten her to consent to allowing Cory and his brother to stay on the farm for a spell. But that had come about simply because she thought Brad needed a safe place to rest up and Dane and Cory were there to help with the planting and harvest. Brittany was a very sharp young woman. She'd soon figure out that there was more to it than that, and then she'd get in the way—or spoil his plans altogether. A frown drew his dark brows in a downward slant as he considered the possibility that he had made a mistake in coming to the Lockwood farm . . . for more than one reason, he mused with a vague smile. The warmth of her body pressed against his and the fragrance of her hair and skin rather confirmed it. The sight of her always stirred his desire, and he knew the longer he stayed, the harder it would be for him to leave.

"What were you doing out here?" he asked, keeping his voice low and lessening his grip on her.

Brittany spun free of him, annoyed that it took so long for him to release her. She hadn't needed his help. She hadn't been planning to walk up to the strangers and ask why they were trespassing on her property. "I might ask the same of you," she spat, then added as an afterthought, "or were these friends of yours on whom I happened at the wrong time?"

When Brittany shifted back a step to set a comfortable distance between them, she unknowingly placed herself in a platinum stream of moonlight, and Dane was quick to notice the transparency of her gown. The ashen beams caressed the firm mound of flesh partially hidden by the lacy cloth, but the rose-hued peaks shown clearly through it, and he absently glanced over his shoulder to the spot where the intruders had disappeared. Those men would have considered themselves blessed if one of them had spotted her behind the tree. She was rare treasure, and they would have eagerly sampled her enticing gifts without thought to her welfare. Suddenly and unexplainably angered by her stupidity, he turned back to her and reached out for her arm. Brittany jerked away.

"If you don't mind, I'll walk on my own," she seethed and quickly started off.

Dane's nostrils flared. "You know, Brittany, someday your willfulness is going to get you in a lot of trouble." He scowled at the direction she had chosen. "Where are you going?"

"Home," she threw back over her shoulder.

"Oh, really?" he mocked. "Well, if you want to get there before sun-up, I suggest you head the other way." He waited until she had stopped and frowned back at him, then jerked his head to his left.

223

In her haste to get away from him, she had forgotten that she had spent the last half-hour or so going nowhere. She had no idea which direction would take her home. Although she would have preferred not admitting it, she didn't much like the thought of roaming about the woods any longer. Her toe ached and she didn't have to look to know her feet were bruised and cut. With nothing left her, she tossed her silky mane and started off the way he indicated, very much aware of the man who followed.

Dane watched the agitated swish of her skirts as Brittany jerked them from side to side to clear her step whenever something lay in her path and she had to go around it. It was then he noticed that she was barefoot, and he opened his mouth to comment on her foolishness. But before he had uttered a sound, he changed his mind and decided to let her realize it on her own—if she hadn't already. Falling back a few paces, he quietly followed her, waiting until a pine needle or sharp rock pierced her flesh. It came only a few seconds later.

A breathless "Ouch!" formed on her lips as she felt the splinter bury itself deeply in the heel of her right foot, and she awkwardly limped to the first big rock she found and sat down. Tears burned her eyes, and she renewed her wish that the ragamuffin suffer a similar fate.

"Maybe next time you'll wear shoes."

Dane's brilliant suggestion awarded him a cold, unappreciative glare. "Next time I won't need them," she hissed. "If I ever see that child wandering about my place, I'll shoot him first before I go after him."

"A child?" Dane tested, kneeling down beside her to examine her foot. It was impossible in the dark. "What child?"

Her injured foot throbbed painfully. She closed her eyes, silently cursed the youngster again and took a deep breath. "I had gone outside to the well for a drink of water and saw a young boy hurrying off into the woods. I called to him, but he kept going. I didn't go back for my shoes because I thought I could catch him quickly enough. Obviously, I was wrong."

"You followed him this far?" He suspected the truth but devilishly wanted to hear her admit it.

"No," she snapped.

"Then why—?"

"I'm sure you've figured that out by now, Dane Remington," she jeered, tempted to slap his shoulder with the heel of her hand and send him sprawling backwards on the ground. He should be made to suffer a little indignity as well.

Dane fought very hard with the smile that tugged on the corners of his mouth. "Actually, I haven't. I had assumed you were on your way to meet someone."

"Dressed like this?" she gasped in astonishment. "Who did you imagine I would be sneaking off to see at this hour, clothed in such a manner?"

He shrugged one broad shoulder, feigning innocence. "Your lover, perhaps?"

"My—!" she exploded. Her gray-blue eyes snapped with rage as she yanked herself up to her feet again. Dane quickly followed, prepared for whatever was in store for him. "What kind of a woman do you think I am?" She cut him short before he could answer. "Well, I'll tell you what I'm not. I'm not the sort of woman who would go running off in the middle of the night to have a scandalous affair!"

Dane didn't respond. He didn't have to. She could read his insinuation in his sparkling, green eyes. She gritted her teeth, lowered her chin, and snarled, "Nor do I wait at home. Contrary to what you'd like to believe, you . . . you viper, I find the idea of such behavior appalling!"

"I'm sure you do, Miss Lockwood," he quickly agreed, though there was a touch of humor in his words. "A lady like yourself expects a man to come calling in the afternoon and only when you're chaperoned. It isn't proper for her to go looking for him. What type of woman would do that?" He stared at her for a long while, taking in her long golden hair, the white, flowing nightgown illuminated in the moonlight, and her bare feet, and she suddenly seemed to him an angel sent from heaven. His mood changed instantly.

"Brittany, I know you have several reasons not to like me or even trust me. I can't argue with that. Our first meeting was rather unorthodox, and after that things got worse. I have no right to expect you to do what I ask, but I must at least try. It was very foolish of you to come out here alone. If those men had spotted you, they probably would have killed you—after they'd had their fun. And you took quite a chance leaving Bernard's last night as well. If you find it necessary to travel away from home, will you at least tell me, so that I may accompany you? For your own protection, if nothing else?"

"Well, it certainly wouldn't be because I enjoy being with you," she rallied. Her foot ached terribly, and all she longed for right now was to go back to bed. "Would you please be kind enough to lead the way? I fear we'll travel in circles if you don't."

"Will you promise me first?"

"And if I don't, does that mean we'll stand here for the rest of the night?" When he didn't answer, she figured that was exactly what he intended. "All right," she sighed. "I promise."

"Good," he nodded, and before she realized what he was about to do, Dane bent slightly, caught her around the waist and the back of the knees, and swooped her up in his arms.

"Put me down!" she demanded. It was bad enough just having to stand next to him without allowing him to touch her. Every inch of her flesh burned. His nearness made her head spin. She silently cursed the young boy a third time. If it hadn't been for him, she wouldn't be in this predicament. "Did you hear me? I said for you to put me down. I can walk on my own."

"You can," he replied, concentrating on the path he took

through the trees, "but it would take us twice as long. And I don't know about you, but I'd like to get some sleep. I have a lot of work to do in a few hours."

If it had been her father offering his assistance, Brittany would have snuggled close in his arms, thankful that she didn't have to put any weight on her foot. With Dane, she remained stiff and held her breathing to a minimum. It seemed that anything she did excited him, and she was in no condition to fight him off. She was drained of strength and knew he wouldn't have much of a struggle if his mood turned amorous. A short time later, he carried her into the clearing behind the house, across the yard, and up to the front door. It stood ajar, and after he nudged it open all the way, he took her into the parlor and gently placed her on the deacon's bench near the hearth. Brittany frowned as she watched him light a candle and bring the taper to the end table beside her, put it in the holder, then kneel down on one knee before her.

"What are you doing?" she questioned when he reached for her ankle.

He squeezed the delicate bones when she tried to pull away, gave her a challenging look, then studied the extent of her wounds. He shook his head disgustedly once he saw all the cuts and bruises and the thorn protruding from her heel. Plucking it from her foot, he rose, told her not to move, and left the house. Brittany did as he bade more out of curiosity than fear. A few moments later, he returned carrying a small bottle in one hand, the bucket of water in the other. Setting both on the cupboard, he poured a small amount of the water into a large bowl, grabbed a cloth and bar of soap, and came to settle himself on one knee before her again. Lifting her right foot off the floor, he gently put it into the water to soak while he lathered up the rag.

Brittany watched his every move in silence, marveling at his gentleness. Ordinarily a man as big as he would be clumsy. But Dane Remington moved with grace, and his methods in tending to her wounds hinted at the probability

227

he had done this kind of thing countless times before. There was a lot about this rogue she had yet to learn. She intended to find out about his plans where the revolution was concerned simply by spying on him. But to know the inner man was something she'd have to ask him about. She'd start by finding out why he had been in the woods just now.

"How did you know where to find me? That I wasn't in bed asleep?"

Dane continued with his ministrations and didn't look up. "I heard you call out to someone and came to see who it was. By the time I left the barn, you were gone." That wasn't completely true . . . he had heard her shout at Dooley, but he hadn't left the barn right away. He figured the midget didn't need any help and would get away without any trouble. About ten minutes later, the dwarf showed up at the barn doors to tell him that Miss Lockwood had managed to get herself lost and because they didn't want her to recognize Dooley, he couldn't go to her and point the way home. Dane would have to do it himself.

He was glad he had. Otherwise he wouldn't have known about the strangers. He would have liked to follow them and learn where they were going and who they planned to meet and why, but he couldn't risk it with Brittany along. He'd have to follow their tracks by daylight, although he had already guessed where they'd take him.

Brittany winced when the harsh lye soap burned the cuts on the bottom of her foot. "Did you recognize those men with the cart?"

A brief frown flitted across his brow and disappeared. It was almost as if she had been reading his mind. "No."

"Do you have any idea why they were there? They were trespassing on my property." Brittany hadn't believed him. Now that she had time to think about it, he had been very insistent that they leave. And it had taken him too long to catch up to her if he had left when he said he had. It didn't quite fit, and she suspected he was already there waiting to meet with them when she stumbled upon them.

Dane took her foot from the water and patted it dry with a towel he had retrieved from the cupboard along with his bottle of salve. "No," he answered simply, wondering if she was testing him. He had the feeling she knew why.

"Oh," she murmured, then jumped when he rubbed the balm into the wounds. It burned a little at first, then faded into a warm, soothing tingle. "Where did you learn that?"

"From Higgins," he replied without much thought.

"Higgins?" she repeated. "Who's he?"

Dane straightened with a faraway look in his eye. He hadn't thought about the man in years. In fact, he wasn't even sure if he was still alive. "Our butler," he finally responded.

Brittany was taken quite aback by the discovery that Dane Remington came from a family of wealth. She tilted her head and studied him, differently this time. "You're not from around here. I would have heard of the Remingtons."

Dane smiled over at her, his green eyes sparkling in the candlelight. "No. We're not from around here."

"Then where?" she pressed, anxious to know.

His first reaction was to lie. He didn't want her to think he sympathized with the British just because he was raised on their soil. But then, if she thought that, perhaps she would think he could be trusted and willingly tell him everything she knew about the goings-on around her place. Lowering his eyes, he screwed the lid back on the bottle, picked up the towel, bowl, soap, and rag, and stood up to carry them to the cupboard. "England," he finally told her, purposely neglecting to add that he and Brad had sailed away from her shores more than ten years ago and that most of his relatives lived in America now.

Brittany could have sworn her heart stopped beating in that moment. His admission rather confirmed her ideas about him. His loyalties were with England, yet he wanted everyone here in the colonies to think he was on their side.

He was a spy! A hard knot had formed in her chest, making it difficult for her to breathe. She pressed a hand over it and started to rise.

"I—I think I better go to bed now," she whispered, waving him off when he hurried to her side and seemed ready to pick her up again. "You've done enough, thank you. I can manage from here."

Dane watched her hobble toward her bedroom door with a frown on his handsome face. His answer appeared to upset her rather than please her, and for a moment he considered the possibility that he might be wrong about her. His gaze absently lowered to her slim hips veiled in white cotton, and the frown disappeared. He hoped so. He wouldn't like having to advise the Sons of Liberty that Roan's own sister was working against them. They could make things very hard on her. Worse than that, Dane would have to explain their actions to Roan.

With her back pressed against the closed bedroom door, Brittany held her breath, listening for the sounds that would tell her that Dane had left the house. It frightened her to think that she had a spy living on the farm. Those kind of men were capable of doing just about anything, including murder. She closed her eyes and fought back the wave of panic she could feel churning in her stomach. And if she became a threat, he probably wouldn't hesitate to dispose of her.

Her body began to tremble, and she hurried to her bed to lie down. Hidden beneath the covers, she stared over at the bedroom window and the moonlight shining in. She wanted to find Roan and tell him what she suspected, but without proof he wouldn't believe it. Roan liked Dane Remington; he trusted him. Otherwise he wouldn't have asked Dane for his help. She'd have to gather the evidence she needed all by herself. A curious frown drew her brows together as she contemplated asking Miles Ingram's assistance. Bartholomew, his father, worked for the Crown, which meant Miles

230

probably agreed. If Dane was doing something underhanded, then the Ingrams would want to know about it. Maybe she lacked the solid evidence that would get the eldest Ingram to act upon it, but at least they'd be aware of something funny going on.

Satisfied with her decision, she rolled onto her side and closed her eyes. But a moment later, she was staring at the ashen streams of light coming into her room and feeling somewhat sad about the whole affair. She didn't like what Dane was doing, and he needed to be punished—he could be a threat to her brother's very safety—yet the gnawing ache in her bosom told her that she'd never be able to forget Dane Remington and the passion he had stirred within her.

Chapter Nine

In the eastern sky, the rising sun spread its vibrant colors across the earth to chase away the last few lingering shadows among the trees. Low clinging fog curled about their trunks and played tag with the bright rays of light as if reluctant to surrender to the warmth of the day. A spattering of clouds in the otherwise flawless blue sky teased the brilliant yellow orb, hovering close in an effort to choke out the beams of light and delay the coming of dawn a bit longer.

Brittany would have enjoyed lounging in bed this morning, since she had had very little sleep. But the bright, glowing streams flooding into her room lay heavily against her eyelids and the moisture-laden air made her perspire. It promised to be a warm, uncomfortable day, and since she had a lot of planning to do where Dane was concerned, she begrudgingly gave in. Flipping off the thin sheet, she sat up and stretched, vowing that this evening would find her in bed earlier than the one past and that no matter who came to visit, she would cover her head with the pillow and blatantly ignore him. Thinking of the child that had been her reason for losing sleep and the subsequent hike through the woods, she gingerly swung her feet to the floor, wincing when she expected to endure a painful experience. To her surprise and relief, the salve Dane had used soothed away the sting and any discomfort she might have had. It didn't, however, remedy the embarrassment she'd felt last night at having him learn she had gotten lost or lessen it any as she recalled it now.

Feeling a hot blush rise in her cheeks, she left her bed and went to the dresser for her hairbrush. Once she had pulled the long, golden tresses over her shoulder and prepared to untangle the knots in them, her eyes caught sight of her reflection in the mirror and her humiliation increased. Her tiny chin dropped the instant she saw the way the thin, lacy fabric of her nightgown clung revealingly to her bosom, positive that even in the ashen glow of moonlight, Dane had been able to see what she was looking at right now. A flood of color darkened her cheeks.

She slammed the brush back down on the dresser, turned to hurriedly pick up her robe, and donned it, swearing never to leave the house without it again. In fact, if the youngster should test his luck a second time and reappear on her property and somehow manage to fall in the well, she would let him drown before she'd put herself in a situation similar to the one last night. The boy's only salvation as far as she was concerned would be if Dane heard the child's cries for help and came to pull him up. The vision of such an event flashed to mind, and an impish smile brightened Brittany's lovely face. If such a thing were to occur and she found Dane leaning over the stone edge of the well with his back to her, she'd be willing to forget her robe for the chance to push him in on top of the youngster. They both needed a lesson: Dane deserved to cool off as well. Just the idea of such a reward lifted her spirits, and without bothering to brush her hair, she left her bedroom, crossed to the bucket Dane had left on the cupboard, grabbed its rope handles, and stepped out into the front yard on her way to the well. She'd take a leisurely bath, fix breakfast, see Dane off to the fields, and then figure out a way to gather the proof she needed. Perhaps she should return to the place in the woods where she had seen the strangers and follow their tracks. The answer to her questions about Dane had to be linked with those men and what they were transporting in the cart.

With the bucket in one hand, her skirts in the other, and her attention on where she walked and what she would do once the breakfast dishes were washed, Brittany didn't look up until after she had rounded the side of the house and the well was in clear view. Once she had, she stopped dead in her tracks, for there next to the well stood Dane. He had stripped himself of his shirt and was splashing cool water over his neck and face. Silver droplets clung to his hair and glistened on his wide shoulders and chest. The muscles in his arms rippled with each move he made. Morning sunlight enhanced the bronze of his flesh, and her head began to spin the moment he sensed her presence. He glanced up and smiled with a perfect set of white, even teeth. Hadn't the scoundrel *one* imperfection she could criticize?

"Good morning, Miss Lockwood," he greeted casually as he shook the remaining drops of water from his hair and combed his fingers through the thick, dark mass. "I didn't expect you to be up this early." Without waiting for her answer and expecting none, he gazed up at the blue sky. "We're in for a warm one today, I'm afraid." His penetrating green eyes fell on his companion again and leisurely took in her attire. "If you haven't fixed breakfast yet, don't bother. I'd like to get out in the fields and get as much work done as possible before it gets too hot." He reached for the shirt he had hung on the handle of the well and slid it on over his shoulders. "And I would suggest you cook whatever you were planning for supper this morning. I don't mind eating a cold meal. That way the house won't get too hot. Don't you agree?"

The hammering of her heart lessened a bit once Dane had fastened up the last button on his shirt and tucked the tail into his breeches, although she wished he had hooked the one at his neck as well. As it was, the fabric lay open at his throat

235

and she could see the beginning of the dark curls which covered the wide expanse of his chest. Just the mere thought of the strength in those muscles and the titillating excitement they aroused whenever she ran her fingers over them made her pulse quicken.

"Are you all right, Miss Lockwood?"

The question brought her out of her thoughts almost instantly. She blinked, swallowed the knot in her throat, and focused her attention on his face. His rugged brow was furrowed in a frown, his green eyes showed concern, and the realization that he had closed the distance between them and stood very near to her now made her jump.

"What?" she asked, unconsciously clutching the lapels of her robe tightly over her bosom.

"I asked if you were all right," he repeated. "You look a little pale."

"Oh," she laughed nervously. "No, I'm fine." She hurriedly moved past him toward the well and set her bucket on the edge, trying very hard to keep her mind and her eyes on her chore rather than on him.

"Did you sleep well last night?" he asked, taking the handle before she had the chance to lower the bucket herself. "Did the salve help?"

Brittany preferred not to be reminded of the events of last night, but could see no way around the issue. If she didn't answer him, he'd press even further. She was sure of that. "Yes," she replied, thinking a simple response would suffice.

Dane watched her out of the corner of his eye and smiled secretively to himself. Something was bothering her, and from the bright color in her cheeks, he guessed it had something to do with him—if not entirely. He doubted she had expected to find him at the well just now or she would have changed into something more suitable. He was glad she hadn't. She was even more ravishing in the pale light of early morning, and the filmy white gown and robe did little to cloak her shapely curves. Raising the bucket to the end of the

236

rope, he leaned in and pulled it over to pour the water into her pail. But when he started to lift it off as a silent offer to carry it for her, Brittany thanked him for his help, took the bucket from his hand, and set off toward the house at a brisk pace. An amused grin parted his lips as he watched her go, for in her haste to be gone, she sloshed water up over the rim of the bucket and down her skirts. The wet cloth clung to her long, willowy thigh and calf and reminded him of how sensual she looked without anything marring his view. Shrugging resignedly, he turned toward the barn, doubting that he would ever have the opportunity to observe her silky flesh and lush curves at his leisure again. Brittany wanted it that way.

The episode at the well quenched Brittany's desire for a bath. Knowing Dane was awake and moving about the farm made her nervous. She didn't want him to catch her in the tub, which she was sure he would try to do if he guessed the water was for just such a purpose. Thus she merely dampened a cloth, sponged herself off, and hurriedly donned fresh clothes, the coolest outfit she owned. Then, just as soon as Dane left for the fields, she planned to search the woods for the place where she had seen the strangers and their cart, positive that it would give her all the proof she needed about Dane. Yet while she tugged on her stockings and shoes, a sadness and strange hopefulness came over her. She honestly didn't want her suspicions to be the truth.

Opening the shutters on the front window, she peered outside at the barn, wondering if Dane had already left and knowing she'd have to be sure before starting off on her adventure. If he spotted her heading into the woods, he'd follow her out of curiosity—or worry, if what she guessed about him was true. A moment later she stood outside the empty barn trying to decide which direction to take.

In the daylight it was easy to follow the trail deeper into

the woods, and about ten minutes later, she came upon the tree where Dane had found her. Beyond, she could see the narrow path the horse and cart had followed, and with its discovery a chilling revelation gripped her very soul: this was the trail her father always used whenever he took the ox and wagon and traveled into the dense stand of trees surrounding the north side of the farm to cut wood. It wasn't far from here that she and Roan had found him crushed beneath a fallen tree. That same horrifying, heart-rending vision exploded in her mind, and she closed her eyes in an effort to fight back the tears that burned her throat. Shaking uncontrollably, she twisted around, leaned back against the tree, and sank to the ground.

Brittany had accepted her father's death as an accident. Roan at first was too upset to think about anything. But after a few days, once their father had been buried in the Boston cemetery, Roan began to spend every free moment he had at the spot where they had found Patrick Lockwood. It was his way of mourning his father's passing, but it also awakened in him the notion that what had happened out here hadn't been an accident at all. For one thing, Patrick Lockwood wasn't a careless man. He was skilled at felling trees. He never would have trapped himself the way it appeared he had. But above all that, the fact that Roan had never been able to find the ax Patrick had taken with him led Roan to believe someone else had been there besides his father. The ax hadn't sprouted wings and flown off! Brittany had argued long and hard with her brother about his speculations, pointing out that she couldn't think of a single soul who would want him dead. The Lockwood family kept to themselves, and even though Patrick disliked the taxes the Crown imposed, he had never told anyone other than his children. What possible motive could there be?

A single tear stole between Brittany's lashes and raced to her chin. Angrily wiping it away, she opened her eyes and glanced over her shoulder at the narrow path. Maybe Roan had been right all along. Maybe their father had done much the same thing she had done last night. Maybe he had accidentally come across the men who chose to trespass after sunset so that they wouldn't be seen. But her father had obviously stopped them and demanded to know what they were doing on his property. Her chin quivered and her tears started anew as she envisioned the scene. They had killed him for it!

Brittany clamped a hand over her mouth, fighting desperately not to give way to her grief. She knew that once she started, she wouldn't be able to stop crying, for it seemed the weight of the universe was pressing down on her just then. Her father was dead, her brother had gone off to join the revolutionaries, and she had had the misfortune to meet up with someone who was very likely responsible for the whole mess. It seemed to Brittany that her entire life had turned upside down. She was alone, friendless, and facing the likelihood that it would always be that way. And of course, the odds were against her hanging onto her father's property. If she lost that too, there would be nothing left for her to live for. Raising her face to the sky, she sucked in a long, trembling sigh and angrily determined to get ahold of herself. Things didn't have to be that way, not if she didn't want them to be.

Her strong will surfaced again, and deciding that the best place to start was right here, she pushed herself up, wiped the tears from her face, shook off the dirt and leaves clinging to her skirts, and started out around the tree. But just as she was about to step into the open, a flash of color caught her attention and she ducked back down out of sight to wait, fearing that what she saw only briefly was the men from last night returning from wherever they had gone. Holding her breath, lest the sound of it reveal her, she held perfectly still, her eyes riveted on a spot through the underbrush where she could see the path in the narrow clearing.

A moment or two later, she espied the black shoes, dark

blue hose, and cotton navy breeches of a man about to pass in front of her. The dense foliage in which she crouched blocked her view of his upper torso and face, and she had to force herself not to shift positions for a peek at him, knowing that if she did, she very well could give herself away.

In the minutes it took for him to pass on by, the deafening stillness drummed loudly in her ears. Her chest ached, and a scream was working its way up her throat. This was almost as frightening as the time she spent hiding from the British soldiers in Bernard Patterson's attic!

Finally, an instant before her fear took hold and threatened to send her flying, the man moved past where she hid and offered the chance for her to stick her head out far enough to get a look at him. However, what she saw no longer frightened her . . . it made her furious.

Dane Remington! she seethed. The cad lied to me. He had no intention of working in the fields this early. He was coming here all along!

Brittany started to rise to confront him. She wanted an explanation. Yet before she had, his reason for lying suddenly dawned on her: she had been right about him when she guessed he was probably an associate of the strangers and that she had intruded before they were able to conduct their business. He had waited until now to talk to them so as not to raise suspicion by leaving some time last night and have his absence discovered by sheer misfortune. That dreadful knot tightened in her belly as she watched his long, sure strides take him further away. She rose slowly and stepped out into the clearing. A frown marred her smooth brow when she realized he was walking in the opposite direction of where the men had gone and that he didn't seem in any hurry to return to the farm or the fields. And from the way he repeatedly glanced down at his feet or off to the side of the path, Brittany soon deduced that he was backtracking the strangers' journey . . . though she couldn't understand why. Curious, she moved back into the cover of trees and

ACCEPT YOUR FREE GIFT AND EXPERIENCE MORE OF THE PASSION AND ADVENTURE YOU LIKE IN A HISTORICAL ROMANCE

Zebra Romances are the finest novels of their kind and are written with the adult woman in mind. All of our books are written by authors who really know how to weave tales of romantic adventure in the historical settings you love.

Because our readers tell us these books sell out very fast in the stores, Zebra has made arrangements for you to receive at home the four newest titles published each month. You'll never miss a title and home delivery is so convenient. With your first shipment we'll even send you a FREE Zebra Historical Romance as our gift just for trying our home subscription service. No obligation.

BIG SAVINGS AND FREE HOME DELIVERY

Each month, the Zebra Home Subscription Service will send you the four newest titles as soon as they are published. (We ship these books to our subscribers even before we send them to the stores.) You may preview them *Free* for 10 days. If you like them as much as we think you will, you'll pay just $3.50 each and *save $1.80 each month* off the cover price. *AND you'll also get FREE HOME DELIVERY.* There is never a charge for shipping, handling or postage and there is no minimum you must buy. If you decide not to keep any shipment, simply return it within 10 days, no questions asked, and owe nothing.

MAIL IN THE COUPON BELOW TODAY

GET FREE GIFT

To get your Free ZEBRA HISTORICAL ROMANCE fill out the coupon below and send it in today. As soon as we receive the coupon, we'll send your first month's books to preview Free for 10 days along with your FREE NOVEL.

—— F R E E ——
BOOK CERTIFICATE

ZEBRA HOME SUBSCRIPTION SERVICE, INC.

YES! Please start my subscription to Zebra Historical Romances and send me my free Zebra Novel along with my first month's Romances. I understand that I may preview these four new Zebra Historical Romances Free for 10 days. If I'm not satisfied with them I may return the four books within 10 days and owe nothing. Otherwise I will pay just $3.50 each; a total of $14.00 (a $15.80 value—I save $1.80). Then each month I will receive the 4 newest titles as soon as they come off the press for the same 10 day Free preview and low price. I may return any shipment and I may cancel this arrangement at any time. There is no minimum number of books to buy and there are no shipping, handling or postage charges. Regardless of what I do, the FREE book is mine to keep.

Name _____
(Please Print)

Address _____ Apt. # _____

City _____ State _____ Zip _____

Telephone ( ) _____

Signature _____
(if under 18, parent or guardian must sign)

Terms and offer subject to change without notice.

Get a Free
Zebra
Historical
Romance

*a $3.95
value*

ZEBRA HOME SUBSCRIPTION SERVICES, INC.
P.O. BOX 5214
120 BRIGHTON ROAD
CLIFTON, NEW JERSEY 07015-5214

quietly followed.

The trail could lead to only one place: the marsh, a parcel of the Lockwood farm that had been totally useless for raising anything other than pesty mosquitoes. Brittany knew it long before Dane seemed to realize it. And once he stood at the edge of the soft, wet soil, he remained completely motionless, staring out across the bog toward the sea further on. Brittany would have given anything right then to know what he was thinking and why the swampland was of interest to him. He turned then as if he planned to head back to the farm and Brittany quickly ducked behind a tree before he spotted her. She stayed there until he had disappeared from view.

Dane wondered how he could have been so careless as not to have sensed he was being watched from the first. It was mistakes like those that got men killed. He should have noticed how the birds quit their singing; he should have felt the quiet that suddenly encased him. But he hadn't . . . not until he reached the marsh and paused. The rustling of dried leaves he heard hadn't been caused by the breeze, for there wasn't any at the moment. And the sound had come from one particular spot, not all around him. Sorely tempted to chase out the spy, he changed his mind when he suspected it might be Brittany. She had come here for a reason, and the only way for him to find out why was to pretend to leave, then turn the tables and spy on her. Choosing the densest part of the woods, he left the narrow clearing and ducked behind a tree. Several moments passed before he spotted her coming from the underbrush, and he felt a heaviness in his heart. He had honestly been praying he was wrong. Warm rays of sunlight filtered down through the leafy overhang and spotlighted her shapely figure standing in the clearing. Her back was to him as she studied the marshland where only a moment before he had stood. He would have liked to know what was going through her head right then, even though he had a pretty good idea. She was probably trying to decide what she should do about him. He was a threat, and she knew that now. He had to be disposed of before he learned what was going on and that she was the mastermind behind it all. A dark brow slanted upward. Well, it was too late. He already knew. Drawing in a long, silent breath, he closed his eyes and raised his chin as he exhaled slowly. Fate had brought them together. He would be the one who would change their destiny.

Nearly a week had passed since Brittany's trek through the woods. Her search after Dane had left awarded nothing. She hadn't been able to follow the tracks of the cart any further than where the narrow clearing joined up with the road on the other side of her property simply because the horse's hoof prints and the indentations of the cart's wheels blended with those already there. She wasn't even able to determine which direction the strangers had chosen to take. Disheartened, for it meant she would have to find some other way to prove Dane's involvement, she had returned to the house to consider other possibilities.

Her days were spent cooking, cleaning, tending the farm animals, and planting a small garden for vegetables while Dane was off working in the fields—or so it was to appear. At night, after they had eaten and she had washed and stacked the clean dishes, she'd slip into her nightgown and lie awake on the bed staring up at the ceiling. The early days of June were unseasonably hot; the nights were unbearable. It hadn't rained in weeks, and Brittany had a new worry. Without the gentle showers, the crops very well could die before they had a chance to grow and then all their hard work would have been for nothing.

She had grown accustomed to having Dane around. The tension between them eased a little when Dane kept his promise and never made any advances toward her. He never even mentioned the time he had appeared at her bedroom door and what had resulted when he had mistaken her willingness. But Brittany never forgot it. The memories of that moment more than the heat of the night air kept her awake. The only good thing that came out of it was the fact that her dream about the Dark Horseman had lessened, and on the occasions when he had come to mind, the vision had ended long before they reached the bedroom door. In a way she was glad. No proper lady would have such thoughts in her head, even though they were only dreams, something she wasn't able to control. But on the other hand, she would awaken feeling that Dane was responsible for her imaginary lover's reluctance to come to her bed. *Dane!* He was the cause of all her frustrations! Why couldn't he just vanish from her life as quickly as he had entered it? Why couldn't she think of him as she did all other men? All except for the Dark Horseman.

This particular night was no different. Sleep wouldn't come and the humidity made her flesh hot and sticky. Without much thought to the possibility that Dane might have the same idea, Brittany tossed off the thin coverlet, picked up her robe from the end of her bed, and headed for the front door. She would walk outside for a while, have a drink of cool water from the well, and then return to bed to get some sleep. However, just as she was about to lift the latch on the front door, she heard the faint sound of horse's hooves cantering off down the lane and changed her mind about going outside just now. Hurrying to the window instead, she peeked out at the dark figure riding off and silently cursed her misfortune in not having elected to go for a walk a few minutes earlier. Whoever it was had ridden beyond where she had a chance of seeing him clearly. Muttering to herself, she went back to the door and swung it wide. She was tired of all her midnight visitors and could blame only one person. After all, things had been very quiet and peaceful on the farm before Dane Remington decided to stay.

Storming across the yard to the barn, she never broke stride once she reached the opened doors. The darkness inside didn't bother her. They would have this out whether she could look him in the eye or not.

"Mr. Remington," she irritably snapped. "I think it's time we talked."

A quiet moment followed during which Brittany sensed she was alone. Tilting her head, she listened for a sound that might indicate otherwise. Nothing answered her. Thinking that perhaps he was a sound sleeper, she called out to him a second time. But when the response was the same, she moved in closer to investigate. The stall where he usually bedded down was empty. So was the rest of the barn, and as she wandered back to the doors, a frown creasing her brow as she stared out toward the road. What did it mean? Had it been Dane she saw riding away? If it was, where was he going at this time of night? A chill embraced her and she hugged herself, wondering if maybe he had gone to meet someone. The men from the woods? Would they be making another trip across her property? That wasn't very smart, if that's what Dane planned. She knew about their little scheme, and Dane knew she did. Why risk doing it again?

A sudden fear tickled the hairs across the back of her neck. Perhaps they didn't see her as a threat. Maybe they had agreed that at the first sign of trouble, they'd dispose of her. The very thought of it chilled her to the bone. Could Dane actually kill her after the way he'd treated her these past weeks? She hadn't noticed any hatred in him for her. Was it all a front? Had he been plotting out a method to get rid of her and make it look like an accident? The same way her father's death had looked like an accident? Tears sprang to her eyes. Suddenly afraid to be alone in the barn, she bolted through the doors and raced for the house to lock herself inside. She'd have to tell someone what she knew. It would be her only insurance. But who? Who would believe her? She doubted she'd be able to locate Roan soon enough.

"Miles Ingram!" she breathed aloud. She had seen the way he looked at her. He might not have marriage in mind, but he certainly didn't want to see any harm come to her, either. Yes . . . that's what she'd do. She'd talk to Miles Ingram first thing tomorrow.

In all the years Brittany had lived next door to the Ingram estate, she had never been invited inside the manor. She had often studied its elegant structure and the grounds surrounding it from afar. As children, she and Roan had ofttimes sneaked away from their chores to hide in the woods adjoining their properties to stare in silent awe of it while they imagined what it would be like to live in such a place. Though a little envious, they had always agreed there was more warmth and love inside their small farmhouse than in all those rooms combined, and after each visit they had returned home feeling a little better about their poor lot in life. Without the security of a family, a castle would be nothing more than an orderly pile of rocks.

The memories of those stolen moments with her brother came to mind the instant Brittany rounded the last bend in the road and the Ingram mansion came into view. The neatly manicured front lawn, the sculptured hedges, the multiple flowerbeds in a riot of color, and the tiny pond in the midst of everything added to the stately beauty of the three-story brick mansion. Facing east, it caught the morning sun and highlighted the stained-glass windows, radiating a friendliness Brittany doubted was real. But her business was of great importance, and she looked upon the place as nothing more than a cold brick building. She hoped those who inhabited it wouldn't treat her with the same indifference.

"May I help you?" the butler asked once he had answered her summons and given her a quick once-over.

Brittany wore her best dress and had styled her hair in a most fashionable way. She realized she still had a long way to go to present an appearance likened to the grand ladies this man was accustomed to meeting on the doorstep, but his silent disapproval was uncalled for. Why couldn't the rich— and their loyal servants—understand that wealth had nothing to do with the kind of person someone was? Just because they couldn't afford the same luxuries in life didn't mean they were any less respectable.

"I wish an audience with Mr. Miles Ingram," she politely replied.

"And who shall I say has come calling?"

"Miss Brittany Lockwood," she informed him, then added devilishly, "And do hurry. I haven't all day."

His reaction was what she expected, and she fought hard not to laugh out loud.

"Yes, miss," he answered stiffly, his shoulders squared, his nose raised high in the air as he turned aside and indicated that she should enter. "If you'll kindly wait in the parlor, I'll tell him you're here." He motioned toward a door and as she crossed the white marble floor he glanced back outside to confirm that she had arrived on foot. Learning that she had, he closed the door with an imperious expression, waited until she had gone into the parlor, and turned for the wide circular staircase at the end of the long front hall, reasonably certain Mr. Ingram would have him return with his apologies. His employer seldom had time for commoners.

Brittany was glad the butler hadn't accompanied her into the room. It would have been very difficult for her to hide her shock at what she saw. The parlor alone was bigger than her three-room house. The walls were done in a dark, rich oak paneling. A huge chandelier hung from the cathedral ceiling with hundreds of sparkling glass teardrops and long, white tapers. A massive black marble fireplace greeted her from across the wide room and above it hung a gigantic oil painting of Bartholomew Ingram. A pure white rug lay at her feet, and Brittany hesitated to step on it.

There were numerous pairs of wing chairs artfully

arranged about the gracious room with their own tables graced by candelabra.

A huge, black-lacquered buffet filled one wall and displayed the largest silver tea service she had ever seen. On each side of it were wine decanters and goblets, two more silver candelabra, large vases of fresh-cut flowers, and bowls of fruit. Brittany guessed fifty guests could easily fit into the space without ever bumping into one another. It was the most beautiful room she had ever seen, but at the same time all she could think of was how much work went into keeping everything clean. What it cost to furnish the place went beyond her imagination. Never having touched a piece of silver before, she was drawn across the room to the buffet by the desire to run a fingertip over its smooth surface. It was there that Miles found her.

Knowing she had come to his home of her own accord brought a pleased smile to Miles's thin lips. He paused just inside the threshold without a word so that he could admire her beauty unnoticed for a spell. She had donned a simple, mint-green dress that clung to her narrow waist and slender back. White lace trimmed the elbow-length sleeves and the collar. Her rich blond hair was pulled high atop her head in a thick knot and accentuated her slim neck. When she turned to appraise another piece of silver on the buffet, he could see the stray tendrils of hair that fell against her temple and his body shook with a desire to place a kiss there. It didn't matter to him that this beautiful creature was of a lower station in life than he. Clothed in the richest of fabrics, Brittany Lockwood would do him proud standing beside him as his wife. Tugging his hurriedly donned periwig into place, he straightened his lace cuffs and started toward her.

"Would you like a glass of sherry, Brittany?" he asked softly, his mind reeling and his heart pounding wildly when she turned her startled gray eyes upon him.

"What?" she laughed, embarrassed that he had caught her admiring his possessions. "Oh no, thank you. It's really much too early, I think."

Miles held out a hand toward a pair of the wing chairs. "Then a cup of tea while we visit?"

Brittany shook her head, smiling nervously as she crossed to where he wanted her to sit. "I haven't the time, I'm afraid. I must return home before I'm missed."

Thinking she referred to her brother, he said, "I wasn't aware that Roan had come home."

"He hasn't," she admitted, sitting down. She waited until he took the other chair before she explained. "Miles," she began, unaware of how the intimate use of his first name affected him, "I must ask your pledge that none of what I'm about to tell you will go any further than this room." She glanced toward the door he had left open. "At least not until I'm ready. Is it safe to talk here?"

Following her gaze, he spied the reason for her concern and quickly left her side to close the door. "You have my word," he vowed, sitting down again, his hands clasped, his elbows resting on his knees.

Brittany frowned, not knowing where to begin. "It's rather confusing and I honestly have no proof of anything . . . yet."

"Proof?" he parroted. "Of what?"

Remembering that Miles had been at her farm the day Dane and Cory arrived, she said, "Do you recall the hunchback and young boy who came to my place looking for work?"

"Yes."

"Well, the boy is actually a young woman and the hunchback is no cripple. His name is Dane Remington. Have you ever heard of him?"

Of course Miles had. But he wasn't going to tell Brittany that. There was a strong rumor that Dane, his brother Brad, and everyone associated with the pair were involved in treasonous activities against the Crown. Because of men like him, Miles had been given the opportunity to increase his wealth. Their efforts to boycott English goods had opened new doors of profit for Miles. He didn't know Dane Remington, but he certainly would like to thank him for his help someday.

"Should I?" he asked, feigning ignorance.

"I guess not. I was just hoping you did. That way maybe between the two of us, we could put him behind bars, where he belongs."

Miles straightened in his chair. "Whatever for? Has he done something to you?"

"Not yet. But I'm afraid he might very soon." She could see that Miles was having a hard time understanding what she meant. "I'd better start at the beginning," she admitted, leaning forward in her chair. "I hired the boy and the hunchback to work the farm for me. A couple of weeks later, I discovered quite by accident that the boy named Cory was actually a girl and the hunchback was Dane Remington. It puzzled me that they had to disguise themselves," she lied, since she didn't want to have to tell Miles the whole truth, "so I asked him. He said something about my not wanting him there if I knew who he was." She shrugged for effect and glanced away. She had never been very good at lying. "Though I can't imagine why. I didn't know who he was anyway."

"So you're afraid he's going to hurt you because you know his identity?" Miles questioned, more confused than ever. "What difference does that make?"

"None," she smiled back at him. He believed it so far, which meant the rest would be easy to tell. Everything else would be the truth. "It's what I discovered about him a short time later."

Miles' thin brows wrinkled. "What?"

"I had a strange feeling about him and his friend from the first, though I couldn't put a finger on it. I suspected he wore a disguise so that someone *else* wouldn't recognize him."

"Who?"

"The Dark Horseman." She waited for the knowledge to

249

sink in, and when Miles' mouth dropped open in surprise, she rushed on. "I think Dane Remington is a double spy. I think he's working for the rebels *and* the Crown."

"Good lord," Miles breathed, "why? What makes you think that?"

"Because of the strange goings-on on my farm lately."

"Like what?" Miles' stomach churned. He sensed trouble.

"One night a week ago, I saw the Dark Horseman leaving my yard. When I went to the barn to ask Dane why the man had come, he and Cory were gone. I believe the Dark Horseman was looking for them and they ran off. But that's not all . . . a few nights ago, I saw a child wandering in the woods near my house. I called out to the boy, but he ran away. I tried to follow him, but he got away from me. That's when I stumbled across something I think you'll find of interest."

Miles could almost guess her exact words. Millicent had warned him that Brittany would be trouble if he didn't get her out of the way. "Me? What could it be that would interest me?"

"I saw two men with a cart cutting through my property."

The muscles across his chest tightened. "Two men and a cart?" He wanted to ask if that was all she saw, since there had actually been ten times that many.

"Yes. And the funny thing was, they had tied rags around the wheels and on the horse's hooves—as if they didn't want anyone to hear them."

"But you did."

"Not really. The only reason I noticed them was that I had stopped to sit and rest. I just happened to see them. But—" She paused, stressing the fact that she wasn't finished. "The best part of the whole thing is that Dane Remington was already there. Whoever those men were, he knew them."

Miles could feel the blood draining from his face. "Why . . . why do you say that? Was he talking to them?"

"No. But he wouldn't let me talk to them either."

Miles felt as if she was holding a loaded gun to his temple and was about to pull the trigger. In dire need of a drink, he rose without comment and went to the buffet for a glass of sherry. "I'm afraid I'm not following you," he said, pouring himself a liberal amount and downing it all in one gulp.

"Dane sneaked up behind me and covered my mouth with his hand before I could do anything. He told me to keep quiet or both of us would wind up dead." She quickly came to her feet and moved to stand next to him. "Don't you see? He couldn't risk letting me know that he was aware of the men and what they were doing."

The sherry relaxed him almost instantly, but he poured another just in case he needed it. "Now let me get this straight. You said all of this happened a week ago or so?" He waited for her to nod, then continued. "And you're afraid you're in danger if he ever figures out that you know what he's up to? Do you know what he's doing?"

"Not yet," she admitted.

"Then why are you afraid? And what do you want me to do? If you have no solid evidence, I can't have him arrested. Maybe you're wrong about him. It's possible he stumbled across the men the same way you did."

"That's exactly what I thought at first. But the next morning I went back to where I had seen them, hoping to follow their tracks and learn where they had gone and what they had in the cart." Brittany was so eager to convince Miles of her suspicions that she failed to notice the look of near-panic in his eyes. "Guess who was already there ahead of me."

Miles feebly shook his head.

"Dane Remington! And you know what I think? I think he had waited until the next morning to meet with them so that I wouldn't know about it. I'm afraid because I believe once he realizes I'm a threat, he'll kill me."

"Good Lord, no!" Miles blurted out. It was what Millicent wanted and he had decided then that it would never happen.

No one was going to harm her!

"It's the reason I've come to you, Miles," she hurriedly went on. "You were the only one I could tell. You're the only one I could trust. Now if anything happens to me, you'll know who to arrest."

The thought of someone murdering Brittany made his hand shake. He nervously raised the glass to his lips, threw back his head, and swallowed the sherry. Brittany's admission left him with two choices: either to get her away from there as Millicent wanted, or change the location of where the smuggled goods were dropped. The latter was impossible; Millicent would simply find a new partner. She had said so before. No, he would have to persuade Brittany to leave the farm. If he owned the land, then he could order Dane Remington off his property and his secret would be safe. His gaze shifted to the beautiful face staring back at him. It sounded simple enough, but he knew it wouldn't be. Brittany would not give up her father's land without a fight and a lot of convincing. And he couldn't tell her the whole truth, something that would make her leave, that her life truly was in danger if Millicent had her way. Setting aside his empty glass, he gently took Brittany's elbow and guided them back to the chairs to sit down.

"I can understand your concern, Brittany," he began, "and I think you're right. Your life could be in danger. But my just knowing about Dane Remington is not going to do you any good. Do you honestly think I could merely sit by and wait for something to happen and then act upon it? I care about you, Brittany. I have for a long time." He dropped his gaze. "I know it isn't mutual, and maybe it never will be. But you're asking too much of me." He looked at her again. "I want you to come and live here."

Brittany was quite taken aback by his proposal. Roan would have told her that Miles had only offered so that he would have a better opportunity to force himself on her, but she didn't agree. There was honesty in what he said and in the way he looked at her. He worried for her . . . and not for his own concern, but for hers. She smiled sweetly in return, thinking that perhaps she had misjudged him all these years.

"Thank you, Miles. That's probably the nicest thing anyone's ever done for me. But I'm afraid I have to decline."

"Why?" His narrow face twisted into a pained, confused expression.

"For a couple of reasons. One is that there is livestock on the farm that has to be tended to, and in the fall the crops have to be harvested if I'm to hang on to Papa's land."

"But I could send someone there to take care of that for you. You don't need this Remington fellow," he argued.

Brittany smiled. "You're too kind, Miles, but I'm afraid you're missing the point. By leaving I'll never be able to prove Dane Remington's involvement in what's going on over there." She quickly raised a hand when Miles opened his mouth to add to his argument. "He's using me, Miles. I don't appreciate that. I want to see that he pays for it, and *I* want to be the one responsible for his getting caught. But more than that, if there's no one around, he'll have free rein. He can double whatever it is he's doing. Don't you see that?"

"Not if I owned the property. I'd order him off and send a couple of my men to see that he obeys."

"It's a fine idea, Miles, except that I'm not interested in selling. And by my leaving, I'd be unable to spy on him. I have to be around to catch him."

Miles knew what her answer would be long before she said it, and he frowned, not knowing what else to say. The threat on her life had nothing to do with Dane Remington, but he couldn't tell her. And the man's presence was more of a threat to Miles than Brittany. Dane Remington was the one who really had to be made to leave. He'd have to come up with some other way to convince both her and Remington that it was safer to live elsewhere. And he'd have to figure it out *before* Millicent learned what was going on.

"All right, Brittany," he sighed. "I'll do whatever you ask.

But I want you to understand that I don't approve of your putting yourself in this kind of a situation." Smiling half-heartedly, he reached over and touched her hand. "And I also want you to know that if you change your mind, my home will always be open to you. I'm sure Father will agree as well."

"Thank you," she nodded with a grin. "I can't tell you how much better I feel knowing you're behind me. And," she continued, coming to her feet, "I'd better get back home before Mr. Remington returns."

"Returns?" Miles echoed as they walked to the door. "Where has he gone?"

Brittany shrugged a delicate shoulder and waited until they had stepped into the foyer to answer. "I'm not sure. I saw him leave in the middle of the night, and when I went to the barn this morning, he wasn't there."

"Is it possible he's decided for us?"

"To live somewhere else?" she questioned. "I doubt it. He was probably off someplace meeting with his cohorts."

Miles frowned thoughtfully. If Remington was indeed meeting with someone, it could mean trouble—for him, not Brittany. She was perfectly safe. "Well, I'm going to pray he has." Miles meant it, but he also realized it was highly unlikely. "You know, Brittany," he added, walking out onto the front step with her, "it's possible this thing you witnessed was a one-time deal."

"Then why didn't he leave the same night?"

"To throw you off."

She shrugged. "Maybe . . . but I doubt it."

"Well, let's hope so." He took her elbow and started down the brick pathway to the lane, coming to an abrupt stop when he realized there was no cart or wagon or even a horse awaiting her. "You didn't walk all the way here, did you?"

Brittany smiled brightly. Maybe Roan didn't like Miles, but her feelings about him were changing. She doubted they could ever be anything more than friends, and distant ones at that because of their difference in station, but she promised herself never to be too quick to condemn a man again because of his wealth. Not all of the aristocracy were snobs. Miles was proving that.

"I'm afraid so. Our horse broke its leg about six months ago, and Papa had to shoot it. I thought it would be easier on foot than riding the ox."

The vision of her sitting astride the huge beast made Miles chuckle. "And more comfortable." His smile vanished as he turned in the direction of the stables. "Wait here and I'll have a carriage brought round."

"Oh no, Miles," she quickly replied, catching the crook of his arm when he started to walk away. "That could mean disaster if Mr. Remington returned home ahead of me and saw me riding up in one of your carriages. He'd be certain to know why I had paid you a visit."

"But it's such a long way."

"I don't mind," she guaranteed him. "I've walked a lot further before, and I'm sure I will again."

Miles wanted to insist, but he realized it would be useless. "All right. But I'm giving in under protest. You will promise, however, that if that man even looks at you in a way that frightens you, you'll come here immediately."

"I promise," she smiled, "and thanks again for your help."

The pleasant, adoring look on Miles's face disappeared once she had turned from him and started down the lane. His help was what had gotten her into this trouble in the first place. Because of greed, her father was dead, her brother had run off after false charges had been brought against him, and she was in danger of losing not only her farm but possibly her life as well. Closing his eyes, he drew in a long breath and lifted his face skyward. And if Brittany ever learned the truth, he would be the one to pay the price. He would lose her even before he ever had her.

Chapter Ten

Pale shafts of morning light spread across the dewy grass and seemed insistent on guiding Brittany's journey home. A smile graced her lips as she walked along, and overhead songbirds filled the air with their cheery tunes. Her talk with Miles had eased her worry somewhat. He had understood her concern, which at first she feared he wouldn't. Her story, after all, seemed absurd. It had taken her several weeks to draw the conclusions she had presented him, and she had even left out the most important parts. She hadn't been fully honest with the man. She hadn't told him how it was she came to meet Dane Remington and his group or that his brother Brad had been shot during a gathering of protesters.

Nor had she told him about the confusing feelings she had for Dane. The sanguine smile faded and a sadness darkened her eyes. She wished more than anything that she could turn back time to the morning her father had planned to take the ox and wagon into the woods. She would have insisted he take along his rifle—in case a wild animal roamed about the underbrush, she would have told him. He would have argued, reminding her that it had been a long time since anything more dangerous than a snake had taken refuge there, but to make her happy, he would take the rifle anyway. He might still be alive today had he done just that.

The chain of events which followed might never have happened, and she wouldn't at this moment be reluctant to return home.

She hurried her pace once she came to the lane that led to the farmhouse. If Dane had gotten there ahead of her, it would be difficult to explain where she had been at such an early hour. But then, she could always ask the same of him. She could claim she had risen early due to the heat—which was true—and had gone to the barn to ask if he'd be eating breakfast before going to the fields—which was partially true. Not having found him there, she would state that she had then gone looking for him—which wasn't true at all. But how could he prove otherwise? Satisfied that he would have no way of knowing where it was she had gone or why, she squared her shoulders and cut through the woods toward the house rather than follow the road which made several turns before coming to the same destination.

When the barn came into view, Brittany was very glad she had taken the time to figure out an explanation for her early morning hike, for there near the doorway stood the cart she had last seen racing off down the streets of Boston with the hunchback snapping the reins. She had mixed feelings about knowing Dane had returned. For one thing, it meant she would have to carry through with her plan to trap him. She didn't honestly want to find the evidence it would take to have him arrested, for in an odd way she felt she owed him. If he and Cory hadn't come when they had, the crops still wouldn't be planted, and by now she'd probably be trying to explain to the creditors why they shouldn't foreclose on her property. Yet on the other hand, he had only helped her out as an excuse to live on the farm. And as for freeing Roan from the gaol . . . well, that could hardly be counted. He had been paid twice for that.

As she stood there at the edge of the woods staring over at the barn, it suddenly dawned on her why Dane had returned with the cart . . . Brad was probably in no condition to ride a horse. Wishing she had never agreed to allow him to stay here while he healed, she gave an exhausted sigh and started toward the barn, deducing that whatever Dane was involved in, his brother and Cory more than likely were too. The thought of Cory having returned with the brothers eased a little of her anxiety. It was possible Dane would keep his word and leave her alone with another woman on the place . . . possible, but not guaranteed. Cory was, after all, a member of Dane's gang of ruffians.

The barn doors stood open and once she reached them, she paused at the threshold to study the activity inside. They had made a bed for Brad in a stall on the straw-covered floor, and although it would be comfortable enough for someone healthy, Brittany frowned at the idea of a man with a shoulder wound lying there. The cool, damp ground beneath him would probably give him a chill and lengthen his recovery. Silently cursing her compassionate nature, she heaved an irritable sigh and stepped into the barn.

"He shouldn't be lying on the ground," she announced, her gaze locked on Brad's pale complexion. Kneeling beside him, she touched his fevered brow. "He's warm as it is." With a disapproving scowl, she glanced up at Dane. "I would think you'd know better." Her gaze shifted to the young woman. "Or you." Without waiting for either of them to reply, she stood and headed for the doors, calling back over her shoulder as she went, "Bring him into the house."

Surprised by her generosity—though her words were laced with sarcasm—Dane and Cory stood mute until after she had disappeared from view. Glancing down at their sleeping companion, then at each other, Cory wrinkled her face and shrugged.

"Ain't gonna argue," she admitted, stooping. "I'm tired of taking care of him anyway. Let her do it for a while. But I'll bet you'll find him back out here in two days. Sooner, once he realizes where he is and she winds up having to fight him off!"

259

Cory's remarks brought a smile to Dane's lips, since he had to agree. Brad wasn't one to let a bullet hole interfere with his flirting. However, he had no idea what he was getting himself into with Brittany. Even a man with the use of both arms had difficulty hanging on to her; he could attest to that. Glancing back down at his brother again, the smile faded, and he was struck with an odd twinge of jealousy. Except for Cory, Brad had always managed to work his way into a woman's arms—and eventually her bed. Unaware of the disgruntled look which darkened his eyes, Dane bent and helped Cory get Brad on his feet. He would have preferred his brother stay here in the barn where he could keep an eye on him, but he didn't want to have to explain why to Cory— or Brittany. Besides, he wasn't really sure of his reason, anyway.

The spare room that her father and brother shared was made ready for its guest in record time. Brittany would have liked having the chance to wash the sheets and pillowcases first and freshen up the bed a little, but necessity overruled priorities at the moment. She had poured cool water in the basin in the night stand next to the bed and pulled back the covers and was waiting at the front door by the time Dane appeared with his brother leaning heavily against him. Dane was only an inch or two taller than Brad and didn't weigh much more, but he handled the half-conscious man as if he were nothing more than a child. Brittany silently marveled at the man's strength and at the love she felt radiated between the two men. If Dane had a weakness, it was his feelings for Brad.

"Put him down gently," she ordered when Dane had helped his brother to the bed. "And take off his shoes, stockings, and shirt. I want him as comfortable as possible." She turned to Cory, who waited at the bedroom door. "When was the last time his bandage was changed?"

"Last night," she replied, failing to understand Brittany's sense of urgency.

"Then start a fire and heat up some water. The wound

should be cleaned and the dressing changed again," she instructed with a dismissing wave of her hand as she rounded the bed to help Dane remove her patient's shirt.

Cory stood there a moment with her arms crossed in front of her, a shoulder leaning against the door jam. "Sure," she said after a while, dropping her hands to her sides and turning to do as she'd been bidden. She honestly didn't see what the rush was all about. Brad wasn't going to die if his bandage wasn't changed in the next two minutes.

"Has he eaten lately?" Brittany frowned once they had tucked Brad under the covers and he seemed at ease.

Dane had been watching her all the while she fussed over his brother, wondering if she would be as eager to help if he were the one lying there. "You'll have to ask Cory," he said, stepping back when she hurried to his side of the bed to dip a cloth in the wash bowl. He watched her wring it out, then dab it against Brad's forehead and cheeks. "We left Boston before daybreak, so I know he hasn't eaten yet this morning. None of us has." As she concentrated on Brad and the bandage, Dane was free to leisurely admire her slender back, the narrow waist and rounded hips thrust out at him while she bent forward over her work. His blood warmed. Had she been the type of woman his brother always seemed to find, he would have surmised she intended to tease him the way she was. But Brittany wasn't aware of what she had done, for if she suspected what was going through his mind at this very moment, she would order him out of the room. Out of the house would be more like it, he thought with a grin.

"Well, ask Cory to fix something, will you?" she asked without looking at him. "He needs to build up his strength."

"You'll be sorry you ever said that," came the remonstrative comment from the doorway, and Brittany sent an angry frown Cory's way.

"If he doesn't eat, he won't get better." She turned her attention back on her task. "And the sooner he's well again, the sooner I'll be rid of the three of you."

Cory found Brittany's remark amusing and wiggled her eyebrows at Dane. "Guess she doesn't know about your brother," she mocked. "Why don't you tell her while I fix the poor man something to eat? We can't have him too weak to sit up when there are more important things he'd like to do."

Brittany glanced over at Cory with the intention of asking her to explain what she meant only to see her disappear into the other room before she could. She settled on Dane, instead. "Well?"

"Cory doesn't appreciate Brad very much. She thinks he's a bit of a scoundrel."

"Being related to you, I can understand that," she scoffed, looking away.

Dane decided to end the conversation, since it wasn't one he enjoyed anyway. Noticing a chair in the corner of the room, he went to it, picked it up by the back rail, and brought it to the bed for Brittany to sit in while she cared for Brad. His thoughtfulness surprised her; he could read it in her eyes. She thanked him, though it was hardly audible, and centered her attention on the ugly but healing wound in Brad's shoulder while Dane crossed to the other side of the bed and sat down, his back leaning against the tall poster. He studied her quietly for several minutes, silently complimenting her on the soft, subtle way she had fixed her hair. He would have liked pulling the pins from it and watching the long, golden tresses cascade down her back. He wanted to draw her into his arms and kiss her. He wished Brad weren't lying in the bed and that they were alone in the house. He'd ignore the fact that it was morning and someone could pay them a visit at any moment. And if he found her willing, as he had those many nights ago, he would strip away her clothes and lie with her upon the soft cushion of down. More than anything else, he wanted to feel her lush curves and silky flesh beneath his fingertips, hear her cries of ecstasy, her words of passion.

He blinked suddenly when he realized where his thoughts

had wandered and shifted uncomfortably on the bed, drawing Brittany's attention. She mistook his fidgeting to mean concern for his brother's recovery.

"He's going to be all right," she pledged with a half-smile. "He'll have to stay in bed and take it easy for a while, but barring a fever or infection, I think he'll make it."

Cory had already assured him of that several nights ago when he came to visit Brad, but he decided not to tell her. There was no sense in irritating her. Besides, she might then question the real reason he found it difficult to be sitting so close to her—with only a bed between them.

The lazy smile on his lips and the warmth in his eyes when he nodded at her statement made Brittany's pulse quicken. She was glad they weren't alone in the room. For some reason she didn't feel that she could trust herself with him. His hair seemed darker and thicker this morning; his eyes much greener; his smile brighter; and his clothes appeared to hug his muscular physique with clearer definition than before. She absently ran the backs of her fingers along the contour of her chin.

"It's warm already, isn't it?" she asked, a bit rattled, and glanced over at the open window with its curtains dancing in the gentle breeze. A frown drew her tawny brows together.

"Here's the water you asked for," Cory announced as she walked into the room carrying a bowl in one hand, clean rags in the other. "And these were all I could find." She dumped the strips of cloth in Brittany's lap and slid the bowl in alongside the one already on the night stand. "If you ask me, he doesn't deserve this kind of attention. He was begging to be shot by walking out in that crowd in the first place."

"Cory," Brittany scowled, "no one begs to get shot. Not unless they're insane."

Unruffled by Brittany's reprimand, Cory tilted her head and clocked a brow at her. "You know Brad better than I thought." Before Brittany could reply, Cory glanced across the bed at Dane. "I think insanity runs in the family."

Neither of them noticed the shocked expression which came over Brittany's face. Cory was silently challenging Dane to disagree and he was thinking of the appropriate answer.

"Must be the reason you hang around," he grinned. "You fit in."

"I'm here because of your cousin," she retaliated. "He seemed to think I could do you some good. However, I don't think he expected me to play nursemaid when he asked me to come to Boston."

"Play nursemaid?" he chuckled. "Is that what you call it?"

A funny half-smile kinked one corner of her mouth. "Wouldn't you? Every time your *little* brother gets in trouble, *I'm* the one who has to take care of him. Somehow I can't believe that's what Beau meant."

Brittany had sat by listening to their exchange, certain neither was aware of the clues they were giving her. Dipping the washcloth into the warm water, she began to cleanse Brad's wound as if she had no interest in what they said and silently hoped they would continue. Obviously, Dane's cousin Beau was a very important figure in whatever it was they were planning—possibly even the mastermind of it. If the opportunity ever presented itself, she'd draw Cory into a conversation about the man and learn more about him—his last name, where he lived, if he would be visiting Boston, and when. That very well could be the connection.

She settled her thoughts back on the strangers and their cart. If she could only figure out what they were transporting and where they were taking it, she might solve the mystery. It suddenly occurred to her that maybe their destination wasn't as important as discovering where they started out. A thoughtful, perplexing frown shadowed her eyes. They came from the direction of the marsh. Beyond that was the sea. Unless they were great swimmers and the cart could float— Brittany stiffened in the chair, her eyes wide, her delicate mouth agape. But of course! What better place to smug-

264

gle goods into the colonies than across the marsh? No one ever went there. Her father had often cursed the land's worthlessness. Worthless, indeed! Those men—and probably Dane—had turned it into the richest piece of property in all of Massachusetts! Feeling a little sick inside, she closed her eyes and took a deep breath. But she'd have to prove it. She'd have to catch them in the act, and that could be tricky as well as very dangerous. Maybe Miles would have an idea. Deciding to ask him, she opened her eyes again and concentrated on replacing Brad's soiled bandage with a fresh one.

Dane had seen Brittany's strange behavior and mentally went over everything that had been said in the last few minutes. Finding no apparent cause for her odd reaction, he motioned for Cory to leave them alone and waited until she had gone into the other room before saying anything.

"Is something bothering you, Miss Lockwood?"

Brittany could feel the blood drain from her face. She had forgotten all about her company. And who worse than the very one who had filled her thoughts and stirred frightening ideas? She forced herself not to look at him while she finished securing Brad's bandage. The brother still slept, and she took comfort in knowing he too couldn't see the worry reflected in her eyes.

"Just a little squeamish," she lied, nodding at Brad's shoulder. "I never was very good at this."

"Patterson doesn't think so," Dane answered her quizzical frown. "The cobbler. The man who assisted you when you took care of Brad. Bernard Patterson."

"Oh, yes," she answered quietly as she stood, lifted the bowl of water she had used to clean Brad's wound and carried it to the window to toss the contents outside. "I had forgotten his name." The memories of how they had come to meet pricked her temper. "I wouldn't have if we had been introduced properly." She returned to the night stand, set the empty bowl on the floor beside it, and picked up the cloth to dip it in the cool water again, intending to dab it against the sleeping man's brow.

Smiling, Dane left his place on the foot of the bed and went to the window to stare outside. He was quiet a moment as he listened to Cory banging dishes around while she prepared them all something to eat. "I apologize for that, Miss Lockwood, but it couldn't be helped. I would have preferred not getting you involved, and had the wounded man not been my brother, I probably wouldn't have stopped."

His confession sounded hard and unfeeling. "Even if it had been *my* brother lying there?" she blurted out, unable to understand how anyone could be so callous.

"Was there a chance it could have been Roan?"

Brittany wished she hadn't opened her mouth. She had no way of knowing why he asked, but she doubted it was out of concern. Wadding up the cloth, she tossed it on the night stand next to the bowl and stood. "If you'll excuse me, I'll see how Cory's doing with breakfast." She turned and started for the door.

"Where did you go this morning, Miss Lockwood?"

His question stopped her cold. She was sorely tempted to tell him the truth. She wanted him to know that it was simply a matter of time before the right people learned about him. But she couldn't, and she knew it. It would ruin everything. "If you must know," she said, looking askance at him, "I got curious when I didn't find you in the barn. I thought perhaps you had already gone to the fields, and I went to look. But I was praying you had left altogether." She smiled sarcastically and went into the other room.

Dane had planned on being back before sun-up and long before Brittany had risen. He wanted to be around should she try and contact someone. But his brother's injury had been a serious one and the ride from Boston uncomfortable for him. They had had to travel much slower than he wanted. Now he was wishing he had gone on ahead of the cart. He didn't believe Brittany had left the house looking for him. He surmised she had paid Miles Ingram a visit, and now there was no way of ever knowing for certain. And starting tonight, he and Cory would take turns keeping an eye on the house. He sensed something was about to happen and he didn't want to get caught sleeping through it.

Having to care for Brad took Brittany's mind off her other troubles. Although his wound appeared to be healing nicely, he wasn't recovering as quickly as she expected him to. He had slept most of the first three days he was there. On the fourth he was able to stay awake for longer intervals, but he wasn't strong enough to lift his head off the pillow, and Brittany had had to feed him herself while she sat next to him on the bed with her arm around his shoulders. What puzzled her was that even though his color was good, there was a sparkle in his eyes, and his wit and humor were always fresh and alert, he still relied heavily on her personal care. It was almost as though he enjoyed being pampered.

On the evening marking the end of his first week's stay with her, Brittany had made sure he had everything he needed, then retired to her own bed shortly after dark. The days of June were not only longer and drier but unbearably hot, and a full night's sleep was becoming a rarity. She had slept for only an hour or two when a noise from the front room startled her awake, and she sat up in bed with her ear turned toward the door, listening. She wasn't sure, but she thought she had heard footsteps. Fearing Dane wanted a repeat of the night he had come to her room, she quickly slid off the mattress, picked up her robe, and tossed it on as she walked to the bedroom door. Bright moonlight trickled in through the window and the front door she had left open to catch what air she could from outside. The light fell across the floor and nearly lit up the entire room, and it took her only a second to see the tall, dark figure standing near the cupboard. Thinking she had been right about Dane, she started to call to him when she noticed that the man was cradling his left arm.

"Brad?" she questioned, stepping further into the room. Her puzzled frown went unseen by the other. "What are you doing out of bed?"

Of all the women he had ever tried to woo, Brittany Lockwood was the most difficult. From the moment his brother came for him at the cobbler's house and told him he would be spending a few weeks at the Lockwood farm, Brad had mentally gone over various schemes to win her heart . . . and hopefully a sweet interlude in bed. He had faked the severity of his injury well enough that even Dane had been fooled, hoping that his brother would insist she allow him to recover in a soft, comfortable bed—preferably inside her house and in a room next to hers. He had hardly believed his ears and good fortune when the idea came from her own lips, and he figured that within two or three days, she would willingly ease the distress he endured that had nothing to do with his shoulder. It hadn't worked out the way he planned it. She had treated him like he guessed she would her own brother. She nursed him, fed him, bathed him, and changed his bandage with the same kind of indifference she would an ailing calf. It frustrated him and put a dent in his ego, and he began wishing there was some way he could bring on a fever. If she found him shaking under a mound of covers, as concerned as she was, she'd more than likely crawl in bed with him to add her body heat to his and chase away the chills. He liked that idea. But he quickly forgot about it, knowing there was no way to pull it off.

By the end of the first week he hadn't gotten any closer to Brittany than when he'd started. The heat of the day and boredom from his confinement had just about driven him crazy. He took to sneaking out of the house at night for a short walk in the cooler air and a change of scenery. During one of his treks to the well, Cory had suddenly appeared at his side and nearly scared him out of his wits.

"My, you certainly made a fast recovery," she had jeered, swinging her slender frame up on the edge of the well to watch him lower the bucket for a drink of cool water. "Does Dane know? Or should I ask if Miss Lockwood's aware of it?"

Brad hadn't liked being reminded of his failure, though he preferred to think of it as a temporary setback. "You know, Cory, if I wasn't so sure about you, I'd say you're jealous."

"Ha!" she exploded. "Jealousy hasn't anything to do with it. I'm smart. I know you haven't a sincere bone in your body. Just as soon as you have your little tumble, you'll move on to the next unsuspecting female. Don't you ever get tired?"

"Of hearing your lectures," he sneered. "Besides, what harm is there if they're willing?" He cranked the bucket within reach and pulled it in. Cupping his hand, he took a long drink, then splashed the rest over his face and neck.

"Do you honestly think that's all there is to it?" she snapped.

Her anger surprised Brad. Turning, he leaned a hip against the stone wall. "Suppose you tell me it isn't."

A deep frown furrowed her brow, and she turned her head away as she heaved an irritable sigh. "I swear God forgot to give you a heart. Or an ounce of intelligence. Haven't you ever considered why these lovely ladies are willing? Hasn't it ever crossed your mind that maybe *one* of them had fallen in love with you and figured there was no harm in giving in to you when marriage was sure to follow?"

"Marriage?" Brad laughed. "I never promised any of them marriage."

"What did you promise them?"

"A night of pure heaven," he smiled, reminiscing.

"God, you're disgusting!" she had raged, jumping to the ground. "It's just a shame you'll never have it happen

269

to you."

"Have what happen?" he had called out to her as he watched her walk back toward the barn.

"You'll never know what it feels like to lose your heart to someone only to have them laugh at you while they lie in someone else's arms."

He had wanted her to explain, but Cory hadn't had any desire to continue their conversation. She had hurried across the yard and disappeared inside the barn, leaving him to stand there in awe of their discussion and the anger she felt about the topic.

The next morning he had awakened to find her standing at the end of the bed, a devilish smile on her lips and a look of justice in her violet eyes. He had quickly looked about the room to make sure they were alone.

"What are you doing here?" he whispered, angered by the feeling he had that she planned to spoil everything for him.

"I just came in to see how you're feeling."

"I'm fine. Now get out." He winced when he tried to sit up.

A silly smirk wrinkled her cheek as she came around the bed to stand next to him. "Now is that any way to talk to a friend? I'm concerned about your health."

Brad glanced over at the door to make sure Brittany hadn't heard their exchange, then glared up at Cory, knowing full well she didn't mean a word of it.

"You know what I decided last night after we talked?" She hurried on before he could tell her that he didn't care. "I decided that Miss Lockwood and I should take turns looking after you."

Brad's jaw slackened and a frown darkened his brown eyes. "Whatever for?"

Cory shrugged, then reached out a narrow hand to touch his brow. He knocked it away. "Well, you seem to heal much quicker when I'm taking care of you. Since you came into the house you've had a relapse."

"Cory," he growled, "why don't you go pester Dane?"

An impish grin sparkled in her eyes. "He doesn't rile as easily as you. Besides, he's already tormented."

Brad looked suspiciously at her. "What do you mean?"

"Well," she began, waltzing away from him, "if you weren't so busy chasing skirts, you'd have seen it, too." She stopped at the foot of the bed and wrapped an arm around the tall poster. "He's having women trouble the same as you."

Brad ignored the pain in his shoulder and pushed himself up, letting the coverlet fall from his bare chest to his lap. "Who?" he had asked. He had never seen Dane with any one woman long enough to get involved.

"Well, let's just say there's likely to be hard feelings between brothers."

The shock of her announcement had shown clearly on his face, and before he had the chance to question her further and learn why she thought Dane had fallen for Brittany, Cory had grinned mischievously at him, spun on her heels and darted from the room. He had spent the next hour going over the times he had been around when his brother and Brittany had been together. As he recalled, Dane had always addressed her formally and their conversations had always been a little tense. Brittany certainly didn't care for Dane. She never flirted with him the way most women did. Brad always figured his brother never allowed himself the pleasure of a woman's company because of Audrey, the young lady back in England who decided not to wait for Dane and married someone else. Dane had cared a lot for the youngest daughter of their neighbor, but not enough to propose after their father died and left his entire estate to the brothers. Her announcement to wed came close on the heels of Dane's purchasing a ship—so close, in fact, that Brad wasn't really sure if she decided to marry because Dane bought a ship or the other way around.

Either way, Dane had been quite withdrawn for some months afterward, and before the wedding took place they

271

had sailed for the colonies. He never spoke of Audrey again, and on the few occasions when they returned to their homeland, he never tried to see her or even ask about her. His affairs with women after that were always brief and scarce. When the rebellion in the colonies grew more intense, they dwindled to practically nothing. But if there was the slightest possibility of some kind of relationship between Dane and Brittany Lockwood, he'd stand aside and give him free rein.

The remainder of the day he spent observing. His brother only came to see him for a short time during the noon break and then while Brittany was outside hanging laundry on the line. He could see her through the bedroom window. Dane had too, and when it appeared she was finished and intended to come back into the house, Dane had hurriedly excused himself and left. He was avoiding her, and Brad knew nothing would ever develop between them if it was allowed to go on. It was then that he decided to help it along. And he had Cory to thank for opening his eyes to the situation. At every opportunity, whenever Dane was around to notice, he'd make his flirtation with Brittany overly apparent.

His task proved harder than he'd imagined. Whenever he had a perfect chance, Dane wouldn't stick around long enough to see it. And Brittany wasn't exactly cooperative. She had an obvious dislike for both him and his brother. But he was sure it was only because Brittany wasn't aware of how Dane felt about her. How could she? He kept his feelings well masked. A bit discouraged, but far from giving up, he had thought of another way. She didn't know it, but Cory would be the go-between. If he had learned one thing about Cory in the year she'd spent with them, it was how much she enjoyed trying to break up his affairs. She seemed to feel a devilish delight in seeing him tossed over for another man. Well, that was exactly what would happen in this case, and the "other man" would be Dane. Every time he saw Cory coming, he'd make a pass at Brittany, knowing the little troublemaker would high-tail it back to his brother with the full account of what was going on. Smiling to himself as he settled down for the night, he had considered suggesting to Dane that Cory be his best man at the wedding. After all, she'd be mostly responsible for it happening, and she seemed to favor a man's style of clothing. No one would even notice.

As usual these past seven nights, the sticky, breathless air played havoc with his sleep, and he had risen with the intention of going outside. He hadn't given much consideration to the likelihood that Brittany contemplated doing the same thing, and once he had crossed the front room on his way to the open door and heard her call out to him, he regretted his carelessness. For a man who hadn't the strength to feed himself, how was he going to explain his ability to be out of bed on his own two feet and without assistance? His mind groped for the right answer, one that wouldn't convince Brittany that he was well enough to do without her aid. She'd send him to the barn with Cory and Dane, and his scheme would become even more difficult to achieve. Without answering or looking at her, he leaned heavily against the cupboard next to him as if he felt faint.

"Brad," she shrieked, running to him and slipping her arms around his waist. "You shouldn't have gotten out of bed."

He laughed weakly and said, "I realize that now, but I wanted something to drink; it was so warm in my room."

"Well, where were you going? Certainly not outside."

Knowing the real reason why his brother had chosen the Lockwood farm as cover, and remembering that Cory had said she and Dane were taking turns keeping an eye open for visitors during the night, he decided what better way to stir things up than to have either Cory or Dane seeing him and Brittany strolling about the yard with her arms around him. It would certainly give them something to think about. Especially with Brittany in her night clothes and he without a shirt!

"Yes, that's what I had in mind. I thought a cool drink from the well would help." He smiled feebly at her as if the gesture took every ounce of strength he had.

"Then why didn't you call to me?"

Standing erect, he feigned dizziness and quickly dropped his arm across her shoulders for support. "I-I didn't want to bother you. You've . . . you've done so much already."

"I only did what my father would have expected of me," she mumbled with a frown. She honestly didn't want his consideration for doing something she felt she had no choice in doing. "Why don't you sit down while I go for fresh water?"

That was the last thing Brad wanted. It wouldn't do any good for Cory or Dane to see her in the yard alone. He had to go with her. "I-I'd enjoy the cool air, Miss Lockwood," he said with a pleading look on his face. "It's not that far to the well, is it?"

Brittany knew it was against her better judgment to agree. This was his first time out of bed since he'd been shot and the short walk might be too much for him. But she certainly could understand why he needed to go outside. If the noise he made hadn't awakened her, it wouldn't have been very long before the heat got to her, too.

"No, it's not too far. But I want you to lean on me. You're not strong enough to make it on your own as yet."

Brad had to bite the inside of his cheek to keep from shouting out loud. Now all he needed was to have it be Dane's turn to watch the house. If Cory was right about Dane—and Brad had an inkling she was—to see his brother half-dressed and coddling the woman he cared about would surely spark some sort of reaction, especially if Cory told Dane that Brad wasn't as sick as he pretended.

"Thank you, Miss Lockwood," he replied softly, taking his arm away. "But I think I'd better walk by myself. I don't want to compromise you should someone happen to see us."

"And who's going to see us?" she snapped, not meaning to

sound so short-tempered. "Cory? Your brother? Do you think I care what they think?" She reached for his hand and wrapped his arm around her neck again, starting them off through the front door.

"Have they done something to anger you, Miss Lockwood?" he pressed, knowing full well her reasons for being upset with the lot of them. She had every right to find their presence on her farm annoying.

"Oh, I don't know," she mocked, turning with him toward the side of the house and the well. "I have a tendency to get angry when I'm lied to and forced into doing something I'd prefer not doing."

"Lied to?" he questioned, sitting down on the tree stump used for chopping firewood. "Who lied to you?"

Brittany straightened before him with her fists on each hip. "You, for one."

"Me?" he echoed, genuinely surprised. "We've hardly talked."

"Well, maybe lying isn't the right term. Deceiving me would be more like it."

Brad was thankful that he was sitting with his back to the moon. She might have seen how uneasy her statement made him. "I-I'm afraid I don't understand." He winced and hugged his arm just in case she had found him out and planned to call his bluff about how ill he really was.

"The first time we met—in the gaol when I came to see my brother—you deliberately led me to believe that a man named Dane Remington would help free Roan. You didn't bother to tell me he was your brother. If I had known, I wouldn't have—" Brittany stopped short when she realized she had nearly told Brad about the deal she had made with his brother. That part of it was over and done with, and best forgotten. She spun away from him and went to the well to lower the bucket.

"Wouldn't have what?" he asked in all seriousness. He sensed the answer would give him the reason for his brother's

275

sudden change in mood. It had been very subtle at first, enough that Brad hadn't really noticed. But later, when Dane insisted he be the one to go to the Lockwood farm with Cory *and* announced that he would be wearing a disguise, Brad had thought his behavior was a little peculiar. Cory had been the one to tell him that Dane admitted he needed the clothes to fool Brittany into letting him stay, though Brad couldn't imagine why. He had helped her brother escape from gaol. She should have been happy to see him. "Brittany, what wouldn't you have done?"

Knowing he probably wouldn't drop it until she gave him some kind of answer, she replied without looking at him, "I wouldn't have asked."

That didn't make any sense. Frowning, Brad mentally traded places with Dane on the night a very beautiful, desperate young woman came to see him, silently going over how he would have reacted when she asked his help in getting her brother out of gaol. The first thing he would have thought was, *what's in it for me?* Dane would have known by looking at her that she hadn't the money to pay for his services, and if she hadn't told him right off that a man named Brad had sent her, Dane wouldn't have been very willing to risk his neck for a total stranger—no matter how beautiful the sister was. And at that point Roan wasn't a member of the Sons of Liberty, so there was no loyalty forcing Dane to help. A devilish half-smile lit up his face as he watched Brittany's slender shape bending over the edge of the well for the bucket. He knew what he would have asked for as payment. The sudden realization that the only difference between him and his brother when it came to a beautiful woman was that Dane was more discreet chased the humor from his lips and made his mouth drop open.

Why, that scandalous rogue, he mused delightedly. Here all this time he had me believing that he was a perfect gentleman. You deserve her scorn. Couldn't you see she was different? You were dealing with a lady, Dane, ol' boy, not a back-street trollop. Or perhaps you have figured it out, but not until *after* she had stolen your heart.

The smile returned to his lips, and he glanced back at Brittany again. That's what she meant when she said she had been forced to do something she'd prefer not doing. He had forced her to give herself as payment. *And* that was the reason why he figured she'd chase him off the farm if she knew who he was. But what about Brittany? he pondered. What were her true feelings for Dane after what had happened between them? He decided to find out.

"I apologize for not being honest with you," he murmured, watching her reach for the ladle hanging on a nail. "If you'll allow me, I'd like to explain."

Having filled the deep-bowled spoon, she turned with it in her hands and came to stand beside him. "Please do," she encouraged, handing the ladle to him. "I'd be interested in knowing why you used me."

Brad winced. "I guess I deserved that."

Brittany smiled mockingly in return and bobbed her head. "And more."

Laughter spilled from him as he agreed. "More than you know," he admitted, taking a drink of the water and pouring the rest over his head. It felt good to be cool again, even if it was only temporary. Running his fingers through his wet hair, he raised his chin in the air and stared up at the stars. "You were the first chance I had to get a message to my brother. I knew you wouldn't be very willing if I told you the truth. I could tell you weren't the type to frequent the docks. So I hoped that by using your brother's predicament you'd find the courage to look for Dane. I realize it must seem now like I used you, and I did to some degree, but I knew Dane would get your brother out as well." He turned to watch her reaction. "As payment for letting him know I was in trouble."

Brittany stiffened instantly and turned her head away. "I think you'd better go inside and lie down. You shouldn't overdo it your first time out of bed."

"His first time?" came a voice from the shadows, and Brad was dearly tempted to fling the ladle at Cory. Her untimely arrival was ruining everything. "Is that what he told you?"

Her tall, sleek figure, dressed in breeches and a white shirt, stepped into the moonlight on the other side of the well. Her long black hair glistened. She would have been a welcome sight had Brad needed her help in getting out of a dangerous situation. This, however, wasn't one of those times.

"No, Cory, that isn't what I told her," he corrected through clenched teeth.

Suspecting he had lied to her again—about his motives at the gaol as well as how sick he was—Brittany cocked her head and glared back at him, her nostrils flared. "But you didn't tell me differently, did you? How often have you strolled out here on your own before tonight? Once? Twice? *Every* night since I took pity on you and brought you into the house?"

"Oh, not every night, Miss Lockwood," Cory volunteered, grinning victoriously at Brad. "Just the past four."

Brittany inhaled a quick breath, ready to hurl every vile insult she could think of. There were so many to choose from that she mentally stumbled over which to say first and wound up stomping her bare foot on the ground out of frustration instead. "You're both alike, Brad Remington! You're both liars, you *and* your brother!" In a rage she whirled away from him, her long, golden hair fanning out around her shoulders in a brilliant array. A second later she disappeared around the corner of the house and the loud banging of the front door advised Brad to find some other source of refuge for the night. He was no longer welcome in her house.

"Thanks Cory. Thanks a lot!" he growled, jerking off the tree stump and wincing when his shoulder truly hurt him.

"Oh, there's no need to thank me, Brad. I wasn't doing it for you." She twisted and perched on the well, watching

Brad slowly make his way toward her and return the ladle to its place on the nail. "I did it for Miss Lockwood."

His dark brow furrowed all the more. "Did what?"

"Wised her up before it was too late."

Brad had a pretty good idea what she meant and didn't want to hear her say it. He shot her a disgruntled look and started for the barn.

"Don't you want to know what about?" she called after him as she jumped to the ground and followed his easy pace.

"I already know, Cory, so save your breath," he snarled.

"I put her onto you. I did her a favor. She and I can be two of a rare breed. We'll be the only two women alive who you never bedded."

That was far from the truth, and he didn't like being compared to a stallion who sniffed around, got what he wanted, and galloped off. He stopped, raised his chin in the air, and waited for Cory to catch up with him. Once she had, he glared over at her. "I don't know where you get all your ideas, Cory Rison, but I'm not as cold-hearted as you make me out to be. Someday, somewhere, I'll come across a woman who'll want nothing to do with me. And she'll be the one I chase. In the meantime, why don't you just mind your own business?"

"You think that woman is Miss Lockwood, don't you?"

Brad heaved a long, irritable sigh and looked away. "No. I don't."

"Then why are you chasin' her?"

"If you're too stupid to figure it out, then you'll have to die wondering." He started off toward the barn again.

"Well, you certainly can't be doing it for your brother."

Surprised by her comment, he stopped and faced her. "And why not? You're the one who told me he was smitten by her. Why couldn't I be helping him realize it by flirting with Brittany?"

A strange, almost hateful look came over her face. "I know more about you than you do, Brad Remington," she

279

said in hardly more than a whisper. "If a pretty face catches your eye, you won't quit until you have her. And it won't matter who stands in your way or gets hurt by it. You've left a trail of broken hearts all the way from England to Virginia to here, and you're so blind you don't even know it." She nodded at his shoulder. "You'd do us all a favor if you got an infection and died." With that parting comment, she turned and headed off into the woods, leaving Brad to stare after her in total confusion.

Chapter Eleven

A single beam of bright sunlight wedged its way in through the narrow slit between two boards on the side of the barn and rudely fell upon Brad's closed lids, rousing him from a sound sleep until the ache in his shoulder reminded him of where he had spent the night. Muttering beneath his breath, he shifted positions on the straw-covered floor and turned his back on the brilliant intrusion, vowing to get a few more minutes of much-needed sleep. In the distance he could hear the rooster crowing and before long the smells of burning wood and frying ham wafted in to make his mouth water. Morning had arrived without his consent, and he knew he could do nothing to prevent it from stretching into a long, hot, boring day.

With his eyes still closed, he curled his lip into a snarl, silently blaming Cory's inventive nature for his having to endure the agony alone, wishing he could shorten it a bit by sleeping another hour or so. He was already sweating and the aroma of hay had never been one of his favorites. Silk sheets, feather mattresses, and breakfast served to him in bed had always been what he missed about living on his father's estate in England.

He rolled onto his back and opened his eyes. But the smile on his lips vanished the instant he saw his brother standing at the end of the stall, arms crossed, a shoulder leaning against the board rail and a look of murder in his dark, green eyes.

"Would you care to explain why you're sleeping in the barn?" Dane questioned, his voice low but tipped with anger.

When they were boys, Dane's size and age had always intimidated his younger brother. It wasn't much different now, especially when Brad knew he deserved Dane's wrath. Struggling to sit up, he slid back against the wall. "You mean Cory hasn't told you?"

"When something involves my brother, I prefer to hear it from him." The muscle in his cheek flexed. "I can always tell when you're lying."

A sheepish half-smile lifted his mouth. He cleared his throat and dusted the bits of straw off his breeches. "I'm here because of a misunderstanding."

"Is that what you call it?"

Knowing now that Cory had already told her version of what happened at the well, Brad mentally went over his options in telling his side of it, stalling for time while he combed his fingers through his dark hair. That damned little mischief-maker! He'd see to it that she regretted ever sticking her nose in where it didn't belong. And now she'd made it impossible for him to shade the truth without Dane knowing it. The way he saw it, he was left with no alternative but to tell exactly what happened and why.

"Well, yes. I'd call it a misunderstanding," he began, choosing his words very carefully. "I hadn't meant to take advantage of Miss Lockwood. I simply didn't want to bother her. I was feeling well enough to go for a short walk, and since I couldn't sleep because of the heat, I decided to go outside where it was cooler."

"How many nights other than this one?"

Brad shrugged his good shoulder and smiled feebly. "A couple, maybe."

"You've been well enough to go for walks for three days and still allowed me to think you weren't out of danger?" his brother observed. "Why, Brad? Are your flirtations that important to you that you'd let your only kin go on worrying about your health when there was no need?"

Brad opened his mouth to deny it, but Dane cut him off.

"Have you any idea what I had to do to get Miss Lockwood to agree in letting you stay here while you healed? This isn't a game, Brad. This is serious . . . deadly serious. Or have you forgotten?"

Brad shook his head. He hadn't, really . . . he had just thought his brother's love life was a little more important. He was wrong, and he knew it. "I apologize, Dane. I was stupid, and I could have gotten the three of us in a lot of trouble. It won't happen again." His words worked magic. Almost before he had finished, Dane had dropped his arms to his sides and swung himself down beside his brother in the stall, the look of anger gone from his eyes.

"I'm glad to hear it. I'm also glad to know you're back to feeling like your old self again." Bending his knees, he laid his wrists across them and idly toyed with a piece of straw. "I think there's something you should know about Miss Lockwood."

Brad perked up, certain he was about to hear Dane's confession of love. "She's a very beautiful woman," he said. It was his subtle way of letting his brother know he approved.

A ripple of laughter caught Dane off-guard. "You never give up, do you? I swear you'd think an old hag was beautiful as long as she was a woman."

"But Dane," he quickly pointed out, "that's why God put them on this earth. For us to love."

Dane suspected there was a deeper meaning to what his brother said. Frowning, he glanced over at him. But Brad had decided to check his bandage and wouldn't look at him. "Well, not all of them," he corrected. "There are a few who find other things more important than loving a man."

Surprised, Brad gave him his full attention. "Are you

283

talking about Brittany?"

It never ceased to amaze Dane how his brother always put himself on a first-name basis with the women he met—whether they wanted it that way or not. Sighing mentally, he pitied the day Brad met up with the woman he was meant to love. Somehow he suspected theirs would be a stormy relationship.

"Yes, I mean Brittany," he acknowledged, flicking away the piece of straw. "I think she's involved in whatever Miles is doing."

"My God, no," Brad moaned. "Not Brittany! Her brother—well, we're sure about him. Why would she work against her own brother? What proof do you have?"

"None so far. Only speculation. And some unanswered questions."

"Like what?"

Stretching out one leg, he leaned back against the wall. "Dooley came here to see me two weeks ago while you and Cory were staying at Bernard Patterson's. Hancock had sent him to keep me abreast of the organization's activities. As he was leaving, Brittany spotted him and followed him into the woods, and he returned to the barn to tell me she had gotten lost."

"But you don't think that's true?" Brad guessed.

"I did at first, but now I'm not so sure."

"Why?"

"Because I found her standing near a tree some distance from here watching two men and a horse-drawn cart moving away from the marsh and heading toward the Ingram estate."

"Only watching?"

"I didn't give her a chance to do anything else," Dane frowned, cursing his reflex action. "I was afraid those men would kill her if they knew she was there, so I stepped up behind her and covered her mouth with my hand."

"But you suspect now that no harm would have come to

her because she knew the men and that they'd be cutting through the woods when they did."

Dane nodded, then rested his head back against the wall and studied the stream of light flooding into the barn through a crack in the wall. "I found it puzzling that she didn't seem at all concerned about the men. In fact, she rather avoided the subject."

"As if she knew all about them and didn't want you to get curious?"

"That and the way she questioned me. It was as if she was testing me, and trying to find out if I had guessed what they were doing on her property."

"*Her* property?"

"Yes. *That's* what made me curious. So the next morning I went back out to the place where I had seen them to investigate."

"What did you learn?"

"For one, the men had quite cleverly, but not completely, hidden their tracks when they left the narrow clearing and moved into an open field heading toward Ingram's manor. Second, they had started out in the direction of the marsh, which leads me to believe the goods they carried came off a ship. But third and most important was my discovery that Brittany had followed me there."

Brad frowned, praying Dane would now tell him how wrong he'd been about her. "And what reason did she give you for being there?"

"None."

Brad's hopes fell. "None?" he repeated quietly.

"That's because she stayed hidden among the trees until after I left, and I didn't call her out."

"But you stayed to watch her."

Dane nodded. "She pretty much followed the trail I had examined, and I can only assume she wanted to convince herself that I hadn't figured out where the men had gone with the cart."

The two brothers were quiet for several minutes, each mentally searching for some logical excuse to clear Brittany Lockwood. Failing that, Brad asked, "Have you ever sat her down and confronted her with what you know?"

"What good would that do, Brad? If she's in this as deeply as I think she is, she'd only lie her way out." He sat up and wrapped his arm around his knees. "And I'd have to tip my hand to do it."

Tilting his head to get a better view of Dane's face, Brad could see the sadness reflected in his brother's frown and in his downturned mouth. "And what makes this whole situation so painful is that you've fallen for her."

Dane's head jerked around to stare in awe at Brad. "What?"

"Oh, come on, Dane. This is your brother you're talking to. I've seen the change in you. Granted, it hasn't been much, but enough for me to know you care about her—and I don't mean in a brotherly fashion."

"Oh, really?"

"Yes, really."

Dane shifted around to look Brad straight in the eye. "If that's what you thought, then why were you making a play for her? Don't deny it. Cory told me what was going on."

"Cory!" he snarled, starting to get up. But the pain in his shoulder made him lightheaded, and he decided to stay put. Grimacing, he cursed the day he so carelessly allowed himself to get shot. "She only told you what you wanted to hear. And you believed her! Do you honestly think I'd try to steal your woman?"

A broad smile parted Dane's lips and laughter rumbled deep in his chest. "My woman? Brad, you obviously don't know a thing about Brittany Lockwood. The last thing in the world she wants is to be my woman. In fact, it's my guess she's fallen for the Dark Horseman."

Brad ignored the burning sensation in his shoulder to stare in wide-eyed surprise, mouth agape. "What makes you think that? When has she ever had the opportunity to get to know him?"

"Remember the afternoon when we rescued John Jacobson from hanging?" He waited for Brad's nod, then continued. "After we split up, I went looking for Brittany. She had been in the crowd that day, and I figured that if I recognized her, one of the soldiers would too and mistakenly assume that she had helped us. It's lucky I did. I found her on her way home and a group of soldiers had stopped her on the road. They weren't acting very friendly, so I intervened."

"As the Dark Horseman."

Dane nodded. "That's really the only time we've been together—I mean, with me dressed as the Dark Horseman. But she said something the other day that really surprised me—she said she was tempted to tell him where he could find me. Out of the blue she brought up his name. And it wasn't so much what she said as the look in her eye as she said it." He shook his head, stretched his long frame out in the stall, and propped himself up on one elbow.

"Dane, do you realize what you just said?"

The oldest gave his brother a funny look. "I should. I'm the one who said it."

"I mean about her telling the Dark Horseman. Everybody for miles around knows he's associated with the Sons of Liberty. She had to, too. Otherwise how would she have known his name? Now, if she thinks you're doing something shady, why would she tell the Dark Horseman instead of the governor? I think she's on our side."

Dane raised a dubious brow at him. "And I think you're crazy."

"Well, there's one way to prove it." Brad grinned suggestively. "And have a little fun at the same time."

"Fun?"

"Well, maybe fun isn't the right word," he admitted, his smile broadening. "But one thing's for certain. You'll be able to prove who she's working for and if she's in love with the

287

Dark Horseman all at the same time."

Dane wrinkled his mouth as if he'd eaten something sour. "Why is it I have a feeling I'm not going to like what you have to say?"

"Probably because you didn't think of it first."

Dane rolled his eyes and sat up. "The world isn't big enough for two people who think like you, and thank God you're the only one. So let's hear it. Tell me your brilliant plan to clear Brittany and make a complete fool out of me."

Excited with his idea, but wanting to make sure neither Cory nor Brittany overheard it, he awkwardly pushed himself to his feet and peered at the front door over the top rail in the stall. Satisfied that it was safe to speak, he sat back down next to his brother and kept his voice low. "Tonight, after everyone's gone to bed, you can don your disguise and pay her a visit."

"Brad—" Dane started to object, but his brother cut him short.

"Just listen, will you? Once in a while I do manage to come up with a good idea. Now, once you're inside, you can let her make the first move. You don't even have to say a word."

"Good," Dane mocked, "because she'd probably recognize my voice if I did."

The enthusiasm over his scheme faded just as quickly as it had come about. "Oh, yeah. I-I never thought about that part of it."

"Obviously," Dane smiled and stood up. "But don't worry. I've thought of something better."

Glancing up hopefully, Brad asked, "What?"

"Why don't you spend the day lounging about while Cory and I work in the fields? By the end of the week you'll be strong enough to help us. And maybe, sometime in between, something will happen to give us all the answers we need . . . without pushing it along."

Brad had sat listening to his older brother's gentle chiding without comment until the last. "Dane, what happens if the

288

answers aren't what we want to hear?"

There was a look of pensive regret in Dane's green eyes as he stared back at his brother. "It's the price we all must pay for standing up for what we believe in, Brad. It wouldn't be the first time someone we cared about let us down."

In silence Brad watched his brother walk away, wondering if Dane might have possibly been referring to Audrey.

Brad spent the rest of the day doing exactly as Dane suggested, not because it had been his brother's idea, but simply because Brad was too weak to do much else. Occasionally, when he couldn't stand the heat in the barn, he'd wander outside for a few minutes, hoping Brittany might be close by. He wanted to apologize for what he had done to her and possibly lure her into a conversation about the Dark Horseman. He couldn't believe she was working for the Crown or anyone else who might compromise her own brother. And he didn't want to see the relationship between her and Dane fall apart before it ever had a chance to grow.

His luck changed a little later in the morning when he saw Brittany hanging up the laundry on the line, and he thought that perhaps this would be his chance to talk to her. But the instant she spotted him, she picked up her basket and went back inside the house, slamming the door behind her as if to tell him not to waste his breath, that his apology would never be accepted. It had discouraged him just enough to send him back to his bed of straw, where he could escape her silent but stinging reminder of his inadequacies. He had slept for a while, talked with Dane, and ignored Cory when the pair came in for lunch, taken another nap, then wandered outside into the yard to sit under a tree when he thought the heat in the barn was hot enough to fry him. Not long afterward he heard the front door of the house open, and he held perfectly still as he watched Brittany, basket of tools in hand, heading toward the garden.

She had donned a pink-and-white-striped dress, bound her long, golden hair high on top of her head, and not bothered with shoes. Just from looking at her it was easy to see why Dane had finally allowed his emotions to surface. Brittany Lockwood might not dress in the rich fabrics of the wealthy women of Boston or London, but she was a grand lady just the same . . . and a smart one, one with principles. She had done everything in her power, even risked her own safety, to free her brother from gaol and prove his innocence.

Thinking of Roan, Brad contemplated the boy's situation. He claimed he wasn't guilty. Brittany set out to prove it. Assuming he wasn't—and Brad had no reason not to believe it—Roan had been falsely charged. Why? Had it been his misfortune to be in the wrong place at the wrong time? Or had someone framed him? Brad's dark brow wrinkled with the thought. Had Roan done something to make someone so angry that he wanted revenge of this kind? Brad shook his head, unable to accept that. Roan was only a boy. And from the conversation the two of them had had there in gaol, Roan talked of nothing but his father, his sister, and working on the farm. He never mentioned a violent argument with anyone. With that thought came another: Roan had admitted to him that he and his sister disagreed about their father's death. Roan claimed Patrick Lockwood was murdered; Brittany said it was an accident. Mulling it over in his mind, Brad couldn't come up with any connection between the man's death and Roan being charged with arson, though something deep inside him wouldn't let go of the possibility. Frowning, Brad decided that once he was well enough to ride again, he'd do some investigating of his own. He liked Roan and he wanted to see the young man cleared.

A flash of pink caught his eye and intruded upon his musings. Blinking, he focused his attention on Brittany again. She was kneeling in the middle of her garden pulling weeds. Her back was to him and he was relatively certain she didn't know he was there. Maybe now would be his chance to talk to her. If he caught her before she had the opening to flee to the safety of her house, he could insist she give him a moment to apologize. Clumsily pushing himself to his feet, he cradled his arm against his chest and headed her way.

Brittany had done a lot of thinking since the episode at the well the night before and couldn't come up with any sensible excuse for Brad's behavior . . . unless, of course, Dane had put him up to it. It was quite probable that he had wanted his brother to win her friendship and trust, then artfully trick her into telling him everything she knew about the men and the cart. She had been too angry at first to think it through, and now that she had she was sorry she'd reacted so. It would have given her the perfect opportunity to mislead them. She could have pretended that just such things happened all the time and meant nothing to her. That way they would have let down their guard and continued with their little scheme, thinking she was too stupid to notice. Yet one thing puzzled her: if this was true, why had Cory ruined it? Surely Dane had let her in on the plan. Figuring it was too late to wonder about it, she dismissed the thought and stood. She'd simply have to find some other way of catching them.

"Good afternoon, Miss Lockwood," the voice behind her said.

Startled, Brittany jumped around, surprised that Brad had managed to sneak up on her. She thought he was still in the barn.

"I didn't mean to frighten you," Brad apologized, smiling softly.

The anger surfaced again. "Well, you did," she snapped, bending down for her basket.

"Miss Lockwood, please," Brad pleaded when she started for the house. "I'd like to explain my actions for the past week, if you'll let me."

"Why bother?" she called back over her shoulder. "What

am I to you except someone who can easily be made a fool of?"

"That's not true," he argued, hurrying as fast as he could to catch up. He stumbled to a halt when she stopped suddenly and faced him.

Brittany hadn't realized the similarities between the two brothers until now. Nor had she truly noticed how handsome Brad was. Although he wasn't as tall as Dane, his well-muscled physique left little doubt that he could hold his own in a fight. His complexion was dark and had a healthy glow. His jaw was square, his mouth full, his eyes the darkest shade of brown she had ever seen. Under different circumstances she might have been pleased to have such a good-looking man chase after her, begging her forgiveness. But Dane Remington was his brother, and that ruined everything.

"Isn't it? Then why didn't I guess what you were up to without having to be told?"

"That's exactly what I mean. Cory made it seem like I was playing you for a fool. It's the furthest thing from the truth."

Clutching the basket in both hands, she cocked her head to one side and said, "Then suppose you tell me what the truth is."

Glancing up at the bright sun, he suggested they move into the shade. Brittany wanted nothing to do with it and shook her head. She wanted him to suffer just as she had suffered, knowing he had taken advantage of her.

"This isn't a social visit, Mr. Remington," she jeered. "Say what's on your mind and be done with it. Then you can stand in the shade while I go inside and start supper."

Feeling the sweat run down his back, he wondered how she could appear so cool. But then she wasn't the one trying to explain. "All right," he sighed. "But promise you'll listen with an open mind." He frowned, confused, when she smiled back at him.

"I don't have to promise you anything."

This was a lot harder than he'd expected. And it wasn't going to be any easier for him when he tried to dance around the real reason he was flirting with her. She wasn't in the mood to hear something as farfetched as his desire to make his brother jealous. Now that he thought about it, it sounded rather weak even to him.

Plucking his damp shirt collar away from his neck, he cleared his throat and said, "From the first day we met, there in that awful gaol, I was quite taken by you. I thought maybe you had figured that out when I talked to you at the courthouse. Then when I awoke at Patterson's and found you bending over me, I thought I had died and gone to heaven." He glanced off to his left as he considered what to say next and missed the gentle smile that came over her face. It had disappeared when he looked back at her. "And when Dane told me that I'd be spending some time here with you, I figured my prayers had been answered. What I didn't count on was that you didn't feel the same way about me. I must admit it hurt my feelings. But once I got over it, I decided to find a graceful way out of the situation and out of your house. Cory took care of that before I had the chance. Unfortunately, it wasn't how I intended. So I apologize for what I did, and I hope you'll understand that it was merely the fever and your beauty that made me lose my head."

Brittany couldn't stop the laughter that tugged at the corners of her mouth or the thought that Brad, in his stumbling way, had solved her problem. She would accept his apology and at the same time win his confidence. The moment he ventured to bring up the matter of her late-night trespassers, she'd pretend indifference.

"Died and gone to heaven?" she giggled.

For an instant he wasn't sure if she was mocking him or actually found what he said amusing. He prayed it was the latter, but in case he was wrong, he stood mute with a silly half-smile on his face.

"Your apology is accepted, Mr. Remington," she grinned, then held out a hand toward him. "Now suppose you come in the house and let me look at your wound. I can't have you getting sick again."

Unable to believe his good luck, Brad stood there dumbfounded until Brittany laughed again and waved him on.

"Well?" she smiled. "Are you coming into the house or would you prefer standing in the hot sun?"

A broad grin stretched across his face. "Anywhere but here," he admitted, holding out his arm for her to take. "Anywhere."

Slipping her hand into the crook of his arm, she turned with him and headed toward the house, thinking that perhaps she had misjudged Brad. Just because one member of the family was a rogue and a scoundrel didn't mean everyone else was.

Moonlight fell into the barn through the open double doors. The air hung heavy with moisture. In the distance an owl hooted, and the only sign of life was the dark figure of a man standing in the doorway staring out at the quiet, peaceful night. Dane hadn't been able to go to sleep the way Cory and his brother had. His head had been filled with too many thoughts about Brittany. He wanted to believe the things Brad had said about her—that she wouldn't have threatened to contact the Dark Horseman if she wasn't sympathetic to the rebels' cause, but there was just too much evidence against her for him to agree. With a shoulder leaning against the door frame, his arms folded in front of him, Dane cast a look back inside toward the stall where his brother slept. There were times when he wished he had as much faith in someone as Brad did. Maybe he wouldn't be standing here now, feeling as if his heart had been wrenched from him. A soft smile parted his lips as he recalled the proud way Brad had told him that he had managed to patch things up with Brittany, hinting that it was something Dane could do if he set his mind to it.

But Brad wasn't aware of the differences which set Dane and Brittany apart. If he was, he'd know why Dane hadn't bothered to try. He hadn't just flirted with her. They'd made love, and he had blackmailed her into it. That wasn't something a woman could easily forgive a man. His dark brows came together suddenly. He wasn't even sure if he cared whether or not she forgave him. If she was guilty of spying, there would be no future for them anyway. How could two people ever hope to share their love if they stood on opposite sides of an issue? And not a minor one like where they should live or what they should name their firstborn, but on the loyalties to an oppressive government!

Listen to me, he thought disgustedly. I'm talking about children and settling down as if I had the choice. A tiny voice somewhere deep within his brain said, And don't you? He straightened at the thought and glanced over at the house silhouetted in moonlight. Yes, I do, he silently agreed. Every man has the right. All I have to do is prove I'm wrong about Brittany. With a devilish half-smile twisting his mouth, he turned and went back into the barn.

A pale shaft of light flickered against Brittany's closed eyelids. She stirred, briefly opened her eyes, and rolled to her side, blocking out the insistent glow. She struggled to fall asleep again, but the sudden realization that it wasn't the sun begging her to awaken rather the flame of a candle brought her straight up in bed. Jerking her head around, a worried, somewhat fearful frown wrinkled her brow when she discovered that the light was coming from the front room.

As quietly as possible she slid from her bed and picked up her robe from the chair. She and Brad had agreed that since he was feeling much better and his wound was healing nicely, it was best if he slept in the barn with the others. In fact, it had been his idea, since he didn't want an unexpected visitor to get the wrong idea should he be seen stumbling from one of the bedrooms in a questionable state of dress. His concern had been honest; she had read it in his eyes. Therefore, unless he had a relapse, she felt quite certain that it wasn't Brad who lit the candle. Slowly edging her way to the door, she stayed to one side so as not to be seen while she peered into the room looking for whoever had the nerve to barge into her house uninvited. All sorts of possibilities came to mind. Cory, for one, though she couldn't imagine why. And of course, Dane. But he was surely smarter than that. He needed a place for Brad to stay until he was completely well again, and Dane knew she'd order them off the farm if he broke his word and tried to force himself on her again. Perhaps it was the young boy from the other night. Maybe he'd gotten so hungry, he'd worked up the nerve to break into her house looking for food. The view of the fireplace presented itself when she leaned just far enough, and once she saw the musket hanging above the mantel, she wished she had had the foresight to prop it up beside her bed before retiring. There was a good chance the interloper might be one of the men from the woods, and he had been ordered to kill her. Trembling, she chewed on her lower lip and glanced about her bedroom for some other kind of weapon, spotting the water pitcher sitting on the night stand. With the former held in both hands, she went back to the door and peeked out.

The room was empty. Even the front door was shut. Was someone playing a trick on her? Did they want to lure her out of her bedroom? Or even out of the house? Absently, she looked at the candle sitting on the table next to the deacon's bench and straightened when she saw a folded piece of parchment leaning against the long white taper. Curious, she put aside the water pitcher and hurried to the table, unable to imagine who had left the letter there and why.

Picking it up, she slowly sank upon the bench and broke the wax seal. The handwriting in blue ink was full and bold. Glancing first at the signature, Brittany's chin dropped. The Dark Horseman! He had been here? In her house? An excited, delicious smile tugged at the corners of her mouth. He had come here to see her? To leave a message? Thinking that perhaps he was hiding in the bedroom, she flew from the bench and raced to its door. But a quick examination proved she was wrong and she returned to the bench to read what he had written, feeling rather disappointed. Her heart fluttered at its intimacy.

My dearest Brittany,

Because of the importance of keeping my identity a secret, I am forced to hide behind a mask, to still the words I long to say to you, when all I really want to do is hold you in my arms and kiss you. I have known since the day I took you from the soldiers that you were special. And unless my mind is drugged by your beauty and my desire to have you, I cannot think that you do not feel the same for me. I ask you—no, I beg you—to meet with me in the meadow. Let us share our love for each other. Let us have those few precious moments together—ones that must last me until I am free to tell you who I am. I will wait until midnight. Forever yours,

the Dark Horseman

Brittany's gaze flew to the mantel clock. Five minutes until midnight! She would have to hurry if she was to make it in time. Jumping up, she raced back into her bedroom, hurriedly brushed her hair, pinched color into her cheeks, and ran for the front door. But the instant her hand touched the knob, she froze. This is real, isn't it? she asked herself. I'm not just dreaming again, am I? She looked back at the flickering flame of the candle and the letter she had laid on the table beside it. If it was just a vision in her dreams, it didn't matter. She'd go to him anyway. No one had ever said such romantic things to her in all her life, and real or not, she vowed to enjoy this to the very last minute.

Hurrying across the front yard, Brittany glanced only briefly in the direction of the barn. There was no light coming from inside or any movement in or around it as far as she could see. The last thing she wanted was for Dane to see her. He'd be nosy enough to stop her and ask where she was going. A soft, hardly audible giggle tightened the muscles in her throat as she thought of an answer.

I'm sneaking off in the middle of the night to meet my lover, she grinned wickedly. I'm doing exactly what I said I would never do. One tawny brow rose capriciously. But that was before the Dark Horseman had asked her to come.

She took the footpath which cut through the woods and led into a field of hay. Bright moonlight lit the way, and the closer she came to the spot where they were to meet, the more excited and hesitant she became. Her actions were scandalous, and for a moment she considered turning around and going home. This was wrong; her father would have been ashamed of her had he been alive to learn about it. Her steps slowed a bit. Roan wouldn't approve either. She stopped and glanced back in the direction she had come. She wanted to go to him. In her heart she wanted it more than anything in the world. But her gentle upbringing and her conscience were telling her no. In the morning he would be gone, and she'd more than likely never see him again. And if she didn't go to him now, the result would be the same. The possibility was very strong that she'd lose him no matter what decision she made.

A row of trees divided the hay field in which she stood

from the meadow on the other side. Hidden within a stand of oaks a black stallion impatiently pawed the ground when he caught the scent of someone near. Nostrils flaring, he reared his head and snorted his seeming disapproval. The dark figure standing off to one side moved to the edge of the sparce stand of trees, making himself quite visible to the young woman in the open field.

Brittany's pulse quickened the instant she recognized his tall, muscular build draped in an ebony cape, tricorn, and mask, and her indecision vanished. She was drawn to him like a magnet, and despite the humid night air, a chill trembled her body. A lean hand, palm upward, was held out to her, the fingers slightly curled. When she came within reach, she slid her hand into his, and the warm touch of flesh against flesh sent her heart pounding. In the moonlight she could see his emerald eyes taking in the sight of her from beneath the silk mask which covered only his forehead, nose, and cheekbones. It was a silent compliment she vowed would last her lifetime. Strong fingers curled around hers and in silence he guided her through the narrow grove of oaks to the meadow on the other side. They stood in the tall grasses bedecked with wildflowers, staring into each other's eyes for several minutes before he let go of her hand to untie the strings of his cape. Fanning it out, he laid it on the ground beside them, then took his hat from his head and tossed it aside before he turned back to her.

The words he had written came to mind as she studied the rugged features of his jaw and full mouth. He did indeed seem familiar to her, and she remembered his need to keep his identity a secret from her. Should the wrong person learn of their meeting, her life would be in danger. They wouldn't stop until they had beaten the information from her. For an instant she thought about telling him that she would rather die than reveal his identity, but the pledge was never voiced, for his sudden nearness when he took her in his arms chased away any desire to talk. His head dipped downward and Brittany raised her face to his, her lips parted, her eyes closed in anticipation of their kiss. Her actions were shameful; she knew that. But at this moment it didn't matter. And if he left her never to return, she would not look back on this brief interlude with regret. Whether it be girlish infatuation in someone else's eyes, this was love as far as she was concerned, and she would carry the feeling to her grave despite what others called it.

His huge hand cradled the back of her head, his fingers entwined within the silken mass at her nape, and his other arm encircled her narrow waist and pulled her against him. Her thin nightgown and gossamer robe did little to shield the heat of his body pressed against her own, and her blood turned to liquid fire. Her head began to spin when his opened mouth, warm and moist, captured hers. Her breath caught in her throat when his tongue lightly teased her lips, then pushed inside. The feel of his hand roaming the slender length of her spine made her knees quiver, and she clung desperately to him, returning his ardent embrace with equal passion. What began as a gentle, tender expression of his desire turned fevered and impatient as though their moments together were limited to one. Their lips still clinging, he slid his fingers across her delicate shoulders, taking the robe and the narrow straps of her gown with them to shimmer down her arms and pool at her bare feet. A wide hand cupped her breast, his thumb gently stroking its peak, while he traced the slim outline of her hip, waist, and buttocks with the other. Brittany moaned in sheer ecstasy and clumsily unfastened the buttons on his silk shirt. It, too, fell to the ground at their feet. An instant later he had shed the rest of his attire and was slowly lowering her upon his cape.

Caught beneath him, Brittany frantically kissed the corner of his mouth, his chin, the strong line of his jaw, then crushed her mouth to his, their tongues clashing while she ran her fingers over his muscular shoulders, the iron-thewed expanse of his wide back. This was her dream come to life, only better. She had never imagined it to be like this. He was here with her, caressing her, kissing her, wanting her more than anything else, even risking his life for her. His knee parted her trembling thighs, and when he pressed his manhood hot and hard against her, she eagerly, willingly accepted the probing staff, arching her hips to meet his first thrust.

The stars exploded in the heavens about her world as he moved long and sure within her. Tears moistened the corners of her eyes. Her heartbeat thundered wildly in her ears. Her flesh burned and her mind called out for it never to end. A hot sensation twisted her insides and spread through every inch of her until her entire body quaked with unbearable pleasure. She could hear his ragged breathing, feel the pounding of his heart against her naked breast; and when they reached the glorious height of their unbridled passion, he moaned her name in a harsh whisper, shuddered in the fury of their rapture, then fell breathless and exhausted at her side.

A loving smile graced her lips as she crept closer within the circle of his arms, her willowy leg draped over his long, muscular ones while she traced a fingertip along the hard curve of his chest. The masculine scent of him filled her nostrils. The warmth of his body next to hers chased away the damp chill in the air. Moonlight gleamed against their naked flesh, and Brittany, unashamed, boldly studied the full length of him, burning the image in her mind, for somewhere deep inside her, she sensed this would be their one and only moment together. Theirs was a love not meant to be. And though she felt the uncontrollable desire to weep, she steeled herself against the need. She would not ruin this special time with a woman's weakness. He would remember her as strong-willed, passionate, loving, and without demands. In the morning he would be gone, but the vision of this night would glow brightly in her memory forever.

He stirred beside her, raised up on an elbow, and kissed her softly, tenderly. His bright smile warmed her soul, and when he handed her her nightgown and robe, she quickly donned them so that she could watch while he pulled on his breeches, stockings, and shoes. Once he had slid on his shirt, she went to him and brushed away his hands so that she could fasten the buttons for him. Gazing up into his emerald eyes, she rose on tiptoe and placed a gentle kiss upon his lips.

"I'll remember this all the rest of my days," she whispered, her fingers touching the silky fabric of the mask hiding his face. "And if it is your desire, I'll be here should you decide to spend your life with me. But know this, too: I will never seek you out or try to learn your name, though the want to know is killing me. It will be your choice alone to make."

A sad, almost pained expression darkened his eyes and he took a breath to speak. But something stopped him, a reason she would never learn. Bending down, he lifted his cape and tricorn from the ground and donned them both, then walked with her to the stallion that awaited them.

Clasping her narrow waist in his hands, he easily lifted her up into the saddle, grabbed the reins, and swung himself up behind her. In silence they rode the short distance home through the hay field, unaware of the dark clouds rolling in from the west and the flashes of light skipping through them. Reining the black steed to a halt in the yard, he turned her in his arms, kissed her long and hard, then caught her waist and gently lowered her to the ground. He stared at her a long while before he finally yanked back on the reins, spun the animal around, and raced off down the road.

Brittany remained in the yard for some time, staring into the darkness that had swallowed him up, praying he would return, yet knowing that he wouldn't. Brushing at the tear which defiantly raced down her cheek, she forced herself to turn toward the house, ignorant of the dark figure who stood in the doorway of the barn watching her as she went inside.

A smile lit up Brad's face as he stepped out into the open, his gaze shifting from the light inside the house to the road where his brother had gone, hoping that the next time they spoke, everything between Dane and Brittany would have been resolved.

Chapter Twelve

The sweet smell of rain in the air and the distant rumbling of thunder should have brought a pleased smile to Dane's lips as he slowly walked his stallion toward the corral in back of the barn, but it didn't. In fact, he hadn't even noticed the approach of a storm. His thoughts were of Brittany and the shattering discovery he had made. Unbuckling the cinch, he pulled the saddle and blanket from the animal, tossed them on the rail, and turned back to unfasten the bridle. He had guessed correctly about her: she was in love with someone she didn't even truly know. And not honestly the man, but the mystery which enshrouded him. What made his brow furrow in a deep frown was knowing that if she learned that man's identity—that the Dark Horseman was Dane Remington—her love would turn to hate. She would blame him for deceiving her and claim it had been what he planned all along.

Having locked the gate behind him, he took the horse's gear and entered the barn through the back door in case Brittany was still awake and looking out the window for some reason. Now that their rendezvous was over, he was wishing he had taken the chance that she might not recognize his voice and asked her what she knew about the men and their cart. He was sure she would have been honest with the

Dark Horseman. This way, he didn't know any more about her involvement than when he started out.

Tossing the saddle over a rail, he haphazardly hung the bridle on a nail and slowly walked toward the front doors as he pulled off his cape and tricorn. Dropping them on the floor near the rest of his things as he passed by, he paused near the entryway to stare out at the dark scenery before him. There had been only one other woman in his life whom he cared about, and Audrey had been unfaithful to him as well. They had discussed getting married before his father died. But Dane had wanted to wait until after his ailing father was feeling better. Audrey couldn't understand why; she was tired of sharing her bedroom with four sisters and wanted a house of her own. When Edward came along and eagerly offered her an escape, she took it. Love had nothing to do with her marriage, and once it had been announced, Dane realized that she hadn't truly loved him either. He was a convenient way out of her troubles.

He had taken it quite hard at first, until he realized that she had actually done him a favor, and from that point on he swore no woman would steal his heart like that again unless he was sure she felt the same for him. It hadn't worked out as he had planned. He hadn't counted on someone like Brittany Lockwood. And what tore at him right now were the similarities between his affair with Audrey and the peculiar one with Brittany. Whenever Brittany looked at Dane Remington, he could see the bitter disapproval in her eyes for him. Yet because of a simple note written by the same man using a different name, she hadn't hesitated in the slightest to go running off to meet him—to make love to him in a meadow where all of God's creatures could bear witness! His gaze drifted toward the dark house. The idea of it angered him, and if he wasn't positive that he'd ruin any chances he had with her, he'd break down her door and tell her the truth. He'd tell her that she was damned fickle! Frustrated and furious, he jerked away from the door frame, spun around, and went to the stall where he bedded down each night. Throwing himself on the pile of hay, he shifted about until he found a comfortable spot and closed his eyes, determined to go to sleep. A moment later, he was staring up at the faint flashes of light reflected inside the barn.

He wasn't sure if he had actually fallen asleep or not before he heard his brother frantically urging him to get up and come to the doors of the barn. The excitement in Brad's tone was one Dane seldom heard unless there was real trouble. Bounding to his feet, he raced to join his brother.

"What is it?" he asked with a frown.

Brad pointed to the horizon. "Over there. Can you see it?"

Where the rough outline of the land met the black sky, a bright yellow glow distinguished the two. It was a good mile or so away, but the dangers were close enough for the two men to reach out their hands and touch it.

"Brad, you'd better go and wake Brittany," he ordered, his dark brows gathered in a fierce frown. "I'll get Cory and see what we can do to stop the fire. If it gets out of control, I want you and Brittany to take my horse and get as far away from here as possible. Do you understand?"

"Four pair of hands are better than two," he argued.

"You're in no condition to fight a fire! You wouldn't last ten minutes. And I won't put Brittany in that kind of danger." Shoving his brother away, he shouted, "Now go!"

The smell of burning hay and dried grass was already drifting toward the Lockwood farm by the time Dane and Cory had armed themselves with blankets and shovels and were sprinting across the potato field toward the fire. A light breeze had picked up, something they had gone without for weeks, and the unfortunate direction it chose was drawing the flames toward them. The closer they got, the more intense the heat and smoke became, and once Dane and Cory got within clear sight of the fire, they both staggered to a breathless stop. The entire width of the hay field was aflame and the flames were rapidly approaching.

307

"We'll never be able to stop this!" Cory shouted above the rumble of thunder overhead. "I think we'd better use our energies praying the storm breaks before this reaches the house and barn."

Dane had to agree, though he didn't want to. Yet he knew something had to be done. It wouldn't be long before the fire swept the bone-dry fields, attacked the buildings on Brittany's farm, then moved on to the woods surrounding them. Every blade of grass, every tree and shrub would go up in flames, along with Brittany's hopes of hanging onto her father's land.

"Dane! Did you hear me?" Cory yelled, her violet eyes squinted, half-shut against the burning smoke that had begun to swirl around them.

"Yes, I heard. But praying never was something I did well." Throwing down his shovel and blanket, he turned back toward the barn as he shouted, "Start digging a path about three or four feet wide. I'm going back for the ox and plow."

"What good will that do?" Cory hollered.

"If there's nothing in its path to burn, we just might not need God's help," he answered, bolting off.

"You're wasting your time!" Cory screamed after him, but Dane wasn't listening.

The pain in his chest and his shortness of breath had slowed him down by the time he returned to the barn. He was unable to talk when Brad came running up to meet him. Motioning for his brother's help, they hurriedly collected the harness and other gear and led the ox from his stall.

"What are you planning to do?" Brad asked as he helped his brother ready the animal.

"Plow a furrow wide enough that the fire can't jump it. It's the only hope we have of stopping it other than the storm. Where's Brittany?"

"I'm right here," she called from the doorway.

"I suggest you gather up whatever you can take with you,"

he said without looking at her. "It doesn't look good."

"I'm not running away," she firmly replied. "This land was my father's dream. I'll not stand aside and watch it go up in flames. I'm going to help. Just tell me what to do."

Dane glanced up briefly at her, then back at his work. But he gazed at her long enough to see the determination in her gray-blue eyes. "And I more than anyone wish he were here right now. He'd pack you a bag and send you on your way."

"And I'd tell him what I'm telling you. This is my home. It's all I have. I'm not leaving."

"I think she means it, Dane," Brad observed.

Dane's brows slanted downward as he mumbled, "I'm sure she does." Having harnessed the ox, he took the reins and hurried the animal outside, his brother and Brittany following closely behind as he headed toward the side of the barn where the plow was kept. "Then I suggest you fill as many tubs, rain barrels, and pots as you can find with water. We just might need them. Then start digging a firebreak." He glanced up at the tall dark trees surrounding the buildings on three sides, frowning all the more when he saw how they swayed in the ever-increasing wind. "But I don't honestly see what good it will do if the fire reaches this far." Once the straps from the harness were hooked to the plow, he faced his brother. "If it does, I want you to throw her on my horse and get her the hell away from here. You understand?"

"You've got my word, Dane," he guaranteed him.

Dark green eyes fell on Brittany. "And I expect you to do everything he tells you. Have you got that?"

Brittany's mouth dropped open as she straightened her spine and started to tell him that no one told her what to do. But the look in those emerald eyes changed her mind. "Yes," she relented.

The moment Dane hurried off through the field on his way back to Cory and the difficult, somewhat hopeless task on which they were to embark, Brad headed for the well. But Brittany hesitated without realizing it. For some unknown reason, she preferred watching Dane's tall, muscular shape until he had moved out of sight. She wanted to hate him, but something inside her wouldn't allow it. Whether he agreed right now or not, he was risking his safety to save her farm when he honestly didn't have to. He took command and didn't look back. Why? she wondered. Why didn't he pack up his things, take his brother and Cory, and ride on? What prompted him to fight in her behalf? A tightness gripped her heart. Was it simply because he cared? Or was there an ulterior motive? A strong gust of wind tore at her skirts and filled her nostrils with the pungent odor of the fire, snapping her back to reality, and she quickly abandoned her thoughts and spun around. She'd consider the reasons later. Right now she had to save her farm from total destruction.

She and Brad worked frantically for the next twenty minutes, filling every available container they could find with water and lugging them close to each building on the premises. They positioned buckets, pitchers, and large pans one could use to hurl water on the flames should the need arise. Once that was finished, they each grabbed a shovel and began to turn over the soil. Thunder exploded all around them. The smells of burning hay and the dense smoke choked them. Lightning seared the sky and in the west the bright orange wall of flame crept closer. The wind increased, whipping Brittany's long hair and full skirts. In the corral, Dane's stallion whinnied fearfully and pawed the ground, then bolted and raced the perimeter of the wood fence. Every animal on the farm and in the woods surrounding them cried out in terror, instinctively aware of the danger closing in on them, and those who were free raced insanely off.

"Brad!" Brittany screamed when the huge horse reared up on his hind legs and wildly pawed the top rail in the corral. "The stallion! He'll hurt himself!"

Covered with sweat and dirt, his face pale from exhaustion, Brad glanced up at her, then at the steed, and finally at the ever-brightening glow in the distance. "Then let him!" he yelled in return. "We haven't the time to stop."

Brittany, too, looked in the direction of the fire, positive now that Dane and Cory had been unable to contain it. Even from this distance she could see the red, yellow, and orange tongues of flame lapping skyward. The stallion bellowed again, drawing her attention to him.

"Brittany, no!" Brad called when he saw her drop the shovel, grasp her skirts in one hand, and race for the corral.

Caring for the animals on her father's farm had always been Brittany's job as a young girl. She'd had a special affection for them, something Patrick Lockwood had seen when she wasn't much bigger than the colt he had brought home. She dearly loved the spirited buck and learned to ride before she had managed to cook a decent meal. The animal's death had been an accident she blamed on herself. She had had a foolish argument with her father that night and took off bareback on the stallion, riding at full gallop through the woods. The steed loved to run, and neither of them paid much attention to the direction they took. Because of it, the buck stepped in a hole, fell, and broke his leg. Brittany had been thrown clear and suffered only a few bumps and scratches. But the pain she endured when her father brought his rifle and put the steed out of its misery was something Brittany would never forget. She vowed then that she would never be the cause of an animal's suffering again. The house and barn just weren't worth this black stallion's life. Upon reaching the gate, she swung it wide, ran inside shouting and waving her arms, and chased him through the opening. Head held high, his tail arched and nostrils flared, the beast galloped off down the road.

"You didn't have to do that, Brittany," Brad scolded breathlessly as he leaned heavily against the handle of his shovel. "He would have jumped when he got scared enough. I've seen him do it before."

"Maybe," she consented, picking up her spade, "but I wasn't going to let him hurt himself trying." Noticing that

311

Brad seemed to be sweating a little harder than he should, she reached over and took away his shovel. "Go sit down for a minute and have a drink before you pass out."

"I'm all right," he argued, making a grab for the tool.

"No, you're not," she snapped. "Now do as I say."

Brad didn't want to admit that his head was spinning and that it took every ounce of strength he had just to stand up. But apparently he didn't have to. Brittany could tell by looking at him. Staggering toward the closest tub of water, he collapsed on the ground beside it.

Every muscle in Brittany's body ached. She had blisters forming on her hands. Her hair and body were wringing with perspiration and the smoke burned her lungs. She had every right to quit, to throw down her spade, to gather all she could carry from the house in her arms and run as fast and as hard as she could away from the raging inferno closing in on her. But Brittany had never been a quitter and she wasn't going to start now.

A loud clap of thunder resounded right above her, preceded by a glaring flash of light. Pausing in her work, she raised her dirt-smudged face toward the sky. "Rain, damn you!" she screamed. "Rain! Dear God in heaven, why won't it rain?" Tears tightened the muscles in her throat and flooded her eyes. A sob shook her body. Raking the long strands of hair back off her brow with her fingers, she looked at the rapidly spreading fire and realized that within a half hour it would reach the ground on which she stood and that even if they were to save the buildings, her crops were already lost. The devastation it would wreak would be so complete that the Lockwood farm would be rendered worthless.

From somewhere amidst the swirling smoke two figures emerged, both coughing and covered with soot, carrying what was left of their charred blankets. Rushing to the tub of water where Brad sat, Cory knelt beside it and frantically

312

splashed the cool liquid over her face and neck, then cupped her hands and took a long, welcome drink.

"What happened to the ox?" Brad asked his brother when Dane had joined the pair and tumbled to the ground beside him.

"I turned him loose," he panted. "The fire's too wide spread. We couldn't stop it." Bending one knee, he propped an elbow on it and rubbed the back of his hand across his jaw as he stared out at the flood of orange light. "Nothing's going to stop it."

"But we have to try," came the strangled cry of desperation. "It's all I have. It's all Roan and I have." Brittany's gray eyes were filled with tears, and when she blinked, they cascaded down her cheeks. "Please, Dane. Don't give up . . . not yet."

She was the most pitiful sight he had ever seen. Her thick, golden hair hung limp and stringy. Her dress was ripped and covered with dirt. But it was the frantic, pleading look in her eyes that tore at his heart. "I won't, Brittany," he promised. "Not until there isn't an ounce of hope left."

Emerald eyes stared into gray ones for a long while, and Brittany thought that if there had ever been a chance for her to love this rogue, then she loved him at this very moment. Brushing away her tears, she smiled gratefully at him, then turned and went back to work.

The foursome labored side by side without a sound or single complaint until the roar of the fire drowned out the roll of thunder in the sky all around them, the glare of its flames outshone the flashes of lightning, and the smoke obscured everything. The trench they had worked on slowed the progress of the fire but still threatened to jump the line, and they shifted their attention to dousing it with water. Each one of them felt a glimmer of hope until the blanket of flames stretched out its long fingers near the corral, scooted across a narrow strip of dry grass, and shot up the posts. The entire fence was aflame before Cory noticed it.

"It's no use," she shouted when sparks ignited the pile of hay stacked near the barn. "We've got to get out of here before we're all killed!"

"No!" Brittany screamed. "Not yet. It's going to rain. I know it will. We can't leave yet!" Dipping her pail in the nearly empty barrel of water, she raced with it toward the pile of hay and the flames which were shooting well above her head. Throwing the contents on it, the small amount of water did very little good, but she was determined to keep on trying. Spinning around, she raced back to the barrel to refill her bucket.

"Dane, she's wasting her time," Brad frowned, throwing down the blanket he had used to beat out the fire. "Cory's right. We've got to get out of here before it cuts us off from the road."

"I know," he sighed, glancing up at the black sky then back to the lane and their only hope of escape. "Take Cory and go. I'll bring Brittany."

"She isn't going to let you," Brad solemnly pointed out, his brown eyes reflecting the sadness he felt for Brittany as he turned his head to watch her last frantic efforts to save the farm.

"Then I won't give her a choice," he replied, stooping to pick up Brad's blanket and dip it in the rain barrel. Wringing it out as he went, he jerked his head at Cory, silently telling her to leave with Brad, then moved to stand in Brittany's way. "There's nothing more you can do, Brittany," he said, grabbing her arm as she hurried past him for another bucket of water.

She yanked free of him. "Until all hope is gone," she reminded him. "That's what you said . . . you promised."

As if to defy her very claim, a sudden gust of wind swirled around the burning pile of hay and lifted large glowing ashes to the roof of the barn. The rest was sprinkled all around, and without waiting for her to admit there was no hope, Dane twirled the wet blanket over Brittany's head and shoulders to shield her from the shower of hot debris, then swooped her up in his arms.

"No!" she screamed, kicking and straining to get free of him. "Put me down! Dane, I beg you." Her demands turned to tearful pleas. "Just a little while longer. I know we could save the house if we tried."

Hugging her tightly to him, he turned with her in his arms and started down the road after his brother and Cory, carefully keeping an eye on the trees to one side of the lane. Many of them were already burning hotly, and there was the threat of one of the limbs snapping loose and falling on top of them as they hurried along. He wished he had the right words to say to her that would ease the torment she was going through, but he didn't. What could he possibly say? There was absolutely no chance of saving anything on the farm, and even if they managed to stop the fire from reaching the house, what good would it do her? The crops were destroyed and in a matter of weeks the creditors would demand the sale of her farmland as compensation for the loans they had given her. There wouldn't be enough left over for her to start again, much less afford a place to live. Maybe the Sons would help. After all, Roan was one of them, and the organization vowed to help its members whenever they needed it. The heartfelt sobs that shook the tiny body he held in his arms cut through him like a blast of cold winter wind. No one needed their help more than Brittany.

By the time they had reached the end of the lane which joined up with the road leading to Boston, they were a good distance away from the worst of the fire. Although the smell of smoke still hung heavily in the air, the sweet smell of rain was mixed with it, and the group paused in their flight to safety to stare up at the dark sky. Within seconds a bright flash seared the black, rolling clouds and seemed to split them in two. Huge drops of rain began to fall on them, and before long, everyone was soaking wet. What should have brought a smile to their faces seemed instead only to add to their frustration. Sliding his arm from under Brittany's knees, Dane gently deposited her feet on the ground, then stood back to watch her. She wasn't crying anymore, and he suspected it was because she hadn't any tears left to shed. Her fate had been decided for her, and there wasn't anything she could do to change it. She knew it. But acceptance wouldn't lessen her grief even a notch.

In silence, with her attention focused in the direction of home, Brittany blindly moved to a huge rock at the side of the road and numbly pulled the blanket from her shoulders as she slowly sank down. She felt as if someone had reached inside her and torn out her heart, then whipped her within an inch of her life. So much had happened to her over a course of a few months, she wondered what she had done that was so wrong to deserve all this. What frightened her was that she had no idea what she would do now. Closing her eyes, she raised her chin in the air and let the steadily pounding raindrops hit her face. Help had arrived too late to do any good, and she didn't have to return to the farm to know her house had been consumed in flames as well. All she had left in the world were the clothes on her back and the love of her brother.

An odd smile wrinkled one cheek. Roan's love wouldn't chase away the hunger or put a roof over her head. She couldn't survive on love alone. Dropping her head forward, the long, heavy strands of hair falling about her face, she couldn't resist the urge to laugh when she realized that even the Dark Horseman wouldn't know where to look for her after this. She'd lost her mother, her father, the spirited buck, Roan, her house, and all her belongings, as well as the one and only man she had ever cared about. Was there any reason left for her to go on living? Drained of all emotion, she slowly came to her feet and started back down the lane toward the house. She'd look upon her father's land once more before she made her last decision.

"Dane," Brad frowned, touching his brother's arm as he watched Brittany walk away from them, "where's she going?"

"Home," he said. "Or to what's left of it."

When Dane just stood there and didn't make a move to stop her, Brad took a step to follow, changed his mind, stopped in the middle of the road, and faced his brother again. "Why? It will only make it that much worse for her."

Reaching up, Dane pushed the wet hair off his brow and smiled softly. "It's something she has to do, the same way you had to visit Father's grave several times after he died. It was your way of accepting what happened. This is her way."

"But couldn't it wait until tomorrow? She's exhausted, and standing in this rain isn't the healthiest thing to do."

"Do you want to try and tell her that?" he grinned crookedly. "Look, why don't you and Cory see if you can round up my horse, if he hasn't hightailed it back to Boston by now, and wait for us at the Bunch of Grapes. I'll stay with Brittany and we'll meet you there later." It appeared that the fiercest part of the storm had already passed, and although it was still raining quite heavily, the wind had died down. "This shouldn't last much longer, but if it should, we'll find shelter somewhere and wait it out. Either way, don't worry about her. I'll see that she's taken good care of. Meanwhile, why not do the same for yourself?"

Brad was reluctant to leave. "Maybe we should stick together."

"So that I'd have two people to look out for instead of one?" Dane asked with a raised brow. "No, Brad. I'd feel much better knowing you're someplace dry and taking it easy. You've done more than your share already."

Brad glanced back down the road toward Brittany again, sighed, then nodded his head. "All right. But will you tell her how sorry I am? That I wish we could have done more?"

Reaching out, Dane squeezed his brother's shoulder. "I

think she already knows that, Brad. But I'll tell her anyway."

Brittany had walked a good distance ahead of him by the time Dane had seen Brad and Cory off and had started after her. His long strides easily brought him close enough to walk beside her, but he chose to stay a step or two behind. She needed the time alone with her thoughts. When she was ready to talk, he'd be there for her.

The ruination of the Lockwood farm was heartbreaking to see. Against a backdrop of ebony sky with bright flashes of light in the distance, the disfigured shapes of the buildings took on an eerie appearance. The roof of the stone house had collapsed and continued to smolder despite the rain, and Dane didn't have to rummage around inside to know everything Brittany owned had been destroyed. The barn had been partly spared, though Dane couldn't understand how that had happened. A section of its roof still stood and offered some shelter to them if he could talk her into using it. The trees in the yard and the first row surrounding the buildings were charred badly enough that he figured they wouldn't make it. As for the crops . . . well, nothing could be done to salvage even a small portion of them. But he doubted that was what Brittany was thinking about. Every keepsake, every token of her past had gone up in flames. All she had left were her memories.

Dane could sympathize with her. After their father died, he and Brad had talked at length about what they would do with their English estate. Although they had been happy living there as children, neither of them wanted to spend the rest of their lives there. They wanted to travel, and when their cousin Beau sent a letter inviting them to spend some time with him and his family on his Virginia plantation, the brothers decided to sell the estate and buy a ship. It wasn't until after they were halfway across the Atlantic that they realized they had broken all ties with home. It wasn't quite the same as Brittany's situation—hers hadn't been done out of choice—but they no longer could roam freely about the lands of their heritage either. Feeling her pain and deciding it was time she got in out of the rain, he slowly approached the place where she stood staring at the remains of the house.

"Brittany," he said softly. "Let's wait inside the barn for the rain to stop."

"It's gone. All of it," she murmured as if she hadn't heard his suggestion. "There's nothing left."

"Then we'll start again," he told her. "The land still belongs to you. If there's a way to rebuild, we'll find it."

An odd smile parted her lips. "And who will sell their goods to someone who can't pay for them? I already owe too many. They gave me credit on good faith, and I'm unable to pay them back. They'd be fools to extend my credit even more."

"And they'd have to be heartless to turn their backs on someone in your situation." He gently slipped his arm around her waist and guided her toward the barn and the remaining section which offered refuge from the downpour.

"Do you really think so?" Her voice sounded queer and childlike.

"Yes," he answered comfortingly.

One third of the structure had been left untouched by the fire once the storm broke loose, providing the couple with a dry place to sit. Pushing her gently down upon the pile of hay, Dane quickly glanced about the space for something to cover her with and espied a blanket folded neatly and lying in the one remaining stall, obviously having belonged to either Cory or his brother. Snatching it up, he whispered his thanks to whomever was responsible and returned to Brittany's side.

"Brittany," he called, waiting for her to look up at him. "I think you should get out of those wet things. I'll cover you with this." He nodded at the blanket he held.

As if in a trance, she stared straight ahead while she numbly loosened the buttons up the front of her dress. "Do you think Roan will be angry with me?"

"Roan?" he asked in surprise. "What about?"

"For not taking care of the farm the way I should have."

"Brittany," he moaned, "this wasn't your fault. You know that. And Roan would never blame you for it."

The soggy material was difficult for her to pull off. Taking her hands, Dane pulled her to her feet and helped her out of the dress and petticoats, then tossed the blanket over her shoulders and set her down again. Kneeling before her, he removed her shoes and stockings, then took the garments and draped them over the top rail in the stall. Having seen to her comfort for the moment, Dane kicked off his shoes, removed his stockings and his shirt, and hung them with Brittany's things before he came to sit beside her in the hay. She sat with her knees drawn up to her chin, her arms and the blanket hugged tightly around them as she stared silently out at the dark, misshapen figure of the house and the rain which continued to pour.

"What started the fire?" she quietly asked after a while.

He shrugged a wide shoulder and ran his fingers through his wet hair, pulling it back off his brow. "Lightning, probably. I've seen it happen before."

She was quiet for some time, long enough for Dane to wonder if she had heard his answer.

"Where?" she questioned, her concentration still focused away from him.

"Where what?" he frowned.

"Where have you seen it happen before?"

"Back home in England," he replied, bending his knees, his ankles crossed and his arms draped over them. "Lightning struck a tree near our stable, ran down the trunk and caught the grass on fire. It had spread to the building before anyone saw it."

"Did you lose the stable?"

"Yes. And several good stallions as well. I was only a boy at the time, but I still remember it—" He stopped suddenly, cursing his lack of foresight. She needed comforting, not

320

being told she would more than likely never forget what happened here tonight.

"Like it was only yesterday?" she finished, glancing over at him from the corner of her eye. "Tragedies like that can never be forgotten." She stared outside again. "Especially by a young boy." She sighed heavily, closed her eyes, and raised her chin in the air. "I know I'll never forget this."

Her thick golden hair hung in long, wet strands, and water dripped steadily from it. Shifting his weight to rest on one knee, the other bent beside her, Dane wrapped the heavy tresses in one corner of her blanket to dry them.

"I know what happened here is painful for you, Brittany, and that you're probably thinking you'll never get over it, but you will. You're a strong woman, and I'm sure you'll overcome it. I'm not a very religious man. There are times I doubt there is a God, but as my father told me that day the stable burned to the ground and I lost one of my favorite horses, God had a reason for letting this happen. It might seem cruel now and totally incomprehensible, but someday it will make sense."

She twisted slightly to look up at him. "Did it to you?"

Dane stared at her beautiful face and those fascinating gray eyes for a moment, realizing the absurdity of what he had claimed. "No," he grinned. "But it made me feel better at the time." Falling on one hip, he stretched out his long frame and propped himself up on one elbow. "And I always believed everything my father told me."

"Doesn't everyone?" she smiled lamely.

A silly smirk wrinkled his cheek as he picked up a piece of straw and twirled it between his thunb and finger. "Not everyone. Brad never believed Father. If the man told Brad the sky was blue, that fool would try to prove otherwise." The humor in his green eyes disappeared. "I think that's part of the reason Brad took his death so hard. Father told him he was dying and Brad wouldn't believe it."

"Maybe it has something to do with his being the second

child," she offered, finding comfort in their relaxed conversation. "I know Roan had a difficult time when Papa died. I think maybe a second child is pampered too much."

"I suppose," he agreed, waiting for another distant flash of light to illuminate the barn and enable him to see her face more clearly. Being so close to her made his heart beat a little faster and sparked the desire to pull her into his arms. He fought down the urge, certain she didn't feel the same, and sat up, deciding it was best they kept talking. It would get his mind off the things he'd prefer doing. "You've never mentioned your mother, Brittany. What happened to her?"

"She died of a fever when I was a little girl. I don't really remember that much about her except that when she died, I came here to the barn to cry."

"It must have been doubly hard on you," he commented tenderly. "A little girl left with only a brother and her father to talk to. Haven't there ever been any women in your life?" He tilted his head to better see her face when she dropped her gaze from him.

"No. I guess that's why Papa always teased me about doing the things a boy would do rather than behaving like a girl."

Dane straightened, truly interested in what she had to say. "Like what?"

"Oh, I don't know," she replied with a half-smile, feeling the blood rush to her cheeks. She hadn't meant to get so personal.

"Please, Brittany. I'd like to know."

She could hear the sincerity in his voice, and since there wasn't much else they could do now and because talking seemed to be relaxing her, she gave in. "Well," she began hesitantly, "I learned to ride a horse before I could peal potatoes. I preferred fishing with Roan to cooking supper. And I can't remember how old I was before I started wearing dresses instead of breeches."

"You're joking," Dane laughed. "One would hardly guess

it to look at you now."

Suddenly Brittany was very conscious of the way she was dressed, and that they were alone and sitting together on a pile of hay in nearly the same spot as the night he came to collect his fee for helping her brother. Nervous, she quickly stood up and pulled the blanket tightly around her.

"I think maybe it's time I went and found Roan," she said weakly.

"We will. But our clothes aren't dry yet," he answered, failing to recognize her reason for wanting to do so at this very moment. "Besides, it's still raining, and you don't know for sure where to look for him. I promise I'll help just as soon as it's light out and we don't have to trudge through the mud to do it." He patted the spot next to him on the hay. "Sit and rest awhile. Telling Roan about this won't change anything."

He was right, of course. Nothing she could say or do would restore the house and barn, and the exhaustion from all her efforts was beginning to take their toll. She would have preferred waiting alone—his presence always unnerved her—but after all his help in trying to put out the fire, he didn't deserve being sent out in the rain. Glancing over at the house, the muscles in her throat tightened again, and she bit her lower lip to still the renewal of tears as she silently told herself that her father would expect her to return Dane's kindness with gratitude. After all, he could have simply taken his horse and belongings and fled, rather than stay behind and risk his life the way he had. And he didn't have to be here now. Heaving a trembling sigh, she slowly sank back down on the hay.

"I didn't think I'd ever be asking someone this again," he grinned, "but are you warm?"

His attempt to humor her worked. "And I didn't think I'd ever be cold again, but I am," she admitted with a smile.

"Do you think I should start a fire?" The expression on his face was quite serious, but the devilish glint in his green eyes made her laugh.

"No. That's quite all right. I'd prefer being cold."

Dane quietly watched her settle herself on the mound of hay near him with her knees drawn up and her arms wrapped around them before he reached over to help readjust the coverlet lying across her shoulders. "It's good to hear you laugh, Brittany," he said. "I don't think I've ever heard it before."

"There hasn't been much reason lately. There isn't now, except it's better than letting this drive me crazy." Her soft gray eyes glanced over at him. "And until a few minutes ago, that's exactly what was happening to me." They stared at each other for a moment. "Thank you. For that, and for your help in fighting the fire. If you hadn't been here, I'd probably be lying in the rubble somewhere. I never have known when to quit . . . at anything."

"There's nothing wrong with that. If everyone was a quitter, the colonies would still be a wilderness."

A sudden gust of wind surprised them both as it swirled about the burnt-out cavity of the barn and brought cold droplets of rain with it to shower on the unsuspecting couple. Shrieking, Brittany scrambled to her feet with Dane's help as he quickly took her elbow and shielded her body from the assault with his own, backing them both further into the darkened recess of the barn.

"For weeks I've been praying it would rain," she laughed, "and now we get too much."

"And too late," he added, pulling the blanket back up over her shoulders. "I was only teasing before, but I'm beginning to think a campfire isn't such a bad idea." He shivered when a second chill wind hit him full across his bare shoulders and raced down his spine. Clasping his arms, he rubbed them vigorously as he glanced over at their garments hanging on the rail. "At least my shirt would dry a little faster."

With each flash of lightning in the distance, his tall, muscular build was silhouetted in the platinum brilliance of the ebony sky for only an instant. But it was long enough to

324

flood Brittany's senses with a mystical desire to touch him, to trace her fingertips along the hardened expanse of his chest and shoulders, to press her lips to his throat, to breathe in the masculine scent of him. The nearness of him, his male prowess excited every nerve in her body and tingled her flesh. Her desire to feel his iron-threwed strength molded against her slender frame was overpowering. Her lips were suddenly dry. Her heart beat loudly in her chest, and her arms ached to hold him. Feeling weak and blaming it on the intoxicating effect he radiated, she closed her eyes and drew in a long, calming breath.

"Brittany," his deep, rich voice called out to her as if in a dream, "are you all right?"

She nodded, yet she wasn't sure if her head had actually moved. She tried to speak, but the words fell lazily across her tongue. What was it about this man that could so easily melt down her defenses? He was a rogue, a traitor, a man she should despise, yet his tenderness and the warmth of understanding and compassion glowing in his eyes attracted her to him like a beguiled moth to a flame. Suddenly his hands were on her shoulders pulling her within the circle of his arms.

Dane had misread Brittany's silence. He had thought that the events of the past few hours had finally hit her, that her soft, tender nature could no longer deal with them, and that all she wanted right now was to be comforted. He had no idea what sensations were going through her mind and body when he gently laid a hand on the side of her head and tenderly forced her to rest her cheek against his chest. He meant to soothe her, to drive away the hurt and pain her loss aroused. Instead, he was unknowingly clouding her thoughts with the stirring passion of a woman. He was ignorant of it all, until her arms came around him, and she lifted her face to look at him. Lightning seared the sky, illuminating the delicate sculpture of her cheek and chin, the grayness of her eyes, and the soft, parted lips begging to be kissed.

"Brittany," he whispered.

Dane no longer felt the chill of the early summer rain or heard it beating steadily against the roof of the barn. He didn't even notice that it had seemed to increase its fury or that the lightning flashed all around them. He was simply too caught up in the turbulent emotions which sent his mind, heart, and passion soaring. He knew that Brittany was extremely vulnerable at this moment, and that he should back away. He shouldn't take advantage of her weakness, for he realized it wasn't him she clung to, but his strength, his compassion, the simple fact that he was here holding her in his arms when there was no one else to turn to. He knew that, but he couldn't bring himself to step away.

Damn the consequences, his mind called out. Tonight she would be his no matter what the reasons.

Locking his fingers in the thick mass of hair at the nape of her neck, he slid his other arm around her narrow waist and pulled her full against him, her firm, round breasts crushed against his bare chest. Their lips met in a fiery urgency that neither of them could prevent nor had the desire to stop. Right or wrong, shameful or glorious, they would share their feelings of the moment, drink in each other's passion, bask in the golden brilliance of their rapture, and then decide. Slanting his mouth across hers, he forced her lips apart and pushed his tongue inside while his hand roamed down her spine to her buttocks, up her hip and waist, then on to cup one breast in his hand. He was only slightly aware of Brittany's touch as her fingers glided over the sinewy ripples in his back, across his waist and lean stomach to the fastenings on his breeches. Then, in the heat of passion, he yanked downward on the golden tresses entwined around his fingers, bringing up her chin to trace hot kisses down the long, slim column of her throat, while his fingers tore at the strings on her camisole. In the next instant, fevered flesh met full length, lips clung frantically, tongues clashed, and hands

326

explored the expanse of naked, trembling bodies. Together they knelt, then stretched out on the bed of straw, no other thoughts clouding their minds except the delirious enchantment of fusing their two souls as one.

The urgency of his desires bade him to hurriedly take her, while in the same instant he wanted this moment to last an eternity, for even though his mind was filled with rapturous bliss and the unbelievable knowledge that this was what she wanted as well, somewhere deep within him he feared it would be their last time together. His thoughts raced with ways to keep her by his side while his hands glided along the silky curve of her waist, hip, and thigh. His breathing quickened as did his caresses. His fingers trailed a burning path along the inside of her creamy white leg to the soft flesh of her womanhood while his tongue sought the sweetness of her mouth. He thrived on the splendor of her willingness, her passion, the way she clung to him and moved in response to his touch.

Brittany's entire being was set aflame by the gentle probing of his fingers, the sweet intrusion of his tongue, and the feel of his naked, rock-hard body pressed full against her. Her passion mounted while the manly scent of him set her mind reeling. She felt no shame, no guilt for what they did. If anything, a glimmer of long-denied love sparked the elusive flame in her heart and quickly filled her with a growing warmth while at the same time it confused her. Was she fickle to give herself to this man so freely while a gnawing in her conscious repeated the pledge to another? His lips moved along the slim column of her throat and she moaned deliriously as she locked her fingers in the thick mass of dark hair and drew his mouth to the peak of her hardened nipple. Then, in a blaze of unsatiable desire, he sensed her need when she parted her thighs to welcome him, and as he raised above her and shifted his weight, she encircled his neck with her arms and pulled him down, arching her hips to eagerly meet his first thrust.

Outside the burnt-out barn the storm raged on. The swirling black clouds were split asunder by a flash of white light that kinked its way earthward to set the countryside aglow. Rain pelted the ground with cold, stinging droplets. The howling wind whipped the trees and shrubs about and filled the air with an eerie foreboding of doom. Yet for all its fury, it failed to compare with the tempest going on inside the shelter which stood rigidly defiant against its wrath.

Chapter Thirteen

Huddled in a blanket draped around her slender frame, her eyes filled with tears, Brittany stood near the edge of the barn watching the ever-brightening glow of sunrise staining the eastern sky. For the first time in weeks, the morning dawned cool and crisp and smelling of rain. The storm had long since passed, but in its wake it had left a vivid reminder of how late it had come. Blackened trees, their limbs charred and barren, stretched upward toward the azure sky as if to mock the serenity of daybreak. A blanket of ebony ash spread as far as the eye could see. But the dismal scenery was not the reason for Brittany's tears. Sometime while she slept, Dane had risen noiselessly, donned his clothes, and left her.

As she thought about what happened only a few short hours ago, she suddenly realized how reckless and totally uninhibited she had been. Her wanton desires for a man she had assumed she hated had overruled all sense of reasoning she might have had, and she could only blame it on her need to have someone, anyone hold her, comfort her, console her during her time of grief. Yet what troubled her more than anything was the simple fact that until she woke to find him gone, she hadn't felt the tiniest bit of guilt or shame. Now, however, those two very strong, very powerful emotions were tearing her apart. How could she have allowed herself to be drawn to Dane Remington when only a short time earlier she had met the Dark Horseman in the meadow, given herself to him, pleaded her loyalty and devotion until her dying day? And what about the Dark Horseman? She fancied herself in love with him and she hardly even knew him! He had never come courting. They hadn't gone for a carriage ride or a picnic along the shore. She didn't even know his name!

A sob shook her fragile body and she bit her lip to keep from crying. And what must Dane think of her? Was it any worse than what she thought? In the course of one night, she had made love to two men! One she loved, and one she hated. Or did she? A tear stole its way down her cheek, and she quickly brushed it away. Perhaps she was only infatuated with the mystique surrounding the handsome stranger who kept his identity a secret, rode a black stallion, and showed an ounce of kindness for her. Maybe *he* was the one who took advantage of her, not Dane. After all, what had Dane truly done to her that was so bad, so evil that he deserved her hatred? He had only collected the payment *they* had agreed upon for his help in freeing Roan. He might not have been totally honest with her at first, but why should he have been? Who was she to him but a stranger, and a foolish one at that? Then, when she needed help with the farm, who came to offer his assistance? The Dark Horseman? No. It was Dane.

He didn't have to come. She knew that, and she wondered now if it had been because he felt guilty over what he had done. And as for her accusations about his involvement with the men in the woods—well, she didn't really have any proof. She was treating him the way the Crown had treated Roan—guilty without a trial. Then there was the fire and his pledge to help her rebuild. He had done for her the things any other woman would have thanked him for. But not her, not Brittany Lockwood. She had done everything in her power to drive him away. Her chin trembled and she lifted her eyes

330

to study the cloudless blue sky above her. And she had succeeded.

From somewhere in the distance, a sparrow called its early morning overture and drew Brittany's attention to the road leading away from the farm. How long ago had he walked that very lane? What thoughts were going through his head? Was he laughing at her? Or perhaps had he decided they could never be together because they came from two very different worlds? She wanted to believe the latter. She wanted to convince herself that he had chosen to leave not because he *didn't* love her, but because he *did*. A frown creased her brow, and she spun angrily away from the scene spread out before her.

You're a fool if you think that, Brittany Lockwood! she silently scolded herself as she hurried to retrieve her clothes from the rail. Why should he love you? What have you done to deserve it?

The distant sound of carriage wheels, horse's hooves, and the jingling of harness straps warned Brittany that she was about to have company. Jerking on her camisole and stockings, then wiggling into her dress, she quickly buttoned up the bodice, stepped into her shoes, and moved out into the bright sunlight to greet her visitor with a puzzled frown marring her lovely brow. She seldom had guests and never did they arrive in such an elegant coach as this. It took her a moment to figure out who it might be, but before the driver had brought the rig to a halt and jumped down to open the door for its passenger, Brittany concluded it could be none other than Miles Ingram. She would have preferred seeing Roan ride up the lane, but oddly enough she took solace in knowing that at least a friend had arrived to comfort her. Lifting her skirts slightly to avoid soiling the hemline in the mud puddles, she started toward the carriage.

Miles's thin face was pinched in a mortified expression as he stepped down from the coach and stood staring at the burnt-out remains of the house. He felt sick inside. He had only meant for the man he had hired to set fire to the crops, not destroy everything on the Lockwood farm. And certainly not chance putting Brittany in any danger! He would hear about this. In fact, Miles didn't intend to pay him. If he was lucky, the fool might escape with his life!

"Oh, Brittany," he moaned, coming to meet her with hands extended, "I'm so sorry. Are you all right?"

"Yes," she nodded, allowing him to gently put his arm around her and drew her back toward the carriage.

"I could hardly believe my eyes this morning when the coach passed by your place and I saw the blackened fields. I never dreamt it had gone this far." He reached and opened the door. "Now I'll hear no arguments from you. You're to come home with me, have something to eat, a bath, if you like, and a long nap. I want you to spend a few days with Father and me. Then we'll decide what to do."

The thought of actually leaving her home—even though there was truly nothing left which resembled a house—made a knot form in her throat. Swallowing hard, she smiled weakly and glanced over her shoulder at the ruins. She realized that it was impossible for her to stay here. She had no change of clothes, the well had been destroyed by the huge tree which had fallen on it, there was no food, and the cow and ox were gone. Maybe if Roan was here they could figure out what to do. But he wasn't, and she had no idea how long it would be before word of their tragedy reached him. Her gaze shifted to the lane. Dane had obviously changed his mind about helping. But then, what else had she truly expected of him?

"Only for a day or two," she agreed, turning back to him. "But I won't stay any longer."

"You'll stay as long as it takes," Miles corrected. "And if you won't listen to me, then I'll have Father convince you." Smiling softly, he extended one hand toward the carriage and put the other under her elbow to help her ascend. Once she was comfortably inside, he looked back at the dull, colorless remains of the Lockwood farm and frowned angrily. Yes, that cretin would pay dearly for his stupidity! Motioning to the driver, Miles climbed in the carriage, closed the door behind him, and took a seat opposite his lady love.

The fancy black rig swung around and headed back down the lane in grand style with its high-prancing mare, gold-plated family crest on the door, and brass lanterns marking the wealth involved in owning such a carriage. But to the one who viewed its departure, the sight of it only instilled anger and pain, and once it had passed by the spot where Dane had moved into the cover of trees, he slowly stepped out into the open to watch it wind its way down the lane and then disappear around the bend.

"Brad!"

The frantic sound of his name upon Dooley's lips startled Brad out of a sound sleep. He bolted and sat upright in the middle of his bed, rubbing his eyes and wincing from the stiffness he felt in every muscle of his body, especially in his shoulder.

"What is it? Is something wrong?" He peered over at the window to confirm that he had slept through the night.

"It's the cap'n."

Brad's head swung back around to stare at the midget. "Dane? What about him? Is he hurt?" Before Dooley could answer, Brad threw his legs over the edge of the bed and reached for his breeches, which were draped over the back of the chair where he had laid them the night before.

"Not so you'd notice," Dooley replied, plucking Brad's shirt off the bedpost and handing it to him.

"What's that suppose to mean?"

"He ain't got any visible wounds, but to look at him, he's suffering from something."

"Is Miss Lockwood with him?"

Dooley shook his head. "He came in alone about a half-hour ago, took his usual place in the back of the room, and ordered a mug of ale. Been drinkin' steadily ever since."

"Did you try to talk to him?" Brad asked, sitting down to pull on his stockings and shoes.

"Are you serious?" Dooley's brows wrinkled together as he straightened his tiny frame. "I didn't go hear him once I saw that look in his eyes. He don't want to talk to anybody. That's why I came after you. You're the only one I know of who wouldn't get their head blown off for trying."

Brad rolled his eyes. "You're probably right on that." Rising, he stuffed his shirttail into his waistband and headed for the door. "And while I find out what's wrong, why don't you order us some breakfast. I sincerely doubt my brother's had anything to eat lately."

"All right," Dooley concurred, following his friend into the hall. "You got any idea what's bothering him?"

"More like who," Brad corrected. "What I don't know is why."

"Miss Lockwood?"

Brad nodded and started down the stairs. "It's a good guess, anyway."

"You mean you think the cap'n's smitten with her?" Dooley observed as he clasped the handrail to steady his awkward descent down the steps behind Brad.

Stopping midway, he looked back at the midget. "Yeah. But keep it between you and me, all right? I'm not sure Dane's aware of it yet, and we don't want to go and ruin anything."

"Oh, I won't tell anyone," Dooley guaranteed him. "But isn't this the same lady the cap'n thinks is smuggling?"

Brad heaved a long sigh, then nodded his head. "And the same lady whose brother is one of us. That's why I find it very hard to believe."

"Want me and Betts to do some snoopin' around? To see what we can turn up?"

"Might not be a bad idea. Just don't let Dane know about it." Bending slightly to peer down at his brother sitting in the far corner, Brad added, "And whatever you find out, tell me about it first. I'll decide whether or not to let Dane in on it."

"It's a deal," Dooley agreed. "I'll see about your breakfast first, then find Betts and be on my way."

Slouched in a tall chair, his legs stretched out in front of him and propped up on a bench, Dane's dark green eyes were shaded by a fierce frown, his mug of ale gripped in both hands and resting on his stomach as he stared out across the room. The place was relatively empty for so early in the morning, but he hadn't really noticed. All he cared about at the moment was that the barmaid continually refilled his cup whenever he drained it. He was in no mood for conversation and preferred the tavern stay the way it was until he passed out from too much ale. Raising the pewter mug to his lips, he took a long drink, settled it back on his stomach, and resumed his black scrutiny of the wall on the other side of the room, unaware of the tall figure who approached, pulled out a chair from the table, and sat down near him.

"Want to talk about it?" Brad asked after a while.

Dane's emerald green eyes moved to scowl at his brother, then returned to study the dark wood graining in the wall again.

"You plan to drown whatever it is that's bothering you?" Brad ventured further when several minutes of silence passed.

Long, lean fingers raised the pewter mug high and tipped the bottom in the air to pour a goodly amount of the brew in Dane's mouth. "Leave me alone, Brad," came the deep, gutteral reply.

"You'd like that, wouldn't you?" the brother snapped in return. "You'd like to sit here all alone and drink yourself numb so you could forget about what's troubling you, rather than standing sober on your own two feet and doing something to correct it."

335

The muscle in his cheek flexed. "Yes. I would." Dane turned his head to look at Brad. "Now will you leave me alone?"

"It's Brittany, isn't it?" Brad rushed on. "You're upset because she wouldn't come here with you."

Dane's nostrils flared as he inhaled an angry breath. "Not exactly." He finished off the ale and motioned for the barmaid to bring him another, ignoring his brother's disapproving scowl.

"Then what is it, exactly?"

Reaching out, Dane slammed the empty mug on the table. "Something I'd prefer keeping to myself," he snarled. "Why don't you go find yourself a willing little whore, take her to your room, and engage in what you do best? And leave me the hell alone!"

"I could," Brad rallied, knowing it was only the ale that had made Dane explode like that. "But I'm not going to. I'm your brother, for God's sake. I care about you. When you hurt, I hurt. If I can help stop the pain, I will. But I'll be damned if I'll walk away!"

The barmaid sheepishly approached the table with a new mug of ale, and when she started to hand it to Dane, Brad catapulted from his chair, grabbed the mug, and flung it away. The sound of pewter crashing against wood startled everyone in the place, and they all stared at the quarreling brothers, eyes wide and mouths agape. Angered by the waste of good ale, Dane dropped his feet to the floor and sat up, his mouth pressed into a hard line, his brow furrowed, and his hands knotted into fists. But Brad didn't feel the least bit threatened. Leaning forward with his hands braced on the table separating him from Dane, Brad returned the other's angry glare with one of his own.

"You want to fight? Is that what you want?" he challenged. "Or are you thinking to scare me off the way you always did when we were boys? Well, I'm not backing off. Not this time. And I'm not leaving you alone until you tell me what's bothering you!"

Dane's anger waned. "And then what? After I tell you what's upset me, then what? Are you going to tell me how sorry you are, that you wish you could do something to change it, but you can't? Well, I'll save you the trouble. You can't. No one can. Not even Brittany!"

Pushing himself up from the chair, Dane started around the table, lost his balance, and staggered into it, and then in a rage shoved the huge trestle table out of the way. Storming the bar and the barrel of ale sitting behind it, Dane grabbed another mug from the shelf in back of it and filled his own when the innkeeper shrank away in fear.

"At least give me a chance to try," Brad argued, following his brother across the room. "Tell me what happened. It might not be as bad as you think."

"Ha!" Dane exploded, carrying his drink to the fireplace, where he stood before the cold hearth and contemplated its darkness. "How could it get any worse?" Wanting very desperately to ease the ache in his heart, he lifted the mug to his lips and drank nearly half its contents in one long swallow. But all he succeeded in doing was making his head spin, and he closed his eyes in an effort to stop his reeling world, sensing more than knowing his brother had come to stand beside him. "I do love her, Brad," he said in hardly more than a whisper. "For the first time in my life, I've fallen in love. What I felt for Audrey wasn't the same. I was hardly more than a boy then. I cared about her, but I really didn't love her. It's different with Brittany." He laughed sarcastically at some secret thought, set his mug on the mantel, and gripped the thick piece of wood with both hands, his arms widespread and his head falling forward between them.

Realizing Dane's confession and frustrations were meant to be private, Brad glanced back at the customers who still watched, spotted Dooley coming from the kitchen, and motioned for him to escort everyone outside. Once the place was empty, he turned his attention back on his brother.

337

"But she doesn't love you?" he guessed.

Dane shook his head and laughed again. "Well, that's the hard part, little brother. She does, but she doesn't." Smiling at Brad, he then turned away from him, went to the nearest table and sat down on it, his feet propped on the bench in front of him, knees bent and elbows resting on them as he stared over at the bright sunlight seeping in through the leaded glass windows of the inn. "Remember your suggestion to prove Brittany didn't love the Dark Horseman while at the same time convincing myself of her innocence regarding the smuggling operation?"

"Yes," Brad replied, taking a like position on the table beside him.

"Well, I might have laughed when you told me about it, but later I changed my mind. I wrote her a note asking her to meet me in the meadow, signed it "the Dark Horseman," and left it in the house for her to find."

Brad suddenly understood. "And she came."

"Uh-huh. Within minutes. She made love to him. To the Dark Horseman, Brad, not Dane Remington. And would you like to know where she is now?" Emerald eyes mirroring his pain glanced over at Brad. "She's with Miles Ingram."

"What?" he breathed. "I don't believe it."

"I wouldn't have either if I hadn't seen it for myself." He reached over and tapped Brad's knee for emphasis. "But believe it, little brother. It's true."

"You mean you've actually seen them together? Where? When?"

Dane rarely told anyone how he felt. There were many incidents he had kept secret from his own brother. His affairs with women were among the more important ones, and he preferred not telling him about what went on in the barn after he'd followed Brittany back home last night. But of all the people who deserved to know the truth, Brad was at the top of the list. As best he could, he related all the events, all his feelings and suspicions about their little rendezvous,

338

praying Brad would see it differently than he had, that Brad had some other reason to explain why Brittany had ridden off with Miles Ingram a few hours ago.

Brad felt as if an entire forest had fallen down on him once Dane finished his story and sat rubbing his forehead. Now he understood Dane's need to get drunk, and if it wasn't so early in the morning, he'd join him. Yet, beneath it all, Brad had to believe there was a logical explanation for Brittany's actions.

"Dane," he began softly, hoping his brother would be willing to listen, "can we discuss this? Maybe between the two of us we can find the real answer."

"Other than the obvious?"

"And how many times have we ignored the obvious to find the truth? What's on the surface isn't always the truth. If that was the rule, we never would have grown suspicious of Ingram. After all, his father works for the Crown. Smuggling English goods isn't exactly in keeping with British authority." He shifted around on the table to look directly at his brother. "Let's start with Brittany's infatuation with the Dark Horseman. Let's say she truly loves him—though I can't see how, when she's only been with him a couple of times. Hardly enough for a solid foundation, but we'll give her the benefit of the doubt. Now if she's working with Ingram, you'd think she'd stay as far away from someone like the Dark Horseman as possible."

"So she isn't too bright," Dane interjected dolefully.

"Wrong, big brother. I say it's because she has nothing to hide."

Dane gave him a dubious look. "Then why did she leave with Miles?"

"Why shouldn't she? Where were you? Where were any of us? You said you told her that you'd take her to Boston to find her brother, then you disappeared. What do you suppose she took that to mean?"

Dane was beginning to understand what Brad was getting at, but it wasn't enough to persuade him. "That I changed my mind."

"Exactly."

"But I hadn't. I just went for a walk to think things out. I was coming back to her to tell her the truth about me."

"How was she to know that? You weren't anywhere around. And Miles Ingram was. More than likely he insisted she come home with him until something could be done about her predicament, and she couldn't see where she had a choice. Now doesn't that make sense?"

Dane shrugged a wide shoulder. "I suppose. But it doesn't explain how she could love one man and fall into the arms of another."

"Listen to you," Brad admonished. "You're talking like there are two men. There aren't. He's one in the same. He's you! Brittany is in love with you. She just hasn't come to realize it yet because you won't let her."

"You're wrong there, Brad," Dane disagreed, shaking his head and pushing himself up from the table to return to the hearth and his mug of ale. "If I told her I was the Dark Horseman, she'd be furious as hell."

"At first, maybe," Brad relented, leaving the table to stand by his brother. "It would be expected. Who wouldn't be when they'd been tricked so completely? But after a while, I'm sure she'd give in to her real feelings about you."

Dane took a sip of his ale, then stared down at the amber brew he twirled around in the mug. "I'd like to believe that," he said after a moment, "but I can't."

"Why? Because you're afraid I'm wrong?" Brad challenged softly.

A vague smile lifted one corner of Dane's mouth, but he wouldn't voice his opinion.

"Then let's find out for sure," his brother suggested. "What have you got to lose? If I'm wrong, and Brittany never wants to see you again, then you'd be no better off than you are right now. But if I'm not, you'll have more important things to do with your time than standing here drinking ale

340

with the likes of me."

Dane had to admit Brad had a point. If the Dark Horseman revealed his identity to her, she would either slap his face and walk away or fall into his arms. He had a fifty-fifty chance. "All right," he said after a moment, "suppose I agree. How do you propose I go about it? I can't very well ride up to Ingram's front door and ask to speak to her."

Grinning broadly Brad said, "Leave that up to me."

In the week that followed Brittany's arrival at the Ingram estate, Miles and his father, Bartholomew, had kept her so busy that she lost track of time. The elder Ingram had been thrilled with the idea of having a beautiful young woman gracing the halls of the manor again; his wife had died some years back and they had never been blessed with a daughter. Brittany's presence added the feminine touch he had dearly missed since Margaret passed on, and gave him the excuse to spend his money on his favorite pastime: showering a lady with gifts. It started with richly tailored gowns, lacy undergarments, shoes, hats, and elegantly coiffed wigs, and went on to pearl earrings and a diamond necklace. Brittany had repeatedly told the older man that she didn't need so many nice things, that a cotton dress or two would be enough, but when he presented her with the gems, she flatly refused.

"This is too much, Mr. Ingram," she told him one bright, sunny morning when the three of them sat around the long, formal dining table having breakfast. "I can't take this."

"And why not?" the older gentleman beamed. "A beauty such as yours demands a complimentary trinket or two."

"Because you've given me too much already," she continued, her gaze locked on the black velvet box and the stunning necklace it held. "I could never pay you back for this. I'm not sure how I'll manage to repay you for all the nice clothes you've already given me."

341

"Repay?" he echoed, his fluffy white brows arched in surprise. "My dear, Miles and I didn't give you the dresses and things thinking to be repaid. They're gifts." Leaning forward, he reached out to touch her hand when she started to object. "Brittany, I'm not sure if your father ever talked to you about our friendship, strange as it might have seemed to everyone else, but I truly admired, respected, and *liked* your father. He was a proud man, too proud to take a loan from me when he needed it most. I guess that's why I thought so much of him. Now he's gone and his daughter needs my help. Maybe he wouldn't accept my assistance, but I refuse to believe he wouldn't approve of my taking you in and caring for you."

"Until I can do it on my own," she corrected.

"Until you can do it on your own," he relented with a smile. "But in the meantime, why not enjoy all the things Miles and I can do for you? Patrick wouldn't frown on it, I'm sure. Especially since you've lost everything you owned."

"Except for her property, Father," Miles cut in.

A sadness darkened Brittany's eyes as she snapped the lid shut on the box. "A lot of good that is. All the crops were destroyed. The only way it would be of much value would be if I sold it."

The two men exchanged glances. "It's something you should consider, my dear," Bartholomew encouraged. "I'd give you a very handsome amount—more than it's worth."

It was quite easy to see where Miles got his looks. He was the image of his father, except that Bartholomew's face had deeper lines around his eyes and mouth. Neither man was very tall, both were thin to a fault, and what they lacked in handsomeness they made up for in style: clothing, good manners, and generosity. Brittany couldn't think of another person in all of Boston who would have eagerly done half as much for her as these two. But selling her father's land wouldn't solve her problems. Just needing money to support herself was the least of her heartache.

"It's very kind of you, Mr. Ingram," she smiled. "But I'm really not interested in selling the farm. It's my home. It always has been, and I can't imagine living anywhere else. Besides, I have no skills to support myself. Once the money ran out, I'd be right back where I started."

"I can appreciate your concern, Brittany," he admitted. "But I sincerely doubt that a beautiful woman such as you will remain single for very long." He settled back in his chair, chuckling. "Why, if I wasn't old enough to be your father, I'd court you myself." He glanced over at his son with a mischievous gleam in his eyes. "How would you like having a stepmother younger than you, Miles?"

"I never intend to find out, Father," he laughed. "Before I'd let that happen, I'd give you a good fight for her hand."

Bartholomew guffawed good-naturedly. "And listen to you. You sound as if I'd be your only competition. If courting Brittany is your intention, son, I suggest you get to it. Once word of her availability reaches our circle of friends, you'll have more rivalry than you can handle."

"I have little doubt of that, Father," he smiled, then glanced at Brittany and winked. "I simply meant I wouldn't stand aside and let an old scoundrel like you have free rein."

"Old scoundrel!" Bartholomew parroted. "Why I'll have you know there's more kick left in me than a newborn colt. Old scoundrel, indeed!"

Their playful bantering was interrupted when the butler suddenly appeared in the doorway, something Brittany greatly appreciated. The conversation, whether in jest or earnestly meant, embarrassed her. It also reminded her that only a short week ago she would have accepted Dane's proposal, had he asked.

"What is it, Jonathan?" Bartholomew asked.

"A message arrived, sir, for your son."

"Well, bring it in," the eldest instructed before reaching for the pot of tea and asking if his houseguest would like a refill.

343

Nodding, Brittany watched Bartholomew pour the light brown liquid into her cup while Miles took the note Jonathan handed him and opened it. A troubled frown wrinkled his pale brow when he had read it, and then, as if he preferred the others sitting around the table not learn of what was written on the parchment, he quickly folded the paper and tucked it inside his waistcoat.

"Thank you, Jonathan," he said, quietly dismissing the servant before lifting his own cup of tea from its saucer. Raising it to his lips, he spotted his father's curious look from over the rim.

"Distressing news, son?" he asked.

Miles took a sip of tea, then set the cup back down and sighed heavily. The arrival of Millicent's request for a meeting in one hour couldn't have come at a better time. By pretending the latter was sent by someone else, he could lie about its contents, and neither of the two watching him right now would suspect otherwise. But more importantly, he could poison Brittany's feelings toward Dane Remington. It had only taken Miles a day or two to realize Brittany cared about the rogue more than she wanted to admit. He couldn't quite say why exactly, only that her grief seemed too intense to be directed solely over the loss of her farm and belongings. She behaved like a woman pining for her lost lover. Several times he had caught her staring out the window in the parlor with a faraway look in her eye.

When a business associate of his father's had knocked on the door, Miles had found Brittany at the top of the stairs with a hopeful expression brightening her face until the identity of the visitor was known, and then she'd turned around to go back to her room, her shoulders drooping, head bowed and a sadness in her step. It didn't take an educated man to figure out who she had hoped had come calling. The little fool had fallen in love with Dane Remington, and Miles had to do something to change that if he hoped to ever win her heart.

"A few weeks back, Brittany came to me about the man she had hired to help with the farm work," he began, "because she suspected he was smuggling goods across her property."

Bartholomew straightened in his chair, one white brow cocked.

"I promised her that I wouldn't tell anyone about her suspicions until she had proof." He shifted his attention to Brittany's startled face. "I apologize for not keeping my word, Brittany, but once you've heard what I have to say, you'll understand why." He set his attention back on his father. "I hired some men to do some snooping around and find out what they could about Dane Remington."

"Dane Remington," Bartholomew repeated thoughtfully. "I've heard that name before, but I can't say where."

"He's just one of the riffraff that hangs around Long Wharf, a pirate, I believe, and one who uses women to his advantage." He knew his statement had probably hurt Brittany, but it had to be said if his plan was to work. "This note"—he patted his side—"confirms what I thought about him. He wiled his way onto Brittany's farm by offering to help with the work as a cover for his real reason for being there. He had planned to use her property to carry goods off his ship."

"Then we should send someone over there to catch him," Bartholomew proclaimed as he wadded up his napkin, tossed it on the table beside his plate, and started to rise. "I'll send Jonathan to see the governor."

Miles raised a hand to stop him. "It's too late, Father. Remington and his crew have left Boston."

"Do your informants know where he's headed?"

"Probably back out to sea where they can steal another shipload of goods to sell. But it doesn't matter. He knows we're on to him. I doubt he'll ever drop anchor in Boston Harbor again."

Brittany wasn't aware whether Bartholomew agreed with

345

his son's observation or not. She was too busy trying to hide the anguish which tore at her heart. Everything Miles had said fit perfectly into place. Dane had only used her to get what he wanted, and she had unknowingly helped him. As for him dropping anchor in Boston again—she doubted it, too. Dane had finished what he'd come here to do. There was no reason for him ever to return. Blinking back her tears, she neatly folded her napkin, laid it on the table, and rose.

"If you'll excuse me," she said softly, "I'd like to go to my room and lie down for a while. I'm not feeling well."

Bartholomew quickly came to her side and took her arm. "Is there something I can have Anna bring you?"

"No, thank you," she replied, forcing a smile. "It's just a headache. I'll be fine after I rest."

"I hope our conversation hasn't upset you," he continued as he escorted her to the door. "It was rather insensitive of us to rattle on like that in front of you as if you weren't even there. I apologize."

"There's no need, Mr. Ingram," she assured him, stopping at the threshold of the dining room. "As Miles said, I had already guessed something illegal was going on. I just didn't know what and had no way of proving it. If anything, I'm pleased to know I was right." She paused a moment to swallow the knot in her throat. "It's just a shame I'll never see him pay for . . . for what he's done."

"Now don't go feeling badly about it," Bartholomew comforted. "Everyone at one time or another gets caught with their guard down. Why, it's even happened to me a time or two. You feel foolish at first, but afterward you're stronger for it." He smiled sympathetically. "And the wiser."

"Oh, I'm the wiser for it. That's for certain," she admitted. "It will be a long time before I trust a man again."

"Surely you're not including me?" he frowned, his white complexion paling all the more at the thought.

"No, Mr. Ingram," she smiled warmly. "That doesn't include you or Miles. I was referring to strangers." And

Dane Remington, she thought acidly. "Now if you'll excuse me. . . ."

"Of course, my dear," Bartholomew consented, walking her into the hall and failing to see the pleased smile on his son's face as Miles watched the couple head for the stairs.

Brittany didn't have a headache, and lying down was the last thing she wanted to do. She would have preferred exchanging the fancy silk gown she wore for a dress more suitable for riding. She wanted to borrow a horse and take him deep into the woods where she could be alone. But in order to do that, she'd have to explain why, and she never wanted to admit to anyone how deeply she hurt and who was the cause.

The room she had been given faced east, the direction of the Lockwood farm. Its French doors were ajar, and a soft, fragrant breeze was spilling through them when she stepped into the chamber and closed herself in. The sweet smell of jasmine filled the air, luring her to the balcony, and as she stood beside the railing staring out at the bright clear sky, a rush of tears flooded her eyes, burned her throat, and made her chin tremble. In a matter of weeks, her entire world had crumbled around her, and she couldn't stop the feeling that she had no one to blame but herself.

Even her father's death could have been prevented if she had had the alertness of mind to insist he take his rifle with him that day. Roan never would have wound up in gaol if she had taken her responsibility as the head of the household seriously and demanded that he stay home where he belonged rather than traipsing off to Boston to join the other foolhardy protesters. And if she had, she never would have met Brad Remington or gone off looking for his brother. She wouldn't have been in town that day to witness the silversmith's escape from execution, been stopped by the soldiers on her way back home, or rescued by the Dark Horseman. Roan wouldn't have run away, she wouldn't have needed help with the farm, Dane wouldn't have had an excuse to be on her property, and they never would have found themselves locked in each other's arms there in the hay. Nothing would have prevented the fire which destroyed the crops and all of the buildings on her farm, but had all the rest been avoided, she still very well might be standing here on this balcony as she was right now. The difference, however, would have been that the tears which raced down her cheeks and the sobs which shook her delicate body would have been an expression of her grief over losing the farm, not because of the betrayal and humiliation she was suffering because of her foolishness. And what tore at her insides more than any of it was her wanton behavior with not just Dane, but the Dark Horseman as well, a man whose identity she didn't even know. Suddenly the sweet smell of flowers, the crisp, cool breeze, and the crystal-clear blue sky turned dark and ugly. Pressing both hands over her mouth, she turned away from the serene beauty of the morning, ran back inside, and threw herself across the bed, there to weep hard and long until exhaustion claimed her and she fell into a restless slumber.

Brittany had no idea how long she had been asleep or what it was that woke her. Sitting up abruptly on the bed, she quickly scanned the room to convince herself that she was still alone, her door shut, her secret safe from inquisitive minds. How could she explain the reasons for her tears when she wasn't truly sure of them herself? She was feeling quite the fool for having allowed herself to be so easily deceived, yet somewhere in the back of her mind she honestly didn't want to accept the possibility that it was true.

She wanted to believe that Dane cared about her, that it was his feelings toward her that sparked his passion, not his need to mask his purpose in being there with her. Collapsing back on the bed, she lay staring up at the bright sunshine reflecting itself on the ceiling, a sad look in her gray eyes and a frown marring her smooth brow.

348

But what truly confused her was her feelings for the Dark Horseman. She had never heard his voice or seen his face. She didn't know his name, yet she had eagerly gone to meet him in the meadow! Dear God, she had lain with him! The only excuse she could find was the magical attraction that seemed to enshroud him. Maybe it was looking into his dark green eyes that hypnotized her. A tawny brow slanted upward. Dane had emerald eyes. Was that what attracted her to him? Not hardly, she deduced, rolling over on her stomach, wrists crossed, her chin resting on them as she stared out across the elegantly furnished room toward the French doors. The Dark Horseman and Dane Remington were as different as night and day. The Dark Horseman had broad shoulders and raven-black hair. His jaw was square, his lips full, his complexion darkly tanned, and he rode a magnificent, ebony-colored stallion. Her head came up off her arms with a jerk when the vision of Dane's black stallion came to mind, the way the animal had reared its head, held its tail high, nostrils flared as he raced off down the road once she had freed him from the corral. Granted, there was more than one stallion of his color, but the similarities were just too convenient! What could it mean?

She came to her feet and idly strolled back out on the balcony, hugging her arms to her when a strange sort of chill ran down her spine. Raven-black hair, emerald eyes, square jaw, tan complexion, and that damnable black stallion! Except for their differences of opinion on how the colonies should be run, the Dark Horseman and Dane Remington could be twins!

"That's it!" she exclaimed aloud. It was the reason she was drawn to them both. Her subconscious had confused the two! Feeling as if an enormous weight had been lifted from her shoulders, she laid her hands on the railing and stretched, sucking a breath of fresh air. But the smile that had finally managed to turn the corners of her mouth upward faded and a frown took its place. It still didn't explain why her heart ached so every time she thought about Dane and the probability that she'd never see him again. She should be furious with him. She should curse his name and her stupidity, not choke every time his image came to mind . . . the way it was now. Sighing heavily, almost forlornly, she twisted and perched one hip on the deeply carved wooden banister surrounding the balcony and set her attention on the artful maze of shrubs, flowers, and sculptured trees in the garden below her.

Suddenly a movement near a cluster of trees caught her eye. Squinting in the bright sunshine, she stared down at the spot where a flash of white showed occasionally among the dense foliage, trying curiously to put a shape to whatever was hidden there. A moment later Miles stepped into the clearing separating the edge of the woods from the gardens. Brittany straightened in surprise, her gaze shifting from Miles to the trees and beyond and back to Miles. He didn't strike her as the type who enjoyed going for an early morning stroll, but she could think of no other reason for his being out there in the woods. Further on lay the Lockwood property, and he certainly had no reason to go there.

And you're making something out of nothing, she silently scolded herself. You don't know anything about Miles, not really. So how can you assume something strange is going on simply because you've seen him coming from the woods? Stop worrying about what everyone else is doing and start making plans. You've stayed here long enough. It's time you tried getting a message to your brother.

"And that won't be easy," she mumbled aloud, unaware that Miles had seen her on the balcony. Roan was still wanted by the Crown, and if he showed up at the Ingrams' front door, Bartholomew would be obligated to arrest him. Lifting the heavy mass of golden hair off her neck, she stretched and stood up. If she was to get a message to Roan, she'd have to deliver it herself. She'd have to figure out a way to visit Paul Revere's shop without anyone going with her. Then she could ask Mr. Revere to tell Roan that she was all right, and that as soon as she had decided what to do with herself, she'd send word. Her face wrinkling into an unflattering grimace, she walked back inside her bed-chamber, thinking that that might take some time in achieving. She didn't have any money to rebuild the house and barn or to fix the well, and if she went to the banker for a loan, he'd laugh at her.

Loan! The word rang loudly in her brain and brought a vague smile to her lips. Her father had been too proud to accept money from Bartholomew Ingram, but only because the circumstances were different then. Without a loan, there was no hope of her ever being able to return to the Lockwood farm, and just as Mr. Ingram had said earlier, her father wouldn't frown on his daughter's asking for help. Brittany was convinced of it. Crossing to the mirror hanging over the dresser, she checked her appearance, fluffed up her hair, and headed for the door.

A disappointed frown wrinkled her brow when Jonathan informed her that the elder Ingram had gone to Boston on business and wouldn't be home until late. She would have liked confirming her decision to borrow money from the man, but realized now that it would have to wait until tomorrow. She hoped the delay in seeing it done wouldn't cause her to change her mind. Thinking to enjoy a stroll through the gardens, she entered the parlor, crossed the room to the French doors, and had started through them when she heard Miles call out her name.

"Are you feeling better?" he smiled, hurrying across the parlor to catch up with her.

"Yes, thank you," she nodded sweetly. "Enough to go for a walk. Would you care to join me?"

Miles's thin face beamed. "I'd be honored," he said,

extending a hand for her to lead the way.

They crossed the flagstone veranda, moved down the trio of steps, and took the first pathway to their right, which wound and curled around the various shrubs, perfectly sculpted trees, and numerous flowerbeds exploding in a riot of color. A soft, cool breeze played with the golden tendrils of Brittany's hair falling against her brow and cheek. The cloudless blue sky lent a feeling of serenity and peace, and despite all the events of the past few months, Brittany smiled contentedly in its dazzling brilliance.

"I always liked going for a stroll," she admitted after awhile when they stopped along the way to let Brittany smell one of the bright pink blossoms. "But it was never like this. I could never seem to find the time to plant flowers. I imagine this was your mother's favorite place to be."

Hit by the vivid memory of Margaret Ingram collecting flowers in a rainbow of blues, yellows, pinks and whites, and then spending hours each day arranging them into various size vases, Miles smiled. Yes, this was his mother's favorite place to spend her days as long as the weather allowed. "You know, I hadn't truly realized it until you mentioned Mother, but after she died, there were never any flowers brought into the house. I guess that's part of the reason Father and I miss her so. But we just hadn't figured out what it was."

"I'd be very happy to change that for you," she smiled. "I might not arrange them as perfectly as I'm sure your mother did, but I'd love to try."

"Then by all means do," Miles grinned. "Father will be quite pleased." Folding his arms in back of him when it seemed to be the only thing he could do to prevent himself from reaching out and pulling her into his embrace, he took a deep breath and let it out slowly. "Father's very fond of you. You know that, don't you?"

Brittany could feel a warm blush rising in her cheeks, and she looked away embarrassed. "I suppose," she relented.

"But I can't understand why. I'm merely the daughter of his neighbor."

"And the daughter he always wished he had," Miles pointed out. "I don't think he's aware I know of this, but I wasn't his firstborn. There was a daughter ahead of me. She died within days of her birth. I was even a little earlier than the midwife expected, and after that Mother was never able to carry a child for more than a few months. So you see, Father's sort of adopted you."

The color in her cheeks heightened with his last comment even though it had been meant as a compliment, and it took her a second to answer. "That's probably the sweetest thing I've ever heard."

An awkward moment followed during which Brittany got the distinct impression that something was bothering Miles—something that had nothing to do with his father or the feelings the old man had about his houseguest. And when Miles frowned suddenly, cleared his throat, and turned his face away from her, Brittany was compelled to ask what was wrong.

"I saw you on the balcony a few minutes ago," he admitted, "and can only assume you saw me. I was hoping to keep my trip a secret, but what that little trek revealed is a matter I shouldn't keep from you."

Instinctively, Brittany's attention shifted from Miles to the woods, mentally seeing her farm just beyond. She honestly didn't expect him to say that Dane had returned, but she couldn't suppress the hope that he would. "Then by all means tell me what you've learned," she managed to say with little emotion in her voice.

Miles glanced worriedly at her, licked his lips, and sighed. "It's about the fire."

A queer feeling knotted her stomach, and for some unexplainable reason, she wanted to turn around and race for her bedroom rather than hear what Miles had to say. She wasn't going to like it. She was positive of that. "What about the fire?"

Brittany's reaction earlier to what he had announced about Dane Remington being a pirate and using women to his advantage had rather confirmed Miles's suspicions that Brittany had fallen for the rogue. Such a revelation had to be painful for her, but knowing the way women's minds worked, Brittany, in time, very well could forgive him, especially if Remington tried to see her—which Miles had little doubt he would. Therefore, Miles realized he must add to her reasons for hating the man. The idea came to him when, after his meeting with Millicent, he spied Brittany on her balcony and knew she'd have to have been blind not to see him. He needed to explain why he was walking in the woods at such an hour, a logical explanation that would settle any curiosity she might have about it, and came up with a solution for both his problems.

"I can't honestly say what made me decide to investigate," he began, purposely averting his eyes. "I think maybe I suspected what I would find, but I went with the hope of being wrong. I wasn't."

"Wrong about what, Miles?" she insisted. The sick feeling she had was quickly changing to anger. "What did you find?"

He sighed again for effect, then faced her and took her hand in his. "I wish I didn't have to tell you this—"

"Just say it, Miles," she snapped. "Tell me what you found."

"A torch," he replied. "I found the remains of a torch lying near the spot where the fire started."

The pain which gripped her heart took her breath away and tears instantly filled her eyes. Miles didn't have to say another word. She knew who had left it there and why. The bloody bastard had set fire to her crops, then had had the audacity to tell her that lightning had been the cause! From there he had proceeded to woo her, and by the cover of night he had dressed, taken his things, and walked out of her life!

354

How could she have been so stupid? No longer conscious of Miles's presence, Brittany turned with her head held high and her shoulders proudly squared and started back down the winding path toward the manor. She didn't know how she'd achieve it at this point, but if it took her the rest of her life she would see Dane Remington hanged!

Chapter Fourteen

Denby Hughs had never been a very courageous man in all of his twenty-three years. When he was a child, his father beat him for things which in Denby's mind were unjust. If he didn't move fast enough or moved too slow to suit his father, the boy was soundly thrashed. If he talked too loud, mumbled in a disrespectful voice, or gave his father the wrong kind of look, he was whipped. And if Denby ever stood up for his rights—well, he was positive that that would be the biggest mistake he'd ever make. His father would have killed him for talking back!

Denby's salvation came the day old man Hughs lost his temper with the boy over a spilled bucket of milk. The cow had knocked it over when she raised a hoof to chase away a fly. But his father hadn't seen it that way; it was Denby's fault, and he was going to get the worst licking of his life! Denby could still remember how red his father's face had gotten as he'd grabbed for a harness strap and prepared to beat his son with it. But before the first blow had landed, the elder Hughs had stiffened, clutched his chest, and fallen to his knees, dying before his stocky frame hit the ground. Denby had been only twelve years old at the time, but the image was as clear in his mind as if it had happened only yesterday.

357

The death of his father left Denby to fend for himself, since his mother had run off with an actor from a traveling show some time back. He hadn't wanted to stay on the farm for the simple reason that it held too many cruel memories, so he had sold the property and headed north, settling in Boston. But his money soon ran out, and he took to stealing or hiring out for any job a wealthy man refused to do himself, such as burning crops. The payment Miles Ingram offered for a simple task had been more than Denby had seen in several years, and he had agreed to do the job without a moment's hesitation.

It seemed everything went in his favor that night. The dry fields caught fire almost instantly, and the wind helped carry it along. The only thing which had worried him was the approaching storm, that a downpour would extinguish the flames before they had finished destroying the crops. His second and most threatening concern had been the man and boy who appeared suddenly to fight the fire. But for once in his life, his luck held. The two strangers had been unable to contain it, and Denby had mounted his horse with a broad smile on his face and ridden off toward town, dreaming of various ways to spend his money.

Mr. Ingram had instructed Denby to meet with him on the south road leading out of Boston one day after the completion of Denby's part of their bargain, and because of his excitement over the thought of all that money, he had arrived early. But when an hour passed and Miles Ingram was still nowhere to be seen, Denby began to worry. He had learned long ago never to do a job unless he had received at least half the payment ahead of time. He hadn't done that with Miles Ingram. He thought he could trust him. And of course Denby didn't have the backbone to object when Miles Ingram flatly refused his suggestion to pay in advance.

He was pacing back and forth across the road, wringing his hands as he went, when he heard the distant pounding of hooves against the hard earth. As the sound increased, so did

Denby's worries. He sensed something horrible was about to happen, that he wasn't going to be paid. He was sure of it the instant he saw the furious look on Miles Ingram's face, saw the riding crop in his hand, and noticed that the man wasn't going to rein his mount to a slower pace. Denby cringed every time he recalled the angry words Ingram had hurled at him, the way he accused him of trying to murder some woman Denby had never even heard of, as well as the threat on his life if he didn't leave Boston immediately. He'd be damned, Ingram had said, if he'd pay Denby Hughs a single farthing.

Denby had barely escaped with his life that day, and now it appeared he was in as much trouble as he had been then. And all because he had gotten drunk and rambled on about his misfortune to a whore, one who went running off to tell someone else. Sitting huddled on the floor in the corner of the room, his knees drawn up to his chest, his eyes wide and his entire body trembling violently, he stared up at the dark-haired man, his brutish-looking companion, and the midget who accompanied them, wondering in fear which of the trio would strike him dead.

"You got a horse, Hughs?" the first man demanded. "Or do we tie a rope around you and drag you through the streets of Boston?"

Denby's chin quivered and tears glistened in his eyes. "I-I got a horse. But-but where are ya takin' me?"

"To see a man who will be very interested in hearing your story first hand," he growled. "Get up!"

Denby meant to obey, but his knees were too weak to support him and there was nothing close by for him to grab hold of. He squealed when the giant of a man leaned in, gripped his shirt front, and nearly lifted him off the floor, making a sound very much like the cry of the young boy who old man Hughs used to beat.

"I-I didn't do nothin'!" he pleaded tearfully. "Ya ain't gonna believe the word of that slut over a man, are·ya?"

Dolly was the least favorite whore to frequent Boar'sInn, a dumpy little tavern on the wharf, simply because she was the ugliest. She'd lost three front teeth some years back when one of her customers decided he didn't like the way she grinned at him. Her faint red hair hung limp and stringy, mainly because she seldom washed it, and she tried to hide the black wart on her chin by using too much rice powder. The result was a ghostly white complexion which she tried to rectify by using dark red lip rouge and penciling in blacker eyebrows. To come upon her unexpectantly in a dark alleyway would scare the life out of anyone, but underneath all the paint, all the feathers, and all the multiple layers of fat was one of the most loyal patriots in all of Boston—and the most informed.

The reason Dolly charged a very small sum for her services wasn't simply because she'd go without customers if she didn't—who'd pay that much for her when a man could buy the companionship of a pretty wench?—but because it would enable her to have many clients, the ones who had the kind of information she wanted to learn. Denby Hughs was one of those, but he hadn't been aware of it. She hadn't been either, at first. She had simply taken pity on the poor drunken slob and invited him to her room for a drink and a tumble. But his tearful confession had sent her flying once Denby gave way to his intoxicated state and passed out on the floor where he had fallen.

Dolly had gone looking for Dane Remington to tell him the little tidbit she had learned about Miles Ingram and had come across Aaron Dooley first. The midget always seemed to know where to find Mr. Remington, and thinking to save time should Denby awake before she returned, she asked Dooley to convey her message while she went back to keep an eye on her informant. Mr. Remington would surely want to hear it from Hughs's own lips, and she wanted to be there to witness it. Everyone involved in the revolt suspected Ingram was working both sides against the middle, and

Dolly wanted the credit for uncovering the first solid piece of evidence against him.

She had been in her room for only a few minutes when a heavy fist against the door practically rattled the portal off the hinges, and when she opened it, she was mildly disappointed to find Dooley, his mute friend, Ernest Betts, and Mr. Remington's brother, Brad. The group had stormed in and circled Denby Hughs's unconscious body on the floor to stare at him for a moment or two before Brad motioned for Betts to dump the basin of water in the young man's face. Denby woke with a start, coughing and choking and rubbing his eyes, but once he had caught sight of the three angry faces staring down at him, he had fearfully retreated to a far corner. He had whined pathetically when Betts lifted him off the floor.

"Mr. Hughs," Brad hissed through clenched teeth, "I would much sooner believe Dolly than a drunken fool who deliberately sets fire to someone's property for a mere tuppence."

"Ain't so," he shrieked, shaking his head and working at the fingers clasped around his shirt. "It was more than that! I ain't stupid."

"Oh really?" Brad challenged. "Well, suppose you hold off thinking that until after you've repeated your tale to my brother. Once he's through with you, I believe you will have changed your mind." Nodding at Betts, Brad waited for the mute to shove Hughs through the door and out into the hall before turning to Dolly. "Thanks, sweetie," he grinned. "I owe ya one."

Dolly smiled toothlessly back at him. "Well, ya always know how ta even the score, Braddy-boy. Why don't ya come back later, and we can settle up."

"And deprive some poor soul out of your pleasures?" Brad teased. "I wouldn't think of it." Leaning in, he lightly kissed her brightly painted lips and exited the room, leaving Dolly to stand there with a lovestruck expression on her face.

More than a few heads turned to watch the group of misfits as they mounted their horses and headed off down the street. But one pair of eyes studied them more intently than the others. Waiting until the group had turned the corner, he bolted off in a half-walk, half-run, keeping the distance between himself and those he followed at a safe, unnoticed measure. He had recognized all but one of them, and it was the man with coal-black hair and immensely dark brown eyes on whom he centered his attention. As soon as the opportunity presented itself, he would step out where Brad Remington could see him.

An expectant, hopeful expression caused the faint line between Brittany's brows to appear as she stood in the middle of Bartholomew's study waiting for his answer. She had broached the subject of a loan with as much tact as she could possibly manage, pointing out her idea on various methods to repay him. Her best, to her way of thinking, would be a form of sharecropping. If he would fund the money to buy the supplies she needed to rebuild the house and barn and the seed for next year's crops, she would work the farm, sell the harvest, and give Bartholomew half the profits. She realized the amount would be small compared to the kind of business dealings he was used to handling, that it would be years before she could repay him, and that there was no guarantee the weather would treat her kindly. But she was willing to commit herself if he was.

The thoughtful, somewhat skeptical look that came over his face worried Brittany. She sensed she had asked too much, put too big a strain on the friendship her father and Bartholomew had had, that she had overstepped the bounds of his generosity. Suddenly feeling like a greedy, spoiled child, she vented a disheartened sigh and turned to the trio of windows. Warm, bright sunshine flooded in through the delicate white lace curtains adorning them, and that feeling of hopelessness washed over her again. If Bartholomew Ingram declined her offer, she would be left with no choice but to sell the property that had belonged to her father.

Of all those with whom Bartholomew had ever dealt on a business level, Brittany Lockwood, he was sure, was the most honest. She had spoken truthfully, explored both sides of the issue, and finally admitted that she realized it wasn't going to turn that much of a profit for him. She hadn't tried to blackmail him, use pressure, or lower herself to the uninventive method of tears. He liked that. He liked her. But then, he always knew he would.

He had liked her father, and Brittany seemed to be cut from the same cloth. What he truly wanted, however, was to find a way of convincing her to stay here at Yorkshire Manor. She had a fragile beauty that was meant to be clothed in silks and furs and complemented with brilliant gems. He'd give her all that if she'd let him. But he knew she wouldn't. She wasn't that kind of woman. Easing his thin frame back in the button-tufted, leather wing chair, he laid his elbow on the arm and rested his chin on the knuckles of his fist. The gentle swish of satin and a flash of mint green caught his eye, and he blinked, looking up. Standing in the bright yellow light stood Brittany, her golden hair shimmering in the sunshine, her face a picture of pensiveness. Perhaps she would agree to a compromise, he thought, something that would give them both what they wanted— even if his side of it would be short-lived. Dropping his hand away, he leaned forward with his arms braced on the edge of the desk.

"You're a very shrewd and perceptive businesswoman, Brittany," he said, pleased that she had refused to wear any of the beautifully coiffed wigs he had given her. Her luscious blond hair shouldn't be hidden.

"Am I?" she laughed, turning her head to look at him. "I was just thinking how I'd refuse such an idea if someone presented it to me. Our crops hardly brought in enough to see us through each year, and I'm offering to give half of it away. I don't think that's being very perceptive."

He smiled softly back at her while he watched her cross to one of the chairs in front of his desk and sit down.

"I wouldn't blame you if you said no," she finished, leaning back against the chair, elbows resting on the arms, her fingers interlaced.

"Well, perhaps it isn't the best deal I've been offered, but I can't resist the temptation of being your partner," he admitted, his brown eyes sparkling. "However—" He raised a hand to stop her when she quickly sat up, mouth open and words of gratitude ready to spill forth. "I'm still a businessman at heart, so there will be conditions to our agreement." He waited for her nod to continue, and once she gave it, he left his chair, rounded the desk, and perched one hip on the corner, his hands resting on his knees as he looked her squarely in the eye. He wanted her to understand every word and to consider them carefully before she gave her consent. "I'll give you the money for the lumber and carpenters needed to build the house and barn, and I'll buy the seeds for next spring's planting, *if*—" He paused to emphasize his stipulation. "If you will agree to continue living here until your work calls you home next April."

Brittany could hardly believe her ears. It was even more difficult for her to speak. "Mr. Ingram. . . ."

"Please . . . call me Bartholomew. Friends shouldn't be so formal with each other." He smiled warmly at her, then rose to pour two glasses of wine. It might be a little early in the day to be drinking, but they needed to seal their bargain with a toast. "Now, I know what you're thinking," he continued as he returned to sit next to her and hand her a glass of wine. "You're wondering why an old fool like me would want to do so much for you. After all, we've never really even talked before Miles brought you home with him." He sighed and got a faraway look in his eyes as he rested his head against the back of the chair. "And to be quite honest, I really don't know why myself, except that maybe I'm missing Margaret more than I realize." He rolled his head and glanced over at her. "She had beautiful blond hair, too. Her eyes weren't the same shade as yours, but they were blue." He sat up and leaned heavily on the arm of the chair. "I guess what I'm trying to do is substitute you in Margaret's place—as the daughter we both wanted but couldn't have." He collapsed back in the chair again, staring straight ahead. "And Lord knows it will be a long time before Miles marries someone. Who'd want a milksop like him?"

"Mr. Ing—Bartholomew," she quickly amended, "Miles isn't a milksop." She liked Miles *and* his father, and couldn't stand to hear Bartholomew talk about his son like that.

"Isn't he?" he chuckled. He cast a sidelong glance her way. "Would you marry him?"

She answered much too soon. "Well, no, but—"

The old man laughed again. "I didn't think so," he admitted as he stared at the wine he swirled in his glass.

"Just because I wouldn't marry him doesn't make him a milksop. You shouldn't talk like that. Miles may be a little clumsy at times and choose to dress in silks and ruffles rather than homespun cotton, but he's kind and generous and very compassionate. He has all the same qualities as his father," she added with a soft smile.

The corners of his mouth turned upward with her compliment, but he elected not to comment. He knew what his son was, whether she wanted to agree or not. He loved Miles as much as he was able to love him, but Miles would never be the son he had dreamed of having. Miles Edward Ingram let people push him around. And in order to stay in high standing with their peers, Miles agreed to whatever was said—whether it was what he honestly believed or not. Miles was a coward.

Yes, he was kind, generous and compassionate, but if someone ever challenged him, he'd shrink away to the nearest corner. And the only woman Bartholomew could ever see him marrying was the boisterous, mean-tempered, bossy sort of female that would be a constant pain in Bartholomew's neck. He didn't relish the thought of the day Miles would bring such a wife into his house, and the only solace Bartholomew had was the thought of the memories Brittany's short stay would give him. He didn't know if he'd go through with it or not, but if she refused his part of the deal, he wouldn't give her the loan. He'd find some way of making her stay. And who knew? Maybe in time Brittany would come to enjoy living at Yorkshire Manor so much that she would decide to stay indefinitely of her own free will. Sitting up, he twisted in the chair to face her, his glass held up in front of him.

"Well? Do we have a bargain?"

Brittany honestly couldn't see where she had a choice. If she didn't agree, she'd be forced to sell her father's land, and as she had already stated, the money she received in the transaction wouldn't last her the rest of her life. Before long, she'd wind up looking for a job as a housekeeper or cook. It wasn't that that sort of employment worried her. It was just that she preferred hanging on to her father's dream as long as she possibly could. Smiling, she raised her glass and tapped the edge of it against Bartholomew's.

"A bargain," she said.

Bartholomew couldn't remember ever having been more pleased with a simple business deal in his entire career. The strange part of it was that it had nothing to do with the small amount of money he would make off it, but the benefits imposed. Brittany would continue living in his home, and with any kind of luck she'd change her mind about rebuilding the farm.

"Good!" he smiled broadly, his brown eyes sparkling as he took a sip of the wine and watched her sample her own.

She didn't know it, but he'd soon start exposing her to the ways the wealthy society of Boston enjoyed life. He'd invite all his friends and their wives to a masquerade ball right here at Yorkshire. He'd purposely start a rumor about the young, mysterious houseguest he had, that she was new to the area, and that anyone who was someone shouldn't pass up the opportunity of meeting her. It wouldn't take too many lavish balls, elite dinners, theatrical performances, or simple associations with people of class to sway Brittany's mind. Moving back to a three-room house and having to do all her own work would soon grow very unappealing to her.

The figure clad in black, his identity concealed by a tricorn and dark cape, watched Brad Remington enter the Bunch of Grapes with his companions before he shot a quick, scrutinizing glance at the men and women milling about the street. Confident that no one had noticed him, much less recognized him, he moved to the entrance of the tavern and guardly peered inside, hoping to see where Remington had gone. He caught only a glimpse of the dark-haired, handsome man ascending the stairs in the back of the room and frowned, realizing it would be difficult for him to approach Remington without someone seeing him. But the rumor he had heard only a short time ago was too important to ignore. He had to know if it was true, and if he could trust anyone's word, it was Brad Remington's.

Pulling the brim of his tricorn down a little further on his head, he lowered his chin and stepped into the tavern, praying no one would glance his way until after he was safely up the stairs. His heart was pounding wildly as he reached his destination and had turned down the hall, but he didn't pay much attention to it, for a new problem had presented itself. The long corridor in which he stood was empty, and he had no idea which of the many rooms lining both sides had received the party of four. Starting with the first door on his left, he pressed an ear to the wooden planks, listening for the voices inside to tell him he had chosen correctly. But when no sound penetrated the barrier, he moved on to the next . . . and the next. . . .

"We found this little guttersnipe sleeping it off at Dolly's," Brad answered in reply to Dane's puzzled look as he sat leaning back on the headboard of his bed. "He made the mistake of telling her how he'd been cheated out of being paid for a job he'd done."

"A job?" Dane repeated, swinging his bare feet to the floor. He had planned to sleep late this morning since his meeting with John Hancock the night before had lasted until nearly daybreak, but he knew Brad's reason for bringing this mousy little creature to his room had to be important or he would have waited until later. Grabbing his breeches off the chair, he quickly donned them, stood and absently ran his fingers through his dark hair. "What kind of job?"

Brad gave the little man standing next to him a jab with his elbow in Denby Hughs's shoulder. "Why don't you explain it, Hughs? That way Dane will hear every detail exactly the way it happened."

Denby shook so badly his teeth rattled. Gulping, he shot a fearful look at the one who had rounded the bed and stood staring back at him with his arms crossed over a wide, bare chest. He knew they'd beat it out of him if he refused, and he was positive they would kill him once he had. He was outnumbered. Escape was impossible, and lying was out of the question. He'd already told Dolly everything, and he was sure she had repeated it word for word. God! He didn't want to die for something he hadn't even been paid for! Fidgeting nervously, his eyes darted from the man waiting to hear his answer to the silent giant at his left, then to the midget sitting on the end of the bed with his feet dangling high above the floor, and finally to the one who had dragged him up the stairs and into this room. Denby drew a trembling breath, wet his lips and said, "I only did what I was told to do. If I know'd he weren't gonna pay me, I wouldn't-a done it. Ya can't kill me for that!"

"I'll kill you if you don't tell my brother the whole story,"

Brad guaranteed him.

"And-and ya'll kill me after I do," he squealed. "Maybe we can make a deal."

"What kind of a deal?" Brad jeered. "I can't see where you have anything to offer."

Denby saw a glimmer of hope. Now if he could only think of something. An excited gleam lit up his dull eyes. "Fer a price, I could kill him for ya."

"Kill who?" Dane broke in.

"Miles Ingram," Denby quickly replied. "It'd be easy ta slip a blade between his ribs."

"If I wanted Ingram dead," Dane told him, his voice low, "I'd do it myself. Now suppose you forget about saving your own hide for the moment and tell me what job you were hired to do." When the little man clamped his mouth shut as if refusing to say a word, Dane nodded his head toward Betts. "Either of your own accord, or I'll have Betts hang you out the window by your heels."

Denby's narrow frame straightened instantly. His eyes grew into wide circles and without another moment's hesitation, he told him everything that had transpired between Miles Ingram and himself, even to the extent of Miles's accusation that Denby had nearly killed the woman living on the farm. Hughs quickly went on to say that it had only been his plan to burn the crops—the way Ingram had instructed—that he didn't know anyone's life would be in danger or that the winds would carry the fire that far. But whether this man believed him or not, Denby wasn't sure and would probably never know, for in that instant the door to the room was thrown open behind him, and when he turned, a body catapulted through the air to assail him. He was knocked brutally to the floor and held there by the weight of the gray-eyed youth whose fingers were gripped around his throat trying to squeeze the life from him.

"You bloody bastard!" Roan screamed, unbridled rage raising the pitch of his voice. "I'll kill you for this!"

"Roan, no!" Brad shouted, lunging for the boy. Together, he and Dane pulled him off the horrified little man, and both had to tighten their hold on him when it seemed he had the strength of ten men in that moment.

"He tried to kill Brittany!" he roared, straining at the arms which imprisoned him. "He destroyed our farm! Let go of me. I want to kill him!"

"No more than I," Dane snarled, his eyes glinting like hard emerald stones. "But we need him." Looking at Betts, he motioned with a nod of his head for the mute to close the door. Then without being told, Ernest clamped a huge hand around Hughs's skinny arm, hauled him to his feet, and shoved him down on the bed and out of Roan's reach.

"Need him for what?" Roan's anger shook his young frame and stained his cheeks a bright red. "What good is vermin like that?" His eyes were still riveted on Hughs, and when Brad let go of Roan, thinking he had calmed down enough for Dane to handle alone, Roan tried to break loose only to find his shirt front seized in Dane's huge fist.

"To testify," Dane growled, shoving Roan up against the wall. "I know how you feel, Roan. I'm just as tempted to slit this slimy bastard's throat as you, but if we kill him, Miles will go unpunished." The wild look in the young man's eyes seemed to diminish with the realization that what Dane had said was true, enough that Dane lessened his grip. "And right now we have more serious matters to concern us than arguing if this one lives or not."

His eyes still glistening with tears, Roan met Dane's gaze. "Like what? What's more important?"

Before he answered, Dane glanced over his shoulder at Betts and instructed him to take Denby Hughs to Brad's room and stay with him while they discussed business. As soon as they figured out what course of action to take, they'd send for him. Touching his fingertips to his brow in salute—his usual form of reply—Betts grabbed Denby by the shirt collar and left the room with him.

"I never liked Miles Ingram," Roan hissed as he stared at the closed door. "I told Brit to stay away from him—that he was dangerous, and that he'd try any way he could to get her in his bed. I guess he succeeded. What I can't figure out is how. What kind of lies did he tell her?"

"Roan!" Brad sharply reprimanded. "You don't know that."

"She's living in his house, isn't she?" he shrieked, the tears, which had until now only threatened to come, spilling over the rim of his lashes and racing for his chin.

"She's there because she had nowhere else to go," Brad argued hotly. "She's your sister, for God's sake, and if I hear you say one more improper thing about her, I'll whip your hide to the bone!"

Since their father's death, Roan had tried very hard to fill Patrick's shoes. He had tried to be a man when his desires pulled against him. But he had somehow accomplished that. He had until now, until all the pent-up emotions, all the grief, all the pain and guilt he felt boiled up and melted his tough façade. He didn't care what these men might think of him. He simply couldn't hold back any longer. Burying his face in his hands, he wept hard and long.

The sounds of Roan Lockwood's agony tore at every man's heart who witnessed it, for they knew there was nothing any of them could do to ease it. No one moved. No one uttered a sound. Yet everyone shared the young man's grief, for in their own individual way each man's heart had been touched by Brittany Lockwood, and they all felt betrayed. All except for Brad, and it was he who finally came to Roan, put his arm around the young man's shoulders, and gently guided him to a nearby chair. He didn't believe Brittany had done anything wrong.

"I think you could use a shot of whiskey," he said, pushing Roan down on the seat. "I think we all could." He glanced up at his brother. "I know I'd like one."

"Over there," Dane replied, nodding at the three-drawer chest and the bottle sitting on top of it.

"I'll get it," Dooley offered, jumping off the bed. He was glad for the chance to turn his back to the others in the room; he was able to wipe the tear from the corner of his eye without anyone noticing.

"Why, Brad? Why did she go there—to his house?" Roan asked. But before Brad could answer, he rushed on. "This is all my fault. I should have stayed home. It was my responsibility to take care of her, of the farm. I let her down. I let Father down. He'd be ashamed of me, if he knew."

"Drink this," Brad strongly ordered, shoving the bottle Dooley had given him into the young man's hand. "I never had the honor of meeting Patrick Lockwood, but I can tell you this—he must have been one hell of a man. He sired two offspring who have more courage, more conviction than a lot of men I know. He'd be proud of you, Roan, not ashamed. You've joined a cause you believe in. You're risking your life every minute of the day, and you don't even consider it. As for your sister—like I said earlier, she had no choice. If anyone's to blame, it's Dane and me. We're the ones who left her alone long enough for Ingram to step in. And I don't think I have to tell you what her reaction will be once she learns who's responsible for the fire. If she doesn't kill him for it, you can bet she'd find someone who will."

The whiskey and Brad's words relaxed Roan and eased his guilt somewhat, and he smiled at the thought of Brit's rage. "Yes. She does have quite a temper." He realized suddenly that Brad had said part of Brit's trouble was because of him and his brother. "What did you mean you're to blame for leaving her alone?"

Brad did not want to tell Roan the whole story. What happened between Dane and Brittany wasn't meant to be shared. Stalling while his mind raced for a suitable answer,

Brad took the bottle from Roan's hand and pressed it to his lips, sucking in a long drink. It burned going down and brought tears to his eyes. Gasping, he turned and crossed the room to where his brother stood staring out the window. Nudging Dane's arm, he handed the bottle to him, then faced Roan again.

"Dane, Cory, and I were living on the farm at the time of the fire. I think you can imagine what kind of chaos was involved. There was a moment when we realized we couldn't save the house, when we all fled for our lives, and sometime during the confusion, Ingram showed up. I'm sure he convinced your sister to stay the night at his manor, since there was nothing left there for her."

"But that was more than a week ago, wasn't it?" Roan pointed out. "I only got back to Boston last night and didn't hear about the fire until a few hours ago. Why is she still there?"

"Where else would she go?"

Frowning, Roan lowered his gaze. "She could have gone to Mr. Revere for help." His head shot upward with a pained expression. "Or here. You would have helped her. You had already. Didn't she know she could trust you?"

Brad laughed nervously, not knowing how to respond without being forced into telling him everything. His hesitation was just enough for Roan to sense something was wrong, and when he looked at the other brother to find him brooding, it rather confirmed it.

"She couldn't, could she?" he stated more than asked as he slowly raised himself out of the chair. "Why not, Brad? Why couldn't she trust you? What had you done?"

Brad smiled half-heartedly, his mouth opening and closing several times as he struggled for something to say. In desperation he glanced at Dooley for help. But the midget was having much the same trouble as he and could only shrug a tiny shoulder.

"He deserves to know the truth, Brad," came his brother's deep voice beside him. "He has a right to know what we suspect."

Brad straightened in surprise and turned to face Dane with a rather irritable frown marring his dark features. "You can't still believe that after learning that the fire was no accident! Do you honestly think she'd allow Ingram to burn her house down just to cover up what you *think* she's doing?"

"What—" Roan started to ask, but Brad waved him off as he would a bothersome child.

"Then explain it to me, for I swear I'm too stupid to undertand your reasoning."

"It's quite simple, really," Dane offered, his emerald eyes concentrating on some object in the street below his room. "She had to get us off her property. She knew we were onto her."

"Wait a minute!" Roan cut in. "Onto what?"

"That's absurd!" Brad bellowed. "And you're a fool to even consider it!"

When Denby Hughs admitted to being hired by Ingram to burn Brittany's crops, Dane wanted to kill the sniveling coward himself. But now that he had had time to think, he realized he couldn't come up with a logical reason why Ingram needed to hire someone to destroy the farm. He wasn't aware that Dane had stumbled across the men in the woods. In truth, he didn't even know Dane was there, only a hunchback named Zachary, unless someone told him, and the only one who knew that was Brittany.

A cold anguish gripped his heart once everything began to fall into place. The farm was in threat of being taken over by creditors, her brother had left her, she needed money, and Miles saw a way to smuggle goods into the colonies. They had struck a deal: her silence and the use of the marsh for his activities in exchange for his paying off her debts. But when Dane showed up to help plant crops, it ruined everything.

374

Brittany had been forced to let Ingram set the fields on fire, but she hadn't meant for her house to go up in flames. That was why she was so believingly distraught when the fire reached the yard surrounding it. Maybe Brad didn't want to accept this explanation, but Dane had a way of proving it. Without further comment, he reached for his shirt, donned his stockings and shoes, grabbed his pistol off the night stand, and left the room before anyone could stop him.

The warm sunshine of late afternoon with its lengthening shadows, bright golden glow, and soft breeze accompanied the tall dark figure of a man making his way in the direction of the wharf. Dane had confirmed his idea about Ingram paying off her debts by visiting every shopkeeper he could think of who might have at some time given credit to one of the Lockwoods, and each told him that just this morning a messenger from the Ingram estate had informed them that Miss Lockwood's debts would be paid by Mr. Ingram. Though each of them thought the messenger surely meant Bartholomew Ingram, Dane was sure the eldest Ingram, if asked, wouldn't know anything about the transaction. Dane had wanted—no, he had prayed the shopkeepers would prove him wrong, that in the course of a few hours he would prove Brittany's innocence. But that wasn't how it had worked out. Actually, it had been much worse.

Along the way he had learned that not only had Ingram paid up her debts, but he'd ordered supplies to rebuild the house and barn, and that in one week's time Yorkshire Manor would be the setting for a very lavish masquerade ball in honor of their new houseguest. To all appearances it seemed that Brittany was in no hurry to leave Miles Ingram's protection. And to think he had very nearly told her all about himself. What might she have done with that knowledge? Would her greed for rebuilding the farm have stood in the way? Would she have told Ingram? A hard knot formed in the pit of his belly. It was something he had to know, something he had to find out. He'd see her one last time. He'd talk to her and then decide. He'd attend the Ingram ball.

"Are you insane?" Brad exploded when Dane announced his intentions later that night. "What if someone overhears you? That place will be filled with Tories! You'll be arrested and hanged before sunrise! I won't let you do it!"

"I think he should," Roan bitterly interjected. "It'll prove how wrong he is about my sister. Turning him in would be the same as betraying me, and I know she won't do it."

"And maybe that's the real reason I'm going, Roan," Dane admitted. "To prove myself wrong." Leaning back in his chair, he waved at the barmaid to bring him a mug of ale.

"Maybe some of us ought to go with you," Dooley suggested. "Not me, of course, but you did say everyone would be wearing masks. Maybe you could talk Cory into wearing a dress. Nobody'd recognize her."

"Where is Cory, by the way?" Rodney Drexler asked. "I haven't seen much of her lately. Not since the three of you came back from Miss Lockwood's."

"Oh, she's around now and then," Dooley answered. "To tell ya the truth, I think she's found herself a beau."

"Now that I find hard to believe," Drexler laughed. "But I have to agree she'd be the best choice to take with you, Cap'n."

"No one's a good choice," Brad cut in. "It's too risky. Besides, I've already come up with a way of getting Brittany alone. And that's what you want, isn't it?"

"Getting her alone won't prove anything," Roan added, his gray eyes centered on the silent one at the end of the table. "For him to prove how wrong he is about her, he's got to tell her the truth in the middle of a crowd of Tories. That way, when she tells him how dangerous it is for him to be there and then helps him slip away—which I'm positive she will—he'll understand why I'm sitting here hating him so much."

With Dane's hurried departure earlier this afternoon without a word of explanation to Roan, Brad had been forced to do it for him. And it had probably been the hardest thing he had ever had to do. He couldn't very well tell a young brother everything his sister had been doing since he'd left home, that it appeared she had fallen in love with the Dark Horseman, then lain with Dane. He simply wouldn't understand or approve. He'd more than likely claim that Dane had seduced her against her will, or worse, that Brittany had lost all sense of morals. Fifteen was just too young to understand the workings of a woman's mind when it was clouded with love. Therefore he had had to leave out the real reasons why Dane was so upset. Brad's only consolation was that in time—once this mess was resolved—Roan could be told the whole story and then decide for himself if he truly hated Dane or not.

"And what if he's right about her?" Brad proposed, though he honestly didn't believe it. "How would you feel knowing Dane had been imprisoned and sentenced to hang because of your sister?" He cocked a brow at the boy and waited. When Roan's face flushed and he averted his eyes, Brad went on, "Or what if we're both right and Dane's overheard by the wrong people? How would you feel knowing he risked his life to clear your sister's name? Instead of sitting there damning him—and I might remind you that he was the one who saved your skinny ass from hanging—why not put your brain to use helping figure out a better way to prove how misguided his thoughts are?"

Brad could see how much his reprimand had affected Roan when the young man glanced up at him, his face pale, his eyes shining with unshed tears; and when he spoke, his voice cracked. "You-you believe she's innocent of any wrong-doing?"

"I think we all do," Dooley cut in with a sympathetic smile. "But there are just too many unanswered questions. You must understand, Roan, that the need for money can turn even the most honest person bad when there's no other way of getting it. *If*—and I stress the word—*if* that's what happened to your sister, you must realize that she did it merely to hang onto your father's property. She's basically a good woman."

"I agree with Aaron," Drexler spoke up. "And I can understand why the cap'n needs to answer those questions. Even you can surely see the incriminating evidence against her. All of your debts have been paid and supplies have been ordered to rebuild the house. That alone makes one wonder what she did to deserve it. I can't see a wealthy Tory going to that extreme for a neighbor unless he's getting something in return."

"Then let me be the one to talk to her," Roan quickly suggested. "She's never lied to me."

"And how would you get near her? She's living with one of the top British officials in all of Boston. You're still wanted for arson, remember? The minute someone saw you, you'd be back in gaol," Dooley frowned. "Then we'd have to start all over."

"Besides," Brad added, "I'm sure Mr. Revere needs you more than we do. We'll take care of this."

Irritated by the way these three were treating him, Roan stiffened in his chair. "Does any of you honestly think I could possibly turn my back on this? She's my sister! If Dane's going to Ingram's ball, then I'm going with him."

Brad, Dooley, and Drexler all voiced their disapproval at one time, each trying to make himself heard over the other until the sounds of their arguments nearly rattled the roof. In frustration, and because he'd have no part of their suggestions, Roan clamped his hands over his ears and shouted, "Stop! I'm not listening! I'm going even if I have to go alone!"

"Dane," Brad groaned, turning to his brother for help, "tell this hardheaded fool that he's staying behind."

A lazy half-smile curled Dane's mouth as he shifted his gaze from Brad to Drexler and finally to Roan. "He might be a fool, Brad, and you'll probably call me one, too. But I like Roan's idea. The two of us will be attending the Ingrams' masquerade ball."

Chapter Fifteen

"Dane, I don't mind telling you how much I disapprove of this," Brad frowned as he watched his brother tug the periwig into place. The neatly coiffed, heavily powdered curls would disguise Dane's raven-black hair, but even the plum-colored mask which came to the tip of his nose and covered his brow and cheekbones could in no way conceal the emerald shade of his eyes. If anything, it highlighted them. Brad had always envied his brother's good looks and felt he himself paled in comparison, but this was one time he wished Dane was short, pudgy, and bald. The matching plum coat and breeches, his ivory ruffled shirt, and the gold brocade waistcoat drew more attention to Dane than Brad liked. It accentuated his broad shoulders and narrow hips and seemed to add inches to his already towering height. More than one lady's head would turn his way when Dane walked into the ballroom, something Brad was fruitlessly praying wouldn't happen.

"You've told me no less than ten times, little brother," Dane grinned back at him in the reflection of the mirror. "And I'll tell you again that there's no other way. If there was, I'd take it."

"Then at least allow some of us to go with you," his brother argued. "If there's trouble, you'll be all alone."

"Roan will be with me."

"Roan!" Brad protested. "He's a fifteen-year-old boy! I'm not sure he knows which end of the pistol to point, let alone have what courage it takes to fire it."

"We're not going armed," came the simple, quiet reply.

Brad threw his hands in the air and turned away from his brother, knowing it was useless to argue with him. Once Dane made up his mind, nothing would change it. "Do you have a preference where you're buried? We've never had the need to discuss it before now."

Dane's green eyes sparkled as he watched Brad flop down on the bed and loop his arm around one of the posts, his mouth curled in a disgruntled snarl, his eyes pinned on the faded rug on the floor without really seeing it. "Well, I always liked the way the Vikings did it."

"Sorry," he sneered, "but the ship is half mine, remember? I'm not setting it on fire."

Securing the mask, Dane forced down the chuckle that tightened the muscles in his throat and turned around. "Well then, maybe cousin Beau will allow me to be buried in the family cemetery on Raven Oaks." He cocked a questioning brow when Brad lifted his angry dark brown eyes at him.

"I'm not finding this conversation humorous, Dane," he firmly told him. "I'm discovering what it's like to have to sit by and watch your brother make a foolish and possibly fatal mistake. And what's worse, I can't do anything to stop it!"

Dane's desire to tease lessened with his brother's confession. "I thought you were the one who was on Brittany's side."

"I am, damn it!" he snapped, jerking to his feet. "But she's not going to be the only one there. Can't you get that through your thick head? I'm afraid for you because of the company you'll have—not because of Brittany. I still believe she loves you and that she'd die before she caused you any harm. But Miles Ingram is a different story."

Dane tried to make light of Brad's concern. "I don't intend to dance with Miles."

"You son-of-a—" In a rage Brad whirled, reached for his jacket, and stormed from the room. Maybe his brother thought it was funny, but he didn't. And maybe Dane would disapprove, but Brad, Drexler, and Ernest Betts were going to the ball!

"Miss Brittany, ye are the prettiest young woman I've ever seen," Anna complimented her when she had finished securing the last pearl-studded pin to the silky golden tresses piled high on Brittany's head. She stepped back to admire her work and added, "Mr. Ingram will be pleased."

A slight frown marred Brittany's pale brow as she stared back at the reflection in the mirror. Anna had indeed worked a masterpiece with the long, thick hair, so much so that Brittany was afraid to move too quickly, lest the mound of ringlets break loose from their pins and cascade down her back. But that wasn't what formed the line of worry between her tawny, finely arched brows. It was the black mark Anna had penciled on her cheek. Touching the tip of her finger to her tongue, Brittany vigorously wiped it away.

"I'm sorry, Anna, but that's not me."

The maid wasn't at all offended. "I agree," she smiled. "But it's fashion and all the ladies wear them. I just thought—" She shrugged and turned toward the bed where Brittany's ball gown lay. "To tell ye the truth, mum, ye don't need extras ter show off yer beauty."

"Thank you, Anna," Brittany blushed, rising from the bench in front of the dressing table and turning around. "It's kind of you to say so." She sighed, glancing about the lavish room, her hands widespread. "It's kind of Mr. Ingram to do this for me—to do all of this for me. However, it's really too much. I don't deserve any of this, but I can't convince him of it."

"Then don't try," Anna replied. "Milord enjoys doin' it for ye. Yer presence here these last couple of weeks has made him very happy . . . happier than I've seen him in a long while. Let him have his fun, Miss Brittany."

Moving to where Anna stood gathering up the yards of ice-blue satin cloth over her arms, preparing to help slide it over the young mistress's head and shoulders, Brittany asked, "How long have you worked for Mr. Ingram, Anna?"

"Oh, since before the young master was born," the gray-haired maid told her. "I helped bring young Miles into this world." Her eyes took on a misty glow. "And I helped bury milord's own daughter as well as his wife. 'Twas a sad time for him, it was. But ye have changed all that."

There was something so permanent in her tone of voice that Brittany couldn't let the statement go unanswered. "He does realize, doesn't he, that this is only until next spring? Once it's time to plant crops, I'll be going home."

"Oh yes, mum. 'Tis what he told me."

The odd smile on Anna's lips as she lifted the gown over Brittany's head hinted that neither Anna nor Bartholomew expected it would ever happen. Brittany knew otherwise. Even though she enjoyed the luxuries of Yorkshire Manor, her real home was the tiny farm near the edge of the marsh, and someday soon she'd return there and pick up where she'd left off.

Well, not quite, she mused, wiggling into the dress, then turning around so that Anna could fasten the tiny pearl buttons up the back. Nothing would ever be the same for her again.

From across the room, she caught her reflection in the mirror again, and for a split second she didn't recognize the young woman staring back at her. She was much too thin, she wore expensive clothes that didn't match her upbringing, and she had a very sad, very troubled expression darkening her gray-blue eyes. While Brittany stared at the image, she searched for the hint of hatred that should have been there, a strong emotion that should have brought a vague frown to her smooth brow and set her mouth in a hard line. She couldn't see it. Yet had there been a way to look inside this stranger, she felt certain she would have found a heart made of stone rather than the empty shell which seemed to be what the mirror tried to reveal. Chilled by the discovery, she blinked and lowered her gaze, not wanting to look at the young woman anymore. But a moment later, black lashes fluttered, then lifted, and Brittany was staring into the face of truth once more. She was empty; her life was empty. She had lost everything and had little hope of ever being happy again.

The soft, sweet strains of violins drifted up to her room from somewhere in another part of the manor, and Brittany tilted her head to listen to the song. It was a slow, sad melody that turned the corners of her mouth downward, and she wondered how she would ever be able to bring herself to smile at all the new people she was about to meet, friends of Bartholomew. He was such a dear man and was quickly becoming a good friend, but her relationship with him wasn't meant to extend any further. She didn't belong with the elite of Boston. She belonged on her farm . . . with Roan.

Roan. She had tried on several occasions to get a message to him. But each time she informed Bartholomew that she would like to go into Boston alone, he had insisted Anna go with her . . . for her own protection. Young ladies should always have a chaperone, he had told her, and because she couldn't tell him the truth, she had had to relent. Anna treated her with the utmost sincerity and was even beginning to confide in Brittany about her own innermost thoughts. But her loyalty to the Ingram family would always come first. If she knew Paul Revere had knowledge of where to find Roan Lockwood, Anna would tell Bartholomew, and both her brother and Mr. Revere would be arrested. Thus she had had to be content with the rumors that were surely flying throughout the city. They were her only way of letting Roan know she was all right.

"Miss Brittany," Anna was saying, "ye'll be the most beautiful woman at the ball. There won't be a gentleman there who won't beg for the chance to dance with ye."

"And that will be a problem," Brittany laughed, sitting down on the edge of the bed to slide on the pale blue satin slippers. "I don't know how."

"Oh, there's nothin' to it, mum," Anna assured her, crossing to the dresser to collect the pearl necklace and earrings Brittany was to wear. "I'll show ye a few steps before ye go down."

Brittany's brow puckered dubiously. "Do you think that will be enough?"

"Oh yes, mum," Anna replied. "The gentlemen will be too busy flirtin' ta notice that ye aren't keepin' time." Her brown eyes twinkled as she crossed the room and motioned for Brittany to turn around so that she could drape the necklace around Brittany's neck and hook the clasp. "'Tis my guess they'll be honored if ye step on their toes."

The maid's lighthearted comment eased Brittany's nervousness a little and she laughed. "At least they'll have something to remember me by."

"Aye. But they'll have more than that, mum," Anna said, handing Brittany the earrings, each a pearl set in a cluster of tiny diamonds. "They'll have the honor of having met the newest, brightest, most beautiful addition to Boston society."

"Oh, Anna," Brittany scolded, "if you don't stop, you'll have me believing that my place is here at Yorkshire rather than on the farm."

Folding her arms over her ample bosom, Anna cast her young mistress a long, serious look. "Yes, mum," she replied. "'Twas my intention."

*   *   *

386

The carriages had been arriving at the front steps of Yorkshire Manor for the past hour. It appeared that everyone of wealth who had heard about the ball and the mysterious young woman Bartholomew Ingram wanted to present to them had donned his finest attire and ventured to the estate to satisfy his curiosity. It proved to be a most elegant affair, one in which the guests were free to abandon the restrictions of proper behavior. After all, who would recognize them? They all wore masks.

"Now remember, Roan," Dane advised as their carriage circled the drive and rolled to a stop, "you must be extremely careful not to let anyone but your sister know who you are. As Brad pointed out numerous times, we'll be all alone in there. If someone recognizes you, I won't be much help in getting you out." A frown deepened the lines in his brow. "And I'd prefer you not tell her I'm here. I'll make my presence known to her when the time is right." Tilting his head, he glanced out the window at the entryway crowded with couples. "And from the looks of things, it will be rather difficult for either of us to get her alone."

Sitting across from him, Roan was able to silently watch his companion without Dane's awareness, something he had been doing since they boarded the carriage. Roan wanted to hate him. He wanted to find some flaw in his character, in his physique. He had the right. Dane Remington had made some awful accusations about his sister, ones that were far from the truth. But during their journey to the Ingram estate, Roan had failed to find a single flaw. He kept thinking of all the stories he had heard about the Dark Horseman and the risks he had taken to free innocent people from the clutches of an unjust British rule. He himself had been freed by Dane Remington. The man was wrong about Brit, but he didn't deserve Roan's hatred. After all, Roan had assumed the worst about his sister when he first heard about her living with Miles Ingram. What made him any different? And wasn't Dane admitting the possibility that he could have

387

made a mistake about Brit by coming here tonight?

A coldness twisted inside him, and he closed his eyes and leaned his head against the plush leather backrest. What if he wasn't wrong? What if Brit was guilty of all those things Dane suggested she might have done? What would happen then? She knew her brother was working with Paul Revere. Would she turn him in? Angered by the thought and refusing to believe it, he jerked himself up and cast his gaze out the window. Brad had refused to accept the idea, and she wasn't even his sister.

"Are you having second thoughts about this?" the deep voice interrupted, and Roan glanced over to find Dane staring at him.

"No. Just having second thoughts."

Dane would have liked to ask Roan to clarify his meaning, but at that moment the carriage lurched forward and rolled to a stop again. The door was opened by one of Ingram's servants. The time for discussion was over. From this point on they both would have to be very careful about what they said.

"Ready, Nephew?" Dane grinned.

Taking a deep breath and letting it out in a rush, Roan nodded. "Ready, Uncle."

Howard Richards and his nephew Charles had just arrived in Boston a few days earlier to conduct a little business before returning home to England—or so everyone was told. Actually there was no such man and no such nephew—only the inventive mind of John Hancock. When Dane had confided in his friend and related the events of the past few weeks, Hancock had come up with the story of Howard and Charles Richards and had managed to obtain an invitation to the Ingram ball. Not only did Hancock want to help Dane clear Miss Lockwood's name, but he hoped Dane's new identity would open a few doors.

If anyone knew what the British were planning next, it was Sir Bartholomew Ingram. The mission was a dangerous one, and Hancock had pointed it out to both Dane and Roan, but neither even flinched. Apparently Miss Lockwood was too important. Hancock could understand Roan's need—she was his sister—and he could always assume Dane Remington thrived on that sort of thing. But there had been more to it than Dane let on. Hancock wasn't really sure—Dane was a very private man—but he suspected there were personal reasons for Dane's desire to be involved. He hadn't, however, liked Dane's insistence that he and Roan go alone, and when his brother approached Hancock with his proposal that he and two others attend the ball, Hancock had eagerly made the arrangements. Thus Ernest Betts and Rodney Drexler were hired as extra wine waiters and Brad Remington would be introduced as Lord Archibald Hayes.

"Couldn't you have found someone else to flaunt as your wife?" Cory snarled as she took Brad's hand and descended the carriage step. "I hate wearing all these corsets and petticoats and things. And I despise these godawful wigs!"

Brad's brown eyes sparkled devilishly. "Now Wilhemina," he chided, "you look ravishing. I fear I'll have to keep a close eye on you lest some overzealous fellow lose control and try to seduce you right there on the dance floor."

"Very funny," she hissed. "And if you call me that ridiculous name once more, I'm going to raise my frilly knee and change the pitch of your voice."

"But I have to call you Wilhemina, my dear," he whispered when they came too close to the group of couples crowding the entryway. "She's Lord Hayes's wife."

"Yeah, well just remember it's in name only," she jeered, her violet eyes glaring up at him through the slits in her black mask. "Once this little tea party is over, you and I go our separate ways."

"Now darling," he cooed, daring to slip his arm around her waist, "you shouldn't talk that way to your husband. Besides, if you gave me a chance, you might learn to like me."

"I doubt it," came the curt reply.

"Well, can you at least pretend you do—for tonight, anyway?"

"I will," she assured him, "but I want you to understand why. I'm doing it for your brother, not because of any feelings I have for you. Now either take your hand off my waist or I'll forget where we are and break your arm."

Brad had known Cory long enough to be convinced that she'd carry out her threat. "As you wish, my dear," he grinned, leaning in to add, "but it will make it rather difficult to dance later if I'm not allowed to touch you."

Noticing how the crowd around them seemed to be closing in, she feigned a sweet smile and said, "You assume too much, Husband."

Brad's merry laughter blended with the excited chatter of the partygoers as he and Cory fell into step with the mass of people moving through the entryway. He wished their reason for being here was simply to enjoy the ball rather than to act as bodyguards for his brother. Cory was quite stunning in all her frills, laces, and silks, and he would have liked getting to know her as a woman, instead of as the sword-wielding hellcat she usually was. There was a lot about her that he didn't know, a lot of secrets she kept buried inside that crusty exterior, and it would be a pleasure unraveling them. But the urgency of their mission wouldn't allow them a moment to themselves, and he knew it. Maybe later, after this affair was over. . . .

The front hall was filled with honored guests bedecked in a rainbow of color and a wide variety of cloth, feathers, powdered wigs, and jewels. Brad realized the wealth to be had within this one large room, but he also realized the difficulty of his job in that moment, for every face was covered with some sort of mask or domino. Spotting Dane and Roan would be simple enough—he knew what clothes they had chosen to wear—but finding Miles Ingram would be another task entirely.

"I suggest we find Dane," he whispered in Cory's ear, "and

stay close by. Unless, of course, you have some uncanny knack for figuring out whose face is behind all these masks."

"I was thinking much the same thing," she admitted, fluttering her fan beneath her chin. "Maybe we should split up. That way we'll stand a better chance of finding him before it's too late."

"That might not be such a bad idea," he said, nodding politely at a couple who stepped in front of them when he and Cory dallied too long going into the ballroom. "And while you're roaming about, see if you can find Betts or Drexler to let them know we're here. There's a good possibility one of them already knows where to find Dane." He lifted his head and glanced over the crowd surrounding them. "I hope he insisted that Roan stay with him. They're both in the same amount of danger being here."

"Give your brother more credit than that," she sighed sarcastically. "The only reason he allowed the boy to come with him in the first place was because he knew the fool would come anyway. This way he can protect him . . . hopefully."

Brad shrugged a shoulder, knowing Cory was right. "Do you suppose Brittany has made her appearance yet?"

"Of course not. How many of these affairs have you attended?" she snapped, tilting her head to stare into his face.

An impish grin slanted his mouth upward and his dark brown eyes sparkled from behind the white satin mask he wore. "None."

Cory shook her head disgustedly and looked away. "This is Miss Lockwood's debut. She'll be the last to join her guests. It's for effect. Chances are she's not even dressed yet." Irritated with the tightness of her corset, she squirmed, squared her shoulders, and added, "I wish I could say the same."

Never one to pass up the opportunity to be of service to a damsel in distress, Brad leaned close and offered, "I'd be honored to help rectify the problem."

391

Cory's response was a quick jab with her elbow in Brad's ribs, one that nearly took his breath away and did, in fact, bring tears to his eyes.

"Don't you ever get the hint?" she snarled from behind her fan. "I'm not interested."

"Can't blame me for trying," he countered, hurriedly scrutinizing those standing nearest them. Not too many wives treated their husbands in public as Cory had, and he was hoping no one noticed. They didn't need any undue attention. "I keep hoping someday you'll cha ge your mind about me. I can be very nice if you'd let me."

"If it were the only way to save my life, I'd start picking out a cemetery plot," she sneered. "Now suppose you concentrate on the reason we're here and keep your hands to yourself."

"Yes, Wilhemina," he nodded, the corners of his mouth twitching with the smile he fought to hide. "But promise I'll have the first dance."

Cory jerked her head around to glare at him, but Brad had already wisely and deftly moved away from her, winding his way through the crowd toward one of the doors at the end of the long hall. Her violet eyes narrowed as she watched him go; she was reluctant to admit that the rogue had his choice of women. The white jacket and breeches he wore fit him perfectly and accentuated his broad-shouldered physique. Of those who might have noticed him, only she knew of the black hair hidden beneath the powdered periwig and the strong, handsome features the satin mask concealed. Brad Remington was an extremely handsome man, and for a brief instant Cory wished things could be different between them. But it was too late for that. He deserved everything he had coming to him. Brought out of her musings by a guest who carelessly stepped on her toe, Cory shot the man an angry look and disappeared within the crowd before he could apologize.

Despite the chaos in the streets, the unrest and ill-feelings of the people of Boston toward their British rulers, the elite of the city turned out in full force for the social event of the summer as a way of ignoring the atrocities. The rich and powerful donned their finest silks and their largest gems, hid their faces behind disguises, and ventured to the Ingram estate for a night of dancing and drinking and wild abandon. They would forget about the pain and suffering of those less fortunate than they, for the hardships of the poor had nothing to do with the noble people of Boston. Thus the mood was light and gay, and few sought to discover the identity of their dance partners or the one with whom they shared a drink or a casual, lighthearted conversation.

The most interesting and jovial of the group was a tall, well-built man dressed in a stunning shade of plum. His speech marked good breeding; he had not long been away from his English homeland. He kept all who listened laughing at his humorous tales of a well-known group of rebels in Boston and the ignorance of such men to think they could outwit the British army. To further his point, he added an anecdote about the mishandled attempt on behalf of the Sons of Liberty to free those prisoners held in the Boston gaol several weeks back, and how all but two of the rebels were recaptured. Did they honestly think a handful of men could change the way the country was run? This remark brought a round of heartfelt laughter from the group and awarded the stranger with the opportunity to step away and confiscate a full glass of wine in exchange for his empty one.

"Are you insane, *Uncle?*" Roan gritted through clenched teeth. "I thought the idea was to blend in—not become the center of attention."

Lifting the monocle which dangled from a delicately braided satin ribbon, Dane tapped the eyepiece against his chin as if considering his companion's disapproval. "I'm sorry if I offended you," he drawled with a heavy English accent and the mannerisms of a fop, "but I figured if word of our attendance reached the wrong ears, what better way to hide than by standing in the middle of them? They certainly wouldn't suspect a dandy like me to be anything more than what I appear. Don't you agree, ol' boy?" Letting go of the monocle, he pulled a lacy kerchief from his cuff and gently dabbed it beneath his nose as if some offensive odor had assailed him. "I wonder when the lady of honor will make her appearance."

"Soon, I hope," Roan admitted with a disgruntled sigh. "I'd like to get this over with."

"As I, my good man." Flipping the frilly piece of cloth toward the open French doors on one side of the room, he added, "Shall we step outside for a breath of fresh air, Nephew? It has grown rather stuffy in here." He glanced back at the circle of men he had been entertaining for the past half hour.

"Yes, Uncle, it has," Roan smiled, taking the lead.

Once they were safely outside where the crowd thinned out, Dane dropped his foppish manner to ask, "Have you been able to find Miles or his father?"

"Not Miles, but I saw Bartholomew. He was talking with a group of men in the front hall when we came in. He's dressed in gray with a black mask. You can't miss him. He has a red ribbon in his wig."

"Well, knowing Miles, he won't be too far away from his father. The man rides on the success of others." His frown went unseen beneath his mask. "That's why this whole mess about the smugglers confuses me. I never thought he had the courage to do it on his own."

"Then you think he's taking orders from someone else?"

Raising his glass of wine to his lips, Dane peered out over the rim of it to study the people wandering about in the gardens. "There hasn't been any indication that he is, but it wouldn't surprise me any."

"But who?"

Finishing off his wine, Dane set the glass on a nearby flower pot. "Well, it isn't his father, that's for sure.

Bartholomew is as loyal to the British as you and I are to the cause. Besides, we've checked him out several times." Dane's attention was drawn momentarily to two men huddled closely together as if they didn't want anyone to hear what they were talking about, and when they burst into laughter, he deduced it was only a witticism they shared and not some plot to make life a little more miserable for the colonists. Exhaling a long sigh, for this sort of adventure set his nerves on edge, he shifted his gaze back to Roan and frowned at the troubled look on the young man's face. "What is it, son?" he gently asked.

"You don't suspect Brit, do you?"

"Of being the one giving Miles orders? No," he guaranteed with a shake of his head. "The first time she was seen talking to him was shortly after we broke you out of gaol. She was on her way to the courthouse when she bumped into him on the street. I doubt they would have been so foolish as to be seen in public like that if they were plotting some sort of smuggling operation. No, we've been watching Miles for a long time, and until that day, your sister's name was never linked to his."

"Then why are we here?"

Roan's question stopped Dane cold. He wished he could tell the boy that the only reason Dane was here was because of the jealousy that was twisting his insides . . . that and the fear that maybe Brittany had fallen victim to the times. Just as Dooley had pointed out, when one's in danger of losing everything one owns, even the most honest person can turn bad. If he thought God would grant him one wish in all those he had been tempted to ask for, he would fall to his knees in this very spot and beg God to prove him wrong about Brittany. The idea of having to turn her over to the Sons of Liberty as a pawn in capturing Miles Ingram tore at his heart. And it would most assuredly destroy the young man who stood staring back at him. Forcing a smile to his lips, Dane reached out and draped an arm around the boy.

"To show what a fool I am," he said, turning with him toward the French doors. "Shall we join the others? I do believe I hear a minuet being played, and I so love to dance."

Dane had slipped back into his dandified behavior again, and Roan found himself wondering if this man truly liked to dance or even knew how. Yet that thought was only secondary, for Roan was inwardly praying Dane Remington would, before the night was out, do as he had said and prove himself a fool for ever having considered Brit a part of Miles Ingram's ploy.

The dance floor was filled with couples twirling and dipping to a sweet melody played by the musicians at the opposite end of the huge room, and Roan and Dane paused in the doorway to watch for a while. Each couple moved with graceful ease and in perfect step with those around them, and although Dane's reason for attending the ball was not the same as those enjoying themselves with wine and dance, his attention was momentarily caught up in the whirl of bright colors before him. The battle ahead of the patriots would no doubt be long and high-priced, but he couldn't help thinking that someday he too would share a glass of wine and a dance with friends the way these people were, and not have to wonder at the reason those within the room chose to hide their faces behind masks. A tightness gripped his heart. Was there any hope that Brittany would be standing by his side? God, he hoped so. He honestly couldn't bear the thought of spending the rest of his life without her, not now, not after having spent so many years looking for her. Closing his eyes, he drew in a slow breath and gritted his teeth, wishing away the thought that within a few hours he would know the truth about her, and that that truth might very well not be what he wanted so desperately to know.

"Are you all right?" Roan asked in a whisper.

Brought out of his reverie rather abruptly and with a certain amount of embarrassment, Dane blinked, chuckled nervously, and nodded. "Too much wine," he lied, purposely casting his attention away from the young man at his side. He couldn't explain to anyone what was going through his head at that moment, and certainly not to Roan.

The minuet had come to an end, and as the dance floor began to clear, the way opened up in front of Dane and presented him with a clear view of a shapely young woman standing alone on the opposite side of the room. She was dressed in black, which made a sharp contrast with the white-powdered wig she wore, and Dane wondered if that had been what had caught his eye. Yet the longer he stared at her, the more he sensed he knew her, though he couldn't figure out why he would. The only women of wealth whose acquaintance he had made were the wives of patriots, and he sincerely doubted any of them would have received an invitation to Ingram's ball, much less attended.

"What is it, Uncle?" Roan asked when he noticed Dane staring across the room. "Have you found Miles?"

"No," Dane admitted. "I'm not sure who she is, but I have the odd feeling I should know her."

"Where?"

Another song had started, and before Dane could point her out to his companion, the way was blocked by couples coming back onto the floor.

"What did she look like?" Roan asked, stretching on tiptoe in an effort to see over everyone's head.

"Like everyone else," Dane chuckled. "This is a masquerade ball, remember? We're not supposed to know what anyone looks like."

"Well, why don't you try and find her again and ask her to dance? Maybe you'll recognize her voice."

"And then again, maybe I won't." Lifting his monocle in front of one eye, he peered haughtily through it at the couples dancing close by, his mannerisms and voice slipping back into that of Howard Richards's. "'Tisn't important, Nephew. She's not the one I'm here to see."

Roan was about to ask why the mystery woman's identity

had been of any importance in the first place when a rather buxom, multi-jowled, heavily rouged woman stepped between him and Dane and nearly crushed Roan's toe beneath the heel of her shoe.

"I've been watching you for some time now, sir," she grinned up at Dane, "and it's quite apparent that you and the boy have come here unescorted. It would be too much to ask, I know, to inquire of your name, but not too bold of me to introduce you to my daughter."

With that, she stepped aside to reveal a young woman. Roan was amazed at how Dane managed not to flinch and contained the laughter Roan was sure was tugging at the corners of Dane's mouth. The daughter didn't appear to be as old as Roan and was a far cry from the sort of lady who, Roan guessed, usually interested his friend. The white mask she wore blended with her milky complexion, except for the spots of rouge her mother, no doubt, had smeared onto her cheeks. The scarlet gown hung limp from narrow shoulders and did little to accentuate her flat bosom, and for a moment Roan wondered if she was truly a girl. Covering his mouth with his hand, Roan cleared his throat and fought back the urge to laugh while at the same time thanking God *he* hadn't been the one chosen to meet this pathetic soul.

"Not bold indeed, dear lady," Dane was saying as he scrutinized the child from head to toe through his monocle. "'Tis an honor."

Both women giggled at Dane's admission, though Roan knew he didn't mean it, and it was all Roan could do to keep his lips from quivering with mirth. He would have enjoyed witnessing Dane's polite escape from the pair, but since other matters were more important than allowing mother and daughter a moment to flirt, he reached out and touched Dane's elbow.

"Excuse me, Uncle, but I believe this is the dance you promised to Martha."

With his nose held loftily in the air, Dane glanced down at

Roan. "So it is," he replied, then cast his attention out over the crowd as if looking for the one mentioned. "And where might she be, Nephew?"

"Oh, I'm sure she'll forgive you this one time," the older woman cut in, grabbing her daughter's arm and shoving her toward Dane. "She certainly can't expect a handsome man like you to stand around waiting for her." She gave them both a nudge toward the dance floor. "Go on."

The desperate look in Dane's green eyes when he glanced back at Roan nearly made the young man choke, and he quickly turned his face away so that neither woman would see. But once he had regained his composure and turned back around to watch the couple dancing, his heart seemed to stop beating. The buxom woman dressed in a gaudy shade of aqua was batting her lashes at him. He smiled weakly and took a quick step to his left, muttering something about needing a breath of fresh air before he spun on his heels and dashed off into the crowd.

The last time Dane remembered having drawn a woman onto the dance floor was at Raven Oaks. Beau and Alanna had just gotten married that morning, and all of Williamsburg turned out to help them celebrate. It had been a joyous occasion, one that Dane was sure he'd remember the rest of his life. Beauregard Travis Remington, the master of a huge plantation, had married one of his indentured servants, something that was considered quite unspeakable. It had shocked the community, but not Dane or his brother. There was something about the Remington men that set them apart from the noble class, and if anything, the people of Williamsburg admired Beau's courage to do as he pleased, despite the outcome. Of course, the result of that union had proved that class had nothing to do with love. Ten years later, Beau and Alanna were still as happy as the day they'd stood before the minister. And they had a beautiful little girl named Victoria to prove it.

Although it had been some time since Dane had taken to

the dance floor, the steps came easily for him, and while he pretended to enjoy his partner's companionship, his thoughts were of Brittany. His cousin Beau would approve of Brittany. She had a lot of Alanna's characteristics. She was headstrong, determined, compassionate, sensitive, and the type of woman who would fight to the death for something in which she believed. It was the only excuse Dane could give for her joining up with Miles Ingram. She had sacrificed one principle for another. Holding onto her father's land was more important than anything else in her life.

The song came to an end, and thinking to rid himself of the skinny young woman who did everything but drool on him, he bowed politely, thanked her for the honor of the dance, and said that it would be rude of him if he didn't make an attempt to find the fictitious Martha. The look on the girl's face was one of obvious disappointment, and rather than have her break into tears—which it seemed she might—he promised her another dance later in the evening, knowing he'd be gone from the Ingram estate long before he fulfilled his pledge. She seemed content with that, and just as he was about to step away, the attention of the crowd around them lifted toward the wide double doors at the opposite end of the ballroom. Curious, he turned in time to see the way open up before him and present him with a clear view of the couple standing at the top of the trio of stairs leading into the room.

In that moment Dane thought Brittany had never looked more beautiful, and his heart ached with the want to go to her, to take her in his arms, to confess his love, and to beg her forgiveness. Memories of the moment they shared making passionate love in the mound of hay while it stormed outside flashed to mind, and he would have given anything to relive that interlude. He would have told her then of his love for her, that no matter what stood between them, together they would tear it down. A round of applause shattered the illusion and snapped him back to the moment. Blinking, he stiffened and quickly stepped within the group that had pulled away from the middle of the dance floor.

In all of her young life, Brittany had never felt as honored as she did at this moment. She was dressed in a rich satin gown with matching slippers and yards of flowing silk and ruffled petticoats. Pearls adorned her earlobes and neck and dotted her upswept hair. She felt like a princess about to be presented to her royal subjects, and all because of the man who stood at her side. At first, when Bartholomew told her about the masquerade ball he was planning on her behalf, she had strongly objected. It was a waste of time and money, she had told him, but he hadn't agreed, saying that Yorkshire Manor was about due for a party anyway and that he would have had one whether she was living in his house or not. It made her feel a little better at the time, but now as she stood beside the eldest Ingram with her fingertips resting on the back of his hand, she got the distinct impression this wasn't just any masquerade ball, it was hers.

A sea of smiling masked faces stared back at her, and Brittany was glad her own was covered in satin and lace. They would have seen her nervousness otherwise. Descending the steps, she nodded back at those who respectfully bowed their heads, smiling graciously at their unspoken compliments as Bartholomew led her to the center of the room. Then, as if on cue, the orchestra began to play again. Presenting her with a deep bow which she returned with a graceful curtsy, Bartholomew took her hand and fell into step with the rhythm of the song. Several minutes passed while those crowded in the hall watched, and Brittany was suddenly wishing her father and Roan could be present. Although Patrick Lockwood had never voiced it, Brittany was sure this was the dream he had always longed would come true.

Hidden within the crowd, a woman draped in black

401

watched the couple gliding effortlessly across the floor, her eyes narrowed and filled with anger. Millicent had told Miles to get rid of Brittany Lockwood. She hadn't meant for him to invite her into his home, to pay her bills, and then see to the rebuilding of her farm. As long as Brittany was alive, she stood in the way of everything Millicent had worked so hard to achieve. Now she was on public display. On the morrow, every person in Boston would be speaking Brittany's name, every eye would be watching her. Miles's stupidity had made it nearly impossible now for her to dispose of the woman. But dispose of her she would . . . with or without Miles's help. After all, she alone had taken care of the bitch's father. Murdering this piece of fluff would be simple. All Millicent needed was the right moment.

The next hour passed in a blur for Brittany. Each time one song ended and a new one began, she found herself with a different partner. Her feet ached, but she didn't have the heart to turn anyone down. Besides, she was having too much fun. She hadn't danced with Bartholomew again, but each time she looked for him she found him standing somewhere close by with a group of his friends, a glass of wine in one hand and a smile on his face, and she soon realized that he preferred she spend her time meeting new people rather than wasting it on him. What puzzled her, however, was the fact that during the course of the evening she hadn't seen Miles anywhere, and as soon as she had the chance, she'd ask his father what was keeping Miles. He deserved a little of the fun she was having, since he was the reason she was here in the first place. An involuntary shudder ran through her as she contemplated how she might have spent the last two weeks had it not been for the generosity of the Ingrams.

Another song ended and before a new partner could beg her to dance, Brittany hurried off toward one of the butlers carrying a tray of wine goblets. With drink in hand, she moved through the French doors and out into the gardens where the air was cool and the ebony sky was filled with bright, twinkling stars. It was hard to imagine that she didn't belong here; everything seemed so natural. Her only regret was that Roan couldn't share it with her. A sadness touched her as she thought about her brother, how things would never be the same for them again.

The day their father died a change began. They were no longer children but adults. They would never again know the joys of being pampered, protected from the harsh realities of life. They had to stand on their own two feet and face them. It didn't seem quite fair to Brittany. Roan was too young; he had been cheated out of his youth and there was no way either of them could ever get it back. The soft strains of the music coming from inside gently intruded upon her thoughts and she smiled. But with Bartholomew's help, she would have something to offer Roan should he ever decide to return home.

Finishing off her wine, she turned back toward the house, thinking that another glass would taste good, when she nearly collided with a tall, broad-shouldered man dressed in a very becoming shade of plum. Laughing apologetically, she glanced up into his face and froze. There was something hauntingly familiar about him, though she couldn't say exactly what it was.

"I beg your pardon, madam," he was saying as he lifted a monocle before his face and peered down at her through the thick lens. "'Twas quite rude of me to sneak up behind you like that. And I assure you it wasn't truly my intention. But your beauty drugged my mind and left me quite the stumbling fool, I fear. Say you've forgiven me."

In spite of his doltish nature, Brittany found him oddly appealing. "No harm done, sir," she answered quietly.

"Splendid," he drawled, then extended a hand toward one of the paths that circled through the elegantly manicured gardens. "Would you honor me with a stroll?"

A warning went off in Brittany's brain. Although the stranger had the manners of a gentleman, going for a walk unchaperoned wasn't quite the same as dancing with him in the midst of a crowd. Hesitant, she glanced back toward the French doors and the scores of people she could see moving about inside the manor, wishing Bartholomew would suddenly come to her rescue. She didn't wish to be rude. After all, what had this man done except ask to go for a walk with her? Knowing that he sensed her reluctance, she forced a smile and raised her empty glass.

"Actually, I'd prefer more wine and the chance to sit down," she lied. "I've been on my feet most of the evening." To her dismay, one of the butlers who continually circled the guests appeared from out of nowhere, and before she could think of an excuse to go back inside, her empty glass was exchanged for a full one.

"I believe I saw a bench not far from here," the stranger smiled as he gently took her elbow and headed them down the first path. "Ah, yes," he commented, his mouth pursed most unflatteringly once he espied the settee made of stone. "There it is."

Although the spot where he took her wasn't far from the few couples standing outside enjoying the cool air, it was a fair enough distance away to give them privacy . . . something Brittany didn't truly want. Nervous, she sat down and sipped her wine, unable to lift her eyes to look at the man standing before her.

"I've been trying all evening to get you alone, my dear," he admitted. "You're rather in demand, I might say. But I knew perseverance would win out eventually."

His confession didn't soothe Brittany's apprehension any, and even though she knew she should thank him for his compliment, she couldn't think of a word to say. Instead, she smiled softly and nodded her head, growing more uncomfortable with every minute.

"Are you enjoying the ball, Brittany?" he asked.

"Oh, yes," she admitted with downcast eyes and failing to notice that he had called her by name.

"You should. You paid a high price for it."

It wasn't so much what the stranger had said that snapped her head up, but the fact that his voice had lost its accent. Staring open-mouthed, Brittany hurriedly studied the strong features of his face for some hint to his identity or at least his reason for the deception. She jumped when he leaned forward slightly, laid his foot on the seat next to her, and propped his upper torso on one elbow braced against his bent knee.

"And before you decide to scream and bring the entire place running here in your defense, I think I should warn you that Roan is somewhere inside milling about with your British friends." The white satin mask loomed closer. "Unless, of course, you've turned your back on him as well."

Brittany's mind whirled; a chill shot up her spine. Her heart began to pound so loudly in her ears that its erratic beating drowned out the soft strains of violins. For the last two weeks she had tried to put her past behind her. She had tried to forget Dane Remington and everything that had happened between them. Now he was here, standing right in front of her, making accusations that hinted she had sold out her loyalties to her family in exchange for Bartholomew Ingram's friendship. How dare he!

"You have a lot of nerve accusing me, Dane Remington," she hissed, slowly coming to her feet, "when it was you who pledged his allegiance, then set fire to my crops." She quickly raised a forefinger and pointed it at him. "And don't try to deny it. Miles found the torch you left behind. What I can't figure out is why you went to all the trouble planting them in the first place when you intended all along to destroy everything I owned." Her rage shook her tiny body. "Or

405

perhaps that was the plan." Tears suddenly burned her eyes and tightened the muscles in her throat. "You wanted to have a little fun with me first. You wanted to see if you could win me over." She blinked and tears ran down her cheeks. "Well, it didn't work," she whimpered, her head held high. "I know what you really are, and I hate you for it."

Angered by her tirade, he roughly caught her arm. "And what am I, Brittany? Am I any bigger a fool than you? You're right about someone setting fire to your crops, but I wasn't responsible. His name is Denby Hughs and the man who hired him is the one who fills your head with lies." In a rage, he shoved her away. "But my guess is you already know that. You allowed it to happen in exchange for all this." His hand swept out to indicate the gardens, the manor, and all that went with them. "You traded your values, your honor, your father's dream for a chance to live like a queen. Tell me, Brittany. Is it worth it?"

"What are you saying?" she demanded, confused by his anger.

"I'm asking what Miles is getting in exchange for paying all your debts."

The opened palm of her hand struck him squarely across the cheek. "You—you bastard," she sobbed. Then, in a whirl of satin and petticoats, she swung around and raced off toward the manor.

Too numb to chase after her, Dane merely stood there with his eyes closed. He deserved to have his face slapped, and he deserved her scorn. He hadn't meant to say what he had. He had planned to tell her the truth, that he loved her, that *he* was the Dark Horseman, that he knew about the smuggling, and that it didn't matter to him. All he cared about was Brittany, and if they had to sail to some faraway island to be safe, then he'd weigh anchor and set a course for the middle Atlantic this very night. But that wasn't how it worked out. He had insulted her, called her a tramp, implied money was more important to her than her own brother. Sucking in a deep breath, he opened his eyes and stared up at the stars. And now she would never believe that he had spoken only out of anger and pain. He would never have the chance again to tell her what he honestly felt in his heart. Casting a rueful look in her direction, he heaved a troubled sigh and turned for the manor. It was time he found Roan and vacated Ingram's property before someone recognized him.

Brittany took a detour at the end of the gravel pathway which led across the patio and back inside the manor. She didn't want anyone to see her tears. She didn't want to have to explain. She needed time to think things out. She needed time to heal, to think rationally. The whole bizarre episode didn't make any sense to her. Veering to the left, she followed the narrow footpath alongside the house until she came to an open doorway. The room inside was dark save the stream of moonlight filtering in around her, but it was enough for her to see the rows of books lining the shelves and to realize that the library was one place Bartholomew's guests would not venture this night. Stepping past the threshold, she hid herself in the shadows and sank down in one of the huge wing chairs before the cold fireplace.

Within minutes, her sorrow overtook her and she buried her face in her hands and wept softly while her mind raced for an explanation. How could Dane—or anyone—possibly think she had given herself to Miles Ingram as payment for the man's kind deeds? And how could Dane even suggest Miles had anything to do with the fire? He hadn't even known about it until the next morning. And what possible reason could he have for wanting to destroy her farm? It was a lie—all of it. Dane was the one who wanted to get rid of her. He wanted her off the property so he could continue with his illegal dealings. Hadn't Miles proven that?

A noise in the hallway outside the study brought

Brittany's sobs to an abrupt end. Fearing she was about to be discovered, she frantically wiped away the tears from her cheeks and prepared to make her presence known when she heard the knob rattle and the latch click open and saw the bright light flood into the room as the door swung wide.

"Are you insane?" she heard Miles ask angrily. "What if someone sees us together and questions me later?"

"Don't worry about that," the strangely familiar feminine voice replied. "I made sure no one saw me coming this way."

The room was plummeted into darkness again, and Brittany wisely decided to stay hidden, resisting the urge to peek around her high-backed chair. From the tone of their words, this conversation was meant to be private.

"Did the shipment arrive safely?"

"Yes," Miles snapped. "Everything's tucked safely away. But I don't understand why you chose to have the ship dock tonight. Someone is sure to have missed me. After all, this ball was to introduce Brittany, and I should have been at her side."

"Yes. I know," the woman grated out. "And she's another matter. I thought you understood what I meant when I said to get rid of her."

The hairs on the back of Brittany's neck tingled, and she bit her lower lip to keep from gasping aloud.

"Yes. I understood. You wanted her off the farm. Well, she's here, isn't she?"

"For how long, Miles?" the woman snapped. "Until your father's hired help has the farm rebuilt? When I said off the farm, I meant permanently! Why do you think I had her brother framed for arson? I knew he'd never be coming back."

Brittany closed her eyes and pressed her tiny frame tightly against the back of the chair, praying they wouldn't discover she was there, cursing the pair of them for what they had done.

408

Crossing to a small table opposite the fireplace, Miles struck flint against steel and lit a single white taper. A faint yellow glow warmed one section of the room and cast eerie shadows about the rest. "I doubt Brittany will ever want to return to that tiny farm once she's had a taste of the rich life. It was my plan all along. I intend to marry her," he declared, turning to glare at his companion.

"How noble," the woman sneered. "But I think you've underestimated her. She doesn't strike me as the type to trade her integrity for a silk gown and diamond earrings. And I certainly don't think she'd want to marry a spineless buffoon like you. She has more spunk than that."

"Spineless buffoon, is it?" Miles rallied. "And whose idea was it to hire Denby Hughs? Who agreed to help you smuggle British goods in the country? Who's run the risk of being hanged should your little scheme fail? Me! That's who!"

"Then prove how brave you are and kill Brittany Lockwood," the other demanded. "She's a threat. Sooner or later she'll find out what's going on and why." The woman's eyes narrowed behind her mask when she saw Miles's nervous reaction. "She already has, hasn't she? Somehow you've managed to foul things up, and she knows about the caravan cutting through her property. You fool!"

"Yes, but she thinks it's Dane Remington's doings," he barked in defense. "She told me so. And I helped convince her of it. I told her he was the one who set fire to the crops!"

"You stupid, arrogant fool," the woman hissed. "All she has to do is tell someone, and they'll laugh in her face. There's hardly a single British official who doesn't know what he is, and once she learns that, the rest will be easy to figure out. You've ruined everything, Miles." Her mouth twisted in a hateful snarl as she moved away from the door and went to the window to stare absently outside into the darkness. Then, as if struck with a brilliant idea, she slowly turned around. "Maybe not," she smiled evilly. "Maybe you've actually helped speed things along. I wasn't sure yet just how I'd get to him, but you've given me the answer. In fact," she sneered, bending forward slightly to lift her black skirt and ruffled, white petticoats to her knee, "you're going to help."

Miles's eyes widened as he watched her pull a small dagger from the scabbard tied around a shapely calf. "W-what are you going to—"

His question was never fully asked, for in that instant, the woman dressed in black took aim and snapped the silver blade through the air with practiced ease. It struck and buried its tip deeply in Miles's chest before he could react, before he could duck out of the way or scream for her not to kill him. His pain was only momentary, the blood on his shirt hardly more than a dot, and his knees only held him long enough for him to stare at the pearl handled weapon protruding from his chest, then at the woman who had thrown it, before he staggered forward, bumped the table and the candle sitting on top, and collapsed to the floor in a lifeless heap.

A demonic smile crept over Millicent's face as she stared down at the unmoving body on the floor. The sniveling coward was dead, but with his demise, he would do her more good than all the carts full of merchandise he had hidden and later sold for her. The murder of Miles Ingram would send the authorities scouring the city in search of his killer. Drawing a kerchief from the sleeve of her gown, she untied the knot and withdrew the coin she had carried in it, the one she kept with her at all times. She knew one day it would serve her purpose. Crouching beside Miles's body, she laid the copper piece in the middle of his forehead, patted his cheek and stood.

"Thank you, Miles," she whispered. "You've been more help than you'll ever know. They'll hang the Dark Horseman, and I'll be there to watch." Turning, she extinguished the flame and moved toward the door. Glancing back only once, she turned the knob and made good her escape. She'd lose herself among the other guests, then quite casually leave the manor. No one would ever know she had killed Miles Ingram, for the copper coin she left behind clearly marked its owner.

Chapter Sixteen

The entire city of Boston had come alive with the news of Miles Ingram's murder. His body had been discovered by a wayward guest at the ball who'd sought a private spot to soothe her wounded pride over her inability to find a dance partner. Since the man's body was still warm, it was concluded that had the guest entered the room only moments earlier, Miles would still be alive, or at the least, a witness would have been able to describe the murderer. As a result, the manor had been sealed off almost immediately and every person there unmasked. But for all their efforts, the only bits of information they were able to obtain had been that from the list of guests, Lord Archibald Hayes, his wife Wilhemina, Howard and Charles Richards, and two servants had escaped unquestioned.

Yet this bit of knowledge proved unimportant once it was discovered that Bartholomew's young house guest, Brittany Lockwood, was missing, for hasty assumptions were made that she had been kidnapped by the man known as the Dark Horseman, the one who'd left his Sons of Liberty coin on Miles's forehead after he had stabbed him. A curfew was immediately enforced, the guests were sent home, and bands of soldiers were ordered to question every known member of the rebel organization. If the Dark Horseman had Brittany,

413

they would find her. But as the sun slowly rose, all hope of rescuing the young woman before harm came to her dwindled. And for all their well-intended motives, no one—including the distraught Bartholomew—thought to search the Lockwood farm.

Brittany viewed the sunrise from within the burnt-out remains of the barn. She had spent most of the night crying and trying to rid her mind of the image of Miles's lifeless body lying on the floor with a knife sticking out of it, and when all her grief was spent, she wearily propped herself up against the far wall where she could keep an eye on the entrance. She had no clue to the identity of the woman who had killed Miles, and therefore couldn't risk her own life trying to get to someone who could protect her. And to whom would she go? Dane?

A tear slid down her cheek when his name came to mind. He obviously didn't care. Otherwise he wouldn't have said all those horrible things to her. And whatever possessed him to come to the Ingram estate anyway? Had he truly brought Roan with him? She doubted it. Roan wouldn't have been so foolish. One mistake on his part, and he'd have been arrested and sent back to gaol. No, if her brother had wanted to see her, he'd have found some other way. Then why had Dane tried to fool her? Was it a way of ensuring she wouldn't scream—just as he had said? It still didn't explain why he had come. A tremulous sigh escaped her and she dropped her head back against the wall, her eyes shut. Was it possible he had tried to warn her about Miles? Did he know who the woman was? Biting her lip, she squeezed her eyes tighter and shook her head. It was all so confusing. All the time she had thought Dane was behind the transporting of smuggled goods, it had actually been Miles. And when she'd stumbled across the operation, who had she run to to tell? Miles! Dear God, he could just as easily have killed her as listened to her. A shudder raced down her spine as she recalled his confession to his partner. He had gone along with the woman's scheme—why, Brittany would never know—but when it came to killing her, he had refused. He had told the woman that he wanted to marry Brittany, and because of it, because he had gone against this woman, Miles had paid with his life.

A strange feeling came over her and she jerked herself up from the floor, her ice-blue satin skirts rustling with each step she took. It was difficult to admit, but she realized now that she was still alive because of Miles and that while someone had attacked him with a knife, she had just sat there. She hadn't done a thing to prevent it. He had given his life for hers. She was ashamed, horribly, unexplainably ashamed of her weakness, her hate at that moment for what he had done. It had stopped her from jumping to her feet and screaming and sounding an alarm that would have brought enough people storming into the room so that Miles would have been spared. Maybe what he was doing had been illegal and immoral, but he had never hurt anyone. He hadn't deserved to die.

"Oh God, listen to me," she moaned, reaching up to pull the pearl-studded pins from her hair. "He was a part of a bigger scheme to ruin my family and I'm standing here defending him!" Numb, she wandered toward the huge door of the barn and stared out across the blackened fields toward the Ingram estate, oddly wishing she could go back. But how could she? She could never face Bartholomew again knowing that she alone could have stopped Miles's brutal murder and didn't. The old man would never understand. He would never forgive her, especially after all he'd done for her.

Sucking in a deep breath, she raised her chin and gazed up at the pale blue of the sky with its sprinkling of clouds and tints of pastel yellows and pinks. It was odd how time merely continued on as though nothing happened. She had felt that strange sensation the morning she and her brother had buried their father. It was almost as if the world didn't care.

Well, she cared. And she owed Bartholomew that much. She was obligated to tell someone what went on inside the library last night, someone who would listen and act upon it. Whoever that woman was, she deserved to be caught and punished.

Brittany straightened suddenly with a chill of worry gripping her heart as she recalled the words the woman had whispered over Miles's body. She had said that the Dark Horseman would hang and that she'd be there to watch. Had she figured out a way to blame the Dark Horseman for Miles's death? Was it her plan to have the wrong person unfairly accused and punished for it? And why the Dark Horseman? Was there a connection? Shaky fingertips reached up to press against her temples. If so—if there was the slightest possibility of that—she had to prevent it. She had to see to it that the right person paid for Miles's murder. But how? What could she do? Tell Bartholomew? To do that, she'd have to tell him everything. And would he believe her? Venting a long sigh and squaring her shoulders, she decided that she at least had to try.

Rather than cut through the fields as she had last night, Brittany followed the road, where it was easier to walk. The dew upon the grasses had weighted down her skirts and soaked through her slippers, slowing her pace, and now that she had come to a decision, she didn't want anything to delay the execution of it. Yet before she had walked very far down the road, she noticed a raspberry bush growing wild at the side of the road. The sight of it reminded her that she hadn't eaten this morning, and although she would have liked continuing on, the temptation was too great. After all, it would only take her a moment or two to gather a handful of berries and be on her way again. Stepping into the thicket, she hurriedly began selecting the ripest.

"Ye mean ye 'aven't 'eard what 'appened over there last night?"

"No, 'arry, I 'aven't," the man's companion replied

disgustedly as they edged their way through the woods toward the road.

"Why, ol' man Ingram's boy was murdered," Harry proclaimed. "Stabbed in the 'eart, 'e was."

"Ye ain't serious?" the other denied, shifting his fishing pole to his other shoulder.

"I am. The constable came knockin' on our door in the middle o' the night wantin' to know if we'd 'eard or seen anythin'. Well, the missus and me told 'em we 'adn't, of course. Been asleep 'til 'e came."

"Did 'e say who done it?"

"Not exactly," Harry admitted with a shrug.

"And what's that supposed to mean?"

"Well, 'e said they were lookin' for Patrick Lockwood's daughter. She'd been stayin' up at the manor since 'er place burned."

"Yeah, so?" his friend urged.

"Well, 'e said they thought she'd been kidnapped by the murderer."

"Kidnapped?"

"Aye. Once Ingram's body was found, she was missin'. But ye know what I think?"

The other shook his head.

"I think she's the one what did it."

"Killed Ingram, ye mean?"

"Aye. And I told the constable that. Everybody knows 'er brother is mixed up with these rebels. So what's ta stop 'er from gettin' 'erself an invitation to live in their 'ouse, then murderin' Ingram when she 'ad the chance?"

"But why would she do that?"

"'Cause Ingram's the one what signed the papers to arrest 'er brother for arson. Revenge, dear friend. She did it for revenge."

"Oh, I don't believe that. She was a nice girl."

"Ha!" Harry exploded. "Ye didn't know 'er. Spoiled, she was. 'Sides, the constable let it slip that they found a copper coin on Ingram's body, a Sons of Liberty coin. And everybody knows who carries 'em. The Dark Horseman. I think she's workin' for 'im."

Brittany neither heard nor cared if the other man replied. All she was thankful for was that the men had chosen this spot to cross to the stream and that it was at this exact time when they freely discussed what everyone else seemed to be talking about. If they hadn't—if she had gone on instead of stopping to pick berries—she probably would have found herself in gaol. Collapsing to the ground behind a tree, she leaned back against the rough bark and closed her eyes. In all her young life, she had never felt so alone . . . so scared. . . .

The lengthening shadows of sunset spilled across the countryside and hid within their arms the passage of a young woman making her way toward the city. In the distance thunder rumbled and the black clouds in the north moved with eerie stealth to cut her off before she had reached her destination. The streets of Boston were nearly empty by the time Brittany had hurriedly traveled the length of Long Wharf and turned down the avenue leading to the center of town, a condition she had prayed for while awaiting the day's end in the barn back on her farm.

Since overhearing the two men on the road this morning, she had spent the time safe within the confines of the burned-out structure where she could fathom what should be done. If what the men had said was true, then not only were the soldiers looking for her, but for the Dark Horseman as well. He must be warned, she knew that, and the only one who could help lead her to him was Paul Revere. Her mission was dangerous and one that must be accomplished with utmost care and secrecy, for one slip on her part and not only would she be caught, but Mr. Revere's covert identity revealed.

Knowing that she couldn't very well walk the streets dressed in her blue satin ballgown without raising an eyebrow or two, and worse the curiosity of someone who might inform the authorities, she had slid out of the garment, loosened her hair, and smeared soot over her nose, cheeks, and chin. It had seemed to be a good idea until she bent down to grab the blanket lying on the mound of hay and a host of memories filled her brain. The last time she had draped this rough piece of cloth about her shoulders had been the night she'd spent in Dane's arms. It had been a wonderful, exciting interlude, and one she doubted she would ever relive. A tear had stolen down her cheek, and she had quickly brushed it away, stiffened her spine, and set her mind on her endeavor. She had spent enough time feeling sorry for herself. Ripping two slits in the blanket for sleeves, she had slipped her arms through them, pulled the edges tightly closed over her bosom and stomach, and tied the cloth at her waist with a piece of rope. To anyone who noticed, she would appear to be a woman whose luck was down.

The silversmith's shop was located in the middle of the block, and as Brittany stepped around the corner and placed the storefront in clear view, she came to an abrupt halt. Three red-coated soldiers were leaving the store and were being followed by a fourth man, a rather plump, dark-haired gentleman who Brittany suspected might be Mr. Revere. Cautiously ducking into an alleyway, she watched until the soldiers mounted and rode off and the gentleman had gone back inside before she hurriedly left her hiding place and dashed across the street to the shop. Her heart was pounding rapidly by the time she reached the front door, and a whimper escaped her before she could regain her courage, for just as she touched a hand to the knob, the light inside the store was extinguished. Rapping urgently yet softly, she guardedly glanced in both directions down the street to ensure no one was watching, then heard the man's reply to her summons.

"I'm closed," his voice called out to her through the thick wooden barrier. "Come back in the morning."

"Please, Mr. Revere," she begged as loudly as she dare. "I must speak with you. I'm Roan's sister."

The lock clicked instantly. The door was swung open, and a hand reached out from the darkness to seize her wrist and pull her inside. Once their privacy was secured, the figure who still held her arm guided them into a back room through a curtained entryway where the shutters were closed over the windows and a single candle lit the small space.

"We've been worried about you, Miss Lockwood," Revere frowned, gently pushing her down in a chair and turning for the kettle hanging over the small fire in the hearth. "Where have you been?"

"Hiding," she easily admitted as her body surrendered to her fatigue and began to tremble. "Is it true? Do they really think I killed Miles?"

Handing her the cup of tea he'd made, Revere smiled. "The ones who matter don't." His dark brows came together briefly as he took in her attire and the dirt smudges on her face. Then, thinking she might be hungry and not bothering to ask, he set about preparing something for her to eat. "Can you tell me what happened?"

Brittany wasn't sure where to begin. Taking a sip of the tea and grimacing at the taste of the whiskey that had been added to relax her, she leaned back in the chair and sighed. "It's a long story, Mr. Revere. It didn't just begin with Miles's death or the day I accepted their kind offer to live at Yorkshire Manor." Dane's cruel accusation came to mind. "Bartholomew Ingram and I had made a business deal. He'd pay off my debts and for rebuilding the house and barn in exchange for half the profits from each harvest until the loan was repaid. Part of the agreement was that I live at the manor until April—planting time, and it's the *only* reason I stayed."

Revere could hear her underlying need to be believed. "No one's judging you, Miss Lockwood. Certainly not I. These are difficult times for the people of Boston—of the colonies.

420

Many of us are moved to do things we normally wouldn't dream of doing." He smiled reassuringly as he set down a plate of food on the table beside her. "So tell me why you ran."

The vision of the pearl-handled knife buried to the hilt in Miles's chest made her cringe, and she took another drink of tea, wishing there was more whiskey in it. "I was there . . . in the library. I had gone there to be alone and was sitting in one of the wing chairs by the fireplace . . . in the darkness. I guess that's why they didn't see me."

"They?" Revere parroted, sitting in the chair opposite her at the table. "Who, Miss Lockwood?"

Staring blankly off into space, Brittany relived the moment in her mind. "Miles and a woman. They had come to the library for the same reason as I . . . privacy. The woman was angry with Miles. She wanted to know why he hadn't disposed of me . . . the way she had ordered him to. He said he wouldn't—that he loved me and wanted to marry me. She called him a coward, and Miles denied it. He asked her whose idea it was to burn my crops, who it was who helped her smuggle goods into the colonies, and who ran the same risk of being hanged should the scheme fail. She called him a fool, told him he had ruined everything." Brittany closed her eyes and choked down the knot in her throat. "I'm not exactly sure what happened then. I couldn't see. But I heard the fear in Miles's voice when he asked what she was doing. Then I heard him groan and stumble, then fall to the floor. I suppose that's when she stabbed him."

Revere reached across the table and gently squeezed her hand. "Who was she, Miss Lockwood?"

A tear stole between her lashes and dropped on the fingers wrapped around her teacup. "I don't know. I was too afraid to move, too afraid to do anything, too afraid to help Miles."

"And rightly so," he urged. "She would have killed you too, had she known you were there. You did the right thing, Miss Lockwood, so don't go blaming yourself. Miles Ingram

421

knew the danger involved in what he was doing."

"But she was his partner," Brittany objected. "And she killed him."

"A partner?" Revere speculated. "I don't think so. From what you've told me, I'd say she was merely using him, and that sooner or later he would have wound up dead anyway." Rising from his chair, he wandered aimlessly around the room, deep in thought. "What I'm wondering is if she's working alone."

"She's not working with the Dark Horseman!" Brittany blurted out, remembering the conversation of the two fishermen.

Surprised, Revere paused in his stroll. "What makes you say that?"

"The coin . . . the one she left behind. She wanted people to think the Dark Horseman was responsible. She said so." Brittany squeezed her eyes shut, trying to remember her exact words. "I heard her thank Miles for his help . . . after he was dead. 'They'll hang the Dark Horseman, and I'll be there to watch!' That's what she said!" Her eyes flew open, and she set her attention on Revere. "I think she was thanking Miles for making her angry enough to kill him and at the same time give her the method to frame the Dark Horseman." Her hand shaking nervously, Brittany set the teacup on the table and rose. "He's got to be warned, Mr. Revere. He's got to stop his escapades for a while. Every soldier in the city is looking for him now and they'll shoot without giving him a chance to surrender! Take me to him, please? Let me tell him what I know."

"Calm yourself, Miss Lockwood," Revere soothed, taking her hands in his. "He already knows, believe me. He's being protected. But I think something must be done about you."

"Me?" Brittany echoed. "What about me?"

"Your life is in danger as well, my dear. Not only do the British want you, but this woman does too, I'm sure. And since you don't know who she is, you can't trust anyone."

"But I can't spend the rest of my life looking over my shoulder," Brittany argued.

"Agreed," Revere nodded. "So the only answer is for you to leave Boston for a spell."

"Leave Boston!" she exclaimed. "But where would I go? I have no relatives except Roan."

"Now don't get yourself in a dither, Miss Lockwood. You're a friend of the Sons of Liberty. We take care of our own. We've been taking care of Roan, haven't we?"

His soft smile eased her nervousness a little, but Brittany still wasn't fond of his idea for her to leave Boston. It meant she would have to depend on someone's help again—the way she had depended on Bartholomew's, even though they had struck a deal—and look where that had gotten her.

"And the first thing we have to do is find you something to wear." Pushing her back down in the chair, he turned for the back door. "You eat your supper while I pay a friend a visit. Then you and I are going to see John Hancock."

As Brittany walked alongside Paul Revere, she wasn't sure if her trepidation was due to her situation or the fact that she was about to meet the great John Hancock. Her father had talked endlessly about the man and how those who opposed British rule looked to him for guidance. He was something of a god in Brittany's mind, and right now she didn't feel worthy of his attention.

"You must thank whoever gave me this dress," she said, forcing herself to think about something other than where they were headed.

"I already have," Revere smiled, leading her down an alleyway that ran parallel with the common in the center of town. "When I told her who it was for, she said she was honored to be of help."

"Honored?" Brittany laughed. "Why would she feel honored?"

423

"Well, because you're Roan's sister. He's thought of quite highly in my circle of friends. They admire his courage and loyalty." He cast her a sidelong glance. "As they do you."

"Me?" she objected. "I haven't done anything to be admired for."

"Miss Lockwood, everyone's aware of how you stuck by Roan when he was in trouble, and because of you, the brother of one of our most valuable men was freed from gaol. Had he stayed in there one more day, he might have been hanged," Revere added with a lift of his brows.

Brittany couldn't imagine who he meant nor was she given the chance to comment, for in that same moment he paused by the back gate of one of the houses in the block, shot a quick glance up and down the alley, then motioned her into the yard. He led her around to a door at the side of the house, checked once again to make sure no one was watching, and rapped three times. A moment or two passed before Brittany heard the sounds of footsteps from inside and a bolt being slid. But before they were allowed entry, the person on the other side called out for Revere to identify himself.

"Silver and gold," he replied in a loud whisper, bringing a puzzled frown to Brittany's brow.

The latch clicked instantly and the door was opened to reveal a man dressed in a butler's uniform who, upon recognizing Revere, nodded and stepped aside to allow them to enter.

"They're in the library, sir," the man informed Revere as he closed and locked the door behind them.

"Thank you, William," Revere replied, taking Brittany's elbow and guiding her through the kitchen and into the hall. "I should have mentioned it to you earlier, Miss Lockwood, but had you arrived at my shop a moment later, I wouldn't have been there. We had already scheduled a meeting tonight to discuss what should be done about you."

"Me? You were going to talk about me?"

"Yes. Your brother asked our help."

Brittany's steps faltered and she stopped in the middle of the hallway. "Is Roan here? May I see him? I have to explain."

"There's nothing to explain, my dear. Roan never doubted you for a second—you should know that. But as for seeing him—well, that will have to wait for a while. We didn't think it was safe for him to stay in Boston. But you'll see each other again. Soon." He smiled encouragingly and pointed to the opened doorway a few feet further on.

The three men who sat leisurely around the desk in the middle of the room immediately came to their feet the moment Brittany and Revere entered. The men shook hands and then all eyes centered on the young woman Revere had brought with him.

"I'd like you to meet Brittany Lockwood, Roan's sister," Revere said with a grin as if he were responsible for having found her. "Miss Lockwood, I'd like to introduce John Hancock, James Otis, and the one staring with his chin down to his knees is Dr. Warren."

That one quickly snapped his mouth shut and stepped forward to offer her his chair. "I didn't mean to gape, Miss Lockwood," he apologized as he watched her sit down. "It's just that our associates have been looking everywhere for you and you simply walk into the house. It doesn't say much for our methods."

"I've been hiding," she smiled softly. "And it's I who should apologize for causing you any trouble."

"Trouble?" Hancock repeated. "It's no trouble to us. After Roan told us what he thought was going on, it became our obligation to help."

"Miss Lockwood," Revere urged, "why don't you tell them what happened last night? I'm sure once you have they'll feel the same as I about your leaving the city for a time." He glanced over at Hancock. "She was in the room when Ingram was murdered."

"You saw who did it?" Hancock asked.

"No, sir. I only heard her voice."

"Her voice?" Otis and Dr. Warren echoed. "A woman killed Miles Ingram?"

"Yes," Revere interjected. "And I'm sure she'll try to get to Miss Lockwood. It's why I think we should get her out of the city."

"But if you didn't see the woman, Miss Lockwood, doesn't that mean she didn't see you? Why would she be after you if she wasn't aware you witnessed the murder?"

"Whoever she is," Brittany began, "she wants me dead and did long before she took Miles's life."

Otis and the doctor exchanged puzzled glances. Hancock settled himself in the chair behind the desk to listen, knowing Brittany's story would be long and involved. The group listened quietly, never offering a comment or flinching while Brittany repeated the tale from beginning to end. When she had finished, Hancock reached for his pipe, packed tobacco in the bowl, and lit it, deep in thought. Finally, after what seemed an immensely long while, he laid his pipe in an ashtray and reached for paper and pen.

"I agree with Mr. Revere, Miss Lockwood," he said, signing his name to the bottom of the letter he had written. "You shouldn't stay in Boston." Sealing the parchment with a drop of wax, then applying his mark to it, he rose from the desk, crossed the room, and called out for William. "One of our members is sailing for Williamsburg, Virginia in the morning. This note will allow you passage on his ship. I've also asked him to contact one of our associates there to provide refuge for you until this matter of the woman is cleared up. You'll be safe there." As the butler came down the hall, Hancock stepped out of the room, handed him the message, and gave him instructions as to where it should be delivered. Satisfied that his orders would be obeyed, he came back into the room and sat down again. "Our next problem

426

is smuggling you on board." He glanced at the men watching him. "Any ideas?"

A light rain had begun to fall by the time Brittany had changed clothes again and was being hurriedly ushered into the back of a cart filled with crates and barrels and furniture in the alleyway behind Hancock's home.

"Keep your head down," the man helping her instructed. "We've got to get you to the docks without anyone seeing you. Put this tarpaulin over you and stay there until I tell you to come out. Understand?"

Brittany nodded.

"Now if for some reason we're stopped along the way and the cart's searched, you're to pretend you're my brother, Billy." He nodded at the shirt and breeches she wore. "That's the reason for the disguise. They'll be looking for a woman, not my younger brother. If it's at all possible, don't say anything. We don't want to run the risk of them figuring out you're not really a boy." He smiled comfortingly at the fearful expression on her face. "By the way, my name's Dennis Holt."

"Thank you, Dennis," Brittany replied weakly.

"Oh there's no need to thank me, ma'am. I'm just doin' what I'm ordered to do." Waiting until she had found a comfortable spot to sit with her knees drawn up and head down, Holt readjusted the heavy canvas over her, waved at the dark figures watching from the window in the library, and climbed into the cart. With a snap of the reins, he started them off down the alley.

Brittany had promised herself she wouldn't cry; it was a weakness she couldn't afford. Hancock, Revere, and the others had gone to great lengths to protect her, and even though she had yet to reach the ship and sail out of Boston Harbor, she felt reasonably sure she'd be safe. Her tears, however, came not from fear, but sorrow. Once the frigate weighed anchor and set a course for Virginia, she would be closing a chapter in her life. She doubted she'd ever be able to come home again, and even if she could, by that time Bartholomew Ingram would have more than likely sold her property for the money she owed him. There would be nothing left for her.

The ride to Long Wharf was bumpy and filled with numerous turns. When Holt had finally drawn the cart in close to the pier, Brittany felt as though she had traveled for days, and when he came around to pull off the canvas, she wondered if the sea voyage would be any more comfortable than this.

"We'll have to row out to her," Dennis was saying as he helped Brittany to the ground. "She's anchored in deeper waters."

"Are you going along?" she asked, hurrying alongside him as he walked her down the pier toward a small boat.

"Aye," he nodded, glancing over his shoulder. "I'm one of the crew."

"And we'll be sailing in the morning?"

"No. Cap'n changed his plans," Dennis replied, jumping into the boat, then holding out his hands to help her. "We're dropping sail as soon as we've hidden you away." He pointed toward the heavy rope. "Undo that, will you?"

Brittany did as he asked, then settled herself on the seat while Dennis took the oars and began rowing them out toward the lone frigate. The rain was coming down much harder now and started to soak through her clothes. Pulling up the collar on her jacket, she readjusted her tricorn to keep the water from dripping down her neck and set her gaze on the huge ship which would be her haven for a time. A shout went up when someone on board spotted them, and before they had tied off the boat and started up the rope ladder, the sails were being dropped and she could hear the clanking of the chain as the anchor was lifted.

"Have any trouble?" someone asked when she and Dennis

stood on the deck.

"No. I think the rain helped. Those dandified redcoats don't like gettin' wet," Dennis laughed as he took Brittany's elbow. "Cap'n say where he wants her?"

"In his quarters for now," the other instructed. "If we're stopped, then she's to come topside and pretend she's standing watch. Those fools would never think to find her working on the ship."

"Good idea," Dennis agreed. "You think of it, Drexler?"

But before the man could affirm or deny it, Dennis stepped away, taking the slim figure dressed in ill-fitting clothes with him.

"I would imagine the cap'n will be down as soon as we've sailed out of sight of the coastline, Miss Lockwood," Dennis said as he opened the door to the cabin. "And I'm sure the cap'n would want you to help yourself to anything he has. If you'd like a sip of whiskey to warm you, you'll find it in the top drawer of his desk, left-hand side."

"Thank you, Dennis. You've been very kind."

His blue eyes softened as he studied her. "Can't help it, ma'am. I like the cap'n too much." Without giving her a chance to ask what he meant, Dennis stepped back and pulled the door shut.

Brittany's puzzled frown was replaced by a grimace from the chill that shot down her spine, and rather than figure out Dennis Holt's ambiguous comment, she decided to do as he offered and help herself to the captain's whiskey. Lifting the tricorn from her head, she shook out the long, golden strands of hair hidden beneath. Next, she removed her wet jacket and tossed both garments on a chair near her before she crossed to the desk and pulled open the drawer. Just as he had said, a bottle of whiskey lay inside. Popping the cork, she poured a small amount into a glass and took a sip. It burned all the way down and made her gasp for air. But within seconds she could feel its warming effect. Jamming the cork back in place, she put the bottle away and walked across the cabin to stare out through the three side-by-side windows at the lights of Boston, drink in hand.

Who'd have ever guessed a few short months ago that she'd be dressed in boy's clothes and standing in the captain's quarters on her way to Virginia? She remembered complaining to her father one time about how uneventful her life seemed to be, but she'd gladly trade it all for the chance to be sitting around the table in their house listening to her father and Roan argue.

And if you don't stop thinking about the past, you'll start crying again, she silently scolded herself. Your brother's a lot younger than you, and look what he's doing with his life. He's trying to change the future. If he can do it, so can you.

Raising the glass to her lips, she threw back her head and swallowed the rest of the whiskey in a brave show of defiance, instantly sorry she had. It seemed her throat and stomach were on fire. The pain in her chest was unbearable, and she thought she would die before she could drag air into her tortured lungs. Tears welled in her eyes and ran down her face when she blinked. Maybe she should leave this sort of thing to the men. They seemed more able to handle it. Wiping the moisture from her cheeks, she turned back for the desk and paused when she noticed the huge bunk on the opposite wall. It looked so inviting. And hadn't Dennis as much as told her to make herself comfortable? Listening to the faint shouts of the men topside as they maneuvered the frigate out to sea, she decided it would be a while before the captain came to his quarters. Setting aside her glass, she went to the bunk and sat down, moaning delightedly at its softness. She'd only take a nap. When the captain returned, she'd hear him open the door.

Sleep came easily for Brittany. She had been so bone-weary with all the events of the past two days that when she laid her head on the pillow, her eyes drifted shut almost instantly, and the gentle rhythm of the rain hitting the deck above the cabin lulled her to sleep within seconds. Visions of home, Roan, and her father filled her dreams. It was winter and a blanket of snow covered the yard outside their home. Bundled in warm clothes, the young brother and sister went outside to play. They built snowmen and forts. They pelted each other with snowballs and went sled riding. Their hands and feet numb, they finally went back into the house to warm themselves by the fire. But their father was gone, and when they called out to him, he didn't answer. Frightened, the children ran back outside to look for him. The snow had melted and disappeared, and spring flowers grew everywhere. The bright colors faded, and in their place the blackened, charred remains of the house and barn and fields loomed up to enshroud Brittany. She was no longer a child, but a woman, full-grown. Cheerful laughter and the sweet strains of violins soothed her for a while. Then a pearl-handled knife glowed in the darkness, and in her dreams she started to scream, but no sound escaped her lips. Fearing for her life, she ran, an endless trek that took her through the streets of Boston. The ice-blue satin gown she wore suddenly transformed itself into breeches and a shirt, and she staggered to a stop, breathless and afraid. Then, from out of nowhere, a crowd began to gather around her, pushing and shoving and carrying her along until they came to the center of town. There before her, she saw the stark silhouette of the gallows against a red sky, and dangling from it was the lifeless form of the Dark Horseman, his hands bound behind him, his neck broken. No-o-o-o! she wailed, clawing her way through the faceless mass who stood mute and uncaring. But before she could reach him, a woman veiled in black stepped out in front of her, and the eerie laughter which assailed Brittany jolted her out of her nightmare.

Damp with perspiration, Brittany sat up in the bunk and buried her face in her hands. The dream had been so real that it had made her tremble. If only she knew the identity of the woman, she might be able to bring this whole affair to an end.

"But I don't," she whispered, sliding back against the wall and noticing for the first time that the lantern light had been extinguished and that someone had covered her with a blanket. How long had she been asleep? she wondered. Had the captain come to his cabin to talk to her and left again without disturbing her? Where was he now? Her gaze shifted to the windows. How far had they sailed? Curious, she slid off the bunk and crossed the cabin to look outside. The rain had stopped and even the dark clouds were gone. Bright, twinkling stars dotted the velvet sky and cast a silver glow in the water, but other than that, she saw nothing that gave her any indication of where they were or how far they had come.

Wide awake now and honestly too upset to try and sleep again—the nightmare might begin again—she crossed to the captain's desk and lit the lantern. Sitting down in his chair, she leaned back to contemplate her future and was struck with a very odd, very unsettling feeling. This was her first time on board a ship of any kind, but her inner senses hinted otherwise. Her gaze quickly surveyed the room. Nothing was familiar. It was just a cabin—the captain's quarters. She studied the desk top. Nothing there out of the ordinary: a spyglass, quill and ink, charts, maps, a compass, and the bottle of whiskey she had neglected to put back in the drawer. Reaching for it with the intention of replacing it, her eyes caught sight of a piece of paper partially hidden beneath a stack of others, and instinct told her to examine it. Pulling it free, she saw that her name had been penned over its surface numerous times: long, bold letters, script, printing, various styles—all done in an unrecognizable handwriting. What did it mean? Who had written this? And why?

The small confinement of the cabin seemed to intensify. The paper in her hand seemed to radiate heat. Dropping it, she darted out of the chair and ran for the windows. In a panic, she fumbled with the lock, freed it, and hurled the sash upward to let in fresh air and clear her brain. This was too coincidental! That feeling assailed her again, but this time it brought with it a vague rationale. It started with something Miles's murderer had said when Miles told her he had convinced Brittany that Dane was behind the smuggling going on.

All she has to do is tell someone and they'll laugh in her face. There's hardly a single British official who doesn't know what he is. . . .

Brittany's knees suddenly went weak and she sank down on the bench beneath the window. He was a member of the Sons of Liberty! It was the reason the Dark Horseman came to her farm that night: he wanted to talk with Dane. And if Dane was a member, then so were Brad and Cory and probably the midget named Dooley. The midget! The image of the child she saw running away from her place flashed to mind. It was no child! It had been Dooley! And Brad . . . she had questioned why a British soldier had shot him if he and Dane were working for England. Well, they weren't . . . that's why he had been in the crowd of protesters. Dear God, she had been wrong about everything!

Numb, she came to her feet and aimlessly walked the perimeter of the cabin. Dane had admitted that Roan was the reason he had come to the farm to help. Roan was working for Paul Revere. Revere was a member of the Sons of Liberty. He told her that other members admired her courage and because of her, she had helped break a member's brother out of gaol. Of course! It was Brad! How could she have been so blind? But the most startling revelation she discovered was the connection she made between that piece of paper on the desk and something Hancock said. *One of our members is sailing to Williamsburg, Virginia in the morning.* It was Dane! This cabin belonged to Dane. This ship belonged to Dane. Tears flooded her eyes. That paper belonged to Dane. Suddenly, unexplainably, a rage boiled up within her. It was obvious he knew all along about Miles and the man's illegal dealings. He knew and he never said a word to her. In fact, he had implied that she was working with Miles. Damn him! Damn him for his lies, his deceit! Well, no more. She knew everything there was to know about him.

Footsteps sounded outside the doorway and Brittany spun around, ready to face him. He had a lot of explaining to do, and maybe—if he was lucky—she'd forgive him. But somehow she didn't think that was possible. Yet as the latch clicked and the hinges squeaked a little, she began to doubt her own words. There was something about him that wouldn't let her hate him—no matter what he had done.

"Brittany."

Her name upon his lips was like music to her ears. The sight of him melted the icy shell she had tried to build around her heart. He really looked no different. He was still broad-shouldered, had raven-black hair, a strong jaw, a sensuous mouth and those incredible green eyes. Yet he wasn't the same. She blinked and forced herself to turn away.

"Are you surprised? Or disappointed?" she asked coldly.

Surprised? he thought. Only that she didn't hurl herself at him with nails bared and ready to claw his face. But never disappointed. She was as stunning as the first time he saw her, the night she bargained her virginity in exchange for his help in freeing her brother from gaol, as the time he found her in the gardens on the Ingram estate clothed in a blue satin ballgown with pearls around her neck, on her ears and sprinkled in her hair, as stunning when moonlight graced her slender form there in the meadow where they had made love. He had spent the last hour on deck trying to figure how to broach his apology and now that that time had come, he couldn't recite the words he had practiced over and over again. They simply sounded too shallow. He moved into the cabin and closed the door.

"Maybe I should be asking that of you," he quietly replied, his eyes watching every little move she made, raking in the beauty of her lithe form garbed in breeches and a shirt.

"Actually, I'm both, if you really care to know," she

answered crisply, returning to the windows to stare absently out at the sea. "Obviously I was quite surprised to learn that the man I thought was using my property to smuggle goods into the colonies was really trying to catch the one who was. I was even more surprised to learn that that same man—the one I thought was an unprincipled cad—was a member of the Sons of Liberty. And I guess my disappointment comes from learning that I was wrong. Or partly so. You're still an unprincipled cad." She cast him a cold, hard look over one shoulder. "Did you truly think I was involved with Miles Ingram? In both senses of the word?"

Her question pained him. He couldn't lie to her. She'd know he was by the look in his eye . . . the tone of his voice. Dropping his gaze away from her, he crossed to the desk and poured himself a glass of whiskey. But rather than drink it, he studied its amber hue while he swirled it around.

"It was unfair. I know that now. But maybe I can make you understand my reasons by explaining what led up to it." Changing his mind about the drink, he set the glass down and turned to perch a hip on the corner of his desk. He was quiet for a moment while he contemplated where to begin. "I've been with the Sons of Liberty for several years now, hiding behind the illusion that I was uninterested in what government ruled the colonies. It was the only way to mask what I was really doing. In order to succeed, I couldn't trust anyone, and it was my job to be suspicious. I know I never gave you the chance to prove yourself, but I wasn't just risking my identity, I was risking everyone's; my brother's, Cory's, Dooley's, that of the entire crew on this ship, and maybe even those of a few merchants in Boston. I couldn't take that chance." He gazed off into space and cleared his throat. "Because of the dangers involved and because we never really know who our enemies are, I began wondering about you . . . especially after we stumbled across the men in the woods and you showed very little interest in finding out who they were. From there, it got worse. I started fabricating all sorts of reasons why. Then after the fire, after you went to live at the Ingram estate, I was sure I had been right about you. You must admit that from my side it certainly looked that way." He shifted his attention on her and frowned at the chilling expression on her face. "Brittany—" He called her name most urgently. "I left you that morning in the barn after the fire not because I was finished with you, but because I needed time to think. I needed to be alone."

"To think?" she inquired acidly. "About what? How long you could go on using me before you were forced to turn me over to—to whoever was interested?"

"No!" he shouted angrily. "I wasn't using you. I had fallen in love with you and had to decide between you and my loyalties. I had to make up my mind to trust you."

"Love?" she smiled, though there was a sarcastic edge to the word. "You fell in love with me." Laughing, she looked away from him and began idly walking the floor. "Is that why you came to the Ingram's ball? To tell me you loved me? Odd," she added, drawing up beside him, one hand on the desk top, the other knotted in a fist on her hip as she glared eye-to-eye with him, "you didn't sound like a man in love when you accused me of sleeping with Miles."

The truth of that statement cut him to the core. But he had gone too far to let the rest go unsaid. "Didn't I?" he posed. "Didn't it sound like a man in love who through blinding jealousy said the first hurtful thing he could think of?"

The possibility hit Brittany like a bolt of lightning. Blinking, she straightened and turned away.

"And yes," Dane went on, "I came to the Ingram ball to tell you I loved you, to warn you about Miles and what he was planning, to ask you to come away with me. At that moment I didn't care if you were involved in his scheme up to your pretty little chin. All I wanted was you, and I would have done anything to have you." Frustrated, he stood and walked toward the windows as he ran his fingers through his dark hair. "I don't know what happened then, but the instant I saw you, the way you were dressed with gems around your neck and in your hair, saw the way every man stared at you, every woman envied you—hell, something inside me snapped. You looked happy—for the first time since we'd met, you seemed happy. And I felt cheated that I wasn't the one who made you that way." He turned to look at her. "You have every right to hate me, Brittany. I was never honest with you, never honest about my feelings for you. And what makes me so guilty is that deep down inside, I really knew you were innocent all along. I was just too stubborn—scared, maybe—to admit it and to admit that a willful, courageous, beautiful woman had stolen my heart. I love you, Brittany Lockwood."

Tears glistened in her eyes, but she blinked them back. He was right when he said he had hurt her, and she wanted him to pay for it. She wanted him to suffer the way she had. Yet she couldn't stop the overpowering sensation building within her to go to him, to slip her arms around his neck and draw him to her. The image of the Dark Horseman came to mind, and she closed her eyes. Yes, she cared for Dane Remington—as much as she would have liked to deny it, she cared. But he wasn't the only man in her life. There was another—one no one knew about. A troubled frown creased her brow. But did she really love the mysterious stranger? Or was she merely infatuated with him? Had he simply been there at a time when she needed comforting, reassurance, tender compassion?

Listen to your heart, Brittany, her inner voice called out. Trust your instincts. Forgive.

Visions of the moment she and Dane had shared in the barn filled her mind, and the memory of how lost she had felt when she awoke the next morning to find him gone played heavily upon her conscience. She had wondered then how she would ever survive without him. She had longed for him to return with arms widespread and words of love upon his lips. She had wanted him then. Was it truly any different now? A tightness gripped her heart and filled her soul with longing. Lifting her eyes to look at him, she instantly knew the truth. No, it was no different now. This rogue, this scoundrel, this man she deserved to hate had found a way to infect her mind, to steal into her thoughts, and to capture her love.

The golden glow of lantern light fell upon the couple standing only a few feet apart and radiated the love shining in their eyes. Without a word, he stepped closer and slowly raised a hand to stroke the delicate curve of her cheek. Moments passed while she savored the warmth of his touch and allowed the feelings in her heart to take hold. Then his other hand came up to cup her face, and their bodies met full length as he pulled her close and tenderly pressed his lips upon hers. Their passion stirred. Slipping her arms up around his neck, she returned his kiss with all the warmth and yearning of a woman in love. Their lips parted, their tongues met, their breath quickened. Feeling her response, he held her tighter to him, afraid to let go, afraid she would disappear and he would awake from his dreams.

He moaned inwardly when he felt her fingers upon the fastenings of his shirt. Not wanting to allow her a moment of thought, the chance to change her mind, he stripped away the clothes from her silken body, then shed his own. In a frenzy he lifted her in his arms and carried her to the bunk, there to fall gently with her upon the soft mattress. Arms and legs entwined, they kissed hungrily, urgently, passionately, their hands exploring the smooth curve of flesh. Their rapture too long awaited, he rose above her, parted her knees with his, and pressed his manhood full and deep within her. A raging fire ignited within them and coursed through their veins, sending them to dizzying heights. Faint from the splendor of their passion, they clung fiercely to each other, her nails clawing his back, his fingers entwined within the golden locks of her hair, while his mouth moved greedily against hers. Then in a wild explosion of ecstasy, their passions soared and took them to greater plateaus, each more intense, more delirious than before. They lingered near the heavens on gossamer wings until the final release sent them floating back to earth, spent, exhausted, and sighing contentedly, breathlessly.

Drawing her within the circle of his arms, he breathed in the scent of her and closed his eyes, vowing never to doubt her again. Yet had he looked upon the beautiful visage nestled against his hard chest, he would have wondered at the sadness reflected in her gray-blue eyes.

Chapter Seventeen

"Dane, you ol' devil," Beau Remington called from the veranda of Raven Oaks as the carriage came to a complete stop in the circular drive and its passengers began to descend. "I never expected to see you here." Smiling broadly, he hurried down the stairs toward his cousin, his hand extended. "Tell me it's only a social visit and that you're not in any trouble. And where's that good-for-nothing brother of yours?"

Accepting the warm handshake, Dane laughed. "He's still in Boston with some of the rest of my crew. But I'll tell him you missed seeing him."

"You do that," Beau grinned, his eyes shifting to the beautiful young woman at Dane's side and subtly taking in her strange attire. "And who's this?"

It was easy for Brittany to see the resemblance between Dane and his cousin. Beau Remington had the same coal-black hair, the same firm set to his mouth, the same strong jaw and muscular physique. The only real differences, aside from their age, were Beau's dark brown eyes and the peppering of gray at his temples. Both men were extremely handsome and for a brief moment she wondered if Dane's offspring would have the same features of his father or her fairer ones. She blinked and straightened slightly when she realized the direction her thoughts had taken her and prayed the light blush she felt rising in her cheeks would go unnoticed.

"This is Brittany Lockwood, Beau," Dane smiled affectionately. "Brittany, this is my cousin, Beau Remington."

"I'm honored," Beau replied, taking her hand and placing a light kiss upon it. "I hope you'll agree to stay here at Raven Oaks for a while."

"Well, it's the reason we're here," Dane cut in. "Brittany needs a place to stay."

Beau raised a dubious brow. "Sounds urgent."

"It is."

"Then let's talk inside where it's cool," Beau instructed. "I assume you rented this carriage." At Dane's nod, Beau turned to the driver, thanked him for bringing his guests, and sent the man on his way. Then, turning with Brittany sheltered between him and his cousin, he started the group up the stairs. "I surmise it has something to do with the way Miss Lockwood is dressed."

"Yes," Dane admitted. "We had to smuggle her out of Boston."

"Are things so bad?"

"Not any worse than usual," Dane explained. "It's just that Brittany got caught up in the murder of Bartholomew Ingram's son, and we had to get her out of Boston."

"Miles Ingram is dead?" Beau queried, pausing by the front door to allow Brittany to enter first.

"Yes. Happened a few nights ago. But I wasn't aware you knew him."

"Not personally. But the Sons of Liberty have been keeping a close eye on him for some time, and the reports of his activities were always forwarded here to Williamsburg. His operation was beginning to cause us real problems. I would never wish anyone dead, but his black market of English goods to the merchants was putting a real crimp in our efforts to boycot imports." He stopped suddenly when he made the connection. "Lockwood," he murmured with a frown. "Now I know why that name seemed so familiar." He turned to Brittany. "Your farm is adjacent to the Ingram estate."

"Yes. And whoever killed Miles was working with him," Brittany replied.

Beau's dark brows rose in surprise. "Really? Sounds as if they disagreed about something."

"They did," Brittany admitted. "Me."

"You?" he questioned, directing them toward the parlor.

"Yes. You see they were using my property to smuggle their goods into the colonies, and I found out about it. His partner wanted me dead. Miles didn't."

"So Hancock decided Brittany should get out of Boston as quickly as possible," Dane finished.

"I don't blame him," Beau added, guiding Brittany to the settee. "How do you know all this—about Ingram's partner wanting you dead?" He crossed to the buffet and poured three glasses of wine, then gave one to each of them while he took his and went to stand near the fireplace.

"It's a rather involved story, but to make things short, I overheard them talking. They didn't know I was there. Otherwise I don't think she would have killed him . . . or at least she would have added me to her list."

"Her?" Beau repeated, genuinely surprised. "A woman? Did you recognize her?"

Brittany shook her head. "I was hiding, and I didn't come out until after she left. But you know something? Her voice sounded vaguely familiar."

Dane perked up instantly. "You never mentioned that before."

"I know. I'd forgotten about it until now. Who do you suppose she could be? I mean, Miles's friends certainly aren't mine."

"I doubt a friend would kill him," Beau pointed out. "She could be just about anyone." He took a sip of wine and murmured, "A woman."

"Surprising, isn't it?" Dane remarked.

Beau shrugged and said, "Not really, I suppose. My wife and I tangled with a woman one time. She nearly ruined our chances of ever being together."

"Yes, I remember your telling me about that. She had Alanna kidnaped, as I recall."

"And she was responsible for the death of my best friend." He took another sip of wine and stared off into the distance. "But that's all behind us. She's living in England now and our lives are much happier for it."

"And richer, I would imagine, since the two of you have a beautiful little girl to show for it. By the way, where are Alanna and Victoria?"

The sadness instantly disappeared in his dark eyes. "They went to visit a neighbor of ours. Mrs. Langworthy just had a baby, and you know my wife," he smiled. "She wanted to help out any way she could. She and Victoria should be home before long. Alanna promised not to be traveling after dark." He straightened as if a thought had just occurred to him. "And if she comes home to find Miss Lockwood sitting in the parlor with us rather than resting in her room, I'll never hear the end of it." He set his glass on the mantel and started for the door. "If you'll excuse me for a moment, I'll have Tilly prepare a room and instruct her to have two extra places set at the dinner table." He paused at the threshold and glanced back at his cousin. "I assume you're not planning to spend the night."

"No, I can't afford the time," Dane admitted, failing to see the disappointed look in Brittany's eyes. "Hancock wants Patrick Henry back in Boston as soon as possible."

"Does Henry know that?"

"I sent one of my men to see him and deliver Hancock's message."

"But you can stay for dinner? If you left without seeing Alanna, she'd never forgive you."

Dane smiled brightly. "I know."

"And a very wise decision, I might add." Beau grinned and pointed to the wine decanter. "Help yourself to more. I'll be back in a minute."

Both Brittany and Dane remained quiet as they listened to Beau's footsteps carry him to another part of the house and his deep voice call out to the woman named Tilly. When the sounds of him grew indistinct, Brittany drew up the courage to talk to Dane.

"Do you really have to go so soon?" she asked, her eyes trained on the crystal goblet she held. "We have a lot of things to talk about, and it could be some time before we see each other again."

"I know, Brittany," he said, setting aside his glass and leaving his chair to join her on the settee. "I wish I could stay a few days. But it's vital that Patrick Henry get to Boston as soon as possible. And I can't see where anything between us can be settled until we've found Miles's partner." When she wouldn't lift her eyes to look at him, he tilted his head down to peer into her face. "You understand that, don't you?"

Brittany shrugged a delicate shoulder and left her place to stroll across the room toward the opened French doors that led onto the veranda. Raven Oaks was like a small town nestled in endless fields of cotton and tobacco with all its buildings, a mill, its own stream flowing by, a blacksmith, livery stables, and row upon row of cabins used to house the slaves and indentured servants. Although she didn't honestly approve of a man owning another human being, she got the distinct impression that living on this plantation, even as a servant, wasn't too bad. After having talked with Beau Remington for a short time, she sensed he was honest and fair when it came to dealing with others. And he was generous. He hadn't hesitated when Dane told him she needed a place to stay for a while. But the idea of living on Raven Oaks for a day or a month wasn't what upset her; it was the feeling that she would never see Dane again. She wanted to tell him what was tearing her up inside, settle their differences, and then be able to admit her love for him openly and freely, without restrictions. But she couldn't do all that in a matter of ten minutes. They needed time, and time wasn't something they had right now.

"Yes, I understand the urgency," she said quietly as she gazed out across the land at the slowly setting sun. "I only wish there was no need. I wish we were at peace. I wish I was still living on the farm with Roan and Papa. I wish you had never walked into my life." A sob caught her unexpectedly, and she swallowed hard, not wanting the tears to fill her eyes or spill down her cheeks as they were. "I wish things were simple . . . the way they used to be." Suddenly he was standing beside her and she could feel every inch of his hardened frame, even though he had refrained from touching her. "I wish you were cruel and insensitive. I wish you'd walk away and never look back. I wish I didn't love you," she murmured, leaning a temple against the cool framework of the doorway as they both stared out at the golden glow of the dying sun.

Two weeks had passed since Brittany's arrival at Raven Oaks and during that time Alanna and her nine-year-old daughter, Victoria, kept Brittany very busy. The petite brunette with the dark eyes had sensed Brittany's love for her husband's cousin almost immediately and realized their separation would be very difficult for her . . . especially after all that had happened to the beautiful young woman.

Each morning they would have breakfast on the veranda, then visit the slave quarters with medicines for the sick, shoes for the children, or baskets of fresh fruit while Beau rode out to the fields to inspect the work being done or met with members of the Sons of Liberty in his study. After lunch, Brittany, Alanna, and young Victoria would go for a horseback ride through the meadow and visit some of their closest neighbors. They'd all have dinner together in the dining room at night, then share a glass of wine on the veranda. It had become a ritual, one Brittany truly enjoyed and something everyone on Raven Oaks came to expect.

The most colorful character she met during her stay was the house cook, Cinnamon. She was a woman about Alanna's age and had at one time been an indentured servant to Beau. She had bright red hair, a face full of freckles, and a fiery temper and personality. She always said what she thought and didn't care who she hurt. Her barbs had stung Brittany a few times and had set her back on her heels. But before long Brittany found it a challenge just to see how well she could fare against the plump woman's criticism, and when Alanna's duties took her elsewhere for a spell, Brittany always went to the kitchen to agitate Cinnamon. It was just such a time this particularly bright, sunny afternoon when Brittany entered the kitchen through a side door and found the woman on hands and knees in the middle of the floor vigorously wiping up the broken pieces of a bowl and the batter that had been inside.

"Have an accident, Cinnamon?" Brittany chided, knowing full well what to expect from the cook.

"No, I just thought it would be fun to see how many times the bowl would bounce before it broke. Yes, I had an accident. You didn't think I did this on purpose, did you?" she barked without bothering to look up.

"Well, I never know about you," Brittany grinned, reaching for a dust pan and broom. "A day hasn't gone by that you don't surprise me in one way or another."

"Well, stick around, honey. There's a lot more to learn."

Brittany was sure of that, but rather than comment, she elected to help clean up the mess, then offer her assistance.

"I would certainly appreciate it. I'm behind schedule as it is," Cinnamon admitted, pushing her weighty form up on her feet. "It's why I was hurrying." She heaved a deep sigh and frowned. "I'm always in a hurry."

"Are the Remingtons expecting company for dinner?"

"No," Cinnamon replied, going to the cupboard for another bowl. "What makes you ask?"

Brittany shrugged then stooped to blot away the rest of the yellow batter from the stone floor. "I just assumed it's why you were rushing." Rising, she carried the rag to the wash pan and began to rinse it out. "They don't strike me as the kind to get upset if dinner is late. Why don't you slow down?"

"Because I've never been late before and I'm not gonna start now, that's why," Cinnamon told her. "Ya start lettin' it slip and before long you're skipping a whole meal." She straightened and gave her ample shape a quick once-over. "Course, I could stand to miss a meal now and then."

"Oh, I don't know," Brittany smiled over at her. "I think you look pretty good the way you are."

Cinnamon gave her a skeptical look. "If you think paying compliments will win my friendship . . ." She paused long enough to knot her fists and rest them on her hips. "You've succeeded."

"Well, it wasn't really my intention, but I'm glad, anyway," Brittany laughed. "I don't really have any friends." Hanging up the rag to dry, she moved to the huge table where Cinnamon had placed the bowl and began measuring out the sugar and butter.

"Now, I find that hard to believe. A pretty girl like you and no friends?"

"Well, it's true. I never really had the time or the opportunity. My mother died when I was very young, so the household responsibilities fell on me."

"And you never went to school?"

"Papa taught us all he could at night after dinner."

"Sounds lonely."

Brittany shook her head. "Not really. We were always too busy to be lonely. Besides, we had each other."

"Well, stay around here a while longer and you'll have more friends than you know what to do with," Cinnamon

448

guaranteed her as she went to the oven and opened the door to pull out the tray of freshly baked cookies.

"I wish I could," Brittany said, picking up a wooden spoon. "But as soon as Dane finds Miles's murderer, I'll be going home."

"To get married?"

The woman's bluntness caught Brittany unawares. Blushing, she drew in a breath and struggled for the right answer.

"Oh, don't go trying to deny telling me you ain't in love with Dane Remington," Cinnamon quickly interjected. "Alanna's told me all about you and him. We've been sharin' secrets for years!" Grabbing a spatula, she artfully plucked the cookies from their tray and placed them on racks to cool. "Course, I must admit I'm surprised you didn't fall for his younger brother." She laughed and rolled her eyes. "That Brad. What a charmer. You know, the two of them came here to live for a while after their papa died, and Brad had every girl on the plantation swooning after him."

"Including you?" Brittany baited, thankful the woman had changed the subject.

"Oh, folderol. I was too old . . . and fat," she admonished. "Course I gotta admit I enjoyed flirtin' with him." The look on her face turned serious. "Every girl did. Especially the sisters." She shook her head with a click of her tongue. "What a shame that was."

Her curiosity piqued, Brittany laid aside the spoon. "What was a shame?"

"Ya mean Alanna ain't told ya yet?" she asked in obvious surprise. "It's the biggest scandal what ever happened here on Raven Oaks, and we still talk about it like it was only yesterday." Setting down the tray and spatula, Cinnamon wiped her hands on her apron and pulled up a long-legged stool on which to sit. "It happened more than five years ago. There were two young girls living here—sisters, about thirteen and fifteen. They were indentured servants and both their parents were dead. Anyway, the oldest—Bethany—fell head over heels in love with Brad the minute she saw him, and every chance she had, she threw herself at him. Now Brad might be a bit of a rogue when it comes to women, but he never took advantage of a girl hardly old enough to know what love was all about. I know that for a fact. There were several times when he came to talk to me—" She grinned somewhat proudly. "I was like his big sister, I guess you could say. Anyway, he trusted me. He told me how Bethany was always trying to lure him to her bed and that one time it almost worked. He'd had too much to drink and Bethany was very persuasive—and pretty. Well, once she got him in her cabin, she threw her arms around him and kissed him hard. It was enough to sober him up and he pushed her away. Then she started to unbutton her dress, and Brad nearly lost his mind. He tried to reason with her, but when that didn't work, he walked out. A few days later, he and his brother left for Boston."

Brittany picked up the spoon and started stirring again. "I wouldn't call that much of a scandal."

"That ain't all," Cinnamon announced. "The worst is yet to come. About three months later, word gets around that Bethany's pregnant and that it's Brad's baby."

Brittany's chin dropped. "But it wasn't, was it?"

"No. I believe Brad . . . the baby wasn't his. Well, Bethany went to see Alanna and demanded that someone contact Brad, force him to come back to Raven Oaks and marry her. Now, being the sort who feels sorry for a young girl in the family way and without a husband, Alanna sent a letter to Brad."

"And he wrote back saying he wasn't the father," Brittany filled in.

"Exactly," Cinnamon nodded. "And when Bethany wouldn't believe her, Alanna showed her the letter. The next day Bethany's younger sister found her hanging from a rope in their cabin. She had killed herself."

"Oh, my God!" Brittany moaned. "That's horrible. Did

450

anyone ever tell Brad?"

"I don't think so. Especially after young Thomas admitted having been with Bethany. Alanna figured Bethany didn't care who got her pregnant, only that Brad married her. And the really sad thing about the whole affair was that her sister, Millicent, would never accept the truth. She was convinced Brad was the father and that because he refused to marry her, Bethany took her own life."

"Where's the sister now?"

"No one really knows for sure. You see, the girls were indentured to Mr. Remington for five years, and because Millicent was so young, he forced her to stay until her time was up. That was about a year ago. The day he handed her her papers, Millicent packed up her belongings and disappeared. But I'll tell ya something. That hate she had for Brad the day her sister killed herself was even stronger the day she walked off Raven Oaks."

"That makes Millicent about—eighteen now, doesn't it?"

Cinnamon thought a moment, then nodded. "Close to, I guess. Why?"

"Well, she's old enough to do Brad harm if she made up her mind to it. Don't you think Brad deserves to know about all this so that he can keep an eye open for her just in case she's decided to get even somehow?"

Cinnamon shook her head and left her place on the stool. "If she wanted to do something, she'd have tried long before now."

"But maybe she didn't know where to find him," Brittany argued.

"Everyone knew where to find him. Gossip about the Remington clan flies around here faster than a leaf caught in a whirlwind. No, I don't think Millicent wanted revenge. She just wanted to hate him . . . and to leave the place that killed her sister."

A frown marred Brittany's smooth brow as she watched Cinnamon gather potatoes from the bin and set about

451

peeling them. Maybe they disagreed about Millicent and maybe Cinnamon was right, but Brittany was going to talk to Beau about it as soon as she got the chance.

"Cinnamon tells me you helped with dinner, Brittany," Alanna smiled as they headed toward the veranda with their usual glass of wine in hand and Beau following close behind. "It was good."

"Thank you. I thought it was about time I earned my keep," she smiled, moving to one of the white wicker chairs and sitting down. "You know, I'm getting very spoiled here. It's going to be rather difficult for me to go home once this mess is over."

"Well, we've enjoyed having you," Alanna smiled. "Haven't we, Beau?"

"We sure have," he replied, lounging in the settee next to the woman. "As for it being difficult to go home . . . I don't think you should worry about it. Dane will be there to help. And Brad."

The mention of the brother's name brought to mind the conversation Brittany and Cinnamon had had earlier, and Brittany straightened in her chair, not sure exactly how to voice her concern. She decided the best approach was straight on. "Beau," she began, her tone serious, "Cinnamon told me about the tragedy that happened here several years back involving Brad and a young indentured servant."

Beau's features darkened with his frown. "Yes, that's exactly what it was—a tragedy."

"Well, from the way Cinnamon explained it, I'm worried for Brad."

"Worried?" Alanna spoke up. "Whatever for?"

Setting down her glass on the table between them, Brittany shifted in her chair to look directly at Beau and his wife. "If what Cinnamon told me is all true, it sounds to me as if Millicent might seek revenge against Brad."

"Revenge?" Alanna's dark, brown eyes widened and she turned to look at her husband. "Beau?"

He shrugged. "It's possible, I suppose. But Millicent left Raven Oaks nearly a year ago. If she wanted revenge, I think she would have tried something long before now."

"I have to agree," Alanna concurred, though the tone of her voice hinted otherwise.

"Besides," Beau smiled comfortingly. "I doubt she could get to him. He's surrounded by too many friends."

Brittany had to admit it was true. But the idea still bothered her. She liked Dane's brother and didn't want anything to happen to him. "I'd feel better if someone at least warned him. According to Cinnamon, he doesn't even know Bethany killed herself or how Millicent blamed him for it."

"I think she's right, Beau," Alanna cut in, her lovely face etched with worry. "I hadn't given it much thought until this very minute, but now it all makes sense."

"What makes sense?"

"Millicent's infatuation with knives. And swords. Don't you remember my telling you how many times I caught her practicing with them?" Alanna turned to Brittany. "She had painted the outline of a man on a tree trunk and would spend hours throwing a knife at it. She always was a tomboy, so I didn't really think too much of it, but instead of playing with dolls, she'd carve herself a wooden sword and fence with the younger boys. No one could beat her."

"What are you saying, dear?" Beau asked. "That she was preparing herself for when she'd meet up with Brad again?"

"It's possible, don't you think?" Alanna added. "And he'd be caught completely off guard. Who'd ever expect a woman to have such skills with a knife?"

The image of Miles's body lying on the floor with a pearl-handled knife protruding from the chest flashed in Brittany's mind, and a chill raced up her spine. Trembling, she shook off the sensation, but not before Beau had noticed.

"Brittany, what is it?"

A cold sweat dotted her brow, and she reached for her wine and took a sip to calm herself. "Nothing, probably," she said after a while. "It's too remote to be connected."

"What?" Beau urged.

Drawing her fingers over her brow and down the side of her face, Brittany stood on shaky limbs and moved to the banister surrounding the veranda. "The woman who killed Miles Ingram used a knife. And from what I heard, there wasn't a struggle."

"Meaning?"

Brittany turned to face Beau. "Meaning, she threw it at him. And she hit him right in the heart. She was a marksman—very skilled with knives."

"Do you think it was Millicent?" Alanna breathed.

"I don't know why it would be. If she was after Brad, why was she involved with Miles? And the woman who killed Miles is after the Dark Horseman. I heard her say so."

Beau and Alanna exchanged startled glances. "Brittany," Beau said, coming to his feet, "do you know who the Dark Horseman is?"

A sadness threatened to reveal itself in her gray-blue eyes. "I wish I did," she murmured, gazing off across the spacious front lawn.

Beau looked at his wife once more, then back at Brittany. "Didn't Dane tell you? I would think he would. It isn't like he couldn't trust you."

Brittany's head snapped around, a frown drawing her softly arched brows together. "Tell me what?"

"That *he's* the Dark Horseman."

Beau's shocking announcement left Brittany feeling as though a thundering herd of runaway horses had just trampled her. Her chin dropped, her breathing stilled, and her knees threatened to spill her to the floor. Grabbing for the banister, she steadied herself and slowly leaned against the rail for support. Dane was the Dark Horseman! The Dark Horseman—the stranger she had fancied herself in love with—was Dane! But of course. It all made sense now: the black stallion; never seeing Dane and the Dark Horseman together; those intense green eyes; the same build, strong jaw, and sensuous mouth; and the fact that she was torn between loving them both. No wonder she couldn't decide. They were one and the same! Joyful tears filled her eyes and she bit her lip to keep from shouting out loud. If only he had told her—but then, she understood why he hadn't. He was afraid of her anger, afraid she would turn away from him because of his deceit. Well, never, Dane Remington, she vowed happily. I will *never* leave you.

"Brittany?"

Beau's deep voice brought her out of her reverie, and she lifted her eyes to look at him. "No. He didn't tell me."

"Well, that could be the connection. Let's suppose the woman is Millicent and that she thinks Brad is the Dark Horseman. She murders Miles Ingram and shifts the blame on the Dark Horseman, the one she believes is Brad. That fits, doesn't it?"

"Yes . . . but it doesn't give her immediate results," Brittany argued. "I would think she'd want something a little more positive."

"Could it be a part of a bigger plot?" Alanna volunteered.

"Like what?" Brittany asked. "And why did she want me dead? I could understand her need to have me off the farm—especially since I knew about the smuggling. But why did she think she had to kill me?"

"Because you know who she is," Beau suggested.

"What?" Alanna gasped, rising from her chair and coming to stand beside Brittany. "Is that true?"

Brittany was quiet for a moment before she explained. "I suppose it's possible. Her voice did sound familiar but I can't place it." She looked to Beau. "And she didn't know I overheard her talking to Miles in the library just before she killed him, so why would she think I'd know who she was?"

"Because you're a very intelligent young woman and she

figures it's only a matter of time before you put all the pieces together—even without having to hear her voice," Beau proposed. "Obviously you know other things about her."

"Then help me," Brittany begged. "Help me figure out who she is!"

"How?" Alanna asked.

"Describe Millicent to me. Maybe I've seen her and don't know it."

Alanna's brow puckered with thought as she selected the best words to delineate Millicent Ashburn. "Well, she could have cut her hair since then, but when Millicent left Raven Oaks, she had very long, black hair that she always wore in a braid. She was tall, very thin, but shapely and had a very odd color of eyes."

"Almost violet," Brittany finished, her face drained of color.

"Yes! Then you've seen her?"

A sick feeling twisted her stomach, and Brittany had to fight down the urge to retch. "Oh, yes. I've seen her. Only her name wasn't Millicent. It was Cory Rison."

It had been close to three weeks since Dane left Brittany in his cousin's care, and with each day that passed, he missed her even more. He was sure she loved him and that their time apart would prove it to her. He was also hoping that she would come to the conclusion that she didn't love the Dark Horseman, that all she had ever felt for the mysterious night rider was a deep-rooted admiration for the man, not an everlasting love. Sitting alone at the table in the back of the tavern, he smiled lopsidedly and plopped his feet up on the bench in front of him. That way he wouldn't have to face her wrath by telling her the truth about the Dark Horseman. But then she was bound to find out sooner or later. Maybe he should send her a letter explaining how things had gotten out of hand before he could admit to being the man she had met

456

that night so long ago in the meadow. At least that way she couldn't make a grab for his pistol and try to shoot him with it. He shook his head, sighed heavily and took a long drink of his ale, knowing he'd have to admit to everything before they could ever be happy together. And before they could even start building a life for themselves, he had to find Miles Ingram's murderer.

Handbills had been passed out all over Boston offering a reward for any information leading to the arrest of the Dark Horseman, and for the past few weeks John Hancock had ordered Dane to stay put and keep his disguise under lock and key. And he was to dispose of his coins! If the Sons of Liberty needed his help, it would be on a very small scale—at least until Ingram's real murderer was uncovered. In that time Dane had grown restless. He missed Brittany terribly and the boredom of staying at the Bunch of Grapes was slowly eating away at his sanity. Brad, of course, always tried to cheer him up and faithfully kept him abreast of any progress his men or the Sons were making in solving the murder, but nothing moved fast enough to suit him. Nor did he like just sitting around while everyone else was wearing out the soles of their shoes trying to clear his name. He was the one accused and he should be the one to prove his innocence.

He was sitting with his head down, deep in thought, when someone approached his table and slapped his feet off the bench. Startled out of his musings, he sat up abruptly with a dark scowl on his handsome face, ready to berate whoever had so rudely intruded. He snorted disdainfully when he saw it was Cory smiling back at him.

"Ya know, Cap'n," she sneered. "I think all that muscle on you is turning to fat. You should see if there isn't some little farm girl who needs help harvesting her crops. You could use the exercise."

Dane's upper lip curled, but he didn't say anything. Cory's biting remarks had seemed to become even more cruel over

457

the past few weeks than usual. Or was he just too sensitive?

"Well, maybe what I have to tell you will help," she went on, glancing around the half-empty room. "Where's Brad?"

"I sent him to check on the ship. There's been some stealing going on at the pier and I want to make sure we still have a mast and anchor. Hopefully I'll be able to go back to Virginia pretty soon and I'd hate to find myself in the middle of the Atlantic because someone stole my wheel."

"Well, you could always swim," Cory suggested sarcastically. "With all that extra lard you have on you, you'd float for days."

"Did you really come here for some reason other than to provoke me?" he growled, putting his feet back on the bench and taking another swig of ale.

"I did. I've got a message from Hancock."

Dane's emerald eyes shifted to look at her, doubting she was telling the truth. "Oh? And what's the message?"

"He wants you and your men to take a supply of guns and powder to the barn at Hound's Head Inn at midnight tonight. There'll be someone there to meet you and take the wagons on to New York."

Dane dropped his feet back to the floor and sat up. "That's a two-hour ride and it's after nine o'clock now. Cutting it a little close, isn't he?"

"I just delivered the message," Cory replied, her hands raised up in front of her as if to ward off his irritation. "But if you're unable to—"

"Don't be ridiculous, Cory," he growled, thrusting his mug on the table and standing up. "Of course I'll do it. Where do we pick up the wagons?"

"The usual place. I've already told Drexler, Betts, and Holt to meet you there, and I'll look for Dooley if you want me to."

"Dooley's upstairs," Dane told her. "I'll get him myself. You go to the ship and get Brad."

Cory nodded and started to walk away. "Oh, I almost

forgot. I won't be going along this time. Hancock's got something else for me to do. Good luck, and I hope everything goes smoothly."

Dane remained where he was for several minutes after Cory had left the tavern. It puzzled him that Hancock had changed his mind about using Dane for something as risky as this, though Dane wasn't about to argue. He welcomed the change of scenery. Glancing at the clock again, he decided he'd have to take Cory's word for it. There wasn't enough time to go and ask him.

It seemed to Brad that this was the hundredth time today his brother had sent him to check on the ship. And just as on the previous ninety-nine trips, he hadn't found anything out of the ordinary. Yes, he had heard there was some thieving going on at the docks, but no more than usual. And the men Dane had ordered to stay with the frigate hadn't abandoned it as his brother had worried they would. Everything was as it should be—as Brad expected—and if his checking it out would ease Dane's short temper a mite, he'd come back again tonight.

Tying off the rowboat to the side of the ship, he grabbed hold of the rope ladder and agilely pulled himself up to the first rung and climbed on board. Waving at the men who sat around a barrel in the middle of the deck playing cards to break the boredom, Brad headed for the captain's quarters. Once inside, he lit the lantern, gave the cabin a quick once-over and crossed to the bunk. He'd stretch out for a while—long enough to guarantee his brother that he had actually come to the ship—then he'd return to the Bunch of Grapes for a well-deserved mug of ale.

Only a short while passed before Brad's eyes drifted shut and his breathing slowed to that of peaceful slumber. He neither heard nor saw the darkly clad figure enter the cabin noiselessly or noticed that the lantern's light was extinguished. Yet as the shape approached the bunk, he stirred, an inner sense warning him that something was amiss. With a start, he came awake. But before he could focus his eyes or push himself all the way to his feet, the quiet figure raised a pistol and slammed the butt of it against his temple, plummeting his body to the floor and his mind into unconsciousness.

"Excuse me, sir," the Ingram butler apologized as he stood in the doorway of the study.

Bartholomew looked up from his papers. "What is it, Jonathan?"

"A message was just delivered," he said, holding up the sealed parchment. "I was told it was urgent and that it should be given to you straightway."

The old man motioned for him to bring it to him. "Who delivered it?"

"Just a boy from town, sir. He didn't say who sent him and I'm afraid I didn't ask."

"That's quite all right, Jonathan. It's late and we're all tired." He popped the seal and unfolded the message.

"Shall I wait, sir?"

Bartholomew nodded as he began to read.

If you want to catch your son's murderer, the Dark Horseman and his men will be at Hound's Head Inn at midnight tonight with a load of smuggled English goods. His name is Dane Remington.

The paper shook in Bartholomew's hand. Until this moment he had never had the proof he needed to convict the Remington brothers, although he had suspected long ago that they worked with the rebel organization. Now all he had to do was gather the men he needed. However, after glancing at the mantel clock, he realized he would have to hurry if he was to arrive ahead of the bastard who had killed his son.

The wagons and his crew were already waiting when Dane rode up with Aaron Dooley hanging on behind him. It was nearly ten o'clock and they could ill afford any delays if they were to reach Hound's Head Inn at the designated hour. Reining in alongside the first two-wheeled cart, Dane helped Dooley dismount from behind him and climb onto the seat. The midget was too small to handle a horse by himself and his skill with a pistol made him more valuable as a guard.

"Where's Brad?" Dane asked after a quick glance revealed that his brother was the only one missing.

"Don't know, cap'n," Drexler answered. "We thought he'd be coming with you and Dooley."

"Damn," Dane hissed beneath his breath as he stretched up in the stirrups and studied the darkened road back toward town. It wouldn't surprise Dane any to learn his brother had found himself a pretty and willing wench and was at this moment enjoying her pleasures in a haystack. "Then we'll have to go without him," he snarled, jerking hard on the reins and spinning his steed around. "We haven't time to wait." Motioning for the caravan to move out, Dane took the lead, his eyes and ears alert for any sign of trouble.

Hound's Head Inn was located on a well-traveled road midway between Boston and Hartford, and because of its popularity as a clean, reliable place to stop, it was not uncommon to see lights shining in the windows no matter what time of night. Thus as the men approached the inn, they gave little thought to the activity going on inside, especially since they assumed those they were to meet with the guns would be waiting for them in the commons.

"Take the wagons into the barn," Dane instructed, "while I talk with the innkeeper."

"Aye, cap'n," Drexler nodded, motioning the lead wagon on. "Want me to come with you?"

"No, you stay with the guns. Everything's gone so well that I'm a little edgy."

"I know what you mean. I expected to meet up with a soldier or two along the way myself," Drexler admitted. "Guess maybe we shouldn't curse our good luck."

"It does seem a little too easy, doesn't it?" Dane frowned.

Drexler shrugged his big shoulders. "Or maybe we're just getting too old for this sort of thing anymore," he laughed. "I'll wait for ya in the barn."

Nodding, Dane reined his steed toward the front steps of the inn and dismounted. But rather than hurry inside, he paused on the bottom tred when an eerie feeling assailed him and he glanced over to watch Drexler and the rest of his crew and the wagons disappear into the darkened cavity of the barn. Maybe he'd just spent too much time sitting and not doing anything to think logically anymore, but the whole situation was really beginning to bother him. Hancock had been very insistent that Dane not get involved with the Sons activities for a while, then he'd turned around and sent him out in the middle of the night without forewarning or any precautions to transport weapons out of Boston. It was too late now to wish he had done things differently, but he should have asked Cory if she'd talked directly with Hancock or if she'd been given a message. Knowing the orders had come straight from Hancock to Cory would ease his apprehension a little. But then, the message had to have come from Hancock. Only Dane's men and Hancock knew about Hound's Head Inn. And as for Brad—well, he never could count on him to be around when the action started. Brad's interests always centered on a pretty face or swish of silk. Dane would be glad when the young man decided to settle down.

That strange sensation hit him again when he stepped up on the second tred. Studying the front door of the inn, then looking to the barn once more, he hesitated, started to turn back around, and changed his mind. If something was

462

wrong, Drexler would have fired a warning shot. Reaching out for the latch, he pushed open the door and moved into the commons.

The dimly lit room was nearly empty, save for a group of three men sitting at a far table having something to eat. Two of them had their backs to Dane. Obviously they were late night travelers; but were they the men Dane was supposed to meet? He glanced toward the bar behind which stood a stranger, and his instincts again cried out for him to be on guard. Simon Jones, the owner of Hound's Head Inn, always worked the place no matter the time of day, and to see someone else standing there wiping glasses made Dane turn around, ready to leave as quickly as possible. But before he had taken a step, one of the men at the table called out.

"Mr. Remington, there's no use in trying to warn your friends," he said. "It's too late for them, just as it's too late for you."

The voice sounded dreadfully familiar and before he looked back to confirm his suspicions, two soldiers, weapons drawn, moved into the doorway from outside the inn.

"How did you know we'd be here, Mr. Ingram?" he asked, allowing one of the soldiers to step up next to him and pluck his pistol from inside his coat.

"Does it really matter? The point is, we've caught the Dark Horseman, all of his men, *and* the carts full of smuggled British goods. Even without the latter, you're bound for the gallows."

"The Dark Horseman?" he laughed. "Smuggled goods? What are you talking about? If you'll examine the barrels, you'll find they're full of flour, not tea. As for my even knowing the Dark Horseman—what proof do you have to connect me with him?"

Adjusting his tricorn on his head, Bartholomew left the table and crossed to where Dane stood. "I believe, Mr. Remington, that I'll have all the proof I need once we've opened the barrels . . . proof of your being a traitor *and* the Dark Horseman." He smiled almost pleasantly and extended his hand. "If you'll kindly lead the way."

Brad's head was throbbing painfully when he finally awoke several hours later. It heightened when he tried to move; he discovered that whoever had hit him had tied both his hands and feet. When he started to call out for help, the foul tasting rag stuffed in his mouth prevented him from doing anything more than just groaning. Resting his head back on the cool wooden planks beneath him, he painfully glanced up at the windows for any indication of how long he had been lying there. But the black sky was all he could see.

Groggy and feeling a little sick, he closed his eyes and silently prayed his brother would miss him fairly soon and come looking for him . . . or at least one of the men on deck who had been playing cards when he boarded. But then why should they? Dane would probably think he was off somewhere with a woman, and the crew would think he had fallen asleep—which he had. The blurred vision of the intruder clouded his thoughts and he wondered how the stranger had gotten past the crew without them stopping to question him. Well, he'd have to ask them once he was free. Pulling on his restraints, he cursed when the coarse rope cut into his wrists. Maybe he'd better lie still for a while until the pain in his head lessened and he had more strength.

The sound of running footsteps across the deck outside the cabin brought Brad out of his half-conscious state. Struggling to sit up, he shouted as loudly as he could when the steps increased in volume; whoever it was was coming his way. Then the door was hurled open and the faint light of early sunrise accompanied the dark figure into the cabin.

"Brad!" Cory exclaimed, rushing to kneel beside him. "My God, what happened?" Having freed his hands and feet and pulled the gag from his mouth, she helped him onto the

464

bunk and turned for the washbowl and a rag to wipe away the dried blood from the side of his face.

"I'm not sure exactly," he said, resting his head back against the wall, his eyes closed. "I came here last night to check the ship like Dane asked, fell asleep here, and then got clobbered. I was out most of the night, I guess." He winced when Cory touched the dark, ugly lump on his temple with the cool rag.

"Do you know who did it?"

"No," he murmured, taking the cloth and pressing it against his brow. "It was too dark and it happened too fast."

"Well, we've got other troubles, Braddy, ol' boy," she remarked, going to the desk for the bottle of whiskey. "Here. Take a big drink and prepare yourself for the worst."

"What do you mean?" he asked suspiciously. "Has something happened to Dane?"

Cory urged the bottle to his lips, then tilted the bottom up until Brad had taken a long drink. Satisfied, she set the bottle on the floor and sat down next to him on the bunk. "Nothing's happened yet. And if everything goes as planned, nothing will . . . except a little surprise."

"What? What are you talking about?" he demanded, holding the cool rag over his temple in an effort to still the incessant pounding in his brain.

"Your brother's been arrested and sentenced to hang in one hour."

"What?" he exploded, springing off the bunk only to stagger and nearly fall to his knees. Cory's quick reaction prevented it from happening and with her arms wrapped around him she guided him back to the bunk. "How? What are the charges?"

"I don't know everything," she said, fluffing up the pillow behind him, "but from what I can gather, someone sent a message to Dane—supposedly from Hancock—instructing him and his men to take a supply of guns to Hound's Head Inn this past midnight. They were to meet someone else there

465

who would take the shipment on to New York. However, Bartholomew Ingram and a band of soldiers were waiting at the inn when they got there. It seems he was given a message, too, informing him where he could find the Dark Horseman and a supply of smuggled goods."

"But they found the guns instead."

"Oh no," she went on, "they found tea hidden in the barrels of flour . . . and cloth and spices—all sorts of things. But the most damaging was the bag of copper coins. Dane's coins. His Sons of Liberty coins."

"Oh God," Brad moaned, dropping his head forward.

"I don't need to tell you what Ingram decided right then and there. As far as he was concerned, there was no need for a trial and he wants Dane executed in the common so the whole city of Boston can watch. He's going to use him as an example."

"We've got to go to Dane," Brad announced, motioning Cory out of his way, but she wouldn't budge.

"It's no use. I've already tried. They're not letting anyone into the gaol. Besides, I'm sure Ingram has soldiers out looking for you right now. Whoever hit you over the head did you a favor. Otherwise, you'd be in gaol with Dane and everybody else."

"Then what are we going to do? I can't hide out here while my brother hangs."

"Don't worry," she smiled. "I've already taken care of that. As soon as I heard what happened, I went to see Hancock. He said he'd make sure Dane wasn't executed while I was to find you. So all we have to do is sit back and wait."

"You're insane if you think I'm going to sit back!" he exploded, pushing her off the bunk. "Whatever Hancock has planned, I'm going to be a part of it!"

"How?" Cory argued. "You'll be spotted and arrested before you leave the dock."

"Well, I can't stay here. They're sure to search the ship."

"Then put a bandanna over your hair and wear an eye patch. And change your clothes." She hurried across the cabin to the sea chest sitting on the floor next to the desk. "I'm sure we'll find what we need in here."

Word of the Dark Horseman's execution at dawn had spread through Boston like a plague. The crowd had already begun to gather near the gallows in the common, a spot purposely chosen by Ingram for the simple fact that it was in clear sight from John Hancock's parlor. What Ingram didn't know, however, was that Hancock wasn't home. He, James Otis, Dr. Warren, and a host of other patriots were meeting at Paul Revere's to make plans. Since neither Cory Rison nor Dane's brother had been found, Hancock could only assume they were hiding out somewhere, though he had truly expected Brad to come bursting in long before now, demanding something be done to save his brother. But whatever reason kept Brad away, Hancock couldn't concern himself with it now. He had to make sure the men understood his orders.

"Now, does everyone know what they're to do?" he asked once the entire scheme had been discussed.

"We're to move in and position ourselves near the gallows and around the soldiers who will be there," one of them spoke up. "Then at the last possible minute—before they put the noose around Remington's neck—we're to overpower the soldiers while Jimmy here helps Remington get away. We got it, Mr. Hancock."

"Good. Then let's get going."

"Are you sure Hancock said he'd know what to do?" Brad asked worriedly as he and Cory worked their way through the crowd toward the gibbet.

"I said he did, didn't I?" she snapped, her eyes quickly

surveying the mass of people for any of Hancock's men. She had worked out every detail of her plan right down to the second they slid the rope over Dane's head. She didn't want anything to go wrong now—not when she was so close to having her revenge. Guardedly, she slipped her hand inside her jacket to the hilt of her knife, and artfully positioned herself on Brad's left. When the time came, she wanted to be sure he was completely helpless while he was forced to watch his brother being executed. This was the moment she had waited for.

A mixture of angry shouts and joyful cheers went up in the crowd when the cart carrying the condemned man was first seen at the end of the street. Brad bolted as if he intended to shove his way through the throng of people toward his brother, and Cory quickly grabbed his arm.

"Stay here!" she demanded. "You'll ruin whatever Hancock has planned if you interfere now. You've got to trust him. He won't let anything happen to your brother. Do you hear me?"

"Yes, I hear you," Brad snarled, his face twisted with the pain and fear he felt. John Hancock was a good man and if he vowed to save Dane, then Brad should stay out of the way. He knew that, but he didn't like having to stand aside while someone else did what he should be doing.

From their position within the mass of spectators, both Brad and Cory were unable to see what was happening around the cart, for if they had, Cory would have sensed that what she had promised Brad was actually coming true. Both sides of the street were lined with people pushing and shoving to get a better view. Yet among those wanting to get closer were several of Hancock's men, and as the cart passed by, they edged their way in between the band of soldiers surrounding Dane with such subtlety that the redcoats weren't aware of what was going on until it was too late. Nor had either one of them noticed the second group of men working their way around the perimeter of the gallows or the young man staring curiously at them from only ten feet away.

As the cart moved closer to the gibbet, the soldiers ordered to accompany it were suddenly pushed aside and separated from it by the crushing mass of bodies surrounding them. Unable to do anything short of firing their muskets in the air and possibly causing a riot, since the majority of the people appeared to be here in protest of Remington's execution, they were left with no alternative but to shove back and demand they be let through.

"Cory, we've got to do something," Brad hissed as he watched Dane being helped from the cart onto the gallows platform. His hands were bound behind him, and from the dark bruises on his left cheek, it appeared he had not been treated kindly during his arrest and resulting stay in gaol.

"We are doing something," Cory sneered, pulling the knife from its scabbard and pressing its tip into Brad's side. "We're watching your brother die."

Brad stiffened instantly at the feel of cold metal against his ribs, but dared not move otherwise. "What the hell does this mean?" he snarled in a mixture of contempt and surprise.

"It means I'm paying you back for what you did to my sister."

"Your sister?" he parroted. "I don't even know your sister. I wasn't even aware you had one."

The tip of the knife pierced the cloth of his shirt and drew a dot of blood. "Well maybe I should refresh your memory. My sister's name was Bethany."

Brad's mind whirled as he tried to recall such a woman. Finally out of frustration he shook his head.

"You don't remember her, do you? You bastard! You should remember her. You killed her."

"Cory, I never—"

"My name's not Cory. It's Millicent. Millicent Ashburn. Now do you remember?"

But before Brad could reply, the angry shouts of the crowd

469

around them drew his attention to the gallows and the gray-haired man who had stepped up on it beside Dane.

"Loyal people of Boston," Bartholomew Ingram shouted, "you are about to witness the execution of a traitor, the one known as the Dark Horseman."

"What about a trial?" someone called.

Leaning forward, Bartholomew clutched the handrail. "He already had his trial. I accused him, found him guilty, and sentenced him to hang, and you who defend him are called upon to watch him die as an example of what you can expect should you go against the Crown." Turning, he motioned for the hangman to loop the rope around Dane's neck.

"Cory, please," Brad begged. "Don't let Dane die because of something you think I did to your sister. He had nothing to do with it."

"It doesn't matter," she spat. "It's part of your punishment. My sister died because of you and now your brother will die because of me. And there's nothing you can do to stop it."

But just as the executioner was about to drop the rope over Dane's head, the sound of thundering hoofbeats rent the air and all eyes turned to see the dark figure of man and beast racing toward the gallows. Clothed in black, his cape flying wide behind him, he leaned forward in the saddle as he kicked the stallion's sides and sent him galloping across the cobblestone street. A strange, paralyzing silence came over the crowd as they watched, for the one who stood accused of being the Dark Horseman now appeared innocent. The rider, mounted on a coal-black stallion, wore an ebony mask, tricorn, and cape, and boldly dared to defy British rule as he reined his animal to a climactic halt beside the gallows. Pistol in hand, he waved the executioner back, then pointed its black bore at Bartholomew Ingram while Dane agilely jumped and straddled the steed behind his rescuer. Then, before anyone could react, the stranger spun the horse

470

around and raced off across the common to freedom.

The crowd, having witnessed such gallantry by one man alone, drew upon his courage and shouted, "Turn the others free! Set them all free! They're innocent!"

"No-o-o!" Cory wailed when the throng of people moved en masse in the direction of the gaol. "They're not innocent! None of them. They're all guilty, every one of them!" Her eyes, darkened by madness and rage, turned on the man whom she still held prisoner. "It doesn't end here, Brad," she hissed. "I'll find him, and when I do, I'll kill him and it will be your fault."

"Not quite, Millicent," the voice behind her announced as the menacing bore of a pistol was shoved in her back. "Drop the knife."

Seizing his opportunity, Brad spun away from her and as he did, he brought his arm around and knocked the weapon from her hand, surprised to find that he owed his life to Roan Lockwood. "My God, what are you doing here?" he questioned, then changed his mind. "Don't bother explaining. I'm just damn glad you are." Bending, he picked up the knife, then grabbed Cory's arm. "Come on. Let's get out of here."

Certain that the crowd would see to it that Drexler, Betts, Dooley, and the rest of Dane's men would be freed from the gaol, Roan agreed and jerked his head in the direction of John Hancock's house.

"The man's waiting for us," Roan revealed. "There wasn't enough time for me to explain before all this happened, so I'm sure he's quite anxious to hear it, now that it's over." He gave Millicent a jab with his gun. "And it will be more interesting coming from her."

Working their way through the crowd, the threesome stepped into the alleyway behind the Hancock house and hurried up to the back door. Then, once their identity was given to the man who answered their summons, they were allowed entry and quickly escorted to the study where

Hancock, Revere, Otis, and Dr. Warren awaited them.

"Brad," Hancock sighed as he left his chair behind the desk and crossed the room to shake his hand, "I'm glad to see you're all right."

"Well, I might not have been if Roan hadn't come when he did. And to tell you the truth, I'm rather confused about the whole thing." He turned to look at Roan. "Mind telling me what this was all about?"

For a young boy of fifteen, Roan looked much older, and Brad deduced that hatred had a lot to do with it. Taking a seat next to Revere, Brad pulled off the eye patch and took the bandanna from his head as he watched the young man escort Cory to another chair and roughly shove her down upon it.

"Her name is Millicent Ashburn. Five years ago her sister committed suicide because she couldn't talk your cousin's wife into forcing you to marry her."

"Me?" Brad echoed. "I—" Suddenly the name struck a familiar cord and he groaned, remembering the letter Alanna had sent him. "Bethany Ashburn accused me of being the father of her child. I wasn't. I never touched her. She was too young." He sighed heavily and ran his fingers through his hair. "No one ever told me that she killed herself."

"Well, whether you were the father or not, Millicent blamed you for her sister's death and began plotting out a way to get even. According to Mrs. Remington, she taught herself how to use a knife and swords and any other weapon that would be helpful in her quest. Then, once she had paid back her debt to your cousin, she left Raven Oaks, followed you to Boston, and changed her name. She wasn't too worried about you recognizing her because you had never really paid her any attention while she was living at Raven Oaks and because she had been only thirteen at the time."

Obviously, what Roan had to say next was the most difficult, for the expression on his face changed. Stuffing his

472

pistol back into his belt, he removed his tricorn and tossed it on a nearby table. "She managed to win your trust—and Dane's," he went on, crossing to the hearth to stare down into its blackened recess, "by telling you that Beau had sent her to help you. Then she set out to get an accomplice—Miles Ingram—although he wasn't really aware of what she needed him for. Together they set up a smuggling operation and used our property to do it. Miles did it out of greed. Millicent did it as a part of her master plan. It's my guess—" He stopped suddenly and swallowed hard as if the knot in his throat would strangle him. "I believe my father stumbled across the men in the woods and they killed him for it." His gray eyes shifted to glare at Millicent. "Or maybe you killed him."

A demonic smile distorted Millicent's mouth. "Very good, little boy," she sneered. "You're not half as stupid as your father. He thought just because I was a woman that I was no threat." She drew an imaginary pistol from her belt. "I just waited until he turned his back and . . ." She raised the phantom weapon high above her head, then swung it earthward as if to crush her victim's skull.

Roan came alive with all the pent-up hatred of a man full-grown. His eyes darkened, his mouth twisted into a snarl, and a throaty growl escaped him. This one woman had singly destroyed his family and his farm, killed his father, and sent Brittany running for her life. Stealthily his hand moved to the butt of his pistol.

"Roan, no!" Brad shouted, lunging for him. "Not this way." Strong arms locked themselves around the younger man's slender frame. "She'll get what she deserves, but don't let her win in the end. If you kill her, she will."

Tears of rage glistened in the corners of Roan's eyes. "But she murdered my father, had our farm burned to the ground, and killed Ingram when he refused to do away with Brittany!"

"I understand, Roan," Brad pledged. "But let the courts

473

take care of her. If you won't do it for me or yourself, do it for Brit."

It took a moment for Brad's words to register, but once they had, Roan seemed to relent to their wisdom. Releasing a trembling sigh, he closed his eyes and swallowed hard before nodding his consent.

"My God," Hancock murmured, shaking his head. "Was there no end to her madness?"

"No," Brad spoke up once he was sure Roan would be all right. He turned and came to stand before Millicent, but she quickly looked away. "It was only the beginning. You're the one who told Dane to take the supply of guns to Hound's Head Inn. You're the one who loaded the barrels with smuggled goods. You're the one who sent the message to Ingram telling him where he could find the Dark Horseman. You even made sure Ingram would find the bag of coins." Reaching down, he roughly grabbed her chin and lifted her eyes to him. "You never went to see Hancock. You never even tried to get into the gaol. And you're the one who hit me over the head, aren't you?"

"Yes!" she screamed, slapping his hand away. "And I'd do it all again, if I could. You deserved every bit of pain I gave you and more."

"But you had plenty of opportunities to just kill me. Why didn't you?"

"Because killing you would have been too swift and merciful. I wanted you to suffer the way I have all these years. I wanted you to watch your brother die, knowing there was nothing you could do to save him, and to know who was responsible." Her face twisted with hate, Millicent slowly came to her feet. "And yes, there were plenty of times when I could have slit your throat, and God knows how tempted I was. But I didn't. I was saving you for something far worse!"

"Paul, James," Hancock cut in. "Take her out of here."

"I hope you live to be a hundred years old, Brad

474

Remington," she screamed when the two men grabbed her arms, "and that every day you'll remember how a fifteen-year-old girl killed herself because of you."

It pained him to see how easily misguided hatred could destroy a young woman's life. He couldn't blame her for what she had done. He could only pity her. "Cory—" he said, reaching out to touch her arm, but she instantly jerked clear, raised her chin in the air, and spat in his face.

With his eyes closed, Brad stood granite-still as he listened to her hurl her vile screams his way while she was dragged from the room. Then with the back of his hand he wiped away the spittle from his cheek and sank down on the chair.

"It wasn't your fault, Brad," Roan said quietly as he came to stand there and rest his hand on Brad's shoulder. "Her sister more than likely killed herself because she was pregnant and without a husband, not because you rejected her. You mustn't let it eat at you."

Smiling weakly, he reached up and patted Roan's hand. "You know, for fifteen years old, you're pretty smart."

"I learned it from a good friend," Roan grinned.

"And speaking of learning, who told you about Millicent and her sister? And how did you know where to find me? And what are you doing in Boston? You were told to stay away until we sent word."

"Lucky for you, I don't follow orders," he teased, ducking out of the way of the huge hand that came up to ruffle his hair.

"So how'd you know?"

"That's obvious. Brittany told me."

The magnificent stallion stretched long and sure and majestically as he raced across the meadow and away from those who wanted to pursue but couldn't. Even with the double weight he carried, he thrilled at the free rein he enjoyed, though one of his passengers wasn't at all pleased.

"For the love of God, Cory, will you slow this beast down before I'm thrown off?" Dane barked, his knees clamped against the horse's sides while he struggled with the ropes tied around his wrists. His skills at riding bareback didn't include doing so with his hands secured behind his back.

They veered off into the cover of trees, following a narrow trail through the tall oaks until they came to a sheltered clearing on the other side, and only then did his companion haul back on the reins. But instead of coming to a smooth stop, the horse jerked sideways, pranced excitedly around in a circle, then reared up on his hind legs and spilled Dane painfully to the ground.

"Damn it, Cory!" he growled, struggling to push himself up on one knee. "I wouldn't think you went to all that trouble saving me from the hangman's noose just so you could break my neck now." A booted foot jutted out, caught him in the shoulder, and sent him sprawling back on the ground. "What the hell—?" Deciding it was wiser, perhaps, to stay put until the young woman had had her fun, Dane sat still and angrily watched horse and rider prance circles around him. But when they came dangerously close, his temper exploded. "All right! All right! I apologize for whatever it is I'm to apologize for. Just quit playing games, Cory. This isn't very funny."

The figure, clothed in black, skillfully brought the animal to bay and leaned forward with her arms folded over the pommel of the saddle, the tricorn shading the color of her eyes as she stared down at him through the slits in the silk mask. Several minutes of silence ticked away while they stared at one another, during which time Dane began to realize that this slight figure wasn't who he thought she was. Frowning, his eyes swept over her—from head to toe and back again—trying to depict one single character that would give him a hint to her identity. Failing that, his irritation grew, and he set his attention on trying to free the rope from around his wrists.

"Maybe you want to sit here all day," he grumbled, wincing when the thick cord cut into his flesh, "but I don't. Ingram's probably gathering an army of men to track us down right now." He looked up to see if his words had had any effect and snarled disgustedly when the stranger simply stared back. "They'll hang you too, you know. They don't take kindly to someone helping a condemned man to escape." That didn't appear to bother his companion. "Well say something, damn you!"

"And what would you have me say?"

The sweet, dulcet voice sparked recognition in his brain, but before he could respond, the darkly clad figure swung a trim leg over the horse's neck and jumped to the ground before him.

"Would you like to hear me say that I forgive you for lying to me?" she asked, taking the tricorn from her head. "That I love you?" The hooded silk mask followed, releasing a flood of golden tresses down her back and over her delicate shoulders. "Would you like to hear me say that I traveled all the way back from Virginia to save your worthless hide so that we could spend the rest of our lives together? Is that what you want to hear, Dane Remington?" Brittany asked, her gray-blue eyes twinkling. "Well, I do forgive you. I love you. And you're the only reason I came back."

"Oh, Brittany," he murmured, coming up on his knees as she knelt before him. "God, I love you."

Slipping her arms around him, she tugged at the knot of rope. "Do you?" she teased, her lips only inches from his. "I wonder. Maybe you should tell me again . . . and again . . . and again."

His wrists free, Dane caught her to him in a wild embrace, his fingers locked within the thick mass of soft curls at her nape. "I love you, Brittany Lockwood," he whispered, his mouth swooping down to capture hers.

LOVE'S BRIGHTEST STARS SHINE
WITH ZEBRA BOOKS!

CATALINA'S CARESS   (2202, $3.95)
by Sylvie F. Sommerfield
Catalina Carrington was determined to buy her riverboat back from the handsome gambler who'd beaten her brother at cards. But when dashing Marc Copeland named his price—three days as his mistress—Catalina swore she'd never meet his terms . . . even as she imagined the rapture a night in his arms would bring!

BELOVED EMBRACE   (2135, $3.95)
by Cassie Edwards
Leana Rutherford was terrified when the ship carrying her family from New York to Texas was attacked by savage pirates. But when she gazed upon the bold sea-bandit Brandon Seton, Leana longed to share the ecstasy she was sure sure his passionate caress would ignite!

ELUSIVE SWAN   (2061, $3.95)
by Sylvie F. Sommerfield
Just one glance from the handsome stranger in the dockside tavern in boisterous St. Augustine made Arianne tremble with excitement. But the innocent young woman was already running from one man . . . and no matter how fiercely the flames of desire burned within her, Arianne dared not submit to another!

SAVAGE PARADISE   (1985, $3.95)
by Cassie Edwards
Marianna Fowler detested the desolate wilderness of the unsettled Montana Territory. But once the hot-blooded Chippewa brave Lone Hawk saved her life, the spirited young beauty wished never to leave, longing to experience the fire of the handsome warrior's passionate embrace!

MOONLIT MAGIC   (1941, $3.95)
by Sylvie F. Sommerfield
When she found the slick railroad negotiator Trace Cord trespassing on her property and bathing in her river, innocent Jenny Graham could barely contain her rage. But when she saw how the setting sun gilded Trace's magnificent physique, Jenny's seething fury was transformed into burning desire!

Available wherever paperbacks are sold, or order direct from the Publisher. Send cover price plus 50¢ per copy for mailing and handling to Zebra Books, Dept. 2326, 475 Park Avenue South, New York, N.Y. 10016. Residents of New York, New Jersey and Pennsylvania must include sales tax. DO NOT SEND CASH.